If I Ruled the World

Also by Amy DuBois Barnett

*Get Yours! How to Have Everything You
Ever Dreamed Of and More*

If I Ruled the World

Amy DuBois Barnett

SIMON &
SCHUSTER

London · New York · Amsterdam/Antwerp · Sydney/Melbourne · Toronto · New Delhi

First published in the United States by Flatiron Books, a division of Macmillan Publishers, 2026
First published in Great Britain by Simon & Schuster UK Ltd, 2026

Copyright © Amy DuBois Barnett, 2026

The right of Amy DuBois Barnett to be identified as author
of this work has been asserted in accordance with the
Copyright, Designs and Patents Act, 1988.

1 3 5 7 9 10 8 6 4 2

Simon & Schuster UK Ltd
1st Floor
222 Gray's Inn Road
London WC1X 8HB

For more than 100 years, Simon & Schuster has championed authors and the stories they create. By respecting the copyright of an author's intellectual property, you enable Simon & Schuster and the author to continue publishing exceptional books for years to come. We thank you for supporting the author's copyright by purchasing an authorised edition of this book.

No amount of this book may be reproduced or stored in any format, nor may it be uploaded to any website, database, language-learning model, or other repository, retrieval, or artificial intelligence system without express permission. All rights reserved. Enquiries may be directed to Simon & Schuster, 222 Gray's Inn Road, London WC1X 8HB or RightsMailbox@simonandschuster.co.uk

Simon & Schuster Australia, Sydney
Simon & Schuster India, New Delhi

www.simonandschuster.co.uk
www.simonandschuster.com.au
www.simonandschuster.co.in

The authorised representative in the EEA is Simon & Schuster Netherlands BV, Herculesplein 96, 3584 AA Utrecht, Netherlands. info@simonandschuster.nl

Simon & Schuster strongly believes in freedom of expression and stands against censorship in all its forms. For more information, visit BooksBelong.com

A CIP catalogue record for this book
is available from the British Library

Hardback ISBN: 978-1-3985-4365-2
eBook ISBN: 978-1-3985-4367-6
Audio ISBN: 978-1-3985-4368-3

This book is a work of fiction. Names, characters, places and incidents are either a product of the author's imagination or are used fictitiously. Any resemblance to actual people living or dead, events or locales is entirely coincidental.

Printed and Bound in the UK using 100% Renewable Electricity
at CPI Group (UK) Ltd

For Kara – who's been there for every chapter and every plot twist, on the page and in life. Thank you for being my home away from home.

PROLOGUE

New York City, Spring 1996

I was a live-for-the-moment twentysomething, like every other twentysomething I knew, until one rainy Friday night in the Krispy Kreme on Twenty-Third Street in Manhattan. I was licking raspberry jelly from the fingers of a very rich, very fine, and very married man, when I looked up to see my parents, shaking rain off their huge umbrella and laughing. I might have been able to salvage the situation if my date—his trademark salt-and-pepper locs unmistakable from any angle—had been a stranger to my parents. No such luck. He was my mother's childhood friend from suburban Chicago. The bond they'd formed as the stray chocolate chips in their high school's huge snickerdoodle had lasted decades, with Mom even toasting the brides at both his first and second weddings.

Dad spoke first, an uncharacteristic curse word exploding from his mouth: "What the fuck is this, Al?"

My date, Alonzo Griffin—husband, father, and, until that moment, oblivious finger suckee—had his back to the door. But he whipped around at the sound of my dad's voice.

"Jesus, what are you two doing here?" he asked, the slight tremor in his voice belying his expressionless face.

"Getting a doughnut, I think," I whispered, shocked into stupidity.

"No shit, Nikki," Alonzo said. He looked at Mom and implored, "Ann, please..."

Hearing her name thawed my frozen mother, who strode over to our table and poked a finger in Alonzo's chest. In a furious tone, she said, "How could you, Al? This is my *daughter*."

Alonzo winced but clearly thought better of rebutting my enraged mom. "Annie," he spoke in a low tone, my mother's name both a question and a warning.

"Don't call me that," she snapped, then turned to me. "And you, what were you thinking? Tell me, please, what *were* you thinking?"

I had no response because I honestly hadn't been thinking at all—unless having a torrid affair with my married boss who was almost twice my age and just happened to grow up with my mother was evidence of deep consideration.

The situation was made worse by the fact that six months prior Mom had called Alonzo, the publisher of *Revolutions*—a venerable music magazine owned by the even more venerable Park Avenue Publishing—to ask him for help with her wayward daughter.

"Black folks rarely make it to the top, so you'll likely get stuck near the bottom where the salaries are dreadful. And most magazines are asinine anyway," she'd wailed when I first brought up my dream of being an editor-in-chief. After I graduated from college, my English professor mom had begged me to find a job in a respectable and secure field—in her mind, journalism, even as an EIC, did not qualify. But after watching me quit a job in finance, drop out of law school, then waitress while trying to get someone to pay me for my words, I think she began to fear I'd never move out of their Harlem brownstone.

What Mom and Dad didn't know was that, during my interview process, Alonzo and I had gone out for drinks, one thing led to another, and I'd found myself in a discreet Midtown hotel watching my mom's old pal unlace his Ferragamo shoes, peel off his Armani suit, and unbutton his Valentino shirt. I'd made love to a few boyfriends by then, but this was something different. Alonzo Griffin had pulled my hair and grabbed my throat and bent me over every piece of furniture in the hotel room, all while whispering that he was going to enjoy taking care of his "good little bitch." As we were getting dressed afterward, Alonzo had tilted my head up to look into my eyes. "Baby-girl, keep this up and you'll be the editor-in-chief in no time," he'd said with a smirk. "But next time I see you, Daddy wants you to have a Brazilian wax. It looks like you sat on a fucking Chia Pet."

I was tall, wiry, and bookish—the child of two professors—with a residual penchant for denim and kicks. I hadn't yet figured out the right products for the wild reddish-brown curls that haloed my narrow shoulders, and my newly acquired contact lenses were still a daily struggle to pop in over backlit brown eyes that matched my hair. I had never even heard of a Brazilian wax, and I didn't know there would be a next time. But Alonzo's declaration had left zero room for debate.

After a few months of working at *Revolutions*—and having clandestine rendezvous with Alonzo—I'd moved into my own studio in Brooklyn. I bought a computer and had even stopped asking my parents for the occasional twenty bucks. At Alonzo's request, I'd made regular waxing appointments, found a local Dominican salon for my blowouts, upgraded my wardrobe to tight skirts and heels, and wore lipstick and mascara to work every day. I wasn't worried about the thousands I'd racked up on newly acquired credit cards because Alonzo promised he'd pay them off.

I'm sure my parents thought I'd finally found my way—until six months later, when they stopped for a doughnut and witnessed their only child literally biting the hand that feeds her.

"Annie, just calm down a second." Alonzo reached out and tried to touch Mom's tensed up shoulder with his sticky fingers.

"I said don't call me that." She glared at him. "You know, I've been watching the music industry do a number on your head for years. I was trying to give you some grace because I remembered that puny kid the white boys beat up after school. I figured you were just sowing your wild oats, making up for lost time, but I was so very wrong about you." Then she turned to me, eyes blazing. "And *you*, I definitely don't know you anymore."

The smell of baking doughnuts turned syrupy and thick as I watched my mother gather herself, grab my dad, and head for the door. On top of being "stubborn" and "irresponsible" in her eyes, I could now add "homewrecking slut." Wonderful. I expected Alonzo to look contrite, to apologize for the situation, to run after his friend. Instead, he watched them leave, dipped a pinkie back into the raspberry filling, and purred, "Well, that was exciting."

I stared at him. "Jesus, Alonzo. That was not exciting. That was humiliating and awful—for both of us." I let my chin fall to my chest. "And what if Mom tells your wife? You consider that?"

"She won't, Nikki. Trust me. Dr. Ann Rose believes in sacred Black love too much to break up my marriage." Alonzo lifted my head and smeared a little jelly on my lip while giving me the authoritative, sexy, boss-man look that got me into this mess in the first place. "Oh, come on, Nikki, you know you like the thrill of danger."

Was he right? I let myself be ushered out of the Krispy Kreme and into Alonzo's silver Range Rover, conveniently parked on a deserted side street. I let him toss me into the back seat while he insisted, "You're going to be Daddy's good girl, aren't you? Get those jeans off now."

It didn't matter to him that I had tears in my eyes, that my shoulders were quivering, that I mumbled, "No, I don't think I want to right now."

It was easier to let him keep going as he yanked off my sweater and pulled down my underwear, as he put my hand inside his jeans, as he ripped open a condom with his teeth. It was easier to let Alonzo remain who he'd always been in our relationship: the initiator, the lead-footed driver of our liaisons. That way, I could continue to hide behind my role as the ingenue, the eager explorer.

When Alonzo grabbed a handful of my hair, yanked my head back, and told me, "You're going to take it all now," I did, only because I couldn't figure out a way to make him stop. I had no idea how to get out of that Range Rover without causing a scene and making it worse. So, I let Alonzo do everything to me that he wanted. And that night, I was everything my mother was afraid I had become.

Any shred of excitement disappeared by Monday, leaving only humiliation, guilt, and rage. Mom had refused my calls, and even my dad, who'd always been reliably on my side, wouldn't talk to me. I pictured them sitting close together on their tatty jacquard sofa, thighs touching, clutching cups of ginger tea, softly bemoaning their only daughter who was once so promising but was now ruined. I imagined them turning the pictures of me on top of their piano face down, throwing away my boxes of childhood mementos, writing me out of their wills. I'd never seen my mother's eyes look that cold or my dad's look that disappointed, so I let myself spiral.

Meanwhile, Alonzo was ringing me every hour to say how turned on he was by the whole situation, illuminating a dirty old-man-ish quality I'd been trying to ignore. Over the past several months, I'd gotten off on his dominance, on acting as if I didn't want him when I did. But instead of feeling satiated and naughty after that night in the Range Rover, I'd cried in the shower when I got home while scrubbing my skin raw.

"Why don't you be a good little girl and meet Daddy in a hotel?" Alonzo repeated some variation of this every time I picked up my phone.

"Alonzo, my parents think I'm a terrible person, and one of your oldest friends believes you're a monster. I can't see you," I finally hurled back, slamming the phone down with what I hoped was enough force for him to leave me alone.

But we worked on the same floor in the Park Avenue Publishing building; it was impossible to avoid him, which was torture because every glimpse of Alonzo's face took me back to that rainy night when

I realized how deeply I was fucking up my life. Meanwhile, Alonzo kept leaving Krispy Kreme doughnuts in my cubicle, like this was all a big joke.

After a couple weeks, I was tired of having oxygen-depriving panic attacks and crying silently into the crook of my elbow in the office bathroom. I wanted my life back—or at least the life I'd envisioned before I'd naïvely fantasized that Alonzo would one day treat me with respect, leave his wife and kids, and elope to the Caribbean with me. Most importantly, I wanted to earn my editor-in-chief title because I was a talented visionary, not because my mom's friend decided to elevate me into the role so he could have his way with me whenever he wanted.

I went into Alonzo's office one afternoon and shut the door behind me. He stood up and ran a hand over his head, smoothing back the graying locs I'd once found so sexy. "Finally! We haven't been alone in a while, but you have been on Daddy's mind," he said, turning to lower the blinds.

"Stop, please," I told him as firmly as I could manage. "Just stop for a minute. I really need to talk to you."

I sat down in one of the oversized chairs in front of his enormous desk. Alonzo's office was typical successful businessman chic, filled with the requisite crystal awards, framed citations, and expensive leather furniture. His three televisions were tuned to BET, CNN, and ESPN. At forty-eight, Alonzo was one of the most senior publishers at the company. He'd been at *Revolutions* for ten years, during which he'd orchestrated a major shift in the brand—changing the magazine's publishing schedule from monthly to weekly, pushing the editor-in-chief to add more music-industry dirt and style content, and launching a cutting-edge website. Alonzo's strategy tripled newsstand sales and advertising revenue, which made *Revolutions* one of the most profitable entertainment brands in the business. Quite a feat for a Black man in a field where African Americans represented less than 3 percent of senior-level management.

Alonzo straddled the rarefied worlds of mainstream publishing and the music industry, where he was equally revered. Even though the EIC technically decided who to feature, everyone knew that Alonzo was the real *Revolutions* gatekeeper. In a rare moment of transparency after a particularly sweaty hotel session, Alonzo shared some of the lengths artists and labels would go to curry his favor. The pop and rock artists preferred to gift him front-row tickets and heaps of blow, but the hip hop artists' ploys were much more elaborate: magnums of Cristal accompanied the cocaine on private jet flights to Saint-Tropez and megayacht trips to the Caribbean, and an endless supply of video vixens willing to do just what "daddy" says.

Having been propositioned and groped by multiple artists and label execs as they passed through the *Revolutions* offices, I could attest to the disrespect and arrogance that would make someone offer up women as payola. But while I'd prided myself on avoiding a disastrous career-destroying turn as a rapper's flavor of the month, here I was, trying to disentangle myself from Alonzo's grasp as LL Cool J rapped "Doin' It" on the television tuned to BET. Then the video switched to a powerful ballad from my favorite singer, Bobbie Washington, about a woman finding herself against all odds, which gave me courage to recite my prepared statement: "What has happened between us is obviously not a good idea, and I no longer feel comfortable. I'd like for our relationship to be purely professional from now on."

Alonzo's expression didn't change as he leaned forward: "No."

"What do you mean, no?" I exclaimed, loud enough so that I could see a couple *Revolutions* team members turn to peer into Alonzo's office through the half-closed blinds. I lowered my voice. "That wasn't a question, Alonzo. I can't do this anymore."

"Sure, you can—and you will, because I'm not ready for it to end."

I stared at him. "Are you telling me you'll have me fired if I stop sleeping with you?"

"That is an interesting question, babygirl," he replied, looking at me so intently I felt myself slipping on the black ice of his gaze. "Either way, you're going to make the smart decision because you love this as much as I do." Alonzo walked around the desk, put both hands on my shoulders and whispered, "You know you get off on being my bitch. Besides, nobody leaves me before I'm ready, Nikki. I know you're young, but you should have known that was part of the deal."

"What deal?" I asked, wriggling out of Alonzo's grasp but worried that my reddening cheeks would betray the desire rising in me despite everything. "What are you talking about?"

Alonzo lifted his right eyebrow. "You're here because of me. That is the deal. So, let's not mess up a good thing."

"Too late, Alonzo," I said as firmly as I could. "We are done."

Alonzo snorted. "You don't get to say no to me without repercussions. So, actually, *you* are done." His expression shifted frighteningly fast from anticipation to exasperation. "I'm not going to be distracted by you every day if I can't have you. Why don't you make it easier on us both and resign?"

My desire drained away as dread knotted my stomach. "But I haven't even been at *Revolutions* a year. How will I get another job? And what about all that money on my credit cards?"

"Not my problem anymore." He put on glasses with conspicuous Gucci logos and started pulling papers from a manila envelope, a signal that he was finished with this conversation and truly done with me. "If you don't want to resign, I'll have you fired tomorrow. Your choice."

"How are you going to explain this to my mom?" I was shaking with fear and anger.

Alonzo laughed. "You really are a child." Then his eyes narrowed. "But since you seem to know nothing about anything, let me school you: You're gonna want to think real hard before you tell anyone about us, because you have literally no idea what I'm capable of. Fuck around and find out, babygirl."

I walked out of his office, straight down the hall to the elevator, right to the human resources floor before I could change my mind. There was only one Black person in HR, and there was no one else I could talk to.

Marie Hyacinthe walked out to greet me with a huge smile. Despite an extensive wardrobe of black pantsuits, her impossible-to-hide curves, flawless cinnamon skin punctuated only by deep dimples, and blond Afro made Marie stand out in any crowd. Even though there was almost a decade between us, we'd become friends during my onboarding process, discovering a shared love of Rollerblading, curried chicken patties wrapped in coco bread, and, most importantly, Mary J. Blige, Sade, and EPMD. I'd even ended up moving into an apartment in her Bed-Stuy neighborhood.

I must have been wearing my awful conversation with Alonzo all over my face because Marie's friendly smile quickly faded. She pulled me into a windowless conference room, shut the door, and asked, "All right, girl. What's going on?"

"It's not a good story." I sighed, leaning on the long glass table. "I think I got myself into a situation."

She sank into a chair. "With Alonzo?"

"How did you know?"

"Please, he's notorious. I have multiple complaints on file, but Alonzo generates so much revenue that the company hasn't wanted to touch him. I thought he'd leave you alone since your families are close. Tell me what happened, then let's figure out how to deal."

"Okay, but this is friend to friend. I'm not doing an official thing here."

"Got it. Not official. Off the record. Shoot."

I gave her the PG-13 version, leaving out my parents busting us in the Krispy Kreme and the subsequent session that left footprints on almost every window of his Range Rover. It was just enough information so Marie could understand my predicament but not so much that she would never look at me the same way again.

"I know, I'm an idiot," I finished. "But he's a lech."

Marie got up and began to pace the room. "I care about you, Nikki, but don't pass the buck here. This kind of thing can ruin you in the industry forever, especially one that's not exactly friendly to *us* in the first place."

"Maybe I don't deserve to be here," I said, digging my nails into my palms so the moisture clouding my eyes wouldn't form into visible tears.

"Look, you got this job on your own merits," Marie said. "All Alonzo did was secure the initial interview. The features editor was legit impressed with your ideas and your edit test."

"But I shouldn't have gotten caught up in this bullshit."

"That is an understatement. But I do know of another opening in the company that could work for you," Marie said conspiratorially. "As for Alonzo, don't say a word. There's no reason for you to go public with this. As much as I'd love to see you get justice, it will blow back worse on you."

"But Alonzo said he'd have me fired tomorrow if I don't resign." I sniffled.

Marie chuckled. "He's all bluster. There's no way for Alonzo to fire you that quickly without incriminating himself. But he does have enough juice to drum up some bullshit reason and fast-track the paperwork." She paused to think, drumming her fingers against her cheek. "Listen, you lie low for a few. Make up an illness and take some time off. But be available to come in for an interview this week. I got you."

Two weeks later, I was packing up my cubicle. I'd just been hired as an editorial assistant at the fashion magazine *StyleList*. The role was a step down from my assistant editor position at *Revolutions*, and I was much more into music than fashion. But *StyleList* was Park Avenue Publishing's crown jewel, with offices literally atop the company's glass-clad Midtown building.

"This is it, Nikki. I stuck my neck out for you. And I can't fix it if this goes left," Marie cautioned me, but she need not have worried. I was scared all the way straight.

The *StyleList* offices were on a floor accessible only via a special elevator bank. On the rare occasion when I spied Alonzo in the lobby, I ducked out of sight—and he never glanced my way. I pushed my expensive miniskirts and bright crop tops to the back of my closet in favor of nondescript clothes in neutral colors and started scraping my hair into ponytails almost every day like I was back in high school. I wanted to be less visible, less desirable, less of a target.

A couple months later, Alonzo left *Revolutions*. Park Ave Pub didn't make clear whether he'd been fired or had walked out voluntarily, but since he was out the door the same day his exit was announced, everyone assumed the former. Alonzo's departure sent shock waves through the building, with the Black employees buzzing about racism and vowing to organize a protest. I nodded and *mm-hmm*ed along with them, knowing full well that, for once, there was more to it than that.

Alonzo had finally slept with the wrong person: a close relative of Park Ave Pub's long-standing editor-in-chief of *Architectural Décor*. When the septuagenarian EIC found out that Alonzo had seduced her precious niece, she reported him directly to Park Ave Pub's CEO, which, Marie told me, was the last straw. The company kept the whole incident so quiet that even Alonzo wasn't aware of why he was summarily dismissed.

Alonzo called me the evening after he was escorted out of Park Ave Pub. "I guess you decided to test me, babygirl." His fury was palpable through the phone.

"What are you talking about?" I tried to keep my voice steady even though I wanted to curl in a ball under the covers.

"Stop playing coy. It doesn't suit you." He was silent for a second and I braced myself. "You know very fucking well that you ran your mouth about us. I'm almost impressed by your guts."

"You think I got you fired?" I had to convince him otherwise. "It wasn't me, Alonzo. Marie said there were others—" I immediately realized my error.

"So, you did talk to HR. And you think you can lie to me about it?"

"No, I . . . I did talk to Marie, but off the record. She's a friend. But she said that other women had complained . . ." I trailed off because I knew I was making it worse.

"If you think you can ruin my reputation along with a career that I've built over two brutal decades, you are either very naïve or you are very stupid." Alonzo's next words would ring in my head for years. "Get ready to grow up, babygirl. You had better hope our paths don't cross again."

ONE

Fall 1999, Three Years Later

Running in four-inch stilettos is not easy. But it can be done. In fact, you can get up to a heart-pounding, sweat-trickling, hair-ruining sprint if you need to. And that day, I *really* needed to. Nobody was late for Wednesday-morning edit review meetings at *StyleList*. So I was running east on Fifty-Seventh Street, at damn near full speed, past the store managers swinging open the pearly gates to Gucci and Chanel and Burberry, past the ladies who lunch (and then blame their retail therapy on a two-Chardonnay buzz), past bored limo drivers smoking cigs and talking shit while they wait for their respective Park Avenue princesses, past slow-moving tourists performing the upward gaze-and-point maneuver like bewildered synchronized swimmers. I was leaping over toy poodles, Chihuahuas, and Yorkies, and narrowly missing Brioni-suited men emerging from breakfast meetings only to watch in amazement as I whipped around them in my high heels.

As a teenager, I developed my style by reading *Teen Beat*, copying Lisa Bonet, and watching music videos on MTV. For years, my outfits were an awkward mix of vintage boho, East Village, and the Boogie Down Bronx. One consistent element had always been a pair of clean sneakers. I had long since shed the confused outfits of my teens, but at that moment, I sure did miss those kicks.

In the three years post-Alonzo, I'd caught a few people in the Park Ave Pub lobby snickering in my direction and assumed that Alonzo had dropped some choice tidbits about me from afar. He had few inroads into the high-end fashion world, so *StyleList* was somewhat insulating, but time had diminished neither the balance on my Visa nor my expectation that he would eventually make good on his threats. Dressing in neutrals, pulling my hair back, and looking over my proverbial shoulder had become a habit. But working in the most stylish office in publishing taught me that if I wasn't going to wear eye-catching outfits, I had better at least have a decent selection of stilettos to give my humdrum wardrobe a modicum of glamour.

I slowed to a trot one block before the marble entrance of Park Ave Pub. Better to be a couple minutes late than risk running into one of my colleagues while panting and sweating mascara down my cheeks. I pushed open the heavy glass doors and hurried inside, trying to tuck my frizzing hair back into a flimsy ponytail holder while the security guard calmly watched.

"Please," I begged him, after searching for and not finding my laminated badge in my overflowing tote. "I am so late. Can you let me through? Just this once?"

"I need your employee ID."

"I know, I know. Dammit." Dumping the contents of my tote onto the security desk, I caught sight of a distinctive tornado of red curls. Lucinda. *Just* Lucinda. No one used her last name, and no one had to because everyone who was anyone in the fashion industry knew who she was. Lucinda, *StyleList*'s editor-in-chief, was formidable and feared. Every designer in the industry practically sank to their knees when they saw her coming, to better position themselves for the ass-kissing Lucinda (Lucifer, as some called her) would demand. To make matters worse, Lucinda was notoriously fickle: One day she loved Dior, the next she adored Balmain, the next she couldn't live without Lanvin. She was like that with her employees as well. Some days she would waltz up to me and pronounce my prose "too, too gorgeous." Other days she wouldn't acknowledge me in the elevator.

I ducked my head, hoping Lucinda wouldn't recognize me today. No such luck.

"Nikki, right? Ah, Nicole Rose," she intoned, bending to pick up my employee ID that had conveniently dropped off the security desk to land inches from her feet. Lucinda handed me the ID while I took in her outfit: a ballet tutu worn with motorcycle boots and a black blazer buttoned over a bright fuchsia bra. Lucinda was known for her excessive jewelry, and on every finger of both hands she'd stacked silver and emerald rings. The whole thing was a little Cyndi Lauper for my taste, but since Lucinda was always way ahead of the trends, I assumed fashionistas across the country would soon be rocking tutus, boots, and bras-as-blouses.

Ignoring my stare, Lucinda fluffed her enormous hair and watched me try to casually stuff my unpaid bills, taxi receipts, and gym shorts back into my tote before she could take inventory. "Aren't you due in my edit meeting? Right now?" she asked.

Shit, there was no way out of this one. "Morning, Lucinda. Yes, sorry. I was having trouble locating my ID and security wouldn't allow me through." I figured I'd peg it on the asshole security guard, but Lucinda wasn't letting me off so easy.

"You should have been there already, doll," she replied crisply.

I didn't say a word, just nodded with what I hoped was the appropriate amount of deference and prayed for an express elevator.

Pissing Lucinda off was not a good career move. First of all, the woman's nickname was Lucifer. The second reason? I was a features-department peon with the rest of the cerebral bookworms. Within the *StyleList* hierarchy, features was near the bottom of the pecking order—after the fashion, beauty, art, and entertainment departments. The one department we trumped was research, and that was only because those pesky fact-checkers insisted on verifying with a doctor or a manager before allowing *StyleList* to print that a big-name actress was bulimic even though the accessory editor's best friend like, *totally* heard her hurling in a bathroom at a restaurant. The third reason was that I was a senior associate editor. Although I'd been excited for my recent promotion, even I didn't know what that title meant. When I was offered the slight upgrade from associate editor, I called Marie in HR and said, "So I'm a jumbo shrimp now!"

"What are you talking about?"

"My new title is *senior* associate editor."

"Oh, your promotion." She'd laughed. "Congrats, jumbo shrimp!"

Of course, that association stuck; Marie's emails to me were always addressed to J.S., and every time I told someone my title, the image of a fried shrimp dangling from Lucinda's fingers popped into my mind.

The fourth reason not to get on Lucinda's bad side—which should probably be the first—was that both the fashion industry and *StyleList* were known for being whiter than white. In Park Ave Pub's one hundred years of existence, they had never named a Black EIC. While street looks from Harlem and Brooklyn were showing up on high-fashion runways, the *StyleList* team felt astonishingly free to dismiss and mock Black people in everything from team meetings to casual hallway conversations. Aside from the receptionist, a couple executive assistants, and our six-foot-eight male bookings director whose head wraps smelled like lemongrass and cocoa butter, I was the only Black person on the staff—though I wasn't entirely convinced that everyone at *StyleList* had processed the fact that I was Black. I thought I clearly looked African American, especially when I wore my curls out, but throughout my life people had questioned what my tawny, freckled skin and penny-colored eyes and hair meant. If I had a dime for every white guy at a bar who exclaimed, "What? No, you're not!" I'd have been retired. The one time I'd given my dad—a wavy-haired, green-eyed Irishman—a tour of my office, he'd confused the matter even more. I could have worn a dashiki to work, and they might have all thought it was just a retro-cool fashion statement.

When the elevator doors slid open on the thirty-ninth floor (or, as some of Lucifer's more jaded employees referred to it, Dante's Seventh Circle of Hell), Lucinda's long-suffering assistant, Mary-Kate, was waiting, folders and fruity-looking drink in hand, her expression petrified as usual. She wordlessly handed the glass to Lucinda, who quickly downed the red concoction (rumored to be acai mixed with some antiaging elixir found only in the chin hair of endangered Sumatran tigers). I was mercifully forgotten.

I dashed to the conference room, hoping for an unobtrusive entrance. But when I swung open the door, all chatter stopped since everyone assumed Lucinda had arrived to deliver her weekly group abuse.

Though I hated to admit it, Mary-Kate and I had something in common: *StyleList* remained an intimidating place to work. The magazine was launched decades after venerable titles like *Vogue* and *Elle*, but *StyleList* quickly became the biggest, hottest fashion magazine in the world. And the fashion fanatics who worked there definitely knew it. They were, after all, the most influential style editors on the planet. They could identify a fake Louis Vuitton purse from fifty paces away; they could distinguish whether an unlabeled lipstick smear was MAC's Viva Glam or Chanel's Rouge Allure; they could tell if a model had gained or lost a pound just by her runway gait. And they wielded their power without mercy. God help anyone wearing last season's Gucci jacket, scuffed Louboutins, the wrong shape pant leg or—yes—the wrong length skirt. If you went to the Midtown Salvation Army on the right day, you could score $750 Jimmy Choos that a *StyleList* editor had dropped off because they were "so last year, ew."

"Only me," I muttered, plopping down in the first available chair while trying to avoid the fashionistas' critical gaze. Unfortunately, the seat happened to be next to my boss, Tara Kinney, the temperamental and rebelliously unkempt head of the features department. Even though she dared to wear fisherman sweaters, baggy blue jeans, and run-down loafers to the office, the fashion girls left her alone. She rarely smiled or complimented others on their work, using her impressive vocabulary to rip apart anyone who trespassed into her features territory. And her bite was as bad as her bark: Tara had once fired someone for using *your* instead of *you're*. Despite successfully pitching, writing, and editing more articles than anyone else in the department, I got the same treatment. Luckily, Tara only had a second to glare at me disapprovingly before Lucinda swept in and took her place at the head of the table.

"Morning, dolls."

"Morning, Lucinda," everyone dutifully replied.

I scrunched down in my seat, hoping to blend in, but Lucinda's eye briefly caught mine as she said, "I hope everyone got *plenty* of sleep last night." The other editors looked around, not sure how to respond, but Lucinda went on before they had to come up with something. "Well, good, dolls, because we have a ton of work to do today. First up, the theme of our January issue: I hate, hate, hate it."

There was an audible gasp in the room.

"But Lucinda, the annual style horoscope package is one of our most successful, and we've been working on it for months," ventured Margaret Lowell, *StyleList*'s executive editor and Lucinda's number two. I always figured Margaret (Muffy to her friends) put up with Lucinda because she truly didn't have to. Along with a duplex penthouse on Fifth Avenue, the Lowells owned mansions in Bridgehampton, Newport, and Nantucket. Muffy preferred Chanel ballet flats and a wide headband in her blond hair and would turn the golf ball–sized diamond on her ring finger toward her palm when she left the office so she wouldn't get robbed by a "thug" in the twenty-three seconds it took to walk from the door to her waiting town car.

"Don't care, doll," Lucinda responded, drumming her fingers on the glass table. "It's yesterday's news. We need something new, hot, sexy."

Immediately, everyone started throwing their pitches into the ring, hoping to capture Lucinda's elusive favor: "The travel issue."

Lucinda rolled her eyes. "Wrong season."

"New year, new you."

"Too boring. I said *sexy*, ladies." Lucinda sighed and leaned back as if bored by this very meeting.

"The jewelry issue."

"Hmm, too narrow."

"Shopping issue?"

Lucinda rolled her eyes again. "Too pedestrian."

Tara threw an idea out: "The health issue."

"Interesting, but not sexy enough."

"The body issue," Tara tried again.

"Warmer, but not hot. I need heat."

There were resounding collective groans when a hapless editor from the largely disregarded website department ventured, "How about a Y2K theme, like technology and style?" We were all exhausted with the endless coverage of the potentially disastrous glitch that could occur in a few months when computer systems moved from 1999 to 2000.

"Fabulous idea: global chaos and shiny low-slung jeans," Lucinda snapped as the digital editor shrunk in her chair.

Before I could stop myself, I raised my hand like I was in kindergarten.

"Yes, Nikki? Would you like to come to the blackboard to write down the correct answer?" Lucinda laughed and the whole room, naturally, cracked up with her.

"The ageless issue," I said, undaunted. "We could do a fashion feature on clothes for different ages or looking sexy without overdoing it. And a health story about how celebrities of all ages take care of themselves. We could run a diet story since everyone loves those." I felt Tara's ire growing as she shifted in her seat next to me, her eyes locked onto my profile, but I was on a roll. "And we could do a package of stories on sex and relationships along with a comprehensive survey. You know, the sexual behavior of modern women at every age with a sidebar on how to keep it hot in bed."

Lucinda looked at me appraisingly, then stood up and slammed a palm onto the table. Smelling blood, the fashionistas got ready to jump into the fray. I braced myself for the feeding frenzy.

"I love, love, love it!" Lucinda yelled instead. "Let's get on this right away. Nikki, you're in charge of the sex-and-relationships package."

Instantly, the attitude of the room toward me changed. People started talking all at once.

"Yeah, awesome idea!"

"So cool!"

"You rock, Nikki! We'll totally need your help fleshing out the rest of the issue."

Only Tara silently glowered at me. I had the nerve to pitch an idea that Lucinda liked better than hers, so I knew I was in for it later.

"One more idea," I said, taking a chance, hoping I could keep riding this positive wave. "We should do an AIDS story." The room went silent again. "AIDS is a huge issue for women along with the gay and Black communities, and fashion titles rarely do in-depth stories on it. We could break the mold and really blow it out, make it a cause *StyleList* embraces."

Lucinda sat back down. "That's not sexy, doll."

"We could do a whole safer sex story—and have a chance to make an impact," I responded, knowing I was losing Lucinda, and therefore the room, by the second.

"Um, doesn't Elton John or somebody have a charity for that?" Lucinda asked dismissively.

"Maybe, but don't you think we could—"

Lucinda shook her head, irritated by my earnestness. "Call Elton's people," she said vaguely, then motioned toward her fashion editors. "Okay, I need a list of January issue designer names by this afternoon. Who screams sex, dolls? Cavalli, Dolce..."

Aware that my time in the spotlight had come and gone, I sat back. Though doing so always made me feel even more self-conscious at being the only chocolate chip in the *StyleList* snickerdoodle, I still tried to pitch one story having to do with people of color at almost every editorial meeting. The reactions I normally got ranged from perplexity to outright derision, reminding me over and over that I was the *only*, while making me more determined to keep trying. How confusing my very presence must have been to those well-connected dilettantes, erudite Ivy Leaguers, and fabulous fashionistas. Only the gay guys in PR laughed at my jokes, though they did so while snickering at my outfits. But no way was I going to let any of them hold me back. So, they would have to stay sick of me.

Tara dug her elbow into my side. "Since you're the genius that came up with the sex survey idea, you will have to figure out a way to execute it along with the rest of the relationship package," she whispered, her coffee breath clouding the air between us. "You have two weeks to get a draft on my desk."

I gasped. "Two weeks! I'm not sure that's even possible."

Tara lifted one shoulder. "Anything is possible if you want it bad enough. And you certainly seem to want it badly."

I spent the rest of the day researching recent sex surveys, emailing sexual health foundations for information, drafting questions, and begging market research firms to take on this monumental project that would require two straight weeks of relentless grinding. I worked through lunch, barely noticing the hours slip away. When I finally glanced at my watch, it was already after seven. I was supposed to meet my boyfriend, Joseph, for dinner at eight.

I sped down the hall to the elevator banks and came face-to-face with Lucinda for the second time that day. She was impatiently jabbing the down button.

"Looks like we're on the same schedule today." It was the most innocuous thing I could think of, but Lucinda was obviously in no mood for my awkward chatter.

"Next time get here before me," she scowled as the elevator doors finally slid open. I had no choice but to follow, standing a little behind her so her eyes wouldn't have to be assaulted by my lowly presence. Lucinda folded her arms and, after a few seconds, rolled her shoulders and said, "Solid idea today, doll."

I got my nerve up and stepped forward. "Thanks," I replied, inwardly wincing at my bright tone. "I've been working on the sex survey all day. I really think you're going to be pleased."

Lucinda said nothing, just nodded, tapping one boot hard on the elevator floor as we were silently whisked to the lobby. I had a critical choice at this point: Stay quiet and let our reasonably positive exchange be the last of the day, or try to chat her up some more. I knew she wasn't exactly in a receptive mood, but my mouth had a mind of its own. I blurted, "So, I have one more idea for you."

I thought I saw her eyes roll behind her sunglasses, but since she didn't cut me off, I pressed on. "Tyisha would be a great January issue cover model." We'd hit the lobby by this time, and I scurried after her. "She's been modeling for years, and her new reality show, *America's Next Cover Girl*, premieres right after the issue comes out—plus she's an AIDS activist."

Out on the street, Lucinda paused. She didn't look up as she took a small silver case out of her bag, pulled out a cigarette, lit it, then blew a long stream of smoke into the crisp evening air. For a second, it seemed as if she might be contemplating my idea. Then she took another hard drag, exhaled practically into my face, and said with finality, "Black girls don't sell magazines."

I watched her take a couple more drags, grind her cigarette under her boot, and climb into the shiny black town car waiting for her at the curb. After her tutu and motorcycle boots disappeared into the back seat, the uniformed driver closed the door and they pulled off with only her profile in view. I didn't say another word, and she never looked back.

TWO

That night, Joseph and I were celebrating his recent promotion to managing director at one of Wall Street's oldest investment banks. By the time I got to Joseph's place, I only had fifteen minutes to make myself presentable before our dinner reservation. At least I'd left my outfit there yesterday. Crashing at Joseph's made sense: Our social life was mostly in Manhattan, plus my tiny studio in Bed-Stuy, with its towering stacks of magazines and books covering most of the available floor space, was a hovel compared to Joseph's two-bedroom Upper West Side spread.

Watching him select a pair of cuff links from his extensive collection, then polish his dress shoes to a gleaming black, I realized that Joseph Burke III was very much like his apartment: mannerly, attractive, functional, above reproach. The Harvard-educated oldest son of the Maryland Burkes, Joseph was a member of one of the East Coast's most distinguished Black families. His mother loved to remind me that her father and her father's father were doctors. Joseph was a "fine catch," as Marie put it. The two of them went to Harvard together, and she'd introduced us a year ago at one of their alumni mixers.

My heart had just been bruised by a guy I'd met right after I transferred to *StyleList*. He was a serious-minded marketer who worked on events for Park Ave Pub's entertainment magazines. A wiry six-foot-six with a penchant for vests and denim overalls, everyone thought he spent his weekends looking for pickup games at Rucker Park. But it turned out that he was too nerdy for basketball and instead spent his free time collecting manga and watching anime—which he found out I loved too when he saw me reading *Dragon Ball* in the cafeteria. He came over to reintroduce himself, then pulled out his copy of *Neon Genesis Evangelion*.

For a few months, we were two happy blerds, enthusiastically geeking out together. And then he got recruited by Roc-A-Fella Records to join their marketing department. Within weeks, he was wearing monochrome baggy outfits with a thick gold chain, canceling our dates to go to industry events, and casually dropping *bitches* and *hoes* in regular conversation. The minute I protested, he unceremoniously dumped me for a Brazilian model.

When I told my sob story to Marie over lunch in the cafeteria, she'd offered to introduce me to her college buddy.

"Yeah, I don't know about your Ivy League friends," I'd said, laughing. "I'm going for a Morehouse man."

"Just come on and meet my boy Joseph. He's fine and paid and straight. It's like the Black man trifecta. And he's in his mid-thirties with no kids." Marie widened her eyes for emphasis.

"Why haven't you gotten with him, then?"

"Maybe I did—a junior-year fling. It didn't even last two weeks, and we've been dogs ever since. It's all good, I swear. Besides, I'd like to see him end up with a nice girl instead of the gold diggers that are always hanging around him."

Turned out the man *was* fine: six feet, two inches of deep caramel with the self-possession of someone who has only ever known success. Joseph tucked in the button-down shirts he wore under his carefully distressed leather jacket; he owned both a silver and a gold watch; his cocktail of choice was a dirty martini; and he spoke with the velvety baritone of a prime-time news anchor, carefully measuring every word like Himalayan salt. Joseph's confidence was even more attractive than his square jawline, broad shoulders, and almond-shaped eyes rimmed with lush lashes.

I had been a little intimidated when Marie first asked Joseph to join us for drinks after work. But it turned out that we had a lot of random things in common: We had both been on our high school track teams; we shared an appreciation for nature and liked to Rollerblade through Central and Prospect Parks; each of us read for at least thirty minutes every night; and we both hated the notion that being smart and goal-oriented meant you couldn't be attractive and have fun.

Marie had rolled her eyes at us. "Sweet baby Jesus, you two are insufferable! Just exchange numbers already."

On our first date, he took me across town to an Upper East Side club where the improbably preppy-looking door guy with the turned-up collar immediately opened the velvet rope. Joseph slipped him a twenty on the way in. "I always hit off the hosts and bouncers. You never know when you need to impress a pretty girl," Joseph had said when he saw I'd noticed.

The DJ was spinning West Coast gangsta rap for a crowd that looked like the grown-up version of my prep school graduating class. Joseph knew half the people in there from the financial industry. As Silkk the Shocker played in the background, Joseph generously shared our bottle of Belvedere with many a blond blazered dude who awkwardly danced over to say hello.

I had never met a man like him in my life. Alonzo had accepted nothing less than excellence, but his energy stayed tensely coiled, as if he were always ready to fight for the largest portion if challenged. Since Joseph already assumed that he belonged everywhere and should have the best of everything, he had an effortlessly calm élan. As a maladroit Black woman with a white father who grew up stubbing my toes on the endless stacks of books decreasing the walkable floor space in my home, my élan was harder to come by. The swanky life Joseph easily proffered was pretty damned enticing.

And, no matter what fancy cocktail party, Ivy League mixer, or European hot spot Joseph took me to, I felt like I belonged, if only because I was with him.

Now, a year later, I was standing in Joseph's bathroom, trying to comb through my sweaty and tangled hair before giving up and shellacking it into a neat bun with loads of gel. I had on a black sheath dress that had been a reject from a recent fashion shoot, black patent pumps, the Swarovski crystal studs I'd worn all day, and a thick silver cuff that Joseph had given me for Christmas. The combination of the sleek hairstyle and carefully applied red lipstick made me look as if I'd stepped out of Robert Palmer's "Addicted to Love" video.

My polished ensemble belied the day's stress still churning my stomach. With "Black girls don't sell magazines" resounding in my ears, I suddenly felt very sick of what was staring back at me in the bedroom mirror. Joseph came up behind me, put both hands on my shoulders, and kissed the back of my neck. Normally, I relaxed under his touch, but tonight my shoulders stayed tight. He dropped his hands. "What's going on with you?"

I forced a smile, faced him, and took one of his hands. "Sorry, I had a stressful day."

"Rough time interviewing Donna Karan? Or did Nicole Kidman want green tea at the shoot and all you had was chamomile?"

His laugh was innocent, but I felt unexpected tears fill my eyes. I went back to fussing with my hair. I was in no mood to defend *StyleList*, but I felt too fragile for his thinly veiled condescension. Rather quickly after we started dating, I realized that the flip side of Joseph's calm confidence was sweeping arrogance. "Yeah, that's it. Donna stood me up and I had to find marmite for Nicole's saltines. Come on, we're late," I murmured.

At that moment, I wanted nothing more than to ditch Joseph altogether. I thought about meeting up with my best friend, Teresa, and my girls Sofie and Denyse, who had invited me out that night. I tried not to picture the three of them laughing it up at Rosa Mexicano, a hangout where we could always count on the bartender, a balding colossus with a Scottish accent and a crush on every female patron, to put an extra shot of Don Julio in our mango margaritas.

Or better yet, I thought of not going out at all. I fantasized about catching the subway home to my own apartment, changing out of my heels and into my slippers and pj's, pouring a bowl of Honey Nut Cheerios, and watching *Law & Order* reruns with fine-ass Assistant District Attorney Paul Robinette.

Anything instead of the long evening that was stretching in front of me...

Then Joseph drew a small box from his pocket and handed it to me. "A promotion present," he said.

"But we're celebrating you tonight. Why did you get me a gift?" I asked, annoyed at myself for reacting to his generosity with impatience.

"Nicole, I want you to share in my good fortune. You're my woman, and you should look like it."

"You mean I'm a reflection on you, so I had better look good?" I could hear the harsh judgment in my voice but had no control tonight. "I'm not your trophy girlfriend."

"No one said you are. Jesus, what's wrong with you? I bought you a present—and yes, as my woman, you should look expensive. I should apologize for wanting my lady to look good?" Joseph sighed and looked upward.

My face grew warm as I suddenly recalled Alonzo intoning, *Be Daddy's good little bitch.* Joseph's imperious word choice was infuriating, but at least I was his lady and not his bitch. I stood up and hugged him from behind. I was almost five eleven in my heels and could kiss his neck without stretching. "My bad. I skipped lunch today and I'm obviously feeling it," I told him, nuzzling his neck.

He grabbed my hands and said without looking back at me, "You know, Nikki, no one has to be nice to you."

Ugh. That was a phrase my mother endlessly repeated throughout my teen years. It stung coming out of Joseph's mouth. "I know that, Joe, I just don't like being told what to—"

Joseph continued as if I hadn't said a word. "And you're not the only one making life choices that have real consequences." He spun around and cupped my chin in his hand. "Right now, I'm choosing you. Not because I have to, because I want to. Now please open your gift."

I wished that my first thought wasn't that he had a point. I saw the looks women on the street threw Joseph's way. And I also knew by the way he would pull me closer when he caught the thirsty glances that Joseph Burke III, for all his high-handedness, truly did care for me. I opened the box to reveal an elongated diamond-encrusted triangle dangling from a thin flat silver chain. It was both elegant and slightly edgy.

"Joseph, this is so cool. It's gorgeous," I said sincerely.

"It reminded me of you the second I saw it," he said, fastening it around my neck. We both assessed my reflection in the mirror. It sparkled against my chest and picked up the shine of the gloss I'd applied over my lipstick.

This had happened so many times before: The presumptuous self-assurance that I'd initially found so fascinating would irritate me. Then Joseph would call to invite me out to some hot new restaurant I never could have afforded on my own, or he'd give me an extravagant present, and my resistance would crumble. He was generous and smart and attractive. And I was damaged goods, a jumbo shrimp with imperfect morals and a mountain of credit card debt. Joseph made me feel like a better version of myself—in part, I hated to admit, because he thought I deserved him.

"I do love it," I said quietly. "And I love you."

The restaurant was right across Central Park from Joseph's apartment, so we were only a few minutes late. I'd grown up in a house governed by the laws of CPT, which meant that my family was indiscriminately late to everything: movies, flights, graduations, weddings. In college, I'd been called out by more professors than I could count for lurching into class ten minutes after they'd begun to lecture. I couldn't tell them that I'd grown up watching my professor parents race to their own classrooms, clutching their jackets over invariably disheveled outfits, papers spilling out of their respective weathered leather briefcases.

I don't know what was more surprising: seeing my parents waiting at the table or that they had made it there on time. I stopped in my tracks, but Joseph's hand on my lower back gently propelled me forward.

"What are they doing here?" I whispered over my shoulder as Joseph and I wove our way through the tables, the suited and bejeweled diners watching us appraisingly. It was one of the most expensive French restaurants in the city, and to the Upper East Side regulars, the Black folks coming into the dining room that evening must have seemed as endless as clowns streaming out of a Volkswagen Bug.

"I invited them," he whispered back. "I didn't tell you because I knew you'd find some reason to cancel."

He wasn't wrong. It had taken my mother months to start speaking to me after that fateful night at Krispy Kreme, and, even three years later, she hadn't fully gotten over the incident. There had been no point trying to explain the anxiety I reflexively felt whenever Alonzo's name hit the industry trades; Mom had no sympathy for me. My dad's reaction was a little more protective, but I knew they both thought I had gotten myself into that mess and would have to deal with the consequences. Spending too much time with them was exhausting.

They had at least saved me some embarrassment by not telling Joseph why our relationship was strained. The downside was that he never understood why I rarely wanted to hang out with my sweet, scholarly mom and dad.

With just a few feet left before we got to the table, I could only grimace at Joseph before turning my head to my waiting parents with a bright smile.

"Joseph, come over here and give me some sugar," Mom said as soon as we got within hearing distance. Her dark middle-parted bob was tucked behind both ears, and she turned her head from side to side, revealing the delicate gold earrings that Joseph had given her for Christmas. It didn't matter that my mother's heavy wool A-line skirt swirled awkwardly around her legs as she stood to embrace him or that she wore a shapeless white blouse and clunky oxfords. A slender five eight with taut mahogany skin stretching over high, wide cheekbones, huge black eyes that seemed to both absorb and reflect the low light of the dining room, and pouty lips, my mother was striking. She never wore makeup and still managed to outshine most women in the room.

My dad was wearing his customary night-out getup, straight from an L.L.Bean catalog: a shabby suit jacket, navy khakis, and brown penny loafers. He and my mom were the most handsome perennially rumpled couple most people had ever seen. Dad stood, gave me a big kiss, and twirled me around. "Ravishing as usual, Nikki," he said, beaming while I hugged my mom.

"Except you're wearing your hair up again," my mom said as she took her seat. "What is the point of having all that hair if you never wear it down?"

Her barbs about my hair never failed to take me back to my childhood. When I was twelve years old, I made my mother remove me from Jack and Jill, an exclusive organization for future members of the Links and the Boulé and their well-heeled parents. My brown-skinned mama hadn't passed their paper bag test when she was a girl but thought her light-skinned daughter would fit right in, not processing that my smudgy glasses, rubber-band braces, bony knees, and pimply cheeks were impressive to literally no one. "Whatever for?" she'd grumbled when I told her I'd had enough.

"The kids are snooty, and there's a girl with blue eyes that all the boys freak out over. At the last meeting, this one boy made me get out of a chair because he wanted her to sit there. That's when I called you to come and get me, and I'm not going back!" As I braced for potential retribution, Mom's face remained weirdly expressionless as she processed the apparent premium blue eyes carried over my frizzy hair. We never spoke of Jack and Jill again, but she stopped allowing me to even get a trim. By the time I went to Howard University, my hair was a waist-length mess. One of the first things I did as a freshman was chop off six inches, which elicited such endless haranguing from my mom that going for a haircut still gave me hives.

Hair had remained a touchy subject, so it didn't help when Joseph chimed in, "Hear, hear," ignoring my glare.

My mom smiled at Joseph while I calculated how many days of "No, honey, I have a headache" he deserved for that comment. But when he gave me a mischievous wink and pulled my chair out for me, I subtracted a day. That man trafficked in charm.

"This necklace is beautiful," Mom said, reaching out for the diamond sparkling in the restaurant's soft light. "Is it new?"

"Just gave it to Nikki tonight," Joseph proudly announced. "I like it when she sparkles."

I expected my mom to deliver a lecture on the disastrous ramifications of blood diamonds, but she gave him a playful smile. "So, when is she going to get a big diamond to wear on her hand?"

"Whoa, whoa," I broke in. "We're getting a little ahead of ourselves here."

Thankfully, Dad noticed the sweat mustache starting to form above my lip. "So, Joseph, tell us about your fancy new job," he said diplomatically.

As Joseph plunged into a long description of capital structure and accounting operations, all I could hear was the "wah wah wah" of Charlie Brown's teacher. I hadn't eaten since my morning bagel, and I was starving. The aroma of butter, garlic, and herbs was making me dizzy, and I fantasized about my steak frites until I felt someone shaking my shoulder.

"Hello, hello? Are you with us?" Mom was asking.

"Of course," I said, having no idea what we were talking about. "Um, Joseph has been working so very hard for this promotion," I tried.

This time everyone laughed at me, including my dad.

Mom shook her head. "You will never change, Nicole. I asked you how your job is going."

"Oh, that. Great. Fabulous. Amazing," I said unconvincingly. "In fact, today I came up with the theme for our January issue. Lucinda loved it. And now I'm in charge of a huge project."

"You didn't tell me that, Nikki. I thought you had a tough day," Joseph said, looking slightly offended. "What was your idea?"

"The ageless issue. And my editor put me in charge of a national sex survey where we look at the sexual habits of women from twenty to sixty." My mom raised her eyebrows, but I kept talking, digging my hole deeper. "I'm on a crazy deadline. I have to find two thousand women who'll answer explicit questions about what they do in bed, and I only have two weeks to finish it . . ." I trailed off with a nervous giggle.

No one said anything for a minute, avoiding eye contact. Finally, Joseph said unconvincingly, "Well, that sounds fascinating."

"Good lord, Nikki," Mom said. "I got a little excited when I heard the word 'study,' but it's about sex?"

"Yes, it's about sex." I sighed. "And it was a big deal that my boss entrusted it to me."

"It just seems so"—she paused, searching for the right word—"vulgar."

I could almost feel the specter of Alonzo Griffin hovering over our table, and I wished the waiter would reappear so I could order a stiff drink. "Mom, you're acting like it's porn or something."

By the time the waiter returned with our appetizers, Mom and I were glaring at each other. As everyone else started talking at once about how great the food looked, I gave up and dug in, finishing every bite of my salad and then my filet mignon and fries in silence. No one noticed because Joseph spent the rest of the night going on and on about his new responsibilities, clients, and office space. Mom kept encouraging his monologue, interjecting with "Tell us more" and "Go on, dear" whenever he took a breath. And when he plunked down his platinum American Express at the end of the meal—without even glancing at the bill—my mom beamed.

Later that night, I sat on the sofa next to Joseph, braiding my hair into long plaits as he watched the news. He'd been too busy regaling his appreciative audience with elaborate stories about his work to notice that I was still upset. I knew I should have been impressed and proud too, but, truthfully, I was a little resentful of the whole thing. He'd invited my parents to dinner without telling me, and then I'd been treated as if I edited *Penthouse* letters for a living. What was worse was how jealous I felt. Joseph's voice never had quite the same passion when addressing me as it did when he talked about his job.

Joseph absent-mindedly reached out for a braid to play with as he drank his scotch, but I pulled it out of his hands, suddenly annoyed by his fixation with my hair.

"Joseph, what if I cut it all off?" I asked, the words rushing out of my mouth. "Real short, Halle short."

"You'll never do it," he said, taking another sip. "You've never had short hair in your life."

"What if I did?" I said with manufactured conviction.

"Please. You won't, Nicole. It's just not you," he said firmly, getting up and walking toward the kitchen. I heard him pour more scotch into his glass.

When Joseph came back into the living room, he shut off the TV and put Portishead's *Dummy* on the stereo. "If anything, you should wear your hair out more," he said. Or straighten it sometime. Do you realize that I've never actually seen your hair straight?"

Naturally, I thought. Every Black man worth his salt seemed to want a woman with flowing locks on his arm. It made their dicks longer or something. I raised my eyebrows and said, "So, you think I wouldn't look good with short hair?"

"All I'm saying is that your hair is beautiful, and I'd like to see it more often." Joseph reached for my hand. "I always figured I'd propose on a boat with your hair whipping in the wind."

"Whatever," I snapped, his presumption making me feel powerless.

Joseph dropped my hand, and I was instantly ashamed; for all Joseph's arrogance, he always looked hurt when I dismissed his periodic hints at marriage. Before I could apologize, he rose and walked toward the bedroom, his face totally unreadable. I hated when Joseph's expression went blank, which I thought of as his "game face." I imagined him pausing to get that face together before entering the old boys' club that was his office.

Pausing in the doorway, Joseph turned and said, "I told you what I like and how I'd like to see you. Either you can continue to be right all by yourself, or you can consider the possibility that not everyone around you is wrong all of the time." With that, he shrugged, downed his scotch, and left the room to shower. I sat still for a minute, then rose when I realized he expected me to follow him.

THREE

"Oooh, finally you're going to let me work my magic!" CeCe exclaimed as I extricated the scrunchie from my knotty hair.

"Well damn, Ce. I didn't realize you'd been feeling so stifled." I winked at her, having already braced myself for what I knew would be an unrestrained reaction to my first-ever request for a silk press and highlights. CeCe had been doing my hair for the last three years, and since hairstylist years are like dog years, she now understood me better than most people. In all that time, I'd only ever allowed her to give me a dusting, not even a proper trim. We'd never shaped my curls, and we'd certainly never blown them out.

"So why the change of heart, boo?" she asked while clipping my split ends. CeCe looked radically different every time I saw her, and that day she was wearing a green vinyl miniskirt, white go-go boots, and a cropped silver sweater that barely covered her bra. Her thick box braids were in a high ponytail, revealing enormous silver hoops that touched her shoulders. Every time CeCe stopped to make a point, she waved her shears emphatically in the air, coming dangerously close to those swinging earrings.

"Joseph wants to see my hair straight," I told her. "I think he's getting pretty sick of the pony."

CeCe caught the slight edge in my tone and briefly put a comforting hand on my shoulder. "It's just a blowout, Nik. Fling it around a little for him, then you can rinse out my brilliant work and go right on back into your ol' curly pony."

She was right. No need to make this more than it was. I closed my eyes and tried to calm down as I inhaled the pungent smell of relaxers and dye mixed with perfumed shampoos and musky candles. It was Saturday morning, prime time in CeCe's Studio, and the place was packed. From the outside, the studio looked like any other storefront Black hair salon. Then you walked through the reception area, climbed a flight of stairs, and entered CeCe's imagination. The second floor was a loft space, tricked out to look like a Middle Eastern lounge with red walls, Turkish throw rugs, scattered beaded pillows, and intricate colorful lanterns hanging from the ceiling. I would not have been surprised if one day gyrating belly dancers offered me a hookah pipe while I sat under the dryer.

The décor was a sharp contrast to the R&B playlist Ce always played at top volume. She was in an Xscape mood that day because "My Little Secret" led into "Just Kickin' It" with "Understanding" coming up right after. Next to me, a couple of Saturday regulars were looking through magazines, waiting for a stylist to get to them. I could hear them chatting over the loud music: "Yo, you know this magazine is kinda hot."

"Please, it's hella ghetto. And what's up with Charli Baltimore on the cover? For real, though."

"Hater. Charli's working it out. That white fur she got on is *lovely*."

"Yeah, but she's not wearing anything else. It's tacky. And look at all these blurry shots of rappers and shit, magazine looking like some glued Polaroids on a page."

The women were seated close together on a red sofa, poring over a thin title I didn't recognize.

"Ce, you seen *Sugar* yet?" one of them called over.

"Yeah," she yelled back, never taking her eyes off my hair, which was now two inches shorter. Satisfied, she pulled out the hairdryer and round brush. "It's kinda janky. And the beauty stories are terrible. The models look like they're on a box of drugstore hair grease."

They all laughed, then a stylist called one of the regulars over to a shampoo sink. The magazine lay abandoned on the sofa while the other woman flipped through a copy of *Hot Hair*.

"CeCe, let me get that magazine, please?" I asked.

"Okay, but quit moving your damn head." She stopped blow-drying my hair to hand it over. We both checked out the cover. *Sugar* was written in thick, swirly, multicolored letters; underneath, Charli was in a long fur coat, lying on a king-sized bed with a glaring purple duvet and matching pillows. The tagline read: "Fashion and Beauty, Baby!" My eyes met CeCe's in the mirror and we both chuckled.

"Well, I like the name," I said.

"And it is kind of a good idea," she said with a shrug.

"Why so?"

"Well, there's no magazine for *us*, you know." CeCe drew the brush through my hair.

"What? Ce, this magazine is not for me!"

"And *StyleList* is?" CeCe raised an eyebrow. She motioned with her chin at a small stack of *StyleList* issues on a side table. "I got a subscription out of loyalty to my girl, but I can't get my clients to pick them up. Don't nobody in here want beauty tips from Gwyneth Paltrow." She paused to glance at my motionless face in the mirror. "Girl, you okay? I didn't mean to be rude."

I barely registered her voice as Lucinda's offhanded pronouncement "Black girls don't sell magazines" scrolled like a prime-time news chyron across my mental field of vision. I thought about a features department meeting earlier that week in which I'd pitched a profile on Bobbie Washington. With her long blond locs, full heart-shaped mouth, and hourglass figure, Bobbie looked like a gorgeous peach, and her new single was in constant play on R&B radio stations. It seemed like a win-win, but Tara shot a withering look my way. "Omg, Bobbie is soooo boring," she'd drawled, then winked conspiratorially toward the rest of the editors seated at the conference table. "I mean, the only way Lucinda would green-light that story is if Bobbie agreed to be photographed in whiteface or something." The entire features department tittered at the thought of the buzz a shoot with Bobbie in whiteface would generate. Everyone except me. Seeing my stony face, Tara put a hand over her mouth in mock contrition. "Whoops, sorry, Nikki."

I shook my head to stop the replay. "But what about *Essence*?" I asked, looking around the salon. Every third woman was thumbing through a copy of the beloved magazine.

"Of course, I love me some *Essence*. Everyone does and always will. But if white girls get to choose between *Glamour* and *Cosmo* and *Elle* and freakin' *StyleList*, why can't I get a magazine that my mom don't read for tips to reduce her fibroids?"

I paged through *Sugar* to see if, despite the wild cover, there was something to it. In the first few pages, I found tons of typos, out-of-focus paparazzi shots, and mismatched fonts in Day-Glo colors. But I also found Black women of all different shades and shapes, fashion by urban designers, beauty tips with melanin in mind. The magazine had been put together with staples and glue and zero respect for either the color wheel or the English language—yet I felt its pure, raw energy flow from the pages into my hands. I thought about how badly I wanted to be an editor-in-chief one day and that *Sugar*, or some version of it, was exactly the kind of magazine I would want to run.

I flipped to the masthead to see if I knew anyone involved in putting together this beautiful train wreck but only recognized the editor-in-chief, Luna Baxter, who'd been a model for years. I remembered her from a tone-deaf fashion spread in *StyleList* titled "Haute Mess." Shot in a grimy Brooklyn diner, she and the other models were styled in garish designer gear with teardrop tattoos on their faces, animal-print eyeshadow, and neon weaves. The pictures were so awful they inspired a short-lived boycott of the magazine. Lucinda, of course, had been elated at all the coverage.

Then I noticed who published *Sugar*: NuVoices Media, headed by Barbara Porter. Now that was a name I knew. Three years ago, Barbara had picked up on the fact that hip hop music and fashion had taken over the mainstream pop scene, so she founded Groove Media and launched *Groove* magazine. She'd hired Alonzo, fresh off his Park Ave Pub scandal, to be the company's president. Together, they swiftly grew *Groove* from a thin magazine you could pick up for free in music stores to an award-winning, provocative publication with a paid subscriber base that had surpassed *Revolutions* in both scale and cultural impact. Barbara and Alonzo had even been the main subjects of a recent above-the-fold *New York Times* article on the power of urban media.

Barbara had surprised the publishing industry by leaving Groove Media a year ago to take over NuVoices Media, a start-up that already housed *Decode*, a sports magazine for Black men, and *Bella*, a lifestyle magazine for Latina women. I didn't know if she'd acquired or launched *Sugar*, and I didn't know if Alonzo had joined her at NuVoices.

My heartbeat quickened as I carefully examined the page again for his name. Not seeing it, I let out a long exhalation. I still took pains not to run into Alonzo, although a couple months ago, I'd made the mistake of going to one of *Groove*'s famous music showcases; along with the up-and-coming talent, Brandy and Monica were supposed to show up, and I was dying to see if the frenemies would make it to the stage to sing "The Boy Is Mine." I'd managed to duck Alonzo until after the performances when I saw him threading his way through the crowd in my direction. I spun around and quickly made for the door, but our close encounter had left me breathless with fear.

I was startled out of my reverie by CeCe loudly declaring, "I have outdone myself, Nik! Ta-da!"

I'd been facing her while she added the finishing touches, so she spun me around to the mirror. My lightened silky hair swirled around my shoulders while the highlights seemed to shimmer under the chandelier's diffuse light. I kept moving my head from side to side, staring at myself as if I were a stranger on the subway. The person staring back at me now resembled my dad more than my mom, which I wasn't sure I liked.

CeCe was waiting for my reaction, so I ran my fingers through my hair and said truthfully, "Honestly, I just didn't process how different I would look." Seeing her crestfallen expression, I quickly added, "Don't get me wrong, you did the damn thing, Ce. No one can touch your skills. I mean, this is crazy."

CeCe shot me a look that said she was aware that I was laying it on a tad thick. Shaking a can of holding spray, she said, "Thanks, girl, but I know you. Let me spray this on real quick so this hair has a chance of lasting at least a few days."

I met her eyes in the mirror. She had me pegged. I was missing my curls before I could finish paying her bill. As I left the salon, I tucked a spare copy of *Sugar* into my bag.

A few minutes after I took a seat at Rosa Mexicano's bar, Teresa made her entrance, swinging a sizable shopping bag. As a public defender, she did not get to bill at a bloated hourly rate like most other lawyers I knew, so Teresa made pennies to their dollars. And I swear homegirl blew half her salary on shoes. She habitually dressed in a sunset spectrum of rich reds, oranges, and purples, but her wardrobe was inexpensive—mostly Old Navy and J.Crew with a few Adrienne Vittadini dresses she'd found on the clearance rack at Lord & Taylor to wear for major trials. In addition to not being able to afford them, Teresa always said she didn't wear expensive clothes so her clients would feel more comfortable around her. A slim-thick five foot two (although her voluminous dark curls added a solid extra inch of height), she justified her shoe habit by saying she needed stature to be more intimidating in court.

I was going to comment on the shopping bag but, true to form, Teresa didn't give me a chance. She took one look at my hair and exclaimed, "Whoa, that is hot! You look like a model, Nik. Or like one of those fashion chicks at your magazine. I swear I wouldn't have recognized you if you walked past me on Broadway."

She spun my barstool around to check out the back, then paused. "You look gorgeous, but like *StyleList* you . . . I mean, you've managed to spend three years there looking like *you* you. I got used to the buns and the ponies. And you know I love a natural." She patted the nimbus of tight ringlets around her own head.

I learned very early on that Ms. Teresa Cruz, the original Bronx Butter Pecan Rican, was incapable of bullshit. I'd met Teresa at a track meet for the best high school track-and-field teams in New York City during our sophomore year. Most of the other girls had cloistered in unwelcoming cliques, but then Teresa bopped in, snapping her gum and twirling short curls that kept escaping a sparkly purple scrunchie. I had on a purple scrunchie of my own and felt an immediate kinship beyond our brown skin and unruly hair. I silently rooted for her as she dominated the 100 and the 200, then anchored the winning 4 x 100 relay team. And I saw Teresa watch as I won the grueling 400- and 800-meter races.

She'd marched up to me afterward and exclaimed, "Thank God you're kind of slow because you powered through those long-ass races. You left those white girls in the dust. Don't ever become a sprinter!"

"The 400 isn't long!" I'd chuckled. "But thank God you've got no stamina because you're fast as hell. Don't come for my mid-distance stats!"

Teresa and I had been tight ever since. During our last couple years of high school, we were inseparable. She'd take the subway from the Bronx, and we'd meet at the 125th Street stop to plan whatever shenanigans we could dream up. Sometimes, we'd walk around Harlem, looping the always hectic 125th Street corridor to flirt with the boys who worked in the fast-food restaurants and sneaker shops. Too many people knew my family to sneak into most of the uptown clubs and bars, but every now and then we could convince a door guy to look the other way so we could hear local MCs like Big Daddy Kane or Rakim or KRS-One and Boogie Down Productions.

When we felt fancy, we'd stay on the subway to Fifty-Ninth Street, where we'd get off to window shop at Fiorucci before going to a movie on Columbus Avenue. But mostly we'd head downtown to Fourteenth Street and decide on the fly whether to bum around St. Marks and sift through the stacks at Tower Records, or walk down to Washington Square Park to score a dime of seed-filled twiggy weed, or trek down Broadway to Canal Jeans to snag some of their famous pinback buttons for our nylon bomber jackets. Every now and then, we'd tell our parents we were crashing at each other's houses and hit a club like the Palladium or Tunnel. Those spots never checked IDs, so if the bouncer deigned to pick us out of the crowd, we could drink whatever silly fruity cocktail we knew how to order. Because the subways were always filled with people, we somehow felt safe dozing off on our tipsy 3:00 AM ride home.

Teresa was a straight-A student and eventually went to Columbia University on a full ride, then stayed through her law degree. We hung out over the holidays and summers when I came home from Howard and then picked up right where we'd left off after I graduated.

I flipped my hair over my shoulder; it hadn't been straight for an hour and I was already getting sick of it. "Yeah, it's the new old me."

"Is it, though?" Teresa was still watching me quizzically. "It's more like the new white you."

"Ouch."

"Don't get me wrong, you look fly as hell," she replied slowly. "But you've always been more of a Denise than a Whitley. And definitely not a Vanessa."

I searched my brain. "Vanessa?"

"Williams."

"Well, don't get too used to it. One ounce of humidity and it's going back. It might be a wrap before I get off the subway," I joked, then let my smile ebb. "It's just weird how no one notices your hair until it's straight. So many guys were staring at me on the walk over here that it started to feel really uncool."

Teresa rubbed imaginary tears from her eyes and played a tiny violin. "You know how guys are. And didn't you say that the blowout was at Joseph's request?" I caught her not-so-subtle side-eye.

While I considered how to reply to her obviously rhetorical question, our regular bartender delivered a couple martinis to some businessmen in the corner and headed our way. He widened his pale blue eyes, did a showy double take, and said in his thick brogue, "What have we here? Is it a special occasion or did you get dolled up because you knew you were going to see me?" He jabbed his beefy thumb into his chest. "The spicy mango 'ritas are on me today, beautiful ladies."

I looked at Teresa, telegraphing *See?* with my raised eyebrows, and we both snorted.

"From now on, imma need you to straighten your hair every time we go out," she whispered as the bartender set our margaritas in front of us with an extra flourish. "How do you think Joseph will like the new look?"

"He's never seen my hair like this." I licked salt from the edge of my glass, then took a big swig. I didn't know how many extra shots the bartender had added, but I could tell it was firewater strong, so I ordered some nachos to soak up the alcohol. "Joe's always on me to wear my curls down more often, and I hadn't processed until the other night that he's never even seen my hair straight. This is the first time a flat iron has touched my head since Alonzo." At the mere mention of his name, every sensation heightened: my denim-clad legs sandpapering together, my hair touching my back between my shoulder blades, my fingers gripping the icy cocktail.

Teresa pressed her lips into a thin line. "And I don't ever want you to get caught up in any ridiculousness like that ever again. Which is why I like it when you do *you*."

"I like it when I do *me* too!" I replied, a little too loudly. "But I also like it when Joseph is happy. It's ... easier."

"He's lucky he's got such a patient woman. He and I would be going at it twenty-four-seven—arguing, not sex!" Teresa laughed, but she put her hand over mine on the bar.

I let out a deep breath. "He would say that I'm lucky to have such a patient man with all my annoying opinions and moody attitude. God knows what he's doing with me."

"Girl." Teresa drew out the word as she turned my head to look me in the eye. "He's with you because the stars aligned for that lucky muthafucka. You are the package, and he knows it. That's why he keeps hinting around at marriage."

"I am so not ready to marry him," I protested, ignoring the first part of her statement.

"And I am so not ready for you to be married! You have to wait until you're at least thirty before I give my consent."

I quietly let myself into Joseph's apartment with the key he'd given me a year ago. "What the fuck!" I heard him yell at the TV. "How did you miss that pop-up, you absolute moron?"

Damn, the Yankees were losing. Well, I was about to turn his evening around.

"Hey baby," I called from the doorway.

"Hey," he mumbled, not turning away from the television.

I went into the kitchen, opened a bottle of Veuve Clicquot I knew he'd been saving for a special occasion, and returned to the living room with two full flutes. I kissed the back of Joseph's neck, handed him a glass, and said, "We're celebrating."

"Nicole, you know I was saving that," he said, then went silent as took me in. Gently, he placed the flute on the coffee table, his expression unreadable.

"Well, say something, Joe," I said, knowing he disliked nicknames. He was the only person aside from my parents and my accountant who called me Nicole.

"Man, you are exquisite, Nicole," he finally said, rising to walk around the sofa. He ran his fingers through my hair, which my tangly spirals had always prevented him from doing. "I admit that I'm surprised. I was starting to lose hope that I'd ever get a blowout. Now I really can't wait to show you off at my client dinner."

Although I'd been looking forward to his appreciative reaction, it was now grating on me. "Was it seriously that bad before?" I asked, taking a swig of the Veuve that I probably shouldn't have opened since I was already buzzed from the extra-strong margarita. "Now I merit an invite to a work event?"

"I'm always trying to get you to go to my work things, but you hate them. You know that!" Joseph took his own gulp of champagne. "I don't know what else I can do to show you how much I think of you."

"Maybe don't say that now that I look like Whitley, you're going to show me off!"

"Whitley? What are you even talking about?" He frowned. "I wouldn't be thinking about a future with you if I didn't like who you are right now. And that's a pretty big deal."

"I'm sorry, what?" I asked, my rapidly shifting mood killing my buzz. I could hear myself overreacting, but his words were hitting a painful target. "So, I should be grateful for your kind consideration?"

Joseph sighed heavily and crossed his arms. "You know what I mean."

I opened my mouth to reply but rushed out of the room instead, not wanting him to see my down-turned trembling lips. I closed the door to the bedroom hard, cracking the paint in the doorway in the process. Joseph hated any damage or mess in his apartment, regularly taking baby wipes to tiny scuff marks on his Farrow & Ball–painted walls.

Joseph let me stew for ten minutes. "Can we please talk?" he asked after I ignored his second knock. "Open up, honey."

I softened a little and unlocked the door. He handed me a fresh glass of champagne and took me in his arms before I could say anything.

"I'm sorry, Nicole. Your hair is amazing and I was just surprised by how different you look. But you were beautiful before too. You're beautiful to me all the time." He held me, his breath warm on my cheek. I felt his hand stealing up my back, touching the long strands.

For a mogul-in-the-making with a killer game face, Joseph had surprisingly little tolerance for conflict and hated for me to be mad at him. He began placing soft kisses up my neck while he gently tugged on my hardening nipples. Ah, there it was: the famous chemistry that had gotten me hooked on Joseph in the first place. Every time I had doubts about whether he would ever really understand me, he'd touch me somewhere sensitive. His emotional declarations and insistence on making sure I was always fully satisfied were a stark contrast to Alonzo's fuck-me-bitch style of sexual domination. Sleeping with Alonzo had been a thrill, but I'd grown tired of his hands pulling my hair while he insisted that he owned my pussy. I wrapped my arms around Joseph's neck, his fingers slipped under my panties, and all was forgotten and forgiven.

FOUR

On Monday morning, I ditched my usual bland, monochromatic uniform and dressed with extra care. My *StyleList* colleagues were world-class experts in all things fashion, with honorary PhDs in cattiness to match. I already stood out like a Day-Glo sign in that office, so a fresh silk press and highlights were guaranteed to spark conversation—both to my face and behind my back. The last thing I needed was for them to turn their razor-sharp eyes on my outfit too.

I shimmied into white Marc Jacobs cargos that were cinched mid-calf with gold snaps, added a matching cropped blazer over a silky tank, and slipped on tan Prada heels that strapped up my ankles. One advantage of working at *StyleList* was the huge designer discounts that the fashion and beauty editors would sporadically allow the features department nerds to use. Plus, I occasionally scored "rejects" from the magazine's fashion closet. Although technically a closet because it was where the fashion department stored clothes for photo shoots, *StyleList*'s looked like no closet I'd ever seen. It was a massive storage space, bigger than my Brooklyn studio, that housed racks upon racks of dresses and pants and tops and jackets, a kaleidoscope of cashmere, silk, leather, and fur. Today's outfit was courtesy of the closet and one benevolent shopping trip to Prada's Fifth Avenue mecca.

Gazing at the walls lined with framed pictures of *StyleList*'s past covers, I hiked down the interminable hall toward my office. It occurred to me that every one of the covers featured a white woman whose hair looked like mine did now: straight, parted on the side. Even though Lucinda liked to stand out in a crowd, her cover taste was remarkably conventional and consistent.

Fighting the urge to scrape my hair into a ponytail, I hurried to my cubicle and pulled out an article I needed to edit for the February issue, comparing five of the most popular diet fads. As far as I could tell the diets were all the same, with different celebrity endorsers. I needed a break from working on the sex survey, but this wasn't the fun respite I'd hoped for. After reading a few sentences, I felt like someone had taken a frying pan to my cranium. I was so focused on rewriting the bland copy that I didn't immediately hear Natasha Gustavsson, *StyleList*'s director of the sacrosanct fashion department, swing around the corner and park herself on the edge of my desk.

Natasha leaned over until her nose was inches from mine. Normally, wide age-range speculation was reserved for Black women since we tend to have taut, wrinkle-free skin until gravity finally gets us in our late seventies. Despite her pallid skin, no one knew if Natasha was forty, fifty, or sixty; she had access to the best cosmetic dermatology in the world, and her Swedish-toddler hair color hid any hint of gray. Up close, though, I could see the difference in skin texture between her face and neck along with a few age spots sprinkled over her bony hands.

"Nikki, darling, I need an enormous, humongous favor." Natasha was always very dramatic, so it was impossible to tell if her request was truly urgent. "Tonight, the president of Saks Fifth Avenue is throwing a cocktail party for Lucinda, and I just found out that I am to give the main toast," she said, voice quavering, standing to pace the tight hall next to my cubicle. I understood why she was stressed; there was no telling how upset Lucinda would be if the toast to her was not appropriately adoring. "We're shooting a punk-princess fashion story at Chelsea Piers in an hour, and I still don't have all the looks," she moaned, not caring that people were craning their necks to see why Natasha was deigning to talk to a jumbo shrimp.

"So, you need me to write you a short speech," I offered gently.

"Oh, would you? Would you?" She ran over and air-kissed my cheek, then turned abruptly at the sound of rolling racks making their way down the hall. Before she sped away to yell at the browbeaten junior editors pushing the racks, Natasha crossed her arms and took me in for the first time. "The hair is to die for, Nikki. You look like you could be in the magazine. Wait until Lucinda sees you," she said, giving me a rare nod of approval. "The party starts at seven. Do this for me and you can come."

"I appreciate that," I said, then continued boldly, "but I also want to shadow you at a couple cover shoots."

I could see her debating whether it was worth it to ask why a features nerd would want to check out a cover shoot. I didn't feel like risking her laughter if I explained that I'd have to know how to put together covers if I wanted to be an editor-in-chief one day.

Mercifully, she decided that questioning my motives wasn't worth her time. "Whatever, fine." With that, she spun around and dashed down the hall.

I look like I could be in the magazine. Of course, it was flattering. But I felt as if what Natasha really meant to say was that I finally looked like I belonged at *StyleList*. The idea that I was now deemed worthy of that honor because I'd lightened and straightened my curls made me want to dunk my head under the faucet in the bathroom sink.

Needing air, I ventured down the hall of framed white women once more to grab a latte from the Starbucks on the corner. The weather had turned cloudy, and as I stepped outside my hair lifted off my shoulders and flapped back and forth like a white flag in the wind.

The party invite was in the back of my mind as I wrote Natasha's toast—*Lucinda, your sartorial sixth sense has amazed and inspired us all... blah blah.* Only the most senior fashion and beauty editors had been invited, and I knew the crowd would be an insular flock of designers, socialites, and celebrities, all dressed to outdo one another. I rarely got invited to events this exclusive and decided to fly solo. I didn't want it to be yet another party where Joseph scoured the room for important people he could convert into clients, or where Teresa would pinch my arm every time she saw someone famous.

The town car pulled up in front of Park Avenue's most exclusive address, a building made famous because the co-op board was among the strictest in the city. The board had turned down several music artists, athletes, and newly rich moguls for the penthouse that the Saks president eventually bought, because they didn't feel the other prospective owners would "fit into their mix."

The doorman led me down a hall that ended in brushed silver doors, where a uniformed elevator operator was waiting to escort me to the penthouse. When the elevator opened into a massive foyer, a Black maid took my coat, a Black waiter offered me a glass of champagne, and another uniformed Black man whose exact purpose I couldn't discern ushered me into the living room. I half expected him to announce me like a herald at court: *All rise for Ms. Nicole Rose, jumbo shrimp from* StyleList.

It took me a second to orient myself, partially because I'd chugged that champagne to calm my nerves. To my surprise, "Can't Take My Eyes Off of You" from *The Miseducation of Lauryn Hill* was playing in the background. I had listened to that brilliant album hundreds of times since it came out, and the familiarity of Lauryn's rich contralto allowed me to relax enough to take in a deep lungful of oxygen and survey the room. If Teresa had been there, my arm would have been black and blue because you couldn't have thrown a paper airplane without hitting an actor, a supermodel, or an infamous heiress.

Trying to appear blasé, I squinted at a squiggle of writing at the base of one of the paintings. Yup, Picasso. The view from the floor-to-ceiling windows that looked over Central Park was almost more spectacular than the museum-quality art. At the end of the room, there was a series of French doors that opened onto the biggest deck I'd ever seen in New York City, big enough to have trees and fountains and a sizable bar with a bartender crafting custom cocktails.

As I stepped onto the deck, a cloud of red hair became visible in the center of a gaggle of *StyleList* editors and boldfaced names. My intention had been to circle the perimeter of Lucinda acolytes, pass the flowery toast I'd written to Natasha, and keep it moving. But Lucinda swung around and recognized me. I could feel her trained eyes passing over my shoes, clothes, and hair like a CT scan. The crowd parted as she moved in my direction, and then collectively gasped as she grabbed me by the shoulders and yelled, "This is the best makeover I have seen in a long time. You, doll, hit the nail on the head."

Lucinda reached a bejeweled hand up and started flipping my mane back and forth over the top of my head. She clearly didn't know to never touch a Black woman's hair.

"Has everybody seen our own intrepid Nikki?" she yelled into the crowd. "So mousy before, and now look! This is what *StyleList* is all about!"

Mousy? So what if I'd worn a ponytail or bun almost every day for the last three years? I'd just about had enough of Lucifer for one night when she grabbed Mary-Kate, who was somehow always within arm's reach, and told her that she wanted an appointment with me tomorrow.

Dodging the daggers I was sure the rest of the *StyleList* team were mentally chucking my way, I surreptitiously gave the toast to Natasha and went back indoors, where the crowd had grown considerably larger. Though my preteen years of fuzzy hair, braces, and glasses had left me with a vague feeling of geekiness that no designer gear or new hairstyle could shake, this party would have intimidated any mortal. I grabbed another glass of champagne from a passing waiter and affixed what I hoped was a confident smile on my face. Then I heard an unmistakably Black woman's voice calling over the din: "Here, sis, let me help you out."

I wasn't sure who the voice was addressing, but I figured the odds were good it was me. Sure enough, a gorgeous willowy woman approached me wearing a skintight Dolce & Gabbana sheath from a spring collection that wasn't yet available in stores. She'd added white stiletto boots and a huge gold bracelet that snaked around her entire upper arm. The crown of her thick black hair was cornrowed back while the rest was in a long loose ponytail. What was most striking in this paparazzi-friendly group was that she wore no makeup, not that she needed it with her flawless mocha skin and killer bone structure.

"I saw Lucifer jack your 'do outside." She laughed, smoothing my hair with her free hand. In her other, she clutched a clipboard with what looked, upside down, like a list of names. When she was done fixing Lucinda's damage, she stuck out her hand.

"Kiara Matsumoro. Matsumoro Public Relations. We're doing this event."

"Nicole Rose. *StyleList*," I replied, shaking her hand. "Call me Nikki."

"*StyleList*? Why don't I know you? I thought I'd met all of you *SL* girls. But your name does sound familiar." Kiara tilted her head. "Wait, did you use to work at *Revolutions*?" Her expression turned more knowing than curious.

"You've really got your ear to the ground," I said, unwilling to reveal more than I thought she might already know. "I was at *Revolutions* before *StyleList*."

"Well, you made it out of there alive," she replied, arching an eyebrow to indicate that she could say more. "What's your *SL* gig?"

"I'm the senior associate editor in the features department."

"Oh, gotcha," she said, lowering her voice. A fashion and celebrity public relations rep with any juice at all would be aware of the departmental pecking order at a magazine like *StyleList*. I was definitely not one of the editors she had to suck up to. But instead of running off as if I had leprosy, Kiara merely waved her hand at the swarm of socialites and celebrities and said, "Well, welcome to the dark side, love. Anyone here you'd like to meet?"

"Not really," I said nonchalantly, immediately regretting my words as I caught sight of a strikingly tall ebony-skinned woman making her way through the vast living room with the easy gait of a former athlete. Her hair was styled in a short natural and she wore a maroon leather jacket with a matching skirt and boots that were almost the same color as the glass of red wine she held. Barbara Porter, the CEO of NuVoices Media, was known for her monochromatic leather outfits.

"I mean, yes," I quickly amended. "Do you know Barbara Porter?" I had become a little obsessed with NuVoices and the media mogul behind it since I'd picked up the issue of *Sugar* at CeCe's Studio, spending hours redesigning *Sugar*'s cover in my mind, filling a fictional table of contents with ideas rejected by Lucinda.

Kiara merely grinned, spoke a few words into a tiny walkie-talkie I hadn't noticed she was carrying, and within a couple minutes, Barbara was being escorted our way by one of the mysterious uniformed men.

"What is this, a coup?" Barbara asked as she kissed Kiara on both cheeks. It did look a bit like we were plotting a revolution—the only three Black women in sight, huddled together in the center of the room. "You know we're going to scare the white folks," she declared loud enough that I knew she didn't care.

"You are a trip, BP." Kiara laced her arm around Barbara's waist.

"You know everyone here knows Barbara Porter, and they're already afraid."

"And who is this?" Barbara turned to me, looking me up and down, taking in my outfit the way Lucinda had but with a markedly different filter. Lucinda was checking my exterior; it felt as if Barbara was gauging my very character.

"You mean you haven't met Nicole Rose yet?" Kiara put both hands on Barbara's shoulders and stared up at her as if she were flabbergasted. It was a little exaggerated, but Kiara was doing me a solid. "She's like the second coming over at *StyleList*, head of features and Lucinda's right hand. Nikki, this is Barbara Porter."

Kiara winked at me from behind Barbara's back, then faded into the crowd.

Barbara and I were suddenly alone. Though I appreciated Kiara's Oscar-worthy intro, I could tell by the neutral look on Barbara's face that this was a woman who made up her own damn mind about people. I took a deep breath and plunged in: "I've admired your career for many years, and it's a tremendous pleasure to finally meet you." Barbara's face remained immobile, so I tried another approach: "America is so ready for NuVoices Media. You really tapped into the cultural zeitgeist."

Barbara took a large gulp of her wine, her eyes starting to wander around the room. I blurted: "Congratulations on *Sugar*. It's a great idea, and even though it's a bit, um, rough around the edges, the magazine definitely has promise."

Well, that was one way to get her attention. I hadn't intended on going down this path, but the champagne had relaxed my filter and my judgment. Barbara let an extra-long silence linger between us while she scrutinized me with amusement. "Oh, you think it has ... promise, do you? Enlighten me, please."

It was too late to turn back, so I ignored her condescending tone and barreled forward. "I mean, there's a whole generation of women who grew up with urban culture and who are defining mainstream culture right now. I'm around high-end designers all the time at *StyleList*, and I can tell you that they are looking to young Black women for inspiration." Barbara was nodding so I felt emboldened enough to ask, "But why is *Sugar* dumbing it down? There's no bona fide style coverage or stories on serious issues. And the design is . . ." I took a breath and looked her in the eye. "I mean, I'm *Sugar*'s target audience, and I think that my friends and I deserve a chic, cool, and smart magazine."

Barbara raised an eyebrow. "Are you the target audience, though? What exactly do you know about urban fashion and lifestyle?" she asked, taking in my outfit again.

"Enough to know that *Sugar* isn't hitting the mark." I shrugged, trying not to look shocked at my own nerve. Kiara might have hesitated to introduce me to Barbara had she known that my first order of business would be to insult NuVoices' newest brand. But Barbara's penetrating glare didn't allow for artifice.

Barbara contemplated my tacit request, pressing her lips together and looking skyward as if she were doing complex math in her head. As an apology was forming on my lips, she handed me a business card. "My assistant's name is Erika. I'll let her know *StyleList*'s 'second coming' will be calling me to discuss *Sugar*." I caught the glimmer of a smile on her face as she walked away.

I decided to leave while I was ahead and made my way toward the elevator. Outside, Kiara was patiently escorting a drunk teenage model into a taxi. Once the girl was safely tucked into the back seat and the driver was given a fifty with specific instructions to deliver her home and nowhere else, Kiara came over to me.

"Poor thing. And that would be a Page Six nightmare. I simply cannot have an underage cover girl fall out at one of my events. You off so early?"

"Yeah, I probably should be a good *StyleList* girl and hang in there, but I'm beat," I said, slightly embarrassed to be called out again on my lack of coolness. I really was tired, though, and they were just starting the part of the evening where various sycophants would deliver their tributes to Lucinda. Since I'd written one of them, I felt I'd done my part.

"Well, you seemed to have gotten enough done in the time you were in there." Kiara winked at me again. This girl didn't miss a trick.

"Thanks again for hooking me up with Barbara."

"Not a problem, love. I have a feeling I'll be seeing you again," Kiara replied, kissing me on both cheeks. She paused before adding, "And you just let me know what you need. Any enemy of that sleaze Alonzo Griffin is a friend of mine."

Our eyes met and we nodded at each other. So, Kiara had heard. My mortification was as real as my gratitude that she was clearly an ally.

As she started to head back into the building, I called out, "Hey Kiara. I have a question for you."

She stopped in the doorway at the sound of my voice. "What's up, ma?"

My curiosity had gotten the better of me: "Matsumoro?"

She laughed and yelled back, "I'm married to Ricky Matsumoro."

The famous real estate developer. Over the past decade, he had been buying hotels and restaurants around downtown New York City, redoing the interiors in a signature chic style, and reopening them to critical acclaim. Even though *StyleList* had covered their elegant wedding, I hadn't registered who she was.

"Lucky girl," I yelled back. We smiled at each other once more, then she disappeared into the building, and I sank into a waiting taxi.

FIVE

Lucinda opened our meeting the next day with: "So, you've been at *StyleList* for three years and this is the first time we've met one-on-one since you were hired."

We were seated on an enormous sofa in Lucinda's thirty-ninth-floor office. I had nearly coughed when I took a sip of the concoction Mary-Kate had given me as I walked in the door, surprised by the presence of alcohol. So this was the elixir to which everyone attributed my boss's youthful glow. But hell, I was cocktailing with Lucinda in her sprawling office that overlooked all of Midtown Manhattan, so I was going to hold my own. I took a huge gulp and nodded.

"And why do you think that is?" she continued.

Because now you think that I look like a StyleList *girl* came to my mind. I'd wanted to wash the curls back into my hair, but knowing that I was meeting with Lucinda, I'd worn it straight again. I nervously wrapped some of the strands around my finger. "Um, I'm not sure, Lucinda. I assume your schedule is hectic, and that your priorities are your fashion and beauty departments."

"Well said." Lucinda got up and retrieved a folder from her desk. "But not entirely accurate." She strolled back over to the sofa, flipped open the folder, and smoothed her skirt over her thighs. Today she was dressed like an urban Inuit in a black leather miniskirt, white fur boots, and a white fur beret atop her fluffed-up hair. Without looking up, she said, "I don't usually meet with my self-sufficient editors who excel. And you, doll, seem to be one of them."

Lucinda continued to skim the contents of the folder while I processed what she'd just said. Though Tara didn't want to acknowledge it, I was her go-to girl: I always had an idea and could be relied upon to hit the most challenging deadlines. I'd produced many of the most talked-about features at *StyleList*, one of which had even won the Oscar of magazine publishing: an Ellie Award from ASME, the American Society of Magazine Editors. Since almost everyone in the office but Lucinda had congratulated me, I'd assumed she didn't know or care that the story had been my baby. But Lucinda was more observant that I'd thought.

"You were responsible for that fabulous package on female sports heroes that won the Ellie. And letters are already pouring in from readers about the sex survey you came up with. Since it only went on sale a couple weeks ago, we don't have final numbers for the January issue, but it looks like the newsstand sales spiked. Not to mention that the impressive sex survey landed me on *Oprah* this week."

In much the same way that I'd had to grit my teeth as Tara sashayed onstage to receive the Ellie (it was a win for the features department, after all), I'd had to swallow my annoyance while watching Lucinda on *Oprah* talking about my survey. I had pulled a couple all-nighters in the office, finishing that massive national survey in only two weeks. But, of course, Oprah preferred the internationally renowned, media-friendly editor-in-chief of *StyleList* over the lowly jumbo shrimp who had actually executed the story.

"I was so honored that Oprah chose to cover that piece. It was important for our readers to have that information," I said carefully.

Lucinda smiled—a rare sighting. "Oh, you are good," she said, emitting a horse's snort of a noise that I assumed was her laugh. "No wonder I never meet with you. You are such a classic overachiever." Lucinda scooted over to my side of the sofa and grabbed my face in both hands. I swallowed the urge to shrug her off during a long minute of examination in which I thought she might pull my lips back to inspect my teeth. "What is your ethnic background?" she finally asked.

"I'm Black," I told her, disentangling myself.

Lucinda waved her hand impatiently. "Obviously, doll. I do live in New York City, you know," she replied, as if I were insulting her. "Black and what else?"

Where the hell was she going with this, I wondered, and was this a potential human resources lawsuit? "My father's parents immigrated here from Ireland."

"Aha!" Lucinda relaxed again. "You're a mélange!"

"Well, yes, my father is white. But I am Black, so..." Enough was enough. I was really trying not be annoyed by her continued close examination of my face. "Respectfully, I'm not sure what my ethnic background has to do with anything we're discussing today."

She got up again, this time to call Mary-Kate, who magically appeared forty-five seconds later with two fresh drinks. As Lucinda took a few healthy swigs, the source of her perpetual unpredictability started to become more clear. "Oh, don't be so uptight, overachiever." She wiped her mouth daintily on what looked like an Hermès scarf. "I have a proposition for you."

At this, I perked up. Crazy as she was, Lucinda was a publishing icon who could make or break my magazine career. I tried not to look too eager as I sat forward to hear her out.

Lucinda finished her drink (an impressive feat since they were presented in tall tumblers with very little ice), and said gravely, "*StyleList* is in trouble." Everything I'd heard about *StyleList*'s performance indicated record-breaking advertising revenue, steady newsstand sales, and rapid digital growth. My face must have registered my alarm because Lucinda quickly continued: "No need to be too concerned, doll." She patted my hand gently, then grabbed it, her nails digging into my palm. "And no need to tell anyone else about our little conversation."

I didn't know many people who could be equal parts motherly and menacing. "I thought we were in the middle of double-digit growth."

"Everyone does," she said impatiently. "And we were for a long time. But over the past couple years we've hit a plateau." Lucinda faced the window, the late afternoon light turning her hair an even brighter shade of red. "The gap between *StyleList* and our lesser competitors is closing. They might even overtake our newsstand numbers if we don't do something."

One of *StyleList*'s claims to fame was that the magazine sold more copies in supermarkets, drugstores, airports, and bookstores than any other fashion title. Not only did we make a ton of money from those sales but advertisers paid a premium to be a part of our success. If that claim was in jeopardy, *StyleList* did indeed have a major problem.

I waited, wary of saying the wrong thing. An editor-in-chief's success is largely based on newsstand numbers, so Lucinda was probably in trouble too. Without turning around, she said, "You seem to have a knack for attention-grabbing stories, which I like. And we need to reach new audiences, audiences that *you* understand better than anyone else." Lucinda summoned her assistant/bartender one more time, took a long drink of her third cocktail, and declared, "I need more ideas that challenge the *StyleList* status quo and generate buzz across demographics—like the sex survey. I'd like to promote you to special projects editor."

I suddenly needed a drink, too, and was grateful that there were two sitting in a row in front of me. Special projects editor was a huge leap, a senior-level title on *StyleList*'s masthead where I would get to conceive and execute major features and multi-issue packages. "Is Tara aware—"

Lucinda interrupted me with one wave of her hand. "Tara will be fine with this. She knows that *StyleList* needs to do more sexy stories that expand our reader base, like the Matsumoro wedding. We got tons of mail after we ran that piece. I want to cover more real-life events in the chic urban crowd."

I allowed myself a moment to dwell on the irony that even though I'd just met Kiara Matsumoro the night before, Lucinda expected me to deliver inside stories on the Black elite. *How typical of white folks to assume we all know each other*, I thought with some irritation. And now I understood: In a desperate bid to save her job, Lucinda wanted me to be *StyleList*'s melanin whisperer to bring in readers who weren't responding to her current stale mix of celebrity diet reviews and the performative diversity of shooting blond supermodels with Maasai tribal members in Kenyan game reserves.

As I tried not to let my face betray my anger at getting asked to be Black on demand, I realized Lucinda was waiting for a response. No one in their right mind would turn this down, certainly not someone whose own goal was to someday run a magazine. I set my drink on the table and stood up. Surprisingly, she stood too, looking at me expectantly.

"Thank you for this opportunity, Lucinda," I said. "I understand the situation and I will do my best to keep *StyleList* on top where it belongs."

"Of course, you will, overachiever." Lucinda clapped me on the back with surprising force. "You didn't ask," she continued, "but the position comes with a significant pay increase. HR will email you the details." With that, Lucinda sat behind her desk, perched teal cat-eye readers on her nose, and started tapping on her keyboard. I realized this was her way of dismissing me. As I moved toward the door, she peered over her glasses. "You know, Alonzo Griffin tried to talk me out of hiring you. I won't lie, he said some very unflattering things. But he'd come on to too many of our in-house models to let him sway me. I told him to go fuck himself." She waited a second to make sure that I was paying full attention, then pronounced with absolute seriousness, "Still, this is when you pay me back."

SIX

I knew I didn't have close friends at *StyleList*, but I didn't know I had so many potential enemies. As word spread that I was Lucinda's new "favorite," the atmosphere on the floor grew chilly, with reactions ranging from pretending I didn't exist to downright animosity. The lifestyle-and-beauty girls rolled their eyes at me as I passed them in the hallways. The copyeditors and fact-checkers who'd always appreciated how detail-oriented I was now gave me skeptical side-eyes. And Tara refused to even look at me, making it clear that Lucinda had been lying about her acceptance of my new position.

Even Natasha seemed salty. When I stopped by her office to ask how that gushing speech I'd crafted for her was received, she said flatly, "Lots of applause, wunderkind." I had a feeling I could kiss my fashion closet castoffs and designer discounts goodbye, which was fine by me, as long as she made good on her promise to let me shadow her on a cover shoot.

When I popped up at the photographer's studio during the next shoot, Natasha begrudgingly described how the *StyleList* team created the covers that had been breaking newsstand records—until recently, apparently. First, we talked about choosing subjects to coincide with major cultural events. *StyleList* would be shooting Julia Roberts that day because she was coming off the success of *Notting Hill* and was about to release her next movie, *Runaway Bride*. The issue would get added visibility because it featured a popular star on newsstands during the peak of her next movie's marketing campaign.

Then Natasha walked me through the importance of well-worded and intentionally placed cover lines. We talked about having a concept and a palette for the cover—we were shooting Julia in a couture wedding dress, so people would think of the movie, against a dark green background that would contrast with her auburn hair. Natasha told me that we'd need enough images for the inside profile, with at least one close-up beauty shot, as well as a vertical full-body shot for the table of contents. Then Natasha showed me the racks of clothing selects and informed me that she always saved the biggest designer for the cover. It was a master class.

Now that I was a senior member of the editorial team, I was also gaining expertise in all aspects of magazine making. I thought I knew a lot after three years at *StyleList*, but now I was sitting in on strategy sessions about long-term issue planning, sponsorable editorial packages for the sales team, possible bookazines and other brand extensions, multi-issue franchise development with prosocial components, and sell-through and reader satisfaction scores. I was getting a PhD in being an editor-in-chief.

While the *StyleList* team was hating on me, everyone else in my life was thrilled: Joseph was excited, my parents were proud, my girls were pumped. But when my expanded responsibilities made me miss one too many girls' nights out, Denyse, Sofie, and Teresa decided to make a surprise evening visit to my office. When the after-hours Park Ave Pub lobby attendant called my desk, I thought my Chinese food had arrived. Instead, my friends spilled out of the elevator with cupcakes and champagne.

As I often thought when we all hung out: We made an odd group. Flaxen blond with icy blue eyes, Sofie was six feet tall in bare feet—which is, apparently, average height in her native Amsterdam. She'd moved to New York five years ago after a semi-successful modeling career in Europe. She and MC WhiteHot, a white rapper whose cred as a gifted lyricist offset the slight corniness of his pale locs, fell for each other immediately. And he bankrolled Sofie's Café, a French bistro on Grand Street with red leather banquettes, mirrored walls, and lighting so low you needed the table candles to read the dinner menu. Sofie added rotating DJs playing hip hop and R&B mixes and curated a cool crowd, transforming the restaurant into a music- and fashion-industry hangout over which she presided in heavily accented English peppered with random urban phrases.

Teresa discovered Sofie's Café after a shoe-shopping extravaganza in SoHo for which she was, naturally, wearing high heels. She'd heard New Edition's harmonies spilling out of the restaurant's open door and hobbled in to give her aching arches a rest. After being welcomed by Sofie herself, who gossiped with her while she recovered from the strain of maxing out her credit card, Teresa was a convert. She brought me and I brought my closest college friend, Denyse, and the three of us had been going there regularly for years—so much so that it had become our Batcave.

While Sofie was a nomad from the Netherlands, Denyse was an old soul from a prominent Bowie, Maryland, family. She'd never failed to make her dorm room bed, cooked nightly, and was dozing with curlers in her hair by 10:30 every night at Howard. I convinced her to go to a few step shows, but she'd prioritized her beauty sleep, her straight A's, and her efforts to make inroads with the recruiters who occasionally visited our campus to find interns and junior hires among the best and brightest.

In addition to being the most driven, Denyse was also the most politically militant among us. Though she was always good for a rant about microaggressions and the lack of diasporic representation at Fortune 500 companies, her real focus was generational wealth for the Black community. Well on the way to her goal of learning on the inside so she could transfer the skills to our people,

Denyse was now the youngest vice president in the marketing department at the third-largest financial institution in the country. With her fresh cacao skin, swingy chin-length bob, and lush figure contained under conservative pantsuits, she looked the part. I could always get a rise out of her by saying she was the token Black woman corporations always trot out in their human resources pamphlets.

Ironically, Sofie was the only one among us who would regularly wear urban gear, like terry cloth minis, NBA dresses, or pastel-colored tracksuits with Enyce or Baby Phat logos splashed on the back. Ordinarily, we would have dismissed her with two snaps and no backward glance. But Sofie was her own free spirit: She gave no fucks about race or sexual preference, and she was always the first person on the dance floor. Sofie was all right in our book and had become the fourth member of our crew.

"The mountain has come to Muhammad," Denyse exclaimed now, brandishing a chilled bottle of Veuve and wrapping me in a warm hug. "I see that look on your face. You can spare thirty minutes for us tonight."

"Oooh, Nik, this place is even more fly than I thought it would be." Sofie high-fived me as she looked around appreciatively. "There have to be flutes somewhere on this fancy floor so we can toast you properly."

Only Teresa slid her eyes around the vaunted offices with more than a little suspicion. "We should toast Lucinda for having the good sense to finally give you an overdue promotion," she muttered, kissing my cheek. Since I'd told Teresa about Tara's "Bobbie in whiteface" comment, she was loaded for bear every time *StyleList* came up in conversation. I knew better than to share that remark with Denyse, who might have burned the place down.

Denyse and Sofie opened the champagne, drowning out my protestations about still having work to do by turning up Destiny's Child's "Bills, Bills, Bills" on the boom box they brought. I relented and the four of us sat in a circle on the floor of *StyleList*'s hall of magazine covers, getting buzzed under their cheerful gaze.

"Yo, the way these women are cheesing, I feel like I've stepped into a toothpaste commercial." Denyse had stood up and was checking out the decades of framed white women. "I swear, I can hear them humming a jingle."

"Welcome to my world." I smiled wryly, then pointed at Teresa. "Don't you say anything!"

Teresa shrugged and pantomimed zipping her lips.

"I mean, they can't be mean muggin' on a *cover*, Denyse," Sofie said, sipping her champagne. "When I was modeling, I used to put Vaseline on my teeth so I could smile through a whole shoot."

Teresa rolled her eyes. "Their bright smiles aren't the issue, boo..."

Denyse jumped in before Teresa could get going. "Oh, chillax, Tee. They obviously promoted Nikki to shake up the place, get some more melanin in the mix."

"Something like that," I demurred, then switched the topic to boys so I wouldn't have to share the mixed emotions I had about the new position that my girls had come to celebrate.

While I now had Lucinda's tacit stamp of approval and more perks—clout, cash, invites to A-list events, a new office—I felt less like I belonged than ever. Kiara had been mining her contact list to give me the inside scoop on the lifestyles of the urban rich and famous, and Lucinda was properly impressed with my sensational exclusives. But every time I pitched a story on anything other than sex, socialites, and rappers, Lucinda's eyes would start to wander. "Doesn't Paris Hilton or Charlotte Ronson have a charity or something?"

Every now and then, I would reach out to Marie to vent, but she was not trying to hear it. Her response was always some variation of: "Blazing a trail is hard, my friend. Suck it up for all the women out there trying to make it."

Three issues after I was promoted, I was finally able to publish a piece I was proud of: I had researched the growing fashion scene in Africa and found several wealthy, fashion-forward African women to profile. It ended up being a groundbreaking special on the continent's most influential women, photographed in looks from emerging diasporic designers shot in Cape Town, Lagos, and Accra. The media coverage was enough to land Lucinda on the *Today* show (an appearance for which she wore a cringey kente cloth dress). It also produced a spike in sales so decisive that Mary-Kate brought me a thank-you gift from Lucinda: a large square box containing a new Celine bag.

When I showed the bag to Teresa, she just shook her head. "Doesn't that cost, like, two thousand dollars?" she asked me, even though she was the biggest label hound in the world and knew, to a decimal point, the retail price.

"This bag could pay my rent, home skillet." I laughed and handed her a glass of Chardonnay. We were having a rare girls' night at my Brooklyn apartment. Lately, I'd been craving more time in the Bed-Stuy neighborhood that always reminded me of the Harlem of my youth. I welcomed the familiar mix of older Black folks dragging red carts filled with groceries, buppies in shoulder pads rushing to the subway with *The New York Times* folded under their arms, intrepid gentrifiers carrying Starbucks cups and pushing fat-tired strollers, teens in puffy jackets with elaborate hairstyles, and dudes in basketball jerseys trying to sell me some dirt weed. It felt like home.

Joseph was working on a major deal and had been pulling late nights for the past couple weeks, so Teresa and I decided to do a classic sleepover, complete with wine, movies, homemade facials, comfy sweatpants, and scrunchies.

I popped a Bobbie Washington CD into my stereo. Her debut was an up-tempo hit with multiple chart-topping singles and a couple club bangers, unusual for a neo soul artist. But that night, I was in the mood for Bobbie's sophomore album, a poignant tour de force written like a series of diary entries.

After Bobbie visited Howard during my junior year to give an acoustic concert and talk to the class about pursuing our passions, I'd been inspired to create a club for aspiring journalists. By my senior year, our club had launched a widely read zine that grew to campus fame for our no-holds-barred op-eds decrying various social injustices. Founding the journalism club had been the first time I'd acknowledged how much I loved to write, but it was producing the zine that changed me. My essays were generating ripples of reaction and impact, and I wanted more: a bigger platform, a larger audience, the ability to deep dive on all the topics I cared about. I started thinking about becoming an editor-in-chief. Bobbie's sophomore album came out around then, which is why its lyrics about finding your voice and being true to yourself felt as if they had been written just for me.

"Oooh, crank that," Teresa said when she heard the first few chords of the lead track, about Black women loving the skin they're in. She sang along for a few lines then stopped to survey me. "Speaking of... are we staying straight?" Teresa motioned with her chin toward my head, her own tight curls pulled into a messy topknot.

"Ouch, heffa. Why I gotta be self-hating because I have a blowout? Although, I do confess to a love-hate relationship with this hair," I replied with a smile that I hoped was convincing enough for her to drop it. But Teresa knew me too well.

I was now scheduling weekly blowouts, and the heavy mop that slipped into my eyes all day was as annoying as the rabid interest it generated from men (including Joseph), who suddenly found me and my flowing locks irresistible. It made me realize that perhaps the blue-eyed girl in my Jack and Jill chapter had not wanted all that attention; maybe she'd felt bad sitting in the chair that her admirer had prevented me from occupying; perhaps she often wore sunglasses so people wouldn't continually comment on a physical feature that others valued more than she did.

"I don't know, boo. Thinking you've really gone to the dark side." She dipped a finger in the mud-colored DIY pore-tightening mask we were mixing in my tiny kitchen, smelled it, and recoiled dramatically. "You know I got you no matter what," she continued. "Like I said when we were hanging in your office, if you're happy, I'm happy. If not, we ride at dawn."

I wasn't sure if we were still talking about my hair. I carefully measured out some more oatmeal to buy myself time. "Everything is going my way right now, you know? Lucinda just gave me the nod, and Joseph has been all over me lately. I'm on a roll, so let me get these silk presses in peace." I laughed unconvincingly.

Teresa frowned at the lumpy substance in the bowl. "Yo, why does this mask look like dog food?"

This time my laughter was sincere. "No idea! But I'm not convinced about putting Purina on my face."

"I'm following your lead. You're the *StyleList* HNIC."

"Yeah, I don't know about this little experiment. I vote for more booze, less beautifying."

"Hear, hear," Teresa agreed. She flopped onto my fraying sofa and tucked her legs under what she considered to be her best feature. "Did I tell you about the cute guy I met on the subway?"

"You mean the Asian dude in the basketball jersey who was reading *One Hundred Years of Solitude* or the Black guy in the suit doing the *Times* crossword puzzle?" With her curves, brains, and easy confidence, Teresa always had men trying to drink her bathwater. An equal-opportunity dater with indiscriminate taste, her only rule was no lawyers. As a public defender, Teresa had to be flinty and focused all day; she needed the release that partying and dating gave her.

"Nah, this guy's Panamanian. Real sexy, runs a music promotion street team for Jive Records. The pro-slash-con is that he's Afro Latino. He gets me and he even speaks Spanish, but he looks like my Flatbush cousins, so I dunno..."

"Yikes, no bueno!" I grimaced.

"I know, right? But he's so fine. I'll let him buy me dinner before I decide." Teresa shrugged. "So, what are you gonna do about Joseph? That nice, fine, rich, boring man wants to marry you sooo bad."

"Ha-ha." I brought the wine bottle over to the sofa, sat down, and topped us off. "All I know is the more people act like marrying Joseph is a foregone conclusion, the less I'm into the idea."

"You love him?"

"Yes," I replied slowly. "We have a million single friends who'd cut off a pinky to be with a guy like him..." I finished half my glass in one gulp. "It's just weird that the less I recognize myself, the more he adores me."

Teresa put down her glass and touched my knee. "Hey, Nik, I didn't know you were feeling this way. Other than having to deal with that big stick up his ass, I thought you were doing okay with ole Joe."

I'd always felt that Teresa's lukewarm attitude toward Joseph stemmed, in part, from the fact that I'd met him through Marie, to whom she'd often referred with the faintest hint of jealousy as my work wife. But despite her snarky words, there was nothing in her expression but concern.

"I really don't know," I muttered, staring into my glass. "I should be so happy right now..."

"Are you having an issue at *StyleList*? I know you're dealing with snobby low-key racists all day, but I thought you were doing okay in that nest of vipers too."

"Now that I'm achieving all these goals at work, I don't know why I'm not more fulfilled. And I can't complain to anyone because I sound like a bougie ingrate." I looked down at my hands, taking in ragged cuticles that I'd been nervously gnawing for weeks.

"Ingrate, no. Bougie, uh... yeah!" Teresa smiled. "But seriously, have you considered that maybe you just don't want any of it? Remember when I was on the partner track at that corporate law firm, and I was fucking miserable? Everyone thought I'd lost my whole mind when I quit. And now I love being a public defender. Well, most days." She took a long drink of her wine. "Sure, I'll be paying off my law school loans until I'm arguing cases in court wearing an adult diaper and using a walker, but I'm helping people."

I had to smile at the image. The reality was that Teresa was whip-smart, with a fearsome ability to think on her feet and a preternatural talent for slicing up opposing lawyers' arguments with Ginsu-like precision. DAs and judges were always underestimating my girl, which was just fine by her, because she had the trial record of a legal prizefighter.

"You were working hundred-hour weeks and your hoo-hah was covered in cobwebs! No way that was going to work for your, ahem, lifestyle," I chortled.

"Hey, I'm a work hard, play hard girl!" Teresa winked, then turned sober. "But that was what I was *supposed* to want, chica. And it was not easy to give up. Even though I got a scholarship, Columbia wasn't free, and it was hard on my family when I went there for seven years straight. Then I give up a fancy job at a fancy firm to help the people my parents were trying to keep me away from?" She exhaled slowly and shook her head.

"I never thought of it that way, Tee. That job just never seemed like you, so I wasn't surprised when you left."

"Well, everyone else was. Which made it even harder for me because I wasn't entirely sure. All I knew was that the longer I stayed, the more I could feel my soul getting hoovered right out of my body."

Teresa was verbalizing exactly how I'd been feeling. "Yep, that's it. It's the absolute worst to get positive reinforcement from the very soul-sucking things that we're least sure about."

"The workaround is not giving a fuck, boo."

I paused for a second, then jumped up. "Let me show you something."

Like most families in Harlem, we'd had *Essence, Ebony,* and *Jet* delivered to our brownstone with utility-bill regularity. Having grown up with a mom too cerebral and distracted to pay attention to fashion,

I used to revere the models in those magazines. For years, I'd been ripping out the pages I found interesting and beautiful, keeping them in meticulous folders.

After Lucinda's "Black girls don't sell" comment, I'd expanded my collection by adding entire magazines that featured Black women. It didn't matter the topic or even the language; I would buy any magazine that put someone who looked like me or my mother on the cover. When I added *Sugar* to the mix, I began to analyze each issue, slapping Post-it notes with scribbles over badly phrased story titles and design disasters, writing down ideas for issue themes, investigative features, and possible covers. I kept everything in a large box, which I hauled out and placed on the coffee table in front of Teresa.

"Is there a severed head in here?" Teresa asked, removing the lid from the box. "What is all this stuff? Is it porn?"

"Oh my god, will you just tell me what you think!" I called over while I looked through my stack of local restaurant menus, settling on jerk chicken with rice and peas from our favorite Jamaican spot. "You want a veggie roti?" I asked.

"Mm-hmm" was all I got back. She was deep into my notes on cover concepts.

By the time I put in our order, Teresa was on the floor, the box's contents surrounding her, and she had rifled through most of it. I had mentioned *Sugar* to her in passing, but this was a whole 'nother level.

"Nik, you put a lot of time into this." Teresa was staring at me hard. "What are we doing here, girl?"

"Don't know, Tee. I can't stop thinking about *Sugar*. Their audience... it's us, right? And I think they—we—deserve better."

"Better than what?"

"Better than the way magazines treat us now. The few paltry pieces a year in *StyleList* about the flashiest Black people in New York or LA are almost worse than nothing because they think they're being so inclusive. I'm sick of being trotted out at sales lunches and investor meetings when Park Ave Pub wants to look like they give a shit." I flipped open an issue of *Sugar*. "And better than this too: Typos on every page and lame Q and As with background dancers counting as journalism."

"So *StyleList* thinks we're irrelevant and *Sugar* thinks we're stupid." Teresa hit the nail on the head.

"Ugh, exactly."

"I guess I never really thought about it. You're right, though," she said thoughtfully. "Where do we belong? Literally nowhere."

I fell silent, this time not sure if we were still talking about publishing. Teresa and I had bonded in our high school years over feeling like outsiders: she, a brown-skinned native-Spanish-speaking immigrant; me, a biracial Black private school–educated Harlem girl. She wasn't Spanish enough, I wasn't rich enough, neither of us was Black enough. We still quoted some of Halle Berry's choice lines from Alex Haley's *Queen* miniseries whenever we felt that we were being treated like impostors.

"Hep me, hep me. I'se nigra." I pantomimed the scene where Halle begs for help in the Black church, which shouldn't have cracked us up the way it did every single time.

"Hep me!" Teresa immediately started laughing. "I needs me a magazine."

"Oh man, we are going straight to hell." I had pantomimed my way into the kitchen so I could grab some chips. Unsurprisingly, the Jamaican restaurant was slow with deliveries, and tonight we had broken our rule of never ordering from them when we were actually hungry. I sat next to Teresa on the floor and plopped the bag between us.

"Laughing burning, burning laughing." Teresa shrugged and grabbed a handful of chips. A minute of contemplative crunching went by before she turned to face me with a more serious look. "You told me that you met the woman who owns *Sugar* at a party, right? What happened when you called her?"

"I haven't yet." Months later, Barbara Porter's business card was still in my wallet. Every time a story I cared about was shot down at *StyleList*, I pulled it out, memorizing every detail of the black matte cardstock, the gold embossed sans serif writing, the shiny outline of a megaphone on the back. Then I'd think about the rare air I was now breathing in the fashion magazine world, how I had finally started paying down my credit card debt, how my parents and Joseph had celebrated my new role. And I'd put it back in my wallet.

"What's the holdup?"

I had no good answer for her. Avoiding her eyes, I mumbled, "Back to the positive reinforcement I'm getting from soul-sucking things, I guess."

"So, you know what you have to do tomorrow," Teresa pronounced. She replaced the lid on the box, leaned over, and hugged me. "Stop fucking around with your life, bonita."

SEVEN

The next day, I closed the door of my office and took a deep breath as I dialed Barbara's direct line. She answered the phone herself, throwing me off guard.

"Well, if it isn't *StyleList*'s second coming," she said crisply. "I thought Kiara was laying it on a little thick at Lucinda's lovefest, then I heard about your promotion. Frankly, I thought I'd never hear from you again after you got the stamp of approval from Lucifer. That's usually how it goes down."

How had Barbara heard about my promotion? "The, um, new position was kind of a surprise to me," I stammered, feeling silly at how nervous this woman made me.

"I bet," Barbara responded. She was not going to make this easy at all.

I cleared my throat. "I would love to get together for lunch."

"Why?" Barbara asked.

I was thankful she couldn't see the sweat mustache forming over my lip. "I'd love to hear your plans for *Sugar*."

"You want to hear *my* plans?"

"I mean, I have some ideas for you, too."

"So, you want to hear my plans, and then give me some ideas—just because you're a nice person." I could feel Barbara smirking.

My embarrassment made me impatient. "Barbara, I've been working at *StyleList* for almost four years. I've seen firsthand how mainstream fashion magazines disregard us. And I don't want *Essence* to be our only other choice. I'd love to see *Sugar* live up to its potential."

No way Barbara Porter would stand for being spoken to that way by a scrub like me, I thought, but she chuckled and replied, "Hold on." Almost immediately her assistant picked up the line and made an appointment for us to have drinks the following week.

I'd never heard of Club Macanudo, the restaurant Barbara had chosen, and when I got there, I understood why. I opened the door and immediately started coughing. Club Macanudo turned out to be an upscale cigar bar that served a few bar bites to soak up the flowing brown liquor. Peering through the thick smoke at the mass of suited white men puffing away on contraband Cubans, I scanned the room for a short natural and leather. On the far wall, an enormous television blared the Giants vs. Patriots game, and the crowd erupted into cheers as the Giants scored a touchdown with the clock ticking down the last seconds of the quarter.

While the suits pumped each other's hands and downed another round of celebratory scotch, I took a seat at the bar and ordered a glass of champagne. The bartender, an incredibly efficient Asian woman with long blond hair and a septum ring, set the flute in front of me in less than a minute. I took a sip then swung my legs around to watch the room, coming face-to-face with Barbara. She was decked out in butter-colored leather pants with a matching suede jacket and a tan fedora sitting low on her head. Feeling plain in my black slacks and black turtleneck, I wished I'd at least added some statement earrings. Barbara took in the flute I was holding.

"Ballin', huh? If it's Cristal, then you, Nikki, may be Black after all."

"I doubt that it's Cristal—" I started, but Barbara waved away the end of my sentence.

"First of all, newbie, always say it's Cristal. No one's got to know you're drinking Moët or prosecco or whatever." Barbara sat on the stool next to me. "I didn't know what to make of how stiff you were acting at Lucinda's party. But when you told me off over the phone, I figured you might have some latent flavor. Which is why, by the way, I decided to meet with you today."

"And I was worried I may have offended you." I hazarded a half smile.

"Please, child. I've been screamed at by three-hundred-pound rappers surrounded ten deep by trigger-happy gangsters armed to the teeth." She pulled out a thin cigar, clipped the end off, and lit up. "You literally cannot scare me."

"I believe that." I sipped my champagne, trying not to look too impressed. "I can't say that I've ever been screamed at by any musical artists, much less rappers with rap sheets." Since that corny comment would not reenter my mouth no matter how much I willed it to, I knew that I deserved Barbara's snort of laughter.

"Miss Nicole *StyleList* Rose, I would be very surprised to hear that you've ever encountered any rappers, with rap sheets or otherwise." Without having to order, a short glass of caramel-colored liquor over ice appeared in front of her. She took a long drink, still chuckling into her glass.

"Well, I did work at *Revolutions* for a year," I said, realizing my mistake as I watched surprise flicker across Barbara's face.

"I knew that, at the very least, this meeting would be interesting." Barbara examined the liquid in the glass in front of her. Apparently dissatisfied, she handed it back to the bartender and said, "Hana, let's do the Courvoisier XO today." A fresh snifter appeared before she could turn to face me again. "Yes, I am pretty curious about your time at *Revolutions*." Since I was already chewing on my tongue, I said nothing, so she continued. "I have to say, you don't look at all like what I expected." Her sweeping gesture toward my outfit managed to convey both curiosity and contempt.

"How do you mean?" I was confused because this wasn't the first time we'd met in person.

"Well, I thought maybe your prim little outfit at Lucinda's love-fest was a fluke. After my last chat with your boy, Alonzo, I half expected you to show up today in a pleather catsuit and Lucite heels." She clicked all five right-hand fingernails on the bar twice, ignoring my frozen expression. Finally, she extended her index finger toward the bar. "Look, our bartender is not especially solicitous to me because of my sparkling personality. Alonzo and I used to meet here all the time—that is, until he cornered Hana outside the ladies' room."

She paused for effect, but I had stopped listening as the possibility of running into Alonzo took hold. Barbara must have noticed my head on a swivel because her tone softened. "He freaked her out so badly that she threatened to call the cops. I had to quietly pay for a semester of Hana's NYU tuition so I wouldn't lose my publisher."

"Look, I don't know what he told you, but..." I stopped talking because Barbara was shaking her head and wagging her index finger from side to side.

"Alonzo isn't special. I know at least ten other equally stupid assholes in and around the music industry. They mostly don't fuck with me for a few obvious reasons, but I see everything." She looked deep into my eyes. "Not excusing dumb behavior, just saying that there are choices. You make bad ones, and we have annoying conversations in cigar bars about your judgment. You make good ones, and no one has to worry about tarnished reputations in these streets."

Barbara's declaration was vaguely protective—even though it was clear that she didn't trust me. I couldn't blame her; I wasn't sure I trusted myself. "Barbara, I—"

She stopped me again. "There's nothing you can say to make it better. The details won't help, so let's skip to the part where you tell me why we're here."

I took what I hoped was a subtle breath. "Urban culture has

taken over mainstream pop culture," I started. "Hip hop music is all over MTV, high-end designers are looking to the young urban for inspiration—"

But before I could continue with the speech I'd rehearsed so much I could envision it scrolling like a teleprompter in my mind, Barbara cut me off for what seemed like the tenth time. "Newbie, I started *Groove* on my living room coffee table. If anyone is aware that rich white kids in the suburbs all want to be the next Jay-Z, I am." She took a sip from her glass while I processed that information. "You have five minutes to tell me why we're actually here."

Trying hard not to dwell on the fact that I could not seem to string two sentences together that Barbara didn't mock, I tried again, abandoning my stiff pitch for a more direct approach. "Young Black women are the hottest thing out there. We drive culture, but we don't have a voice—*Sugar* could fill that void. But that audience is very savvy—they won't buy bullshit. I know that I wouldn't."

"So, you think *Sugar* is bullshit?"

How did I keep putting my foot in my mouth? "Not necessarily," I hedged, "but *Sugar* could truly represent the style and the perspective of smart women of color who grew up with hip hop, are into fashion, who want to do something with their lives, and who still like to hit the club." I paused before delivering my pièce de résistance. "And since you know everyone follows what we do, there's no reason *Sugar* couldn't appeal to all women—Black Latina, white, anyone who loves urban culture. The brand could cross over multiple demographics and open NuVoices to a whole new audience."

Barbara took a thoughtful puff on her cigar. "And why are you the person to run *Sugar*? There are other female journalists with more experience covering music and fashion who have more... urban style."

She cast another skeptical look at my tame outfit, which I chose to ignore, "run *Sugar*" echoing in my mind. I had a moment of panic as I realized that I really did want to leave my swanky new gig at *StyleList*, the biggest fashion magazine in the world, to be editor in chief of a brand-new title at a tiny publishing company almost no one had heard of. As it sank in, I tried not to think about Marie, who had always looked out for me at Park Ave Pub.

I started to talk about my journalistic prowess and fashion connections, but Barbara waved her hand to silence me. She leaned forward and said, "*Sugar*'s readers will be able to tell a pretender from a mile away, and you're talking about a role that goes beyond anything you've ever done. I assume you're decent at what you do, otherwise you wouldn't be creeping up the *StyleList* masthead. My question is: Can you represent the *Sugar* brand to an unforgivingly perceptive and judgmental audience?"

The Giants had just scored another touchdown and I could barely hear her over the yelling, backslapping, and clanking of glasses. One of the middle-aged suits looked over at me at winked. *Not a chance, Thurston Howell*, I thought.

I drained my flute and put it down on the bar. "Barbara, my friends are the audience. *I* am the audience."

"Well, I must say I am surprised by your conviction. I admit that I took you for another Lucifer sycophant." I flinched but kept quiet. "And, so you know, it's not as if I did not recognize that *Sugar* has its problems."

"Oh no, I didn't mean—"

"Yes, you did. And that's okay, because I like opinionated people. But let me repeat: I do see everything."

I wasn't sure what she was referring to but had to assume she meant that she didn't trust me. There was no response other than "Of course, Barbara."

She nodded again. "As I said, I've been having my doubts about the direction *Sugar* is going and the current EIC." Barbara paused to motion for the check. "If I make any changes, I'll be doing so within the next couple months." She finished her drink and put a gold

American Express down on the bar. The meeting was clearly over and we'd both revealed enough cards.

A white Lincoln Navigator was waiting for Barbara in front of Club Macanudo. The uniformed driver hopped out to help her inside as DMX's "What's My Name" blared through the open door. The image of Lucinda's tutu disappearing into her black town car after she'd proclaimed that "Black girls don't sell" contrasted with what was in front of me like a split screen. After she climbed into the back seat, Barbara turned to me and said, "Email me your vision for *Sugar*, Second Coming. Maybe I'll be in touch."

As the SUV pulled away into the freezing night, I could hear Barbara rapping along with DMX: "Here we go again. How many times do I have to tell you rap niggas I have no friends. I'm not a nice person..."

I spent the next couple weeks consolidating my notes on *Sugar* into a fifteen-page document outlining my vision. But I knew that I was really selling myself. Would the readers respect and like me as the face of the brand? Would the urban world trust me, especially since Barbara had already alluded to my tarnished reputation in the streets? Could I fit in and pull it off?

Fitting in had always been a challenge for me, ever since high school. My folks had rolled the dice on our Harlem brownstone decades ago when it was one of the few on the block not filled with squatters behind boarded-up windows. Since then, most of the neighboring brownstones had been refurbished, a coffee shop had opened around the corner, and the folks on the street hollering, "Wassup, Dr. Rose," to my English professor mom and/or math professor dad had gone from being all Black to mirroring my parents' interracial relationship: 50 percent white.

Every morning from freshman through senior year, I'd sprint to the subway at the corner of 145th and St. Nicholas, where my commute to the Upper East Side began. I would race by groups of teens walking to the local high school who'd call me "high yellow ho" only to be bullied by the kids at my private school for living in Harlem, for my frizzy hair and beige coke-bottle glasses, for my scrawny, late-blooming frame, for my good grades.

Turning down an ivy-covered college to go to Howard University was one of the best decisions I'd ever made because it was the first time I felt like I had a real community. But even there, my freshman roommate had tried to make me feel like I wasn't Black enough. She'd grown up in the DMV so claimed the campus as part of her hometown and, therefore, her territory—which was inconvenient since she judged me before I opened my mouth. It didn't matter that I had brought a big boom box and a case of hip hop and house music cassettes for our room. It didn't matter that my collection of kicks was better than hers. It didn't matter that I was from Harlem while she lived with her parents, both doctors, in a huge house in Bethesda with a golf course–sized backyard and pool.

Her skeptical expression never shifted as she watched me unpack my suitcases, taking in my Doc Martens, baggy jeans, collection of multicolored scrunchies, and books. My cheeks burned under her baffled gaze as I stacked my manga collection on top of Toni Morrison's Beloved trilogy, understanding that my roommate couldn't believe that I had brought books to college. I only made it worse by trying to prove myself to her. I'd blast Public Enemy whenever she was around. I got box braids. I declared myself an Alice Walker womanist, tracing her famous quote, "Womanist is to feminist as purple is to lavender," on poster board for our wall. My roommate's rolling eyes confirmed that my overcompensation only made me look like a poser—which I hated as much as being treated like a tourist in Harlem.

Working on my *Sugar* proposal brought it all back. I was the Black whisperer at *StyleList*, but I might not have enough street cred for *Sugar*. Was I cool enough? Was I *Black* enough? How could I prove myself without trying too hard to prove myself? Or would I find my work crew the same way I'd found Denyse at Howard? We met in the housing office at the start of our sophomore year while complaining about our respective obnoxious roommates and decided right then to switch for a suite together. Unlikely friends, as distinct as Freddie and Jaleesa, we learned to appreciate our differences so that by the end of the year, Gilbert Hall had nothing on us.

Only Teresa knew what I was working on. Joseph was so involved in a new mergers and acquisitions deal, he'd barely been home. I justified not letting him in on my conversation with Barbara by telling myself that it was a bad time to bring it up. But I knew that Joseph loved telling people that his girlfriend was a senior editor at *StyleList*. I'd watched him puff up with pride at his finance colleagues' and Harvard classmates' invariably impressed reactions. I couldn't even envision Joe telling his buttoned-up buddies from the office that I ran a magazine called *Sugar*.

I poured my soul into the *Sugar* proposal—citing research, quoting fashion designers, interspersing music lyrics, integrating visual inspiration, listing directional writers, suggesting cover subject ideas and features concepts. I'd even offered up stories about me and Teresa, how we searched for a place to belong, how we needed a voice. When I finally pressed send on the email to Barbara, I tried to put the whole thing out of my mind. It was officially out of my control.

To distract myself, I switched my focus to my thirtieth birthday, which was coming up in a few weeks. I'd always assumed my shit would be together by thirty: My 401(k) would be worth more than six figures; I would have a daily yoga practice; I would not own any undergarments with holes; I'd have a pet *and* pet insurance; my bed would be made every day with color-coordinated decorative pillows; and I'd be happily married. But I hadn't yet experienced the magical transformation my third decade was supposed to usher in. Since my birthday fell on a Friday, I had every intention of partying through the weekend like the unenlightened twenty-nine-year-old I still felt like. Joseph was taking me out to dinner, and we had plans to hook up with some of my friends afterward to go dancing.

I left work early on my birthday to get my hair blown out and was sitting under the hair dryer when I got the call. Seeing the Nu-Voices number was so startling, I immediately sat forward, banging my head on the front of the dryer and dropping the phone on the floor.

"Hello, hellooo," I heard as I finally brought the cell to my ear.

"Yes, hi, hello, Barbara," I stammered, trying to get out from under the hair dryer. "Sorry about that."

"What is all that noise?" she asked after a few seconds. "You sound like you're inside a jet engine."

"I'm at the salon. You know how that is," I said, attempting a conspiratorial tone. Then I remembered she wore her hair in a short natural. Her vibe was more barbershop than salon.

Mercifully, Barbara ignored me. "I have some news for you," she said.

I had gotten up and walked to the front of the salon so I could look out onto the hectic street below. Conversations with Barbara felt like a chess game, with me trying to think ahead a few moves while she kept putting me in check. Since I couldn't come up with an intelligent play, I said nothing, which was probably the best move.

"I've decided to change the leadership at *Sugar*," Barbara continued. "I liked your proposal and your vision, Second Coming. It was smart and insightful."

The salon buzz disappeared behind me and the scene on Broadway felt magnified. It was as if I'd been transported outside and was running through traffic, dodging cabs and bikes and buses, exhilarated and petrified at the same time. Nerves made my voice quaver as I wiped my sweaty hands on my jeans. "Thank you. I put a lot of work into—"

"Yes, yes," Barbara interrupted. She did not suffer yammering fools. "I'd like for you to be editor-in-chief, but I'm still not convinced that you can handle everything this job will bring. I can offer you the job on a trial basis. You have six months to prove yourself."

I had no playbook for how to respond to being *sort of* offered a job. "I appreciate the opportunity," I began. "I just want to be sure I understand. You want me to leave *StyleList* for a six-month trial period at *Sugar*?"

"Yes, that's exactly what I want you to do. Taking this offer will be the first step toward proving to me that you have the mettle to succeed." This time, she paused, and I could hear her gulping something I imagined was brown liquor in a snifter. Then she said pointedly, "Look, you're going to have a lot of obstacles, some that you know are partially of your own making"—Barbara lingered on that phrase long enough for me to know that she was referring to Alonzo—"and some that are simply part of the challenge of running a new magazine at a start-up media company. I'll be able to share more if you join my team."

Clearly, Barbara still didn't trust me. But it was also clear that she thought I might be able to figure out how to succeed. "Thank you, Barbara. I'd like some time to consider. By when do you need an answer?"

"Yesterday," she snapped. "It makes no sense to keep publishing *Sugar* as it stands, which I've already shared with the current editor-in-chief. She's a bit of a live wire, so we'll need to make this announcement quickly before word gets out. You have until Monday. Monday morning." And without waiting for me to say another word, she hung up.

EIGHT

Joseph had kept my birthday restaurant, a well-known Midtown steakhouse, a surprise. Though the conservative environment filled with Thurstons and Muffys would not have been my first choice, my filet mignon au poivre was amazing. But Joseph and I began our meal a little too careful with each other, enunciating everything with exaggerated politeness: "May I please have the pepper?" "Would you care for another roll?" "Could I trouble you for the butter?"

The tension between us started while I was getting dressed for the evening. I'd been extra quiet, too distracted by my conversation with Barbara to chat. After watching me silently pull on an uncharacteristically flashy outfit that I'd let Teresa talk me into buying—tight leather pants, a gold one-shouldered top, and gold stilettos—Joseph finally cornered me in the bathroom. As he watched me layer on plum lip gloss, desire had made his dick swell. My eyes had lingered on Joseph's straining crotch seams then moved up to his muscle-roped arms, exposed by a black tank top—which I'd been seconds away from pulling off when he'd spoiled the moment by asking, "So, what's going on with you tonight? Turning thirty starting to hit you?"

It had taken me a moment to register what he was asking. "No, not really."

"Then what's up? You've barely said a word since you got here. You look like you're sleepwalking."

"I have things on my mind."

"Like?"

I'd realized that I was acting too weird to not offer an explanation, so I told him that I got another job offer.

"Baby, that's great news!" Joseph had exclaimed. "From a rival fashion magazine? Did *Vogue* hear about your promotion and call you? Lots more money?" Without waiting for an answer, he'd started to pace. "Telling Marie will be hard, but if it's a big enough job, she'll have to understand. Or, even better, you can leverage the offer to get more money from *StyleList*."

"Not exactly," I began. "Have you heard of Barbara Porter?"

"Doesn't she have a start-up with a couple urban magazines or something?" Joseph Burke III had little interest in companies unless they hit the Fortune 500.

I bit the bullet and summarized the past few months since I'd met Barbara at Lucinda's party, ending with the editor-in chief offer. Joseph had stared at me with an impassive expression until I finally asked, "Would you please say something?"

"I can't believe you kept this from me all this time," he'd replied in a hurt tone that had unnerved me. I'd been steeling myself for his judgment, not his pain.

"Look, I'm sorry I didn't tell you, but can you honestly say you wouldn't have tried to talk me out of it?" I lowered my voice to Joseph's tenor and scrunched my eyebrows together. "'Nicole, why are you giving up on a great job at a prestigious company to work for a little fly-by-night operation like NuVoices?'"

"Maybe," Joseph admitted. My bad imitation had made him smile, but I could still see the hurt in his eyes. "NuVoices seems sketch to me. Plus, you're doing so well at *StyleList*. This seems like a step back for you after the promotion. And have you thought about Marie? Whatever you do is going to reflect on her. I just want what's best for you, and this doesn't feel like it."

In one fell swoop he'd expressed everything I didn't want to hear:

disdain for NuVoices, skepticism about my leaving *StyleList*, a reminder that I'd be impacting Marie if I did, and concern about what was best for me that implied he knew what that was. Sometimes I couldn't tell if Joseph thought he knew more than me because he was seven years older, because his family's money made him feel superior, because he'd never experienced true failure, or simply because he was a man.

We'd dropped the subject, neither of us wanting to ruin my milestone birthday, and we'd avoided it for the first part of our meal, only our careful communication and overdone etiquette betraying the tension. But after a couple cocktails plus a bottle of excellent pinot noir, we left the restaurant buzzed and laughing, my arm wrapped around his waist and his hand tucked into the back pocket of my leather pants.

After dinner, Joseph directed our taxi to Sofie's Café. When he opened the door, instead of the usual Friday night crowd, I saw approximately forty people gathered near the door. It took me a minute to realize that I recognized all of them: my parents, friends from previous jobs, people I'd met around the city. Even Kiara was there. Teresa and Sofie were in the middle, each holding one side of a huge chocolate cake with lit numbered birthday candles on top proclaiming to the world that I was thirty. But it wasn't until everyone yelled "Surprise!" that I processed that this was my birthday party.

As everyone started to sing Stevie Wonder's "Happy Birthday," I kissed Joseph, feeling guilty about how impatient I'd been at his apartment. Then I turned to Teresa. "You bitch!" I yelled, hugging her. Now I knew why she'd been casually grilling me for weeks about my other friends.

She laughed, passing the cake to Sofie to hug me back. "I got your ass."

After I said my millionth hi, my girls pulled me away from the crowd into the kitchen. I perched on a long metal counter to take off my shoes. "Y'all, this is fucking amazing. But next time, warn a bitch so I can wear more comfortable shoes."

"Hellooo, it's a surprise party. That means it's a surprise." Denyse leaned over and thunked me lightly on the head. "Besides, remember when that poor Kappa who was crushing on you tried to throw you a dinner party for your birthday junior year and you chickened out at the last minute?"

"Oh wow, I totally forgot about that! Wait, why didn't I show?" I said as I massaged my feet.

"Because you were freaked out that he went to so much trouble when you didn't think you liked him."

"Oh my god, that's right!" The memory came back to me. "He had awful breath."

"I spent weeks consoling the dude. Nothing worse than a soggy Kappa. I thought his poor ego would never recover." Denyse chuckled and rolled her eyes. We were all cracking up by that point. "Yeah, we learned the hard way not to throw yo ass a party unless it's a surprise."

Sofie pulled a bottle of Veuve from the enormous metal refrigerator and popped it open. "I have no idea what a Kappa is and that's still the funniest shit I've heard today."

That cracked us up some more. "A Kappa is a pretty playboy," Teresa told her.

"So, you did have the Divine Nine at Columbia?" Denyse asked with exaggerated innocence, knowing full well that the easiest way to get under Teresa's skin was to pretend as if she believed PWIs had zero Black culture. Denyse had never considered going anywhere other than an HBCU.

"Talk to the hand, mami," Teresa warned, always ready to defend her beloved alma mater.

"You guys are ridiculous!" Sofie had no patience for the Teresa and Denyse show. "Let's give Nikki her gift."

Teresa stepped forward with an envelope in her hand. "Here you go, homie," she said, handing it to me. "It's from all of us."

"Yeah, girl," Denyse chimed in. "Now that you're an old woman, we wanted you to be able to relax your weary bones."

Teresa nudged her. "Shh, you're going to give it away. Although Nikki's been hinting about it, so she might already know."

"Okay, Ma, you better open it." Sofie laughed. "It was hard enough to keep the party on the low. Someone's about to figure out how to mess up a present that you got in your hand."

Trying to think of what I'd apparently been hinting about, I tore open the envelope. Inside was a certificate for a year's worth of monthly massages at Bliss Spa. I had been telling Teresa how the stress of my new position was tying knots between my shoulder blades, but I never would have guessed they'd get me a present this extravagant. "You guys, I'm just... I'm completely overwhelmed," I said.

"Please, don't get all mushy on us," Teresa groaned.

"Can't help it. You guys are seriously the best. Thank you so much for this night and for my gift." I got up to throw my arms around all my friends. "Ya know, I might have to use a few of these Bliss certificates on a spa day for me and my fave girls."

"Sheeeet, I know that's right. I'm there!" Denyse exclaimed before Teresa slapped her on the thigh.

"No way, lady. D's just kidding," Teresa said while Denyse mouthed, "No, I'm not," behind her head.

Teresa had better eyes in the back of her head than most moms and pursed her lips to suppress a laugh. "We love you, Nik. You never stop working, and we want you to take some time to relax as you head into your thirty-first year on the planet."

Sofie poured the rest of the champagne, then got a new bottle from the fridge. As she refilled glasses, she added, "With a huge new gig, no less, as the HNIC at *StyleList*!"

"Okay, Sof, imma give you a pass this time, but you would want to discontinue *any* further use of that phrase," Denyse emphasized, slowly shaking her head while Sofie raised both palms in confusion.

Every now and then, her love of urban colloquialisms collided with her language barrier, forming a riptide that pulled her into dicey cultural territory. Since we knew her intentions, we always tried to catch her before she got too far.

My eyes briefly met Teresa's. "My HNIC job is okay, but I have something else to tell you."

"Joseph popped the question?" Denyse guessed eagerly.

I almost shared my misgivings, but my girls were in no mood for a serious conversation about my relationship. So, I poked Denyse's arm and laughed. "Girl, he ain't ready to hear no."

She shook her head. "Why would you ever turn down that lovely, paid man?" She was perpetually looking for a guy who matched the tall, chocolate, suited model she'd cut out of *GQ* and affixed to her vision board. "He didn't come out as a Republican, did he?"

"Joseph isn't the only man in New York City," I shot back. Over the chorus of "Oooooh," I asked, "Now, do you want to talk about Joseph, or do you want to hear my news?"

"Um, Joseph," Denyse said.

"Damn, D, you are single-minded," Sofie cut in. "Let the woman speak."

"Thank you, Sof," I said. "So, I have another job offer."

Teresa exhaled sharply and jumped up. "Is it . . . ?"

I smiled, and before I could get a "yep" out of my mouth, Teresa ran over and grabbed my shoulders. "You did it, Nikki! Wepa!"

Everyone else looked mystified until Sofie asked, "Nikki, can you please get on with the news so we *all* know what the hell you're talking about?"

"My bad." I drained my champagne glass to give myself a second to think about where to start. "So, a few months ago I pitched Tyisha to Lucinda for a cover."

"Girl, what?" Sofie exclaimed. "Even I know Lucinda wouldn't take that idea seriously."

"Well, I should have known too," I replied as she refilled my flute.

"She told me 'Black girls don't sell magazines.'" I made air quotes to indicate that those were her exact words and watched my friends' mouths fall open.

"What? How come you didn't tell us?" Denyse exclaimed, taking off her glasses to clean them on her silk top. "You know I would have organized a protest outside Park Ave Pub that same week."

"Uh, that's exactly why I didn't tell you!" I smiled at the thought of Muffy trying to work out how to get to her waiting town car as a brigade of activists marched in front of Park Ave Pub's doors. "I wasn't ready for DEFCON 2–level action. But it did get me thinking about whether I really wanted to stay there."

"I bet." Denyse huffed. "I deal with microaggressions all the time at work but nothing so blatantly gross."

"Exactly." I sighed. "But then Lucinda offered me the special projects editor position, and I just couldn't turn down such a big job, even though she basically told me straight up that she wanted me to blackify *StyleList* so I could save the business *and* her ass."

"That is some bullshit," Sofie declared, rolling up the sleeves of her pink satin FUBU jacket.

"It was. But it was also flattering to be entrusted with something so huge by a literal publishing legend," I said with a half shrug. "Around the same time, I saw an urban women's lifestyle mag at CeCe's called *Sugar*. It's published by NuVoices, this new media company."

"Barbara Porter runs it, right?" Sofie interrupted. "I had a meeting with her once about sponsoring an event at the café."

"That's right," I continued. "I started obsessing about *Sugar*, then I met Barbara at a fashion party. I went back and forth about what to do until my girl"—I pointed my chin at Teresa—"told me to get off my culo. I sent Barbara some ideas for *Sugar*, which she must have liked because she just offered me the editor-in-chief spot."

There was total silence for a second, then everyone screamed at once. This was the reaction I wanted. I tried to field all the questions that were coming at me:

"Will you have a big staff?"

"Don't know."

"Will you meet celebrities?"

"Definitely a different set than *StyleList*. More hip hop than Hollywood."

"Are you going to get to go to the Grammys?"

"Not sure."

"Are you going to be rich?"

"Ha! No. I think it pays less than I make now."

"What's Barbara like?"

"Street smart and takes no shit *or* prisoners. She told me that she wasn't sure I can handle the job so she's giving me a six-month trial period."

Another silence as I watched them look around at each other. The music outside the kitchen and the loud hum of the commercial refrigerator combined into a head-pounding fury.

Finally, Teresa replied, "Well, then, I guess you had better fucking crush it!"

"I guess I had better fucking crush it." I took a deep calming breath and bumped fists with each one of my girls.

At that moment, the door cracked open and Kiara peeked her head in, her blingy chandelier earrings casting tiny rainbows around the kitchen. "I don't want to interrupt, but I heard some loud screaming in here. Y'all good?"

"Join us." I waved her in. "Come meet my crew."

I introduced Kiara, carefully watching the reactions of my protective besties. Sofie, our peacemaker, was the easiest, enveloping Kiara in a quick bear hug and chatting her up about their mutual connections. Denyse, the most judgmental, scoped out Kiara's expensive, iced-out getup so thoroughly I knew she would have plenty of comments later. Teresa, the hardest nut to crack, was unsurprisingly the most skeptical; she coolly extended her hand, making it clear that no hugs would be forthcoming until Kiara proved her loyalty.

When I told Kiara about *Sugar*, she had the same reaction: a moment of stillness before she yelled and high-fived me.

"I swear I'm psychic. When we first met, I just knew something big was going to happen for you soon," she said, accepting a glass of champagne from Sofie. "I thought it was your promotion at *StyleList*, but this is huge, love!" I could see my girls warming at her unfettered excitement. Kiara turned to the rest of the room. "Your girl is about to become a major player in the culture. Better strap in—this is gonna be a wild ride!"

I lifted my glass. "To wild rides!"

"To wild rides." They clicked my glass and hugged me again. I looked around Sofie's kitchen and thought about the fact that these were exactly the women *Sugar* was for: my smart, cool, fun girlfriends.

NINE

As the glass crashed into the far wall of Lucinda's office, red liquid splashing all over the celadon-and-pink-striped wallpaper, I was oddly touched by the ferocity of her reaction to my news.

"Are you going to one of our competitors?" she screeched. "Is it *Vogue*? *Elle*?"

"Um, no, Lucinda. I—"

She cut me off, rising menacingly out of her chair. "If it's *Harper's Bazaar*, I'll kill you myself!"

"No, no, it's not," I said quickly, tensing my muscles in case she lunged for me. I calculated how long it would take for me to reach the closed door of her office, factoring in the distance, the myriad artfully positioned floor cushions I'd have to vault, and my uncomfortable high-heeled suede boots. I nervously fingered the sleeve of my sweater. "I'm going to NuVoices Media."

Lucinda plopped back down in her chair, cocked her head to the side, and stared at me. "NuVoices? Isn't that an *urban* company?" She said *urban* like it was roach pesticide or a past bankruptcy—something undesirable that one didn't talk about in polite company.

"Yes, it is," I told her. But before I could explain my new job, Lucinda interrupted again.

"You mean to tell me that after I've given you the promotion of a lifetime, you're leaving to go work at some upstart *urban* company?"

"Yes. I'm going to be the editor-in-chief of a magazine called *Sugar*." Since Lucinda was clearly uninterested in the details, I didn't elaborate further. "But I truly appreciate the opportunity you gave me here."

"You, overachiever, are a fool. If you hadn't already ruined your career with this dumb move, I'd tell you you'll never work for a major magazine again." She leaned forward to deliver the next sentence with chilly precision. "No one leaves *StyleList* after getting promoted by me personally. No. One."

With her flushed cheeks and wild hair, Lucinda, who normally looked like a stylish leprechaun, was infused with an energetic fury that made her almost attractive. She summoned Mary-Kate, who appeared thirty seconds later with a fresh drink. From the sympathetic look she shot me, I gathered that the commotion was audible outside Lucinda's office.

"Mary-Kate, please escort Nicole out." Lucinda swiveled in her chair to face away from me, her threat to kill my career serving as our sentimental goodbye.

By the time I got to my office, there was a security guard waiting. I had exactly ten minutes to get my personal belongings together—the rest would be heaped into a box and mailed to me. As I packed, taking extra care to remove the precious picture of me with Bobbie Washington on the Howard campus from my bulletin board, a small crowd of fake-sympathetic rubberneckers gathered. Looking around at the wan, designer-clad fashionistas waiting to pounce on my remains, I was surprised by how excited I was to get out of there, potential career doom be damned.

I hoped to escape without any further confrontation, but I rounded the corner to the elevator bank to find Marie waiting, arms crossed. Since Marie had been at my birthday party, I'd asked my girls not to spread the news about *Sugar*, and I'd been putting off the conversation ever since. Now I was busted.

"Marie, I really—"

"How could you let me find out this way?" Marie marched over and jabbed me a little too hard in the shoulder. "How are you going to let Lucinda of all people tell me that you're leaving? And why wouldn't you let me help you navigate your exit?"

"She called you?" I managed.

"Who else was she going to call to arrange for your exit documents, and your security escort?" she said, motioning toward the burly uniformed guy who was hovering behind me. "It's okay, Boris, I got it from here." Marie waited until he left, recrossed her arms, and lit into me again. "So, what are you thinking? Do you truly understand what you're giving up?"

Under her livid gaze, I felt like a third grader caught cheating on a quiz: ashamed and scared. But even in my mortification, I realized that it had been more than cowardice that had kept me from telling her; I still held some insecurity about my decision to leave the Park Ave Pub ivory tower, and I knew that Marie was one of the few people who could get me to see my folly. "I'm so sorry. I . . . I was afraid to call you after everything you've done for me here," I told her.

"Yeah, okay, Nikki. But again: Do you have any idea what you're giving up?"

"The gig wasn't as amazing as it initially sounded." My words sounded ungrateful to my ears, so I tried to clean it up. "You know that I had a lot of problems with Lucinda."

Marie turned away and rubbed a hand over her side-parted and slicked-down blond Afro. She looked toward the ceiling and loudly said, "Are you kidding me right now? Did you think it was supposed to be easy?"

I winced, feeling more and more foolish. "I didn't think it was supposed to be easy, but you know Lucinda is a closet racist."

Marie swung back around and shook her head in disbelief. "Big deal, Nikki. What are you, a child? You think you're the first Black person to deal with racism on the job?"

"How could you say that? Isn't HR supposed to say the opposite? Isn't it your job to protect me?"

"Oh, so now I'm 'HR.'" Her air quotes drove home how weak I sounded. "Well, my role as HR is also talent development, which I was doing by putting you in a position to blaze a trail at *StyleList*. You were breaking ground, so what did you think it was going to be like? The first one always has it bad. I just thought you were strong enough to deal with it."

"I didn't exactly quit for some cushy gig, you know." My eyes were getting damp. Marie must have noticed, but she didn't let up.

"No shit. You left to work for Barbara Porter, who, by the way, is no easier than Lucinda. But since you didn't bother to give me a heads-up or ask if I had any intel, you probably don't know the stories."

I had nothing to say to that. I couldn't ask what she was talking about even though I was dying to know what I'd gotten myself into.

Dropping her voice to an angry whisper, she said, "I could have at least coached you on how to tell Lucinda so you didn't burn your bridge with her and Park Ave Pub. She was furious when she called me."

"I know. She threw a glass at a wall, spilled her drink all over her silk pillows."

"No! I would have paid good money to see that." She cracked a small smile.

"Yeah, it was crazy. She totally lost it."

"Apparently." Her face turned serious again. "But I wouldn't be so smug about making Lucifer lose it. She's a formidable enemy. Frankly, for a mild-mannered bougie girl, you are racking up a lot of enemies."

My hands squeezed into fists. "That's not fair, Marie. You know what happened with Alonzo."

"You know what I know?" she asked, punching the elevator button. "I know that you seem to have a habit of making rash decisions.

And you need to think about that, Nikki. One day something's going to happen, and you will not get off so easy."

"It already has. Alonzo already told Barbara and, apparently, half the urban world that I'm a slut who'll do anything to succeed."

"Uh, you don't think I know that, Nikki? I've been shielding you for years. I know you've always wanted to be an editor-in-chief, and you think you'll fit right in at NuVoices, but I'm not so sure that you've made the right calculation." The elevator arrived and Marie motioned for me to get in, saying only, "I will be rooting for you from afar." The doors closed on her sad yet stern face, leaving me to escort my sorry self out of Park Avenue Publishing for good.

Barbara had pooh-poohed my request to give *StyleList* their full two weeks' notice—or perhaps she'd understood that I'd immediately be shown the door like a drunk brawler at a nightclub. Either way, she had insisted that I go to the NuVoices office for a morning meeting that Friday to rally the *Sugar* staff, and I was to start my new job the following Monday. I'd dreaded telling Lucinda I could only give her a week to transition, but since she and *StyleList* wanted no part of me, I now had a few days off to prepare.

Within five minutes of setting foot in my Brooklyn studio, I'd put on sweats, ordered Chinese food, and had my phone in hand to call my mother. Since I was already persona non grata at Park Ave Pub and had upset my one work friend, I thought I might as well piss off my mom too. It was bad enough that she couldn't talk me out of journalism as a career. No way, I thought, would she endorse my departure from a stable job at a prestigious company to work for an unknown brand. It was like leaving an executive role at the Coca-Cola corporation to run a lemonade stand.

I dialed her number, gave her the news, and braced for impact. There was a long silence before Mom exhaled and slowly asked, "Okay, does it pay as much as your position at *StyleList*?"

"The base is about the same." My new job actually paid almost five thousand dollars less than my *StyleList* salary. I was taken aback when Barbara told me, but she wouldn't budge. The only thing she promised is that if I lasted a year, she would consider giving me a raise and a bonus. However, I had negotiated one solid perk. "But I do have a clothing allowance!"

"Then, we'll have to go shopping," she said. "You'll need some suits."

"Suits! Whoa. Mom, I don't think—"

"Suits," she repeated firmly. "You'll have an entire staff to oversee, and you should look authoritative, Nicole."

And that was it. No recriminations or cautionary lectures. I almost wanted her to go in on my decision so I'd have a reason to defend it—to her and to myself. Instead, I was alone with my thoughts, and suddenly terrified all over again. I ate my kung pao chicken in front of the TV, letting *Law & Order* and ADA Robinette eventually lull me to sleep.

My mother, whose entire wardrobe came from a catalog, improbably insisted that we go to Bloomingdale's. The whole thing seemed ludicrous. I was going to run an urban lifestyle magazine, not *Town & Country*. She kept yammering about someone on *The Oprah Winfrey Show* saying that female bosses needed to dress a certain way to gain respect. I tried to remind her that my boss (well, former boss), the most respected and feared EIC in the business, regularly wore tutus to work. "Bloomingdale's. Suits. See you at eleven" was her only reply.

I gave in and showed up for our shopping expedition in ripped jeans and Stan Smiths, ready to build the foundation of my editor-in-chief look. I was surprised when my mother climbed out of a taxi looking polished. Her tan slacks were neatly pleated and devoid of lint; there were no stains on her white button-down shirt; her black loafers had minimal scuffs; and she'd finished the look with a black handbag that she only dug out of her closet for special occasions. When she walked up to me, Mom kissed my cheek and said stiffly, "Nicole, how many times have I told you to dress well when you're shopping in better stores?"

Since we didn't shop in "better stores" growing up, those words had never come out of her mouth. But I was too grateful that she hadn't yet questioned what the fuck I was doing with my life to point that out. As we browsed the racks, I quickly realized that my mother was way more nervous and overwhelmed than she let on. While she may have expected her academic prowess to transmute into shopping ingenuity, my cerebral mother barely made it thirty minutes before beads of sweat started to form on her forehead.

A few hours later, after having enlisted the aid of several efficient saleswomen, I was the proud owner of a black blazer with leather lapels and a matching pair of leather pants, a cropped navy jacket, a few bright blouses, and a cream-colored pantsuit that would have fit in beautifully with the associates who worked at Joseph's Wall Street investment bank. But Mom kept telling me how important it was to look professional when you lead a team. And I was too nervous about starting my new job to keep objecting.

In the middle of our late lunch at a Midtown Italian restaurant, I couldn't hold it in any longer. We'd been casually chatting about my mother's classes and students that semester, Dad's new computer chess game, and Teresa's latest case, but I kept feeling like she was waiting for the right moment to tell me how idiotic all of this was.

"Mom, what is the deal?" I blurted out halfway through our main courses. "Why aren't you saying anything negative about *Sugar*? I know you must be thinking it."

"Do you really assume I'm going to criticize you all the time?" she asked, putting down her forkful of veal piccata.

"Well, kind of." I was wilting under her gaze, but I really needed to know what was up. "You never seem to think anything is worthwhile compared to academia. You didn't want me going into journalism in the first place, and you thought the whole fashion magazine thing was silly. And right when I got a position that you didn't seem to think was beneath my intellect, I quit to go work for a start-up. I just can't believe you haven't said boo about it."

Mom's brow furrowed. "Your father and I have always thought that you were destined for great things. You're smart and beautiful, and we assumed you were going to take over the world," she retorted, her terse tone contradicting the compliment. "The challenge is that the only world the two of us really know is academia."

"I'm so very aware, Mom." I suppressed a smile. "But that's *your* world. What you wanted for me has never been what I want for me."

"I did the best I could with the data I had," was her pedagogical reply. Then Mom heaved a big sigh, her face softening. "What can I say? I'm sorry, sweet pea." She hadn't called me *sweet pea* since I was a little girl, and my eyes suddenly welled up. "I know that I haven't exactly been overflowing with enthusiasm about your career in journalism, but only because I didn't understand it. And I was worried that you would never get to the top. Then the whole thing with Alonzo happened... and you can't blame me for questioning you and the entire magazine industry at that point."

When she said Alonzo's name, the tears forming in my eyes spilled over. In the three years since my parents had caught us in Krispy Kreme, we mostly avoided the subject. Hearing his name come out of her mouth not only brought back the humiliation of that day but also reminded me that I was now outside the *StyleList* cocoon and back in Alonzo's world.

To her infinite credit, Mom passed me an extra napkin without questioning why I was having such an extreme reaction. After giving me a second to catch my breath, she continued, "I've watched the shift in how you've comported yourself since you got to *StyleList*. Clearly, you're excellent at what you do and respected in your field, otherwise these opportunities would not be coming your way."

Why was every formidable woman in my life so skilled at double-edged compliments?

"I know my start in journalism was... inauspicious at best," I acknowledged, seeing her eyes crinkle at my use of one of her favorite words. One thing my mother and I shared was a love of beautiful language. "But you're right. I've worked really hard to get past the nightmare of your childhood friend—and to prove myself in my industry."

Mom involuntarily flinched at "childhood friend." As we stared at each other across her veal and my penne alla vodka, emotion chipped away at my mother's implacability until her eyes got moist as well.

"Nikki, I'm just so glad you're out of there." Mom reached over to grab my wrist. For the first time, I noticed that the skin on the back of her hands was thinner, the bones and veins slightly more visible than before. "I've hated that you were still at Park Avenue Publishing this whole time, even with the *StyleList* promotion. And I don't know that I'll ever forgive myself for bringing Alonzo into your life."

"What? I thought you were impressed by how well I was doing at *StyleList* and Park Ave Pub."

"Yes, but I absolutely hated you being in that... haunted building, even after Al left." Mom paused to signal to the waiter. He'd been staring at her from across the room as men often did and lit up at the signal that she needed him. As he made his way toward us, she told me, "Am I concerned for you? Yes, and I probably always will be. But I also see that this is a fresh start."

I didn't want to tell her about Alonzo's increased influence in my new world—or my six-month trial period. And I kept thinking about Marie's remark: What "stories" about Barbara had I not heard? Compared to the toxic environment that was Park Ave Pub, NuVoices could turn out to be Chernobyl. "I hadn't thought about *Sugar* as a fresh start, but I hope you're right." I chewed on my cuticle, then stopped because I knew Mom would recognize my nervous tell. "It's also a leap of faith, and I'm jumping without a parachute."

"You will simply have to rise to the challenge, Nicole." This was my mother's version of *you'd better fucking crush it*. She looked past me to the waiter who'd scurried up to our table. "Hi there." She smiled brightly at him with the confidence of someone who's been naturally pretty her whole life. "We'll need a new napkin, the dessert menu, and two glasses of champagne. Today, we're celebrating my daughter's new job."

TEN

Friday morning, my stress began to work over my stomach an hour before my alarm was supposed to go off. By my third trip to the bathroom, I was regretting the Mexican feast we'd had for dinner the night before. Joseph finally knocked on the bathroom door.

"You going to be all right in there, Nicole?" he asked.

"Fine. Great. Just getting ready," I replied quickly, turning on the faucet and the fan. I had tried not to wake him, but after several visits to his marble-wrapped sanctuary, there was no hiding the situation. I held my head in my hands and tried to will my nerves-addled digestive system into submission. But my deepest fears were running like a news ticker across my mind: *You'veneverdonethisbeforewhatif theyhateyouwhatiftheythinkyou'reafraud*... It was like watching the news in hell.

Finally, with eight minutes left to get dressed, I put on a black blouse and my new pantsuit, grabbed a black Gucci bag—my last score from the *StyleList* fashion closet—and ran for the door. I hadn't asked Barbara about the office dress code, and though my outfit was more stuffy than I would have liked, it did make me feel like a boss. It was only in the elevator that I realized a cream pantsuit was possibly not the best choice given the time I'd already logged in the bathroom that morning, but it was too late to change. I headed outside into the chilly morning, praying fervently to the gods of fashion and digestion.

By the time the taxi pulled up in front of the NuVoices office building, I felt a lot calmer. I'd talked to myself all the way downtown like a coach to his football team before the Rose Bowl. "You know your shit. You're a badass. You got this job for a reason . . ." I said it out loud with my eyes closed, trying to kill that news ticker of self-doubt still broadcasting in my brain. *Just be a leader and give it everything you have. Go make* Sugar *the success you know it can be. Let's go!*

The building was on Fifth Avenue just south of Seventeenth Street, in a neighborhood that was a lot less uptight than Midtown. A chubby olive-skinned guy whose Knicks jersey could not hide the fact that his baggy jeans were losing a battle with gravity headed into the NuVoices building. He stopped in the doorway to rub a minuscule scuff from his Air Jordan VIs and pull his wavy black hair into a low ponytail.

"Got to keep it professional for work, right?" he called over to where I had stopped to gather myself. A half smile tugged one side of his mouth up as he looked me up and down with interest. "You need some help, mami?"

"No, I'm fine." I squared my shoulders and followed him inside.

He and I soon discovered we were heading to the same place: the twelfth floor. I don't know what I was expecting when the elevator doors opened, but it sure wasn't Wu-Tang Clan's "Protect Ya Neck" blaring at top volume. While I figured the NuVoices office might be a culture shock, I didn't expect to be waving my arms in the air like I just don't care at ten in the morning.

"I got to tell Barbara about this bullshit," the guy muttered, holding the door open for me while taking note of the empty reception desk. "Tisha's not supposed to leave her area uncovered or play her music so goddamn loud first thing in the a.m. Damn, that girl is stupid."

I didn't say anything—in part because I didn't know who Tisha was and in part because I was too busy checking out the surprisingly masculine office. It looked like a garage that had been converted into a man cave, complete with an overabundance of black leather furniture, the requisite steel and red accents, and a pool table that was positioned too close to a large red bookshelf to properly use. The stark white walls were decorated with poster-sized recent covers of *Decode*, *Bella*, and *Sugar*, including the infamous Charli Baltimore cover I'd seen in CeCe's Studio. I couldn't help wondering how Barbara could have put together this decidedly unsexy space.

"Hey, you know where you're going?" the Knicks guy asked, as it became increasingly obvious that this was my first time in the NuVoices office.

"Not really," I admitted. "I'm here to see Barbara Porter."

His eyes widened and his smile grew. "Wait a minute. Are you the new *Sugar* lady?"

"Editor-in-chief. Yes."

"Oh shit. *You're* Nicole Rose." He put a hand in front of his mouth and looked around, clearly bummed no one was in the area to witness the moment. "Yo, we have been waiting on this day. I'm Jorge. I'm your guy if you ever need something delivered or fixed—or a male model for one of your fashion stories." He struck a pose then said, "You better come with me so you don't get lost up in here."

As we passed through the reception area into the main room, I realized how different NuVoices was from Park Ave Pub. Putting the masculine décor aside, the office was already humming with energy. All three magazines were on one floor, and, with the open design of glass-walled offices surrounding a thick tangle of cubicles, I could see every bit of chaotic activity. Music was playing in all corners. Folks were laughing loud and shouting to each other from cubicle to cubicle. Racks of clothes and shoes filled every vacant space. There was even a small dog barking its head off in one corner. Letting the image of *StyleList*'s serene, perfumed halls waft through my brain, I had a fleeting thought: *Well, Dorothy, you're definitely not in Kansas anymore.*

The commotion subsided as everyone turned to watch Jorge walk me into Barbara's office. I tried to look calm and confident, but I could feel every eye on me, probing my silk press, makeup, bag, shoes, and—oh, yeah—ridiculous outfit. Everyone was wearing jeans or a tracksuit. Every. Single. Person. In my tailored pantsuit, I looked like an IRS auditor coming to bust them for faking taxi receipts or something. "Thanks, Mom," I grumbled under my breath.

Despite the scrutiny and mayhem, I liked the environment—mostly because the office was straight out of a United Colors of Benetton ad. I had never worked somewhere where I wasn't the minority, but here, it seemed as if almost every ethnicity and shade were represented.

Jorge, who clearly enjoyed shepherding me across the floor, handed me off to Barbara with a little flourish, then ran off to enjoy his privileged status as the only one who had firsthand info about *Sugar*'s new EIC. Barbara, resplendent in a royal-blue leather outfit with enormous shoulder pads, stood to shake my hand, then closed the door firmly behind me.

"So, how does it feel to be working in the ghetto?" she asked, motioning for me to sit on her black leather sofa. *What the hell did this woman have with leather?* I wondered, settling in with a loud squeak as Barbara perched on her desk.

"Great!" I exclaimed, falling right into the trap. "I mean, not like this is the ghetto, of course."

"Not exactly. But closer than you've ever been, I'm guessing," Barbara replied. I started to remind her that I grew up in Harlem, but she went on. "Don't get defensive, Nikki. I obviously wouldn't have hired you if I didn't think you could hang. The question is whether *you* think you can hang because that's the only way you'll ever relax enough for the folks in this office to get to know Harlem Nikki instead of *StyleList* Nikki."

Barbara let that hover in the air between us for a moment, while I wondered again why it was my fate to deal with women whose insults and compliments sounded exactly the same. But I was glad that Barbara at least remembered where I grew up. And she was right: I'd spent so long repressing my Harlem upbringing at *StyleList* that I had no idea how to be myself at work. Again, I regretted walking into that office looking like I'd just climbed out of a Park Ave Pub town car.

"Well, I'm looking forward to getting started," I told her. "I've got ideas for my first issue and the cover, plus a few special packages I think I can pull off quickly."

"I'm sure you do, Nikki, but you might want to focus on your staff first. They're a little burned out from producing issues under Lunatic."

"What's Lunatic?"

"Not what, who. Lunatic is Luna Baxter, *Sugar*'s about-to-be-former editor-in-chief." Barbara plopped down on the sofa with me, seemingly exhausted by merely mentioning this woman's name. With a peeved sigh, she continued, "You probably know that Luna modeled for a while. When she aged out, she talked her way into running *Hot Hair* magazine. I decided to overlook that *Hot Hair* was a hot mess and made the mistake of thinking the skills she'd developed as a fashion model were transferable." Barbara closed her eyes and pressed her fingers into her temples. "But you don't make the mistake of underestimating her. She may not be the strongest technical editor, but Luna knows the urban market like the back of her hand, and she has shrewd editorial instincts. Most of all, Lunatic does not care what she has to do to succeed." Barbara rose and brushed off the front of her pants. "You're going to need to make a few staff changes, but there are some good people on that masthead. Luna just made it hard to tell who is who."

"Maybe she and I can meet to discuss the magazine's direction and who on staff was performing the best," I replied, trying for diplomacy. Kofi Annan would have been proud, but Barbara just laughed.

"Puleeze. Luna Baxter is a serious handful," she said, striding back to her desk. "You need to be careful with that one 'cause she's going to try *something*."

Before I could ask what she meant, Barbara's office door burst open to reveal a slender six-foot-tall chestnut-brown woman wearing low-slung white jeans tucked into Fendi boots and a white fur bomber. She sauntered in and sat on the edge of Barbara's desk, tapping her red talon-like acrylics on the shiny surface. Her bright green contact lenses and butt-length blond weave were gilding the lily, as Luna was drop-dead gorgeous.

"Is the buzz going around the office true?" she said in a loud voice, then stood to deliver a dramatic curtsy. "Is this the great Nicole Rose?"

"Watch it, Luna." Barbara's tone held a stern warning. "Nikki, meet Luna Baxter."

The tension in the air and the wrathful look on Luna's face made sense now. Trying again for peace, I stuck out my hand. "So nice to meet you. I'd love to talk to you about *Sugar*'s editorial calendar and the next issue you have planned."

Luna looked down at my hand and turned to Barbara. "What, you didn't warn Miss *StyleList* about me? You're slipping." Luna turned back to me and declared, "Girl, you on your own with *my* staff and *my* magazine. Nothing is planned so you'll be starting from scratch on Monday. But come on, let me introduce you to the *Sugar* team."

I wasn't exactly eager to be left alone with Lunatic, but it didn't seem that I had much choice. Luna led me out and down the hall without a backward glance. We rounded a corner, and she opened a door to a conference room where the *Sugar* staff had already gathered. The sixteen people seated around the large glass table were mostly Black, with a couple Latinas, one Asian guy in a Public Enemy snapback, and a lone white woman.

"Well, team, our great"—Luna paused to glance at me and shrug with exaggerated confusion—"I'm-not-sure-what savior has arrived. *This* is the famous Nicole Rose." She turned to me and said in a saccharine tone that didn't match her smirk or the dead fury in her eyes, "I've already informed my *Sugar* staff that you have *graciously* decided to step down from your perch at *StyleList* to come to lowly NuVoices Media to save us from ourselves."

"I'd hardly say all that," I replied, chafing at her *great white savior* reference.

"Oh, I would," Luna retorted. "And I'm sure the staff is so very grateful. Aren't you?" Luna beamed a huge, shit-eating, I'm-taking-you-down-with-me-bitch smile. She'd obviously planned this little exchange in advance. Before I could think of an appropriate comeback, Luna tried to nail my coffin shut. "Sure you are. Everyone knows we Black folks can't manage on our own, so we need a *StyleList* princess to tell us how it's gonna go down. And, from what I've been hearing, you have plenty of experience going down."

It was dead quiet until I broke the silence. "Excuse me, what did you say?" It was a real question, but I could tell from all the averted eyes in the room that Luna was referencing the rumors Alonzo had spread about me.

"Don't be ashamed, Nikki," she carefully articulated, laying on fake empathy as thick as a double-decker club sandwich. "I mean, you must be very skilled at what—or who—you do to be an editor-in-chief so young." Luna looked expectantly around the room, waiting for the pile on. "Come on, y'all. Gather round, introduce yourselves. This phenom obviously has loads of things to teach you, and possibly show you." She giggled and looked around. "Just be careful not to spill anything on her swanky suit."

Luna giggled some more. And the staff started to laugh with her, at first behind their hands, then outright, obviously not giving a damn what I thought. There were a few folks who weren't laughing, but they weren't looking at me either. Only one person regarded me with any real sympathy: a slender guy with a russet Afro and a solar system of freckles on his bronze cheeks. His arms stayed crossed across his untucked white button-down as he slowly shook his head and rolled his eyes. I was momentarily distracted by his chic leather sports jacket, waxed jeans, and polished Doc Martens. He looked like he could have been equally comfortable at *StyleList*, which I was missing quite a bit just then.

It was at that moment that the gods of digestion let me down. I could feel the rumblings beneath my suit jacket and, though I wanted to have it out with Lunatic then and there, I had to make a quick exit to find a ladies' room. I could hear the laughter get louder as I hurried away.

I was in a bathroom stall, licking my wounds and wondering how the hell to come back from that humiliation, when I heard two women come in, talking about yours truly.

"I give her a month," one said, entering the stall next to mine. I tucked my feet up so they would think they were alone. I needn't have worried; they were so involved in their conversation they didn't even bother to check if anyone else was in the bathroom.

"Girl, I give her one week. Did you see the way she took off? I couldn't believe Luna had her on the run like that."

"Maybe it was because Luna insulted her fancy getup. Did homegirl think she was going to work at Condé Nast or something?"

They both laughed while my cheeks burned.

"Clearly. Is she even Black?"

"Must be. Barbara's not stupid. But you know massa got up in the field house very recently 'cause she is mad pale."

"And she was flinging around a lot of hair that I don't think were bundles."

"I dunno. You almost can't tell a weave these days."

"Girl, you must be smoking dick if you think Miss Priss is the Brazilian silky type."

"True true. But speaking of dick..." They both cracked up.

"I bet she didn't think she was gonna be called out on day one for being a straight ho."

"Luna may be batshit crazy, but she tells it like it is."

As my "we are the world" dream dissipated, they laughed some more, washed their hands, and walked out, leaving me to ponder the raging dumpster fire that was my first morning at *Sugar*.

I wanted to collect my thoughts by myself in the reception area, but the freckled guy was sitting on the leather sofa, waiting for me. He stood up and stuck out his hand. "I don't believe that counted as a proper introduction. I'm Von."

I smiled at him, grateful that his tone was professional instead of patronizing, and shook his hand. "Nikki. Very nice to meet you."

My face must have betrayed how shook I felt because he leaned in and whispered, "Don't worry about Lunatic. She's like a cornered rabid dog right now: determined to fight her way out and unafraid to chomp on anyone in her way."

"I think I got that part." I shuddered, looking back in the direction of the conference room. "Is everyone still in there?"

"No, darlin'. They've dispersed to spread your tale of woe to the far ends of NuVoices."

"Great," I blurted, thinking about how embellished my already mortifying intro to the *Sugar* team would get by the third or fourth retelling. "Well, at least you're honest."

"Not to worry," Von assured me. "Everyone on the floor knows how extreme Luna is. And we are all too aware that she wouldn't have gotten her ass booted if *Sugar* had been doing better." He linked his arm through mine and led me down the hall back toward Barbara's office. "Why not give it a rest for the day? You come back on Monday, right? Maybe let the nonsense die down and talk to the staff again then."

Von was making sense because I wasn't feeling up to reintroducing myself to that pack of laughing hyenas ready to eat my innards while I was still alive. "You know what? Excellent idea. I'm going to say goodbye to Barbara and go have a liquid lunch." I inspected him with curiosity, realizing I had no idea what he did. "So, Von, what is your position at *Sugar*, anyway? You're the only person in here aside from Barbara wearing a leather blazer. Let me guess: fashion?"

He grinned and then bowed deeply. "I am your new assistant."

Barbara was unfazed to see me leave so fast. "Let me know now if you don't feel like you can handle this job," she said when she saw my purse in my hand. I wondered if Luna had run off any other EIC candidates.

"Not to worry, Barbara. I've got the situation under control," I said with a lot more confidence than I felt. "See you Monday."

"Not so fast," she said, motioning for me to close her office door. "I just got off the phone with Alonzo."

My heart started beating in my throat as I realized my already shitty day was about to get worse. Barbara stared at me, waiting for a reaction. For once, I decided to play it cool. "Oh yeah? How's he doing?"

"Well, he's running the media company that owns the biggest urban magazine in the world, so I think he's doing all right. He's always crowing about *Groove*'s revenue numbers."

I forced a smile but said nothing, waiting for the other shoe to drop.

"So," Barbara continued after it became apparent that I wasn't going to take the bait, "he is really not a fan of yours. I am a little surprised that Alonzo Griffin would feel it important enough to call me a second time about an assistant editor at his former magazine."

"Barbara, I think you know why," I replied weakly.

She regarded me carefully, then tapped her index finger on her pursed lips. "He tried to double down on some bullshit about your work ethic, but I already told you that I know the deal." She leaned across her desk to flick some dark fuzz off my collar. "Now, I'm not going to hold whatever happened against you, but I want to remind you that I see everything that goes down in this office."

I hoped she couldn't see the sweat creating huge circles under my arms. "I understand."

"Good. Because we can't afford any scandals right now." She walked around her desk to perch on the edge of the sofa where I had sat down. "I mean, we literally cannot afford any scandals at all."

I hadn't thought that Barbara would have even been capable of an expression and tone so subdued. "Is there something happening, Barbara?"

"NuVoices is not growing at the rate we need to satisfy our board. If the investors pull their money, we will not be able to survive on our advertising revenue alone. We have six months or so to prove that *Sugar* can increase its audience and be profitable or I'll have to shut down the entire company." Her matter-of-fact declaration made the words even more alarming.

I was instantly afraid—and also angry. "So you hired me for a six-month trial period knowing the company only has six months to survive?"

Barbara smiled and the fire came back into her eyes. "No. I hired you for the opportunity of a lifetime to turn this ship around. I don't think you know how to fail, Second Coming. So I need you to do what you do best and overachieve on *Sugar*'s ass."

Another backhanded compliment. "I just...I just wish you had told me so I could be more prepared."

"And how would you have done that?" She snorted. "Look, I brought you here because you know what the best looks like." She waved dismissively toward the floor outside her office. "Most of them have never seen the best of anything, certainly not in publishing. You have. Show them."

"I'll be honest, Barbara, this is really not what I signed up for."

"It never is. Now go and have a restful weekend. Come in on Monday ready to fight."

ELEVEN

Walking to the train station, I called Teresa to tell her how hideous my morning had been. She must have heard it in my voice because next thing I knew, she and I were sitting in a hole-in-the-wall Vietnamese restaurant in Chinatown, tearing through an early lunch. The criminal court building where Teresa worked was a few blocks away and this was her favorite local cheap eat—a good find for her since she could barely afford Mickey D's after her latest purchase of Jimmy Choo boots.

"I can't believe how hungry I am," I said, finishing off a lettuce-wrapped spring roll in two huge bites. My stomach had finally calmed down and I couldn't eat fast enough.

"Sounds like you have reason to be. You basically ran a marathon this morning," Teresa said as she dug into the lemongrass beef. She'd reacted just as I expected to my exchange with Luna: pissed as hell. She shook her head through the whole story, saying when I was done, "That bitch does *not* want me coming in her office. I will get so goddamn Bronx on her ass."

I smiled to myself, thinking that Teresa vs. Lunatic would be like *Alien vs. Predator*.

"Shit, it did feel like a marathon," I replied, helping myself to seconds of pan-fried noodles. "I'm just so mad I didn't see it coming."

"Yeah, well, Barbara is obviously hazing you."

"I don't know about that, Tee. She seemed dead serious about NuVoices shutting down." I stopped eating long enough to take a big swig of my Singha beer. "I really don't know how I'm going to 'turn the ship around' while dealing with that team."

Teresa nodded. "You're going to have to work on your street smarts for this gig, Ms. Park Avenue Publishing. NuVoices could really be a once-in-a-lifetime opportunity. But you gotta play the game."

"You got that right. I need to stop thinking *StyleList* and start thinking *Sugar*."

"And fast," Teresa said, staring intently out the window onto the street. Suddenly, she started waving.

"What the hell are you doing?" I asked as Teresa banged on the glass.

"My boy is walking by," she said, standing up to greet a tall man in a narrow-cut charcoal-gray suit who strolled in and swooped Teresa up in a hug. Judging by how far down he had to bend, he must have been at least six foot three. With his muscular build, flawless chocolate skin, and neatly trimmed goatee, he was one helluva sexy man. I watched enviously as Teresa planted a kiss on his cheek.

"What's up, Tee. Nice to see you out here slumming it."

"You got jokes today? This is the cheapest restaurant in the neighborhood, and Jimmy Choo stole my lunch money." She socked him in the arm. "Derek, meet my best friend, Nikki. Nik, this is Derek Mills from New York County Defender Services. We tried that four-month serial burglary together. Thank god for second chairs because it was in the middle of my breakup with the psycho boy. Derek held me down so I wouldn't tank the trial. And then he knocked it out of the park with his summation." Teresa turned to Derek, who was waving away her praise. Then she looked at me. "Actually, you and my brother from another mother over here were giving me the same relationship advice that whole time. It was like being in the most annoyingly sensible echo chamber ever."

Derek chuckled and leaned forward. "First of all, there's no way we would've gotten the acquittal if you hadn't beat up that detective so bad on cross." He rested the book he'd been holding on the table to shake my hand. "Nice to meet you, Nikki. Any annoyingly sensible friend of Teresa's is a friend of mine."

As I shook his hand, I snuck a peek at the book title: Joan Morgan's *When Chickenheads Come Home to Roost*. It had been published a few months ago and I'd already read it; the author's layered observations about hip hop culture and the modern Black woman made me realize anew just how fucked-up my relationship with Alonzo really was.

"That your book?" I couldn't resist asking.

"Yeah, the title caught me in Barnes and Noble and I couldn't put it down."

I stared at Derek, processing that he'd voluntarily bought a book about feminism. "I read it in one sitting. It really, um, hit home for me."

"I bet it did," Derek replied carefully. "The book was very clear about how complicated the world is for educated, goal-oriented, independent Black women. And while I love hip hop from my soul, Joan made me think about misogyny in the lyrics in a totally different way."

I nodded slowly, unwilling to reveal more to a total stranger—even as I had a feeling he might understand.

"Sheeet, you put a good beat under 'Bitches and hoes and hoes and bitches' and my ass will be on the dance floor." Teresa shrugged as we all started laughing.

"That might be part of the problem, girl," I said lightly, although I wasn't entirely kidding.

"We're all a little bit complicit, right? But no disempowered community should bear the responsibility for fixing the dominant culture." Derek sounded so earnest that I started to feel the edges of suspicion. No man could be that damn evolved.

"Well, I'm not relying on a man to end my oppression," Teresa shot back, clearly used to sparring with Derek.

He raised a power fist. "Hear! Hear!"

"All this advocating for the underdog makes you guys sound so public defender-y." I smiled at them, clearly in their element.

After shifting gears to chat with Teresa for a few minutes about a new case he had, Derek kissed both of us on the cheek and took off toward the courthouse.

My girl normally had indiscriminate taste in men: knuckleheaded gym rats, lying adulterers, sheltered Upper East Siders looking for an exotic thrill; Teresa had dated them all. But this time, I thought she'd hit the jackpot. This guy was handsome and smart and gentlemanly. I held up my hand to high-five Teresa. "Tee, that man is hot," I said. "You did good this time. Why didn't you tell me about him?"

She laughed. "He's my boy, not my man. We're just friends."

"Yeah, right. He is way too fine to waste on some platonic nonsense."

"I swear. We're not each other's type. He's too geeky for me, always reading in his spare time. And I keep it way too real for him." She signaled the waiter for our check.

"Whatever, Teresa. Just because you have a photographic memory doesn't give you the right to make fun of the rest of us who actually have to read things." I rolled my eyes and pointed at her. "All I know is that you need to get in there and help yourself to a big serving of Derek Mills before some other chick does."

She raised her eyebrows. "I saw the way you were looking at him," she said. "You want a lil' spoonful for yourself?"

"Nope. I'm heading home now to get ready to meet my own man for a date later."

She shot me a knowing look. "Okay, chica. My bad."

When I called Joseph to fill him in on my morning from hell, he "oh no"ed and "oh wow"ed through the story, making me feel for a minute that he might have understood how deflating the day was. But then he said, "Well, at least they didn't pat you down or make you pass through a metal detector on your way in," chuckling at his own joke.

I swallowed my irritation at his snarky tone, but then he reminded me that we were going to dinner with another one of his bank's managing directors at seven. I had been looking forward to going to his house, ordering a pizza, and watching a movie. The very last thing I wanted to do was hang out with some suit and his trophy girlfriend of the month. But it was obviously important to Joseph, so I told him I'd meet him at the restaurant. I figured if I closed my eyes for a few minutes, I'd be fine. But a few minutes turned into a few hours.

I woke with a start at 6:30. I'd crawled out of my suit and into comfy pajamas and gathered my hair into a messy bun. My makeup was smudged and would have to be redone. Hell, I probably needed to shower. No way was I going to make it to Midtown in thirty minutes, so I called Joseph to let him know I'd be late.

"Dammit, Nicole," he exploded. "This is not some random dinner. We're meeting Peter Boatswright and his girlfriend, Nina Hilman—you know, of Hilman hotels."

"Well, tell Peter Boatswright and Nina Hilman that I've had a stressful day and I will be along shortly."

"And how am I supposed to explain your day?" he huffed. "Should I say that you nearly had a bathroom accident on day one at a media company they've never heard of?"

I was so stunned by the venom in his voice, I almost couldn't respond. My hurt quickly changed to anger. "You know what?" I spat. "Why don't you and your socialite friends have a lovely dinner tonight. And don't bother calling me this weekend. I'm not in the mood."

I slammed the phone down as my fury turned to disbelief. But I was also almost grateful we'd fought because my brain was still fried. I really didn't want to reapply mascara, put on heels, and come up with pithy small talk. Pepperoni pizza and a night of DVDs sounded much better.

I rolled into CeCe's Studio the next day with my unfortunate morning at NuVoices still looping endlessly through my mind. I tried to refocus on what I could possibly do to get the *Sugar* staff to trust me, but all I could think about was their downcast eyes as Lunatic mocked that stupid suit, everyone snickering at the slander that I slept my way to the top, the bathroom bitches trying to revoke my Black passport, and Barbara staring into my eyeballs as she told me that I could either save or tank NuVoices.

CeCe got an earful as she trimmed my hair. She'd been so excited when I got the gig, making me promise to book her on all the beauty shoots, so her face was crestfallen in the mirror as I told her the real real. I shared the entire story except the part about the company being in financial trouble. Though Barbara didn't tell me that it was confidential, NuVoices' imminent downfall was clearly privileged information.

"This is the worst story I've ever heard, Nikki. Like, what the fuck?"

"I know, right? It started unpleasant and kind of confusing, then descended into hell real fast." I forgot I was getting a trim and let my head fall back, barely missing CeCe's scissors.

She bonked me on the head with her knuckle. "How's about we not make it even worse by sending you to work on Monday with a random chunk of hair missing."

"I can't even believe I've got to go back there on Monday." I groaned.

I dropped my head into my hands as A Tribe Called Quest's "Can I Kick It?" played, and I longed for the simple times at Howard when Denyse and I did the Cabbage Patch to this song at frat parties.

"Jesus be a snow day, girl, because you clearly need a sec to get your mind right." CeCe tugged a corner of my hood under the salon robe. She'd known something was up right away when I showed up in a ratty green tracksuit with saggy bottoms and a broken zipper that I normally only wore around the house.

"First of all, it's April. Only Prince thinks we might get snow." I allowed myself a small smile. "Second, I have to take it like a... woman, so I have forty-eight hours to figure out how I'm going to handle Monday."

"Well, bite that bullet, girl."

"Grinning and bearing it," I returned.

"Suck it up, buttercup!"

We were both smiling now, and my relief at feeling my face muscles relax was palpable. CeCe bent over to whisper in my ear. "You want some tea on Luna? I heard from another client that she slept with every member of Jagged Edge within the last year."

"I don't know about all that," I replied. I had zero motivation to defend that malicious beautiful woman, but given the bogus back-fence talk floating around about me, I resisted the urge to pile on. "Although that witch does seem completely out of control. They literally call her Lunatic. And now I have to deal with a staff conditioned to crazy."

"Maybe they'll be grateful to work with a sane person for a change," CeCe said, smoothing serum into my hair.

"They didn't seem particularly grateful when I met them."

CeCe squinted at me in the mirror, then put both hands on my shoulders and gave them a little shake. "You need to pull yourself together, Nik. Yes, Luna is a hot mess, but you gotta remember that also means that those poor people at *Sugar* haven't had a real leader in a while. Give them a reason to follow you, and I bet they will."

She went back to fluffing my hair while I digested her wisdom. I pulled out my *Sugar* notebook and began to make notes... and ended up writing all weekend. I kept a rotation of hip hop CDs blasting from my boom box, initially ricocheting between A Tribe Called Quest and Public Enemy, Biggie and Nas, KRS-One and Tupac. But after a while, I found myself playing female artists on repeat: MC Lyte, Foxy Brown, Queen Latifah, Lil' Kim, Da Brat, the Lady of Rage.

I took a couple breaks to walk around Brooklyn, absorbing what made it the cultural hub of Black New York City. With all the hipsters moving in, Bed-Stuy was feeling less Do or Die every single day. But the old-school community was still the soul of the neighborhood. On Saturday, I made my way from my apartment through adjacent Clinton Hill all the way to Fort Greene, where I got most of my local inspo from the artsy people hanging on the sycamore-lined streets. The true center of Black bohemian life, that neighborhood was as vibrant as the cultural mecca of Harlem must have been during the Renaissance years. I swung by Spike Lee's 40 Acres and a Mule Filmworks production company and his shop, Spike's Joint, then wandered around the local clothing boutiques, Caribbean restaurants, record stores, and bars. My utter mortification at wearing a pantsuit on my first day at NuVoices only increased as I checked out the sea of luxury tracksuits, baggy overalls, headwraps, cropped jerseys, slip dresses, bucket hats, and oversized bombers. I had no idea why I thought the office of an urban publishing company would look more like a corporate law firm than my own hood.

On Sunday, perched on a bench in Fort Greene Park with a bagel and a coffee, I took in a breakdancing crew windmilling for dollars on a nearby corner. Somehow, there was always music in Fort Greene: teens rapping on stoops, drums coming from a basement, a boom box blasting across the park. It reminded me of watching hip hop's decisive takeover from the stoop of my family's brownstone. My own obsession with music started in this more innocent time, when Kurtis Blow, Run-D.M.C., LL Cool J, Queen Latifah, and Will Smith were releasing joyful party songs that still got people to the dance floor, when the vibe was funky-fresh fun. But hip hop had now morphed into something more violent, more woman-hating, more complicated to love.

As much as Brooklyn—and New York City—seemed like the

center of the world that weekend, I knew that *Sugar* had to appeal to women outside the borough, outside New York City, hell, beyond the coasts. NYC and LA could be aspirational, but I didn't want to alienate women in Atlanta or Chicago or Houston. *Sugar* had to be cool and cutting-edge but also approachable and fun. And I had to figure out how to integrate hip hop culture in a way that felt empowering instead of demoralizing.

Back in my studio, I organized my notes into a document very different from what I'd sent Barbara. More manifesto than marketing plan, it was a rallying cry for me and my new team. It was about values and tone and style and mission. I even filled a folder with inspiration for a visual redesign. I'd realized over the weekend that the *Sugar* team needed to be invested enough in my vision so they could be optimistic about the future. Otherwise, I would be written off as another out-of-touch suit—and I would fail.

On the walk home, I'd stopped by a huge outdoor newsstand to look at the newest issues of my faves. After forcing myself not to pick up the issue of *Black Enterprise* featuring none other than Alonzo's unsmiling face on the cover, I'd lost an hour, perusing *Trace, i-D, Essence, Architectural Digest, W, Vibe, Rolling Stone, Paper, The Source, Teen People, The New Yorker, Travel + Leisure, XXL, Elle, Untold,* and *Vogue*. Scanning the tables of contents and flipping through cover stories and style features, I read the first few paragraphs of interesting articles and studied the mastheads to see if there had been any major changes in leadership. I'd wanted to be an editor-in-chief for as long as I could remember, and I knew the names of every EIC at all the major magazines on the newsstand. Failure was not an option.

By the time I cracked open a bottle of pinot noir on Sunday night and popped Massive Attack's *Mezzanine* into my stereo, I'd produced a declaration of editorial independence into which I'd infused every ounce of passion I had for *Sugar*'s audience, for my career as an editor, and for the opportunity to create a space where I belonged.

I was so focused that I didn't register until I was getting ready for bed that I'd heard crickets from Joseph. We hadn't spent an entire weekend apart in months, yet I felt ambivalent—except for missing our reliably good sex. When the batteries ran out in my vibrator, I almost broke down and took the subway into Manhattan to beg for that fine man's forgiveness. But it would have inevitably turned into an argument about his business dinner. He'd been insulting, but I knew I'd acted like a child. Though I realized my silence was adding a sprinkling of coarse salt into Friday night's open wound, I decided to go to the bodega for batteries instead of dialing Joseph's number.

TWELVE

Monday morning, I marched through the NuVoices doors at exactly 9:59 AM. Although the elusive Tisha was still nowhere in sight, Lil' Kim's "Queen Bitch" was booming when I stepped off the elevator. I took it as a good omen.

I stopped in the reception area to straighten my clothes. That morning, I'd pored through the remains of my *StyleList* stash and settled on a Dolce &Gabbana sleeveless black turtleneck with loose-fitting camouflage pants tucked into black boots. My hair was in a high ponytail that exposed chunky hoops. It wasn't jeans and Timbs, but I didn't look like I worked on Wall Street, nor sexy or flashy enough to trigger more slut-shaming.

Teresa took the morning off to ride the subway with me to work. She bought me a bagel and coffee, then walked me through a plan of action to project confidence at all costs. It was a pep talk worthy of a heavyweight prizefighter's corner man in the last round of a title bout. The last thing she told me as we walked out of the subway station on Fourteenth Street was, "Imagine the feeling of leaving the office at the end of the day like a champ, knowing those bitches saw you were a force to be reckoned with. Imagine your team starting to see who you are and why you are the only person who can take *Sugar* to the next level. Imagine knowing that you fucking crushed it as you walk to the subway tonight. Visualize it and keep that energy, bonita. You got this!"

With my mind right and my I'm-not-fucking-around-anymore outfit in place, I dabbed on some red lipstick and sauntered as casually as I could right up to Barbara's office. "Morning. Just wanted to check in before getting to work."

Barbara nodded approvingly at my outfit and resolute expression. "Nice to see you, Nikki. The next issue you need to work on is June. I'll have the production department schedule a meeting with you to go over deadlines for the rest of the year. Show me your edit rundown when you get it together. As you are aware, we have a lot of work to do and limited time in which to do it."

I definitely did not need a reminder that the clock was ticking.

"Barbara, does anyone else on the *Sugar* team know how little time—" I began, but she cut me short.

"What do you think, newbie?" Barbara threw her hands up. "Keep your mouth shut."

I nodded and, without another word, headed straight down the hall toward the area where the *Sugar* team sat. Von was on the phone in his cubicle across from what I assumed would be my office, but I didn't look inside to see if Luna was still there. I rapped lightly on the cubicle wall, startling Von, who nearly dropped the phone when he saw me. I realized that he hadn't known if I'd ever darken NuVoices' door again.

"Morning, Von. Would you please assemble the team for a meeting in fifteen minutes? I'll be waiting in the conference room," I told him, taking off before he or anyone seated around him could react.

The *Sugar* staff trickled in, checking me out with obvious curiosity before taking seats around the glass table. I said a calm hello to each person as they entered, remaining composed as Lunatic herself glided through the door.

"Well, I'll be!" she exclaimed in an exaggerated Southern accent. "Thought we mighta seen the last of you, *StyleList*."

I deliberately looked her up and down—this time she was all in pink, from her bedazzled baseball cap to her Timberland boots. Despite the over-the-top outfit, Luna looked annoyingly stunning. "As if," I said with a tight smile.

"Puleeeze," she retorted, neck swaying back and forth. "Luna Baxter always gets what she wishes for."

Why don't you wish for a new job, boo, I thought but held my tongue in case there was a chance we could solve this peaceably. Instead, I asked, "So, what can I do for you?"

Luna snickered and looked around the room as if she couldn't believe her ears. "What can *you* do for *me*? I know you're not serious. I came in to see if you needed some help. Oh, and whether you were wearing another three-piece suit."

As she started to laugh, heat rose from my stomach to my neck. This was not about to be a repeat of Friday. "Yeah, all right, *Lunatic*. You really are living up to your reputation," I fired back. "Don't you have something else to do other than hang around this office?"

Her eyes widened for a second, then quickly narrowed. Both hands on her hips, she snarled, "Who the hell do you think you are?"

"The new editor-in-chief of *Sugar*." I stood up and put my hands in my pockets, an intentionally nonchalant gesture that I'd always thought held more power than the defensive insecurity of crossed arms. "Which means that you are no longer needed here."

She started toward me, but I held my ground. This confrontation was not ending like the last one. One of us was leaving and it wasn't going to be me. When Luna saw I wasn't moving, she stopped in her tracks. "You don't know what you got yourself into, ho," she spat.

"Maybe, but I do know what you got yourself *out* of—and that seems to be NuVoices. So, why don't you take off and let me talk to *my* team." I took the seat at the head of the conference table, proud of myself for not flinching at being called a ho to my face.

Luna stomped out. We could all hear her cursing and banging stuff around outside.

"Von," I said, "close the door, please." As he shut the door with a firm click, I handed out a single sheet of paper to each person in the room. "Now that we've taken care of that," I said, winking at Von, who gave me a small thumbs-up, "let's move forward. In your hands you have *Sugar*'s new editorial mission statement."

The team looked at each other with raised eyebrows, but I pressed on. "Let me read it to you: *Sugar* is *the* media brand for smart, stylish, and cool Black women, ages eighteen to thirty-four. Recognizing that our audience isn't just a part of culture but that we define culture, *Sugar* will inform, embolden, and entertain our readers with content that reflects their power and potential: cutting-edge fashion and beauty; insightful features on social issues, relationships, career, and health; and access-driven coverage of the hottest celebrities. *Sugar* is the new voice for young urban women who want to set big goals, achieve their wildest dreams, have full and fun lives, and look fly while they're doing it."

The concise little paragraph summed up so much of my conviction and my own wildest dreams. I was certain everyone would be inspired, but instead of the standing ovation I'd hoped for, there was silence. "Come on, people," I said, looking around the room. "I know some of you have *plenty* to say."

There was some throat clearing, then the Asian guy piped up: "So what does 'urban women' mean?"

"Glad you asked," I replied. If they were talking, they were engaged. "Make no mistake, *Sugar* will be written for Black women. But Black people drive urban culture, which drives pop culture, and *we* drive style. Any woman interested in culture and fashion might want to check out *Sugar*."

"So, you *are* Black?" came a high-pitched nasal voice to my right that I immediately recognized as one of the women kiki-ing at my expense in the bathroom on Friday. As she drummed her fingers on the table and popped her gum, I took in her smooth tawny skin stretched over wide cheekbones, short red twists, and large hazel eyes.

"Without a doubt," I pronounced, looking around the room, then directly at her.

A second harsh voice to my left cut in: "Why do we need a new mission statement, anyway? Isn't this"—she waved the paper I'd given her in the air, then slammed it back onto the table—"what we already do?" I swung around to see a petite woman with purple locs and a nose ring.

"Yes and no. Listen, *Sugar* has the potential to impact culture and be a real voice for women across the country," I said. "We just need to build off what you guys are already doing and raise the bar, starting with a top-to-bottom redesign."

I was on a roll, but she interrupted again, this time standing as she spoke. "Ain't this a bitch," she exclaimed, her locs cascading over her crossed arms. "Why do we need to redesign a brand-new magazine?"

I'd had about enough of her. "Because the way it looks right now isn't advertiser-friendly, and it won't reach the entire audience we could attract. Tell me, what is your position here?"

"I'm the art director," she flung back, "and I don't think *my* magazine needs a redesign." Von was seated next to her and tried to put a calming hand on her arm, but she shook it off, telling him, "Look, you know the only time I hold my tongue is when I'm at the dentist." She turned back to me. "Even if I did want to do a redesign, I'm not at all convinced that *you* would have a clue how to make *Sugar* better. Honestly, I don't even know how you got this job since you sure aren't Barbara's type."

I stood as well and examined her coolly. "Then I guess it's fortunate that you are no longer the art director at *Sugar*."

Someone in the back loudly whispered, "Oh snap," while everyone looked at each other, wide-eyed and frozen like a troop of lemurs.

"Are you actually firing me?" she sputtered. "You can't be serious."

"As a heart attack. This is your last day. You can leave."

As she stormed out, dead silence fell over the room. "Anybody else?" I scanned each person in the conference room, but no one so much as blinked. "Good, then let's get started. We have a lot to do to close June."

That was the understatement of the century. I had just over two weeks to ship the June issue to the printer, and the Wall—the uninspired name for a literal wall where magazine editors affixed pages of whichever issue they were currently closing—was disturbingly empty.

During a magazine issue's production process, editors hang miniature versions of finished stories on the Wall, according to where they fall in the magazine, to review the overall layout. So, every month, we'd literally see the magazine coming together in front of our eyes. The first week of production, there would be a page or two of the FOB (front of book, the beginning section of a magazine with all the ads) on the Wall. The next week, most of the FOB would be there, along with maybe one feature. By week three, we'd really get going and most of the well (the section with style spreads and longer articles in the middle of the magazine) would go up. Week four was for the last couple well features, the cover story, the BOB (back of book, the last pages of a magazine where the features in the well spilled over), and the cover itself.

Miniatures of at least half the June issue's stories should have already been hung up by now. I would have to put together a table of contents and figure out a cover subject that the team and I could deliver in two weeks. The only thing I was totally sure of at that moment was that I didn't have a second to spare.

While I hadn't expected an extravagant Lucinda-esque setup, I was unprepared for the grimy, cramped, rectangular space that assaulted my eyeballs when Von unlocked the door of my office after the Monday staff meeting: a hot-pink leather swivel chair peacocked behind a scratched desk; matching magenta guest chairs were artfully placed in front of the desk to hide the scuffs and grooves pockmarking its fading black paint; a dusty plywood bookcase was filled with gossip and hair magazines in front of which lay a threadbare floral-print rug spotted with stains whose origins I did not want to contemplate. Two of the walls were painted bright fuchsia and covered in framed posters of Dru Hill, Jodeci, and Boyz II Men. The décor was obviously Luna's handiwork.

With a master yogi–level exhalation, I turned to Von, who had been waiting for my reaction. He couldn't take it any longer. "I know, boss lady. It's tragic in here."

"Von, it's so much worse than tragic." I tried to channel the two pranayama breathwork classes that Sofie had dragged me to before she'd finally processed that I was more of a kickboxing girl.

"We need paint and upholstery and a new rug, stat," Von insisted, pulling out a notebook.

"What we need is to burn some sage," I replied, running my hand over the top of the desk, then examining the thick dust on my fingers. "And cleaning supplies. Lots of cleaning supplies."

Of course Luna left the place a mess. I kept finding evidence of her presence everywhere, like mouse droppings: nail clippers, a curling iron, tampons. I located some rubber gloves in the kitchen closet and got to work alongside Von, much to his surprise.

"I have this, I swear," he protested after I kicked off my boots.

I motioned to his monochromatic cream-and-gray outfit anchored by cashmere sweatpants and a matching knit jacket. "Are you serious? I want to wrap you and that fabulous outfit in plastic wrap. If anything, you're the one who should be sitting out this gross cleaning session."

"I'll take that as the highest compliment, boss." Von did a little twirl. "My last girlfriend used to work at Ralph Lauren and scored this fab fit."

"Well, your last girlfriend had killer taste," I said, trying to keep my surprise that he liked women out of my voice.

"I know, right?" Von shot over his shoulder as he removed all the copies of *Hot Hair* from the bookcase. "She was so stylish, I probably would have stayed with her forever. But we broke up when I accidentally spilled cranberry juice on her white Shabby Chic love seat."

My hoot of laughter startled the *Sugar* staffers, who were finding reasons to walk by while we were cleaning. It was hard to tell if the incredulity on their faces meant they were impressed or horrified by the sight of me on my knees, scouring the underside of the desk. It took Von and me a few hours to scrub the office enough so that I would even sit in the desk chair. We were both spattered in so much dirt that the undersides of my nails turned into black crescents, and it became hard to distinguish between Von's freckles and dots of grime. I sent him to buy new pillows and an inexpensive rug, and we planned on painting the next weekend. I was determined to make the space mine.

In stark contrast to the unglamorous spectacle of me plucking hairballs out of drawers, deliveries from local florists were arriving almost every hour. *Sugar*, while obviously in need of a reboot, had still made waves as the only magazine for urban women, and there were apparently tons of folks interested in its future. Congratulatory flowers came from record labels, beauty companies, streetwear fashion lines, and even a couple former Park Ave Pub colleagues.

When Von brought me an arrangement of sunflowers so tall we had to place it on the floor, I was surprised that they were from Joseph. I'd sent him an email that morning to apologize and to ask how the dinner went. Joe's curt reply told me that he was still mad, but the flowers implied that he wanted to forgive me.

Tucked in among the bouquets was an enormous vase filled with calla lilies in a purple so deep that they appeared almost black. I wondered who had sent me something so original. Then I read the card:

Well, well, Nikki, aren't you the surprise contender? Congratulations on becoming the newest target in a world predisposed to hate you. Watch your back, and your front. And watch out for Barbara...

All my best,

Alonzo

Von was watching as I read, so instead of freaking out, I said, "From L'Oreal," and excused myself to go to the ladies' room. I was hyperventilating as I locked the stall door. It was a full twenty minutes before I was ready to face anyone. As I turned to walk out of the stall, I realized that my hand was still gripping Alonzo's card. I ripped it up and flushed it down the toilet.

THIRTEEN

Sitting in the editor-in-chief chair meant being the center of attention all the time. I'd frequently lift my head from my computer to see someone scurry off, or I'd round a corner to find a few people huddled in a conversation that would immediately stop when they saw me. I began to wonder if I was unknowingly collecting enemies in every corner like the dust bunnies I had cleared out of my office. It didn't matter that I had grown up in the long shadow of the Apollo Theater or that I now bought incense and bean pies on the street in Bed-Stuy, I still had to earn their respect. I came in with no street cred and my name had been dragged through the mud. I was getting zero passes.

Theater or that I now bought incense and bean pies on the street in Bed-Stuy, I still had to earn their respect. I came in with no street cred *and* my name had been dragged through the mud. I was getting zero passes.

Someone leaked the new mission statement I had written to Robert Jameson, a journalist who covered Black media brands with the intensity of a *New York Times* ombudsman. When he added it to his weekly newsletter, the reaction was instantaneous. There were a few haters and Luna loyalists who questioned my background and Blackness and motives. But it mostly got love from supportive women who sent me encouraging letters and emails. A few singers and actresses caught wind of the growing buzz and publicly expressed their excitement, which took the furor to new levels; I had more visibility than I'd ever experienced, and I understood how much I was under a spotlight. Unlike at *StyleList*, where no one cared what I did, my success or failure at *Sugar* would be playing out in the public eye. And I didn't have a lot of time to get it right.

After two sixteen-hour days, I finished the June issue story lineup and gave it to Barbara. She pushed back on a few concepts, but had to admit that my presentation was more thorough than anything she'd ever seen. By the end of the first week, I'd produced a draft editorial outline for the entire year and had started outreach to music labels and Hollywood PR firms about album and movie releases for future cover subjects. I kept the file on my desktop, and the printouts were in a locked drawer so no one could leak the covers and editorial specials I had planned.

Though the *Sugar* staff was taking their time warming up to me, even the hardest among them couldn't deny that generating cool ideas was my sweet spot. Luna hadn't been doing regular editorial meetings with the team, so that was the first thing I changed. The team couldn't be invested in a magazine they didn't have a real hand in creating.

The first meeting was awkward and unproductive, with most of the team gaping at me, arms crossed, not believing that I was actually interested in their input. The more daring among them popped their heads up to voice a few thoughts. But the minute I questioned an idea or asked for more information, they'd retreat like crabs on the beach, leaving me staring at bubbling holes in the sand. I ended the meeting early and asked everyone to bring story ideas the next time. It was during the second brainstorm that I saw glimmers of what the team could be. I'd decided to put on some music in the background and caught the surprised yet appreciative looks when I chose BDP. I'd figured KRS-One rapping would mean less weird silence to fill. I didn't consider that it might give me a shred of cred. The meeting started on a much more energetic note.

"Okay, I think we have a bomb FOB for the July issue!" I exclaimed after thirty minutes. Almost everyone had offered an idea, and they let me work with them to refine them until we'd put together a smart, cool, and buzzy front-of-book section filled with emerging artist miniprofiles, fashion shopping pages, new tech products, movie and book reviews, and album releases. "Let's work on the well. Who's got a feature concept?"

An associate editor with red glasses perched on top of a dense mass of wiry curls and a thick Trinidadian accent raised her hand. I remembered Lucinda making the *StyleList* team crack up by asking me if "I'd like to come to the blackboard to write down the correct answer" when I did the same thing in an editorial meeting. So I gently told her, "No need to raise your hand, Felicia. Just jump on in. What do you have?"

She nodded gratefully. "I was thinking about how women get treated on the street. Like, I can't take two steps down Flatbush without some dude yelling out his car."

I knew exactly what she meant. The catcalling in Brooklyn was almost as prevalent and creative as it was in Harlem. "Yep, I bet a few of us here can relate. Tell me more."

"Well, we're working on a summer issue, which is catcalling season. What if we did a roundup of the, um, best lines we've heard?"

"Whew, I've heard some crazy lines on the street—" I began, but I was interrupted by a salty copyeditor.

"Oh, okay, Nikki. It's hard to imagine dudes were *hangin' out the passenger side of their best friend's ride, trying to holla at you* on Fifth Avenue or wherever Park Avenue Publishing is," she said, quoting TLC with a smirk. "Tell us where exactly you've heard these crazy lines?"

There were a few low snorts. "Mostly in Harlem, where I grew up, although it's open season on the streets of Bed-Stuy, where I live now," I said calmly. "In high school, I used to take the train at 145th. I was tall and looked older than I was, so every day, I'd walk down that long-ass block between Convent and St. Nicholas, hearing a new and even more creative set of lines. I think my fave was 'Hey, white chocolate!'"

"You grew up in Harlem?" someone else asked.

I ignored the skeptical question and continued, "Although I also enjoyed 'How am I supposed to admire all your beauty when you walkin' faster than a fat kid looking for fried chicken?'"

The whole room had to laugh at that one. Then every woman chimed in.

"I'm partial to the ol' classic, 'Hey baby, you'd look prettier if you smiled.'"

"What about 'I'm married, but I'm sure the good Lord would make an exception for you.'"

"Someone once yelled 'What's up pumpkin spice?' to me."

"But there are also the creepy lines like 'Screw the gym, baby, I'll give you a workout,'" another editor added. "Or 'You look like a filet mignon I'd like to sink my teeth into.'"

"That's true, it can be really disturbing. I think we need more than a roundup of lines." I thought for a minute. "What if we deep dive into the history of catcalling? Where did it come from? Why is it more prevalent in communities of color?"

"Oh, I like that! We could add a debate on whether catcalling is good or bad. I bet some of those dudes don't think they're being disrespectful."

"What if we interview a notorious catcaller?"

"And we could add a service sidebar on how to react if you're getting catcalled on the street."

"Love this! This was such a great idea, Felicia!" She beamed back. Maybe I'd promote her to senior associate editor so she, too, could be a jumbo shrimp.

The *Sugar* staff basically fell into three categories: teacher's pets competing for my attention, skeptics willing to be converted, and Luna devotees who couldn't believe their queen had been deposed. The first category was easy to deal with: I gave them tasks and let them slug it out. The second was my favorite because they kept me on my toes and made my game better. I didn't mind when they asked question after question because this was the group that truly loved *Sugar* and the women we were trying to reach. I knew they only wanted the magazine to be the best, and I respected that.

The last group was an enormous pain in my ass. I'd catch them whispering in groups, smirking over every editorial change they didn't agree with, secretly calling Luna to fill her in on the dirt. At least they were obvious enough that I knew within weeks which staffers I had to replace. Barbara had given me free rein to fire whomever I needed, and some folks had to go before they poisoned the whole team and any chance I had to save the company.

I found a new art director quickly. She'd been at a cool indie magazine for the past few years and would bring an edgy sensibility to *Sugar*. Just as I finished negotiating that hire, the beauty director, QT Jones, started to act out. Luna had brought her from *Hot Hair*, and she had the models in *Sugar*'s beauty stories looking like they were auditioning to walk in one of those Detroit hair shows, in massive beehives shaped like a helicopter or the Chrysler Building.

When I gently suggested to QT that she focus on hair and makeup that the average girl would want to rock, she had wiggled her neck and said, "Maybe at *StyleList* y'all like the models to look like bankers, but at *Sugar* we supposed to keep it real." Then she had looked at me defiantly, like: What you gonna do about it?

Clearly, homegirl had a short-term memory problem. I put both hands on her desk and leaned in. "You see anybody walking around the *Sugar* office with hair shaped like a skyscraper on their head?" I looked around for emphasis. "Yeah, me either. So why don't you think about it and let me know whether you still want to work here."

Luckily, *Hot Hair* offered QT her old position, so she left without too much drama. But I soon found out how few Black beauty editors there were. I finally remembered a lissome bay-brown associate editor at a teen beauty magazine whom I'd met at a journalism conference. She'd been in the game way too long not to have a senior position, so I lured her with a director title and the promise of an office with a door.

The next casualty was Jennifer Hobart, the entertainment editor. J.Ho, as she was known around the office, had a reputation for sleeping with every major male star she interviewed. According to NuVoices lore, homegirl had even bedded one or two of the female celebs. She was maybe five feet tall with short round legs, a thick neck, and enormous breasts, the top half of which were in full display every day, jiggling like Jell-O above low-cut shirts. I didn't want to believe the whispers since urban culture loved to brand women as "hoes," and having an ample chest and a penchant for button-downs a size too small didn't automatically make her promiscuous. But it was a little suspect that Jennifer lived in a West Village loft, owned a condo in Miami, and had an extensive wardrobe of designer bags on her meager editor's salary.

One afternoon, I found her faxing our working July issue rundown.

"Where are you sending that?" I seethed.

"Uh, my apartment, so I can work at home?" she said too quickly, her voice lilting so her statement ended in a question. I glanced at the outgoing number: It was a Brooklyn exchange.

"Jennifer, you told me you live in the Village. And why would you have a fax machine in your home?"

"Well, see, I...um, sometimes work at a friend's house, a friend who lives in Brooklyn and doesn't have a printer, so I'm sending these there," she stuttered.

J.Ho was out of there that day. I quickly pitched my vision for *Sugar* to my girl Sondra Lopez, a veteran entertainment writer and celebrity booker languishing in a junior role at *People* magazine. Sondra agreed to take a risk and join me at NuVoices, where I promised that she would now get to cast covers and write features.

I also had to make a major change in the fashion director, Cindy Bonham, the only other person on the *Sugar* staff with mainstream fashion magazine experience. Although I wasn't particularly impressed by the fact that she'd been fired from her job as the assistant to the associate fashion director at *Vogue*, she carried the Condé Nast title's name around like it was a crocodile Hermès Birkin bag filled with gold bars. Cindy was petite, with pinched features and acne-pitted skin, and she layered on foundation and dressed in off-season designer gear every day as if she might run into Anna Wintour in the elevator. It was obvious from the beginning that Cindy resented my presence because she valued having the lone claim to being a "real" fashion magazine editor.

She'd heave an irritated sigh every time I asked her anything. "Just let me figure it out, Nikki," was her standard offhand response. "I can only imagine you have *much* more important matters to deal with."

One afternoon, Barbara burst into my office while I was writing an article assignment letter for a freelance writer and shut the door behind her. "Have you been accepting gifts from fashion designers?" she blurted without prelude.

"What are you talking about, Barbara?" I'd replied, stunned. "High-end designers hardly know we're alive. They're certainly not sending me gifts."

"And have you been raiding the *Sugar* fashion closet?" she demanded next.

"Not to be rude, but we don't have anything but sweatsuits." My smirk disappeared when I realized these questions weren't coming out of nowhere. In a more serious tone, I asked, "Where exactly are you getting this information?"

Barbara hesitated, then proceeded to spill that Cindy was the occasional mistress of NuVoices' notoriously adulterous CFO and had apparently been telling him monstrous tales about me. After another ten minutes of interrogation, I finally gave Barbara an incontrovertible piece of evidence: "Will you please look at what I'm wearing?" I motioned toward my *StyleList* closet outfit of a Versus by

Versace minidress and tall Doc Martens. "Do you actually think that I'm going to pilfer our precious supply of velour hoodies? Seriously, Barbara, why would I do that?"

"Look, I don't trust anyone until they've proven themselves to me," she retorted. "You and I are in the process of getting to know one another, and as far as I'm concerned, the jury's still out."

Barbara was living up to her tough-as-nails reputation. The only thing that prevented her from being as bad as Lucifer was that she didn't have the same mind-fuckingly unpredictable mood swings. Instead, Barbara was consistently and unrelentingly difficult. Ultimately, the logical evidence of my wardrobe full of designer *StyleList* rejects prevailed. Barbara agreed that Cindy was clearly holding a grudge and had to go.

Fortunately for Cindy, the CFO still liked having her around, so she was shuffled over to *Bella*. While she was spared from being fired, she had unfortunately not been declawed. So, I'd added another enemy to my growing collection.

It was worth it, though, because CeCe hooked me up with Frederika "Freddy" Douglas, a celebrity stylist who'd worked with everyone from Mary J. to Eve to Gwen Stefani. I was astonished that Freddy was interested in a position at *Sugar*, but she seemed truly committed to young women of color. "Besides," Freddy told me in confidence, "a sister is pushing forty over here, and following the latest spoiled brat singer around on tour is not as sexy as it was back in the day. Nahmean?"

The last key person I had to find was an executive editor. Barbara had handed me a folder of undesirable candidates: former *Groove* editors with an axe to grind, newspaper reporters who were decent writers but had no style or flavor, fashion editors who had plenty of style and flavor but who'd never edited a sentence in their lives. And none of them would be able to perform the real function of a number two: have my back.

One afternoon, as I was poring over the mastheads of every

magazine Von could hold in two arms, looking for candidates, Denyse left a message on my work line. "I know you're in the middle of running thangs, but in case you need some help, I just talked to my girl Imani McKnight, who was in my NAACP leadership program. I told you about her—she's the one who dated that fine-ass Alpha who's into historical fiction. Anyhoo, she's a freelance writer now, and I gave her your phone number because she wants to pitch an AIDS feature. Hope that's okay. She's mad cool, Nikki. Smart and funny. Give her a shot. And call a sister when you emerge. Love you."

Imani called the next morning and came in that afternoon. With her waist-length locs dyed a light sandy shade that matched her gold-flecked eyes, flowing tunic, and kaleidoscopic ethnic jewelry, I presumed she might only be interested in poetry slams, incense, and world music. But our conversation made me feel stupid for being so shortsighted.

"So, what's your profit model based on: Newsstand sales or advertising revenue?" was her first question.

I didn't exactly want to reveal trade secrets to a virtual stranger, so I tried to be glib. "I, um, well, newsstand is very important," I said, faltering.

"I see," Imani replied. "So then, what percentage of your circulation is newsstand? Do you have a website?"

Thrown off guard again, I stumbled through my response. "I think the newsstand is about eighty percent of circ. Kind of high but that will shift toward subs as the brand gains awareness. And we have a site, but it's pretty basic. We'll need to redesign it along with the magazine."

"Of course," she said patiently. "And how do you plan on differentiating *Sugar* from its competitors: *Groove, Essence, Glamour*...?" Homegirl was no joke. I thought she'd come in to pitch me on a feature, but here she was, cross-examining me on my growth strategy. She turned red, laughed self-consciously, and said, "Wow, I'm sorry. I'm acting like Five-O or something. I'm just very interested in magazines, always have been. I read *MediaWeek* and *The New York Times* on Monday—when the media news comes out like it's *Entertainment Weekly*."

"Why aren't you on staff somewhere?"

"I have been, both as a writer and an editor, but I'm freelancing because there are no magazines I'm really into right now."

"Really..."

I assigned Imani the AIDS story, which she handed in a week before her deadline. It was well researched, insightful, and she'd captured exactly what I'd envisioned the *Sugar* voice to be: smart but accessible, funny but not corny. I took her out to lunch, and we talked about how we felt the magazine could serve an audience we both loved—and be a viable business. She and I were on the same page, and I trusted Imani because she was friends with Denyse. It took me just one day to convince her to be my executive editor.

I'd sorted my colleagues into friends versus foes and built a small team of hungry, gifted overachievers in record time. I was working around the clock, ordering pizzas for lunch, eating dinner from the kitchen vending machine, and watching the lights of downtown Manhattan recede behind me as my taxi rolled over the bridge to Brooklyn after midnight. I'd go home to crash for a few hours, shower, rinse, and repeat. I couldn't stop to call my friends or thaw the frost between me and Joseph. I was all too aware of the limited time I had to show that *Sugar* could be successful—and before Alonzo would rear his head again. I was busy watching my back and my front.

FOURTEEN

"Are you screwing me over?" I raged into the phone. "That's all I want to know, Manuel. Are ... you ... screwing ... me?"

I paced my tiny office with a white-knuckle grip on the receiver as I let loose on the publicist at the other end. Really, the question was rhetorical as he was definitely screwing me—or at least making his best effort to do so. Manuel managed Sinclaire, an actress-turned-singer whose buzzy debut album was dropping in a month. He was trying to weasel out of our cover shoot at the last minute because he had just gotten a cover offer from *Onyx*, a magazine with a much bigger audience. Though I understood where he was coming from, there was no way I was about to let him off the hook, because I didn't have the budget or time to find someone else. And he was about to make me look like a fool on my first actual cover shoot.

"You already accepted our cover offer two weeks ago and the whole shoot is already planned—with all of Sinclaire's crazy requests in place," I yelled over his weak protestations. "We've already ordered the lemon jelly beans, the peanut-butter-and-bacon sandwiches, and the friggin' aquarium for her dressing room, so you had both better be at the studio on Friday!" I slammed down the phone and looked up to see Barbara's amused face in my doorway. She was wearing a forest-green leather trench coat and holding a matching tote bag. It was near the end of the day, so she must have heard the ruckus on her way out. I was too upset to hide my stress and could only put my head in my hands. "I'm sorry, Barbara. Until my new entertainment director starts, I'm it. And these publicists are seriously testing my patience."

When I'd started to yell, a small crowd that probably assumed I was in real trouble had gathered outside my office to witness the carnage. But Barbara only laughed. I'd forgotten the hell she must have gone through during the inception of *Groove*. "This is just the beginning. Right now, *Sugar* is low on their list of priorities, so you better get used to being treated like a second-class citizen." She plunked down in a chair in front of my desk. "This is what you do: Call Manuel back and tell him that if Sinclaire doesn't show up, you'll put out a press release revealing that she's on our July cover. And you'll pull a pic from Getty that you really *cannot* guarantee will be flattering that will be paired with a write-around story that you also *cannot* guarantee will be positive. Hell, you may even interview that girl she was feuding with on her last movie set. *Onyx* won't want to follow us so Manuel will lose their cover anyway, and the press opportunity they have in hand will go from glowing to snarky." She paused to survey my face. I was stunned by the level of her gangsta, but learning. "To soften the blow, let him know that Jean Paul Gaultier agreed to send looks for the cover and that you got Pat McGrath on the glam squad."

"But I have neither lined up," I squeaked.

"Well, get them," Barbara replied with an eye roll. "You have to act important to become important, Nikki."

I made the call to Manuel with Barbara still in my office. He had some choice words for me, but I had him backed into a corner. He angrily capitulated, then immediately switched his tone to chat about glam. We ended the conversation like two BFF's about to braid each other's hair.

Barbara waved my thanks away. Apparently, screaming matches with record label execs was just another Tuesday to her, and she was on to another topic. "So, what are you doing tomorrow night?"

"Not sure. Why?" I lied. Joseph and I had bought theater tickets months ago for a show that evening. He and I had crafted an uneasy peace that allowed us to coexist in relative harmony, have sex, order Chinese food on Saturday nights, go to boring plays—while not discussing anything deeper than the very basics of our days. I had a feeling that Barbara was about to propose something a little more fun.

"Oh nothing, just MC RedHot's annual Red Party." She paused to let the words sink in. MC RedHot was known for throwing the hottest parties from New York to Ibiza, and everybody who was anybody went to his annual Red Party. Platinum rappers, box office blockbuster actors, fashion designers, rebellious socialites—they all showed up wearing red from head to toe, expecting the Cristal to be flowing, the music to be pumping, and the weed brownies RedHot passed around himself to be extra strong. I'd heard about it like everyone else but had never come close to being invited.

"I think you need more exposure in the entertainment industry. Plus, all those gossip forums like *Lipstick Alley* need to know who you are so they can stop slandering you for being an ambitious seductress and start vilifying you for having the audacity to run the next big media brand." Barbara smiled. "You want to go with me?"

While I didn't love the way she'd framed the invitation and wasn't particularly excited at the prospect of partying with Barbara, I was dying to go. Trying to look cool, I told her, "Yeah, sure. I can go. Great, thanks."

"Good." She stood to leave. "Meet me in the office at ten PM. I've got a limo picking us up here. We're rolling together and we need to cover a lot of territory, so don't bring anyone."

"Fine," I said, thinking Joseph would not be happy to miss the Red Party. "Uh, what should I wear?"

Barbara was heading out the door and turned to look at me like

I had two heads. "Nikki, I think you'll want to wear red." Then she disappeared down the hall to go wreak havoc on the *Decode* team.

Predictably, Joseph was not at all pleased that he wasn't invited, so I was shocked when he offered to go shopping with me the next day. Though he was one of the rare straight men who could tolerate shopping, I never thought he'd volunteer for an afternoon of searching for an all-red outfit that looked neither cheesy nor sleazy—the shopping equivalent of scaling Mount Everest in stilettos with only Diet Coke and saltines in your backpack.

Joseph scoped out a red ruffled miniskirt at our very first stop, the exclusive department store Jeffrey in the Meatpacking District. Next stop was the boutique Kirna Zabête in SoHo, where I found a sheer wraparound red top that was cropped above my waist and a matching red bra to make the outfit street legal. In a tiny shoe store on West Broadway, I spotted some cute red ankle boots in the window. Ordinarily, I would never be caught dead in head-to-toe red, but with some statement jewelry and a decent clutch, I had to admit that this outfit could work.

I still had some time before I had to meet Barbara at the office, so Joseph and I walked over to Sofie's Café, where we found the proprietress in her typical hip hop music video extra getup, complete with a Kangol pulled low over her blond hair. Sofie hugged us both, brought over a couple craft beers, and peeked into my shopping bags.

"Let me guess, you're going to the Red Party."

I'd forgotten about all the places she'd been with her man, MC WhiteHot. "Yeah, you?"

"Hells no." Sofie sighed deeply. "WhiteHot and RedHot are, like, mortal enemies. I went once but now I'm forbidden to go. It's da bomb, though. All kinds of crazy shit goes down. Last year, I heard the Marquette twins—you know, the actress and the DJ—did a striptease together on top of the bar..." Sofie trailed off, looking at me quizzically. I was shaking my head slightly while making wild eye motions toward Joseph. "Uh, but it ain't all that," she said, finally catching on. "Nothing you haven't already seen. No biggie, really. No special—"

"Okay, okay, we get the picture," I interrupted. Joseph may be a lot of things, but stupid was not one of them.

"I'm going to leave you two alone now. The waitress is on her way over. Holla before you leave," Sofie said with relief and loped off toward the bar.

Joseph and I ate our meal in what I thought was companionable silence. I was lost in thought about who I could put on my August cover when, out of the blue, Joseph took my free hand and said, "Nicole, I wonder if you might be getting in too deep here. It might be time to make some decisions." I looked at him uncomprehendingly. "About *Sugar*. It might be time to make some decisions about *Sugar*."

"What are you talking about?" I asked, shaking my hand loose and putting down my forkful of Caesar salad. "I've barely been there a month. I haven't even seen my first issue yet."

"I know. But I wonder if you might be rethinking this whole thing yet."

I knew this day had gone too easily. "No, I'm not. The exact opposite. I feel tired and drained and anxious. But I'm more excited about this than anything I've ever done in my life," I told him calmly.

Joseph put his cheeseburger down, took a slow drink of his beer, and said with equal calm, "Then maybe you should rethink your decision to be with me."

These words should have made my stomach drop. Instead, I was instantly exasperated. "Are you breaking up with me over *Sugar*?" I snapped. "Is my ambition that much of a turnoff?"

Joseph wasn't taking my bait. "No, I want to be with you. But I'm not convinced that you want to be with me."

"Why would you say that? We just made up."

"Yeah, but you're in the office all the time or going out without me now. I feel us moving in different directions." Joseph's voice wavered for a second but then he got his game face back together. "And I haven't seen you enough lately for you to convince me otherwise."

Blood rushed to my head. What was the distinction between my schedule and the sixteen-hour days Joseph would often spend working on various deals—other than a couple zeros on a paycheck? "Convince you?" I spat. "Why don't you try to convince me that you can be supportive of what I'm trying to do?"

"What the hell are you talking about? I've been shopping with you all day for a party I'm not even invited to." He looked down to adjust the lapels of his jacket while slowly exhaling, then continued in a more measured voice. "Nicole, you won't talk to me about anything but *Sugar*. And you haven't asked me about my life in ages. Has it even occurred to you that I may have things going on as well? If you had shown any interest in how I'm doing, you'd know that I just lost a major client, which is not exactly a great move for a new managing director, certainly not a new Black managing director."

"Shit, I didn't know, Joe," I murmured, instantly contrite.

"Yeah, I'm well aware. We barely talk. I bet you know more about your work friends' lives than I do about yours right now."

An image flashed through my mind of Von showing me the mood board he'd built for his Red Party outfit while he told me all about his new girlfriend, who was part of RedHot's street team and had gotten him an invite. I didn't say anything, guilt flooding my system like contrast dye. I knew I should have gotten up right then to sit on his lap like I used to when we went to clubs; I should have taken his handsome face in my hands and kissed him, sucking gently on his lower lip, which always made his dick swell; I should have asked him to tell me everything. Instead, I surreptitiously looked at my watch to see how much time I had to get ready for the party. My distraction made me insensitive and edgy.

"I'm busting my ass right now, Joe. Can't you be patient for a little longer?"

Joseph cocked his head and stared at me for ten seconds that felt like ten minutes under his searching gaze. "I'm not sure how going to the Red Party in a miniskirt is exactly busting your ass," he finally replied.

I threw my napkin on the table and stood up. "Wow, okay. I knew this day was too good to be true." My eyes were welling up, and I didn't want him to see me cry. "How am I supposed to care about what's happening in your world when you don't value what's important in mine?"

I grabbed my shopping bags and took off before the tears could spill over.

My subway ride to Brooklyn felt endless. Everything that had been going on between me and Joseph hit all at once. *Sugar* and my insane work schedule had been like emotional codeine: I knew there was something wrong, but I had felt very little pain—until now. I was suddenly terrified at the prospect of being alone.

It was not the best night for a trial by fire at one of the hottest events of the year, but there was no way I was backing out. I took a quick shower, slapped my own cheeks, and made myself get dressed. After I put on the last of my makeup, I surveyed myself with some satisfaction. This was my first big outing as *Sugar*'s editor-in-chief; I was representing the brand, and I was about to head into the stronghold of the rumor mill where so much speculation about me had originated. I knew I had to bring it. I'd given myself a deep charcoal smoky eye and added a shimmery gold lip. With my two-week-old blowout in a taut ponytail, the shoulder-grazing gold hoops I wore looked even cooler. All in all, the red outfit was kind of hot. *Red-hot,* I said to myself, smiling, taking one final look, and heading out the door.

FIFTEEN

The limo Barbara had ordered turned out to be an enormous black Yukon Denali that had a stereo system so loud, the side mirrors vibrated with each bass note. In her red leather skirt, matching jacket with no shirt underneath, stiletto boots, and red fedora, Barbara was giving sexy pimp vibes. When I climbed in, she looked me up and down appreciatively.

"Nicely done, Nikki," she told me. "You represent well, and that's a good red-carpet look."

The thrill I got at finally receiving a qualification-free compliment from Barbara mixed with panic. "Red carpet?"

She laughed. "Yeah, Second Coming. All those photographers will be curious to see who I'm with—especially when I hype *Sugar* and its new EIC."

Barbara wasn't lying. From the moment we pulled up in front of Hades, a hot new club in the West Village, flashbulbs started popping. I'd never experienced this level of photographic enthusiasm or anything like the overall scene. As we lined up to walk the red carpet, we joined a scarlet throng of boldface names, many of whom were slit-eyed and tottering sideways as if they had been pregaming before the event.

"Hey, Barbara!" the photographers called, jockeying for attention. "Over here. Look over here. To the left, please."

Barbara smiled as if she'd been doing this all her life, then grabbed me by the hand. "Hey, everyone!" she yelled over the din. "Meet Nikki Rose, the new editor-in-chief of *Sugar*, the hottest magazine to hit newsstands since *Groove*!"

The flashbulbs started popping in my direction. "Over here, Nikki. Smile for us. Who are you wearing? To your right, please. Who made the shoes? How do we spell your first name?" I felt like a star and a total geek all at the same time. From the corner of my eye I could see Barbara watching me, gauging my performance. I had no idea how to pose, which way to turn, or who to answer first. I plastered a huge smile on my face and told them I was wearing Catherine Malandrino, Barbara Bui, and Sergio Rossi. Then I put a hand on my hip like I'd seen celebs do in paparazzi photos—hoping that I didn't look like a complete fool—and called out, "And my name is Nikki Rose. N-I-K-K-I."

Barbara smiled approvingly, then led me inside, where I knew for certain that my life had truly changed. Hades was designed to look like, well, hell. The jaded New York City clubbers' version, of course. Flames shot up the bloodred walls, torture instruments hung from the ceiling, and women in red leather dominatrix outfits danced in suspended cages. There were also seven different rooms representing the seven deadly sins. Walking past the lust room, I caught sight of what looked like a tangle of human flesh writhing on the dance floor and on every available sofa. As I grabbed a glass of champagne from a waitress who wore only a red bra, boy shorts, and thigh-high boots, I sure hoped God had a sense of humor.

The red sea of hard-partying celebs was also like nothing I'd ever seen. Every time I turned, another celebrity would come into view: Usher, Will Smith, at least two of the Spice Girls, Nelly, Aaliyah, Lenny Kravitz, Lil' Kim, Justin Timberlake. Not one person had defied MC RedHot's strict dress code.

The first person I knew was one of the senior editors from *StyleList*'s entertainment department. She kissed my cheeks, never actually touching me lest our makeup be smudged, and asked, her voice full of sympathy, "How's it going, Nikki? Are you *okay*?"

"Hey, Suzanna. Everything is great. Wait until you see my first issue."

"Of course, everything is great," she enunciated carefully, patting my shoulder. "You just keep it up."

I had no time to react because I felt someone pulling at my hand. I swung around to find Barbara standing in front of me next to a man with deep umber skin and shiny black curls, wearing a form-fitting red tank top that showed off his muscular arms and diamond-encrusted watch. He looked me up and down, then ran a hand over his short ringlets, whistling low.

"Barbara Porter, you have outdone yourself this time," he said.

"You are *stupid*," she said, punching his shoulder lightly. "This is Nikki, *Sugar*'s new editor-in-chief. Nikki, this is Jerome Jermaine, songwriter and music producer extraordinaire."

Barbara widened her eyes for emphasis so I knew that this was someone I needed to know. Good thing he seemed pretty eager to know me too. "Well, hello, my dear. Aren't you the perfect embodiment of a *Sugar* woman—smart *and* sexy," he said, bending down to kiss my hand. "Call me JJ."

"Why thank you, JJ," I flirted back, trying to get the hang of mixing work and pleasure. "You are too generous."

"You have no idea." He chuckled wickedly. "We should have lunch or, better yet, dinner sometime soon."

Luckily, Barbara came in with the assist before I had to conjure up a response. "Yes, we'll all have to hang out soon," she said, silky smooth. "Now I'm going to take my new girl around." She winked at him. "See you later, JJ."

Barbara proceeded to introduce me to enough music label executives, celebrities, and well-lubricated party people to fill the *New York Post*'s Page Six for years. I had met a few famous people at *StyleList*, but this was a different crowd, more *Vibe* and *Village Voice* than *Vogue* and *The New York Times*. After a couple hours, my head was spinning from all the famous and infamous hands I'd shaken and cheeks I'd air-kissed—as well as the champagne I'd been nervously drinking like it was Perrier. Von appeared at that exact moment, girlfriend in tow, with an extra bottle of water. He was rocking red hammer pants and a loose V-neck knit sweater that revealed a tangle of gold chains against his freckled chest. I gratefully chugged the water while he and his girlfriend had some words in the corner. She stormed off and Von dejectedly shuffled back to me.

"What happened there?" I yelled over the music.

"I was two hours late to pick her up," he yelled back. "Now MC RedHot is mad at her, and she's furious at me. We're probably a wrap after tonight."

I was starting to detect a pattern. "Von, how long is your average relationship?"

"About a month. But I once dated a hand model for three months—until I lost her English bulldog in the park."

He looked glum again, so I pulled him onto the dance floor. The DJ had just mixed Q-Tip's "Vivrant Thing" with 702's "Where My Girls At," and I needed to keep my mind off my relationship issues as well. I only lasted a couple songs because my new boots were no match for my energy. Desperate for a break, I found a cerise leather sectional sofa in a corner and perched on the edge. Taking another glass of champagne, I was about to get comfy and people watch for a while when I heard a shrill voice behind me.

"Excuse me. *Excuse* me." The earsplitting voice carried over the loud music.

I turned to see where the yelling was coming from and was confronted by a svelte woman with long jet-black hair, toasted-almond skin, and gray eyes. From a distance, she was beautiful, but as she leaned over to me from where she was seated on the other side of the sofa, I could see her hooded eyelids, the brown lip liner sloppily drawn to make her lips look fuller, the tracks of her weave.

"Are you talking to me?" I asked, not sure what to make of the tone of her voice.

She turned to her friends, seated around her like ladies-in-waiting, all tall, striking women in identical tight dresses, and smirked. "Am I talking to her? This bitch don't even know," she said. They all laughed. Through the clamor, I thought I recognized a voice. On the sofa's far arm perched Luna, wearing a low-cut red catsuit.

"Tell her, Serena," Luna egged the tall woman on.

"Did we invite you to sit here?" Serena wiggled her neck at me, her face inches from mine.

"I didn't realize I needed to be invited to sit on a sofa in a club," I said defiantly.

The women all cackled in unison. Serena calmly looked me up and down. "Bitch, this is a *reserved* area. Puff Daddy"—she practically genuflected when she uttered his name—"is on his way over here and he don't want to see your sorry ass up in his private VIP, exclusive, *reserved* section."

As Luna and her model crew laughed, I debated whether to mock the absurd redundancy of that sentence and stand my ground or roll my eyes and confidently flounce off. Opting not to be at the center of a bar fight at my first Red Party, I stood to leave. When I felt another hand on my arm, I assumed it was Barbara wanting me to meet some more people, but I turned to see Kiara, looking amazing in a red Balmain dress with rubies in her ears.

Kiara hugged me hard then twirled me around to check out my outfit. "*Fabulous*, love! Next time let's go shopping together. Maybe we can score some showroom freebies." Then she looked past me to survey the scene on the sofa. "And what do we have here?" It was clear that Kiara and Serena were not exactly girls.

"I was just leaving. Apparently, Puff Daddy is on his way over and I'm not invited to sit on his special, VIP, exclusive, reserved, private sofa," I told her, emphasizing every word.

Kiara started to laugh—clearly at Serena, Luna, and their ridiculous pronouncement. "Well, love, I'll tell you what. Let's head on over to my reserved banquette." She motioned with her chin at the most crowded area of the room. Photographers were going crazy, trying to shoot whoever was sitting behind the crush of onlookers. "Puff is already hanging over there, along with Paris, Usher, and Gisele. Oh, and you can leave your champagne glass here. I've got bottles of Cristal coming all night."

I threw a triumphant backward glance at Luna and Serena, who couldn't hide their envy, and followed Kiara to her table.

"Don't worry about those party hags, love," she whispered when we were out of sight. "They're over-the-hill former models who have already played musical chairs with every rich modelizer in New York City. Now everyone's seated and they're still left standing—with no man and no prospects. You're their worst nightmare."

MC RedHot got up on a table and yelled into a mic, "Who throws the best muthafuckin' parties in New York?"

"You do!" we screamed back.

"Who throws the best muthafuckin' parties in the world?"

"You do!"

"Who throws the best muthafuckin' parties in the universe?"

"You do!"

"Then party, muthafuckas. *Party!*" he shrieked.

And we did. I spent the next couple of hours hanging out with Kiara at her table, thinking about how surreal it was that I was doing shots and dancing on a table next to Jay-Z and Naomi Campbell. Every now and then I would catch a glimpse of Luna slinking through the crowd in her red catsuit, pretending to ignore me. I was feeling smug, until I saw her head my way—with Alonzo.

As the president of Groove Media, Alonzo had a lot of influence and power—so much so that he had ignored the red clothing rule, opting for a black suit with a crisp white shirt. The red polka dots on the handkerchief tucked into his jacket pocket were the only nod to MC RedHot. The crowd was clearly feeling his defiance and juice as a small throng of sycophants gathered around him to pay homage.

Puff stood to greet Alonzo as he approached, leaning forward to exchange a few private words. Alonzo laughed and clapped him on the arm as Mary J. stepped up to say hello. No one spoke to Luna, but she didn't seem to care. Her eyes were fixed on my face, waiting for my reaction.

As I looked for an opening to step away from the far end of the table, hoping for a quiet exit, I could hear Alonzo's deep voice booming over the music: "Have you met Luna, *Groove*'s new deputy editor?"

As Alonzo introduced Luna around the table, I tried again to slip away. I'd managed to get off the table, but I couldn't get out of the banquette without literally bumping into him. Luna smirked as the introductions got to me.

"It's so good to run into you, Nikki," he said, raising an eyebrow at my short skirt and sheer top. "I just knew we'd see each other again. And I know you and Luna have met."

"Nice to see you both," I lied. "Excuse me," I said as I attempted to squeeze past Alonzo.

"Oh, don't leave. I see you've already got this area staked out, so we'll go. And it's your very first Red Party," he said condescendingly. "I want you to have a good time. Enjoy this while it lasts, babygirl."

By the time Alonzo and Luna sauntered off, I had sweat through my shirt, exposing my red bra even more. I asked the hovering waitress for a glass of ice water, then held it to my forehead.

"That was hella uncomfortable, love," Kiara said low in my ear. "But you and I both know that Alonzo is a notorious prick. And he's gotta be pissed that the ether he tried to spread about you didn't relegate you to obscurity. It's driving him crazy to see you at a RedHot party! Don't worry about him, at least not right now."

"Agreed. I would definitely like to enjoy the rest of this night," I whispered back, wondering how much of Alonzo's smear campaign had reached her and how long it would actually last.

The party was still raging at 3:00 AM. And given all the drinking and drugs and hooking up that was still going on, it could have continued for hours. But suddenly, the DJ lowered the music and MC RedHot got back on the stage with a mic.

"Everybody chill out," he yelled. "Five-O is in the hizz-ouse." One of his many red-suited flunkies went over to him and whispered something in his ear. "Ah, shit," he said, turning to look at the club's doorway. Through my slightly buzzed haze, I could see some uniformed guys streaming in as RedHot said pleadingly in the mic, "Please, Mr. Fire Marshal, please don't shut down the sexy. Come on, man. Look at all the honeys up in here. You and your boys stay. Drinks on me."

But the fire marshal was having none of it. The lights turned on and folks started making their way toward the door. I found Barbara, who looked like she'd been enjoying the open bar, with a mystery woman wearing a crimson tuxedo. Barbara didn't bother to introduce me, just climbed into the waiting Denali with the woman and slurred, "You don't mind taking a taxi, do you? Brooklyn is so out of the way."

"Of course," I replied, unsure that they'd even heard me since the door to the SUV had slammed shut. "It's all good."

As I hobbled toward the corner in my too-tight boots to look for a cab, a white Bentley pulled up next to me. A bald guy with a thick beard whom I vaguely recognized from Kiara's banquette leaned out the back window, the diamonds in his ears and encircling his neck in thick ropes gleaming in the streetlights. "Yo, Nikki, right? You want a ride?"

"Oh, hey. No, thanks, I'm okay."

"Nah, climb on in." He opened his door and motioned for me to get in. "I'll have my driver drop you wherever you want."

I hesitated because I was spent and buzzed and in no mood to hail a yellow cab. But my Spidey senses were going off. "Honestly, I'm alright."

The guy's expression darkened. "What, I'm not good enough for you? Shit, Alonzo said you'd be down for anything. But now you want to be shy?" He sucked his teeth and slammed the door. But before he took off, he left me with these choice words: "Bitch, imma see you again."

The Bentley sped off into the night. The second his taillights disappeared, I leaned against the wall of the nearest building, willing my heartbeat to slow down so I wouldn't pass out. "It's all good," I whispered again to myself as tears formed in my eyes for the second time that day.

SIXTEEN

I called Barbara over the weekend to tell her what happened with the Bentley guy, expecting outrage and sympathy. Instead, the line was so silent, I finally had to ask if she was still there.

"Yeah, I'm here, trying to figure out why you're so freaked out that you would call me on Saturday morning after the party of the year," she griped. "Hang on." I could make out a woman's voice in the background, then Barbara whispered a reply, her hand clearly over the receiver to muffle the sound. Then she got back on the phone. "Okay, Nikki, seriously, what is the issue?"

I was almost too stunned to answer. "I just... feel threatened by what happened. Clearly Alonzo is telling people stuff that could put me in a dangerous position."

I heard dishes clanking and the low whirring of a coffee grinder in Barbara's background. "It was probably Leo Roberson. He's bald and has a white Bentley. Leo runs the promotions department at Too Loud Records."

"Wait, you know this guy?

"Everyone knows Leo." Barbara blew out a long breath. "The whole Too Loud crew is notorious for their aggressive womanizing. Shit, the whole music industry is known for womanizing. Alonzo may have whetted their appetite, but you're the new pretty young

EIC, so lots of thirsty guys in fancy cars are going to roll up on you after industry parties."

"Barbara, I did not sign up for rape-y dudes dripping in diamonds threatening me when I turn them down."

"Actually, that is exactly what you signed up for, Miss *StyleList*. You signed up for it when you abandoned your common sense to mess with Alonzo and then when you left your ivory tower to slum it with me at NuVoices."

"Are you saying that it was my fault?"

"Jesus, Nikki. Of course not. But urban music is chock-full of a certain type of guy who wants what he wants and is used to getting his way. You obviously know this from personal experience, so you shouldn't be so surprised." Barbara slurped her coffee. "Now, if you'll excuse me, I'm going to go enjoy my day."

"But what am I supposed to do?"

"You're supposed to act like you didn't just fall off the turnip truck and toughen the fuck up. And you should do a write-up on the Red Party for the magazine."

Before I could say anything else that Barbara would clearly interpret as whiny, she hung up, leaving me feeling vaguely stupid and totally naïve for being upset.

Apparently, Barbara's exasperation with me did not dissipate over the weekend. She stormed into my office early on Monday, closed my door with a loud thud, and demanded, "What is this I hear about you putting Soleil on *Sugar*'s August cover?"

Soleil was a neo soul singer who'd released a critically acclaimed album a couple years prior, and her sophomore effort was coming out in July. Soleil was pretty, talented, and all her songs were empowering to women.

"Her CD comes out the week the August issue hits newsstands," I explained.

Barbara rubbed her temples, then made herself comfortable in one of the chairs in front of my desk. "Nikki, let me school you," she said, like she was explaining fractions to a kindergartner. "*Sugar* is a magazine. Magazines can make a lot of money from newsstand sales. To do that, you need to put someone on the cover who appeals to a lot of people who will buy a lot of copies." She paused and I waited for a second to see if Magazine 101 was over before responding.

"And I take it you do not think Soleil will sell a lot of copies," I replied slowly as Barbara put her index finger to her nose: bingo. "But why? She's like the ideal *Sugar* woman."

Barbara stared at the new rug I had laid down that week and pressed both index fingers on the innermost corners of her eyes. Finally, she looked up. "Nikki, Soleil's first album sold like three hundred thousand copies. That's not even gold. She might be the ideal *Sugar* woman to the crystal-gazing, incense-burning, head-wrap girls in Brooklyn, but the rest of the country, i.e., ninety-eight percent of *Sugar*'s potential readership, doesn't have a goddamn clue who she is."

"But Soleil is so positive. You don't think she's a good role model?"

"Of course she is. So give her an inside story, profile her, review her album or something," Barbara said firmly, standing up. "Just don't put her on the cover, for god's sake—that is, if you want to reach anyone west of Philadelphia and east of California."

My instinct was to push back, because I loved Soleil's vibe. But Barbara had a point. *Sugar* was not only for me and my friends. "Okay, Barbara, I get it. You know what sells better than I do."

"Yes, I do. And you had better learn quickly. We don't have time for me to hold your hand while you get this right," she barked. "You're coming up on two months here. A little over four months left..."

I said nothing, my thoughts drifting back to my last conversation with Marie. She did warn me. Barbara's lessons were valuable, but she was not a natural teacher. She had no patience and clearly preferred to manage me like a mouse, using electric shocks versus cheese rewards.

Barbara eyed me appraisingly. "One more thing, newbie. I heard that Alonzo hired Luna to work on *Groove*. This might turn into a dogfight." With that, Barbara stomped out of my office to administer more electric shocks across the NuVoices floor.

Pulling Soleil off the cover broke my heart, and I hated having to call her publicist. After I apologized profusely, the publicist graciously accepted a six-page inside profile. But now I didn't have a clue what newsstand sales–generating star I could book for a cover ASAP. I'd already shot Sinclaire for July, but the August issue needed to be finished in a few weeks. In the magazine world, we ideally worked on three issues at a time: assigning stories for one, editing the stories for the next, while putting the third issue to bed. I was already behind deadline and dangerously close to missing my printer deadline, which would mean missing my newsstand date, which would be certain death for that issue—and for me.

As I was typing a panicky message to my entertainment editor, an email from Barbara flashed on my screen. It read: "I've called Jerome Jermaine, the producer you met at the Red Party. He's taking you to dinner this week and schooling you some more on what constitutes hot. JJ's got his hands in everything, and he'll get you up to speed fast."

When I called Kiara to get her take, she chuckled into the phone. "He is a playa, love," she cautioned me. "Have fun, but don't get caught up or caught out there."

"What are you talking about? I've got a man," I said, even though I wasn't sure that was still true. After the Red Party, I was too shaken to be alone, so I'd gone to Joseph's apartment instead of home. He'd taken one look at me and kindly pulled back his bedcovers for me without a word. Over the weekend, we'd fallen back into a tense coexistence—but it felt like we both knew it wouldn't last.

"Exactly," Kiara replied. "Exactly."

Joseph hit the ceiling when I let him know I was having dinner that Thursday with JJ. I told him casually while I was in his bathroom, washing my face. There was silence for a second, then Joseph appeared in the bathroom doorway.

"How is this cool, Nicole? Even I know Jerome Jermaine's reputation," he exclaimed.

"It's just work, Joseph," I tried to reassure him. "He's going to school me on the music industry—who's out there now and how to identify up-and-comers."

"Oh, he's going to *school* you," Joseph shot back. "Baller 101."

"Fine. I get your point. But Barbara set it up so I have no choice, okay?" I squeezed by him to go into the bedroom. Hoping to distract him, I unzipped my work bag. "But take a look, honey. It's my first issue. Now at least you know what I've been killing myself over."

I passed him the magazine with a huge smile. My new art director hadn't finished the redesign, but she and I had labored over the pages and *Sugar* already looked drastically different. For my first cover—June's music and summer style issue—I'd landed an interview with internationally renowned DJ Cassius and his wife, Latika, who was the star of a popular network sitcom that featured five Black women living in Atlanta. I couldn't believe they'd agreed, but Tika had a new movie premiering and Cassius was about to head out on a world tour; the timing was perfect. It didn't hurt that Barbara had shown a lot of love over the years to Cassius's Jam Rock music label. Some people even credited her with the explosive success of their main artist, Sabryna, because Barbara had championed her back when she had a bad weave, a thick Caribbean accent, and zero hit records in sight. Jam Rock owed Barbara and, therefore, *Sugar*.

I had to put the June issue to bed within a couple weeks of joining

NuVoices, so I didn't have time to book a photographer and studio. But I was able to use some never-before-seen outtakes from a photo shoot the couple had already done to promote the movie and tour. DJ Cassius and Tika were in black tie on the cover; she shone in a gold Dior gown, and he looked clean in a classic tux, his signature diamond C pendant glittering under the studio lights. I'd done the interview myself and had gotten Tika to reveal for the first time that she was pregnant. It was a coup that yielded an explosive cover line, sure to make the issue fly off newsstands.

Joseph scanned the cover, then flipped through, reading nothing but taking in every page. He was the first person who'd seen it other than the NuVoices crew. When the box of preview issues hit the office, the entire *Sugar* team had erupted into cheers. Even the doubters couldn't hate on the cover or the rest of the issue. We had tons more work to do, but the shift was already dramatic. Barbara came out to see what the commotion was about, and the office had fallen silent while she surveyed the cover and carefully turned each page of the magazine. She'd obviously seen mock-ups, but it was another thing entirely to hold a fresh-off-the-press issue in your hands.

"You've nailed your debut, newbie. This is solid work," Barbara proclaimed, her normally unsympathetic expression relaxing. It was a brief reprieve as her next words were, "I'll schedule a meeting with you this week. We'll do a page-by-page postmortem so I can tell you where you fucked up." My joy had ebbed a little, but then Barbara winked at me. She turned to my team and said, "You guys all did a great job! Lunch is on me today."

The office had breathed a sigh of relief, and someone played Nas's song "If I Ruled the World." Von high-fived me as the team sang Lauryn Hill's verse, "If I ruled the world, I'd free all my sons. Black diamonds and pearls. If I ruled the world..."

Now, I was dying for Joseph's reaction. I waited while he surveyed the ad on the back cover for a little-known beauty brand that specialized in additive-free products for natural hair. He stared at the model's glorious locs, and said slowly, "Well, it's not exactly *Style-List*... but I can tell you put in a lot of work. The cover is great and I'm sure the next issue will be better than this one." I must have been visibly frustrated. "*Even* better than this one," he amended, then reached out to draw me into bed. "I'll read the whole thing tomorrow," he said, pulling me on top of him. By the time he unhooked my bra and was gently licking the tips of my nipples the way he knew I liked, my resistance had broken down. I ripped off his boxers and rode him until I had a dizzying orgasm that blew everything else out of my mind.

SEVENTEEN

"We'll take another, my man," JJ told the waiter over my weak objections. There was already an empty bottle of Cristal sitting on the table and we hadn't even finished our appetizers. I was feeling lightheaded and could have used a sparkling water, but the waiter, who'd clearly identified my dinner companion as a big spender, practically bowed before speeding away to get the second bottle. JJ tilted his flute at me and continued to eat his lobster salad.

JJ had chosen Chakra, a trendy Asian fusion restaurant in NoHo that I'd been dying to check out, but I'd never been able to get a reservation for between 5:00 and 10:30 PM. He'd asked for a bottle of Cristal the minute we sat down, not bothering to inquire if I'd prefer a cocktail or wine. Then he wouldn't let me look at the menu. I could only watch as he called over the obsequious waiter and ordered a ridiculously expensive feast: lobster salad, spring rolls stuffed with foie gras, seared tuna toro, and Kobe beef that cost fifty dollars per ounce. I felt slightly disregarded and completely pampered all at the same time.

For all his obvious wealth, JJ had shown up in ripped jeans, a black hoodie, and a black leather jacket. Of course, the hoodie looked like Maison Margiela, and the jacket was probably Gucci, but still. That night, JJ's hair was neatly cornrowed, though his motorcycle boots and silver belt chain looked more rocker than rapper. The thin yet very noticeable diamond chain around his neck was the only flashy indication of his wealth. I had to admit it: The man was *very* good-looking. I was trying to hold Kiara's warning in my mind, but watching JJ's muscles ripple every time he reached for the Cristal to fill up my glass was messing up my program.

I hadn't been sure of what to wear that evening, but instinct told me to glam it up. I dug my black leather pants out of the closet and paired them with a glittery green bustier that I wore under the black blazer from Bloomingdale's. As I'd strapped on my stilettos, I'd felt some guilt about how hard I'd worked to put together my outfit. Then I remembered how Joseph still hadn't picked up my first issue of *Sugar* again, even after he'd promised to read it. I added an extra coat of mascara, some gloss over my lilac lipstick, and left my apartment.

Once I got to Chakra, I was glad I'd dressed up because it was a scene, crawling with celebs, models, and artists. And after the Red Party, I understood how critical a part of my job it was to represent *Sugar*. On the way to our table, JJ had said hello to at least five urban entertainment industry baller types, identifiable by their seemingly uniform diamond-encrusted cross pendants, watches, and pinkie rings, the empty bottles of Cristal in front of them, and the requisite prepubescent Zac Posen–clad model clinging to their arm. When he introduced me to each one, they'd looked me up and down appraisingly. I had no idea if the ballers recognized my name from the gossip mill, if they were curious about the newest EIC of *Sugar*, or if they were just very blatantly checking out JJ's flavor of the week. So, I couldn't tell if showing up for dinner with JJ was helping or hurting my reputation.

Once JJ and I sat down at our table, I kept waiting for him to live up to his reputation and act like the playa everyone said he was (or to allude to Alonzo, because there could be no doubt that he'd heard the scandalous tales about me). Instead, he was respectful and polite, asking me questions about where I was from, how I'd gotten my start in journalism, how I came to be at *Sugar*. Never once did he venture a question about my romantic life. By the time we'd finished half of our second bottle of Cristal, I'd shared more about my life and dreams with JJ than Joseph and I had talked about in years. And we were making each other laugh nonstop.

"Biggie," he insisted.

"No way. Tupac," I said, taking another sip of champagne.

"What do you know, bougie girl? Pac is the truth but it's all about Biggie."

"Whatever, music producer *extra*ordinaire," I enunciated, imitating Barbara. "Any man who can write 'We'll have a race of babies who hate the ladies that make the babies' is my man. I don't care what you say."

JJ laughed at me. "All right, be like that. But you know Barbara wants me to teach you what's hot, so you're supposed to be listening to me."

"I am listening to you. I just don't agree!"

We grinned at each other. I reached for my champagne glass but changed my mind at the last moment, taking another bite of the beef and gulping some water instead. The room was already starting to spin, and more Cristal would not help the situation. JJ reached across the table and gently lifted my chin with his index finger.

"You're cute when you're stubborn," he said, letting his grin fade into a spicy smirk.

"And I bet you're stubborn when you think a woman is cute," I responded, keeping the smile on my face to defuse my comment but removing JJ's hand and placing it back on the table. I nervously picked up my fork and tried to skewer a shrimp dumpling, but the dumpling skittered off my plate to the floor and rolled under the table next to us.

JJ had the grace to ignore my runaway dumpling and horrified expression. "Yeah, well, not to worry. Barbara told me you've got a man," he said, forking a piece of meat into his mouth. Without missing a beat, he continued, "But ma, you are fine."

His grin had turned a little sheepish, and I couldn't help but think how attractive he looked now. We both glanced away, then JJ saved the moment by giving me some behind-the-scenes details: how a CD gets made, the artist development, the marketing efforts, the radio promotions. By the end of his music industry tutorial, I understood that you could tell if an artist had a real shot at blowing up by how much heat (music-ese for promotional dollars) the label put behind them. JJ was in the middle of talking me through the marketing process when I heard a familiar voice above me. I looked up to find Joseph standing above us, so drunk he was practically swaying.

"Isn't this cozy?" he slurred, loud and belligerent, then stuck his hand out in the general direction of JJ's head. "I've heard a lot about you, Jerome. In case you're wondering, I'm Joseph, Nicole's boyfriend. I guess she likes J's."

I was mortified. The only other time I'd seen Joseph drunk was when he'd stumbled home from a friend's bachelor party missing his shoes, tie, and all the money in his wallet. We'd agreed the next afternoon that excessive alcohol was not his friend.

"Joseph, please," I warned.

But JJ merely shook Joseph's outstretched hand. "What's up, brother. How you livin'?" he asked smoothly.

"Not as good as you, *brutha*," Joseph sneered, holding the side of the table for balance. "Since you are having dinner with my woman."

"Jesus, Joe. Enough," I said sharply. "You need to leave."

"Why, Nicole? You don't want me to meet your new friends? Or am I interrupting something?" He stumbled slightly, knocking my champagne flute to the floor. As it shattered, a few people at nearby tables turned to see what was going on. "Whoops, sorry about that," he hollered, nudging the glass away with a Ferragamo loafer. "But I'm sure Jerome can afford another bottle. Can't you, *brutha*?"

With an apologetic glance at JJ, I stood and grabbed Joseph's arm. "Let's go. Now."

Once we hit the street, I let go of him and crossed my arms in front of me, waiting for an explanation. Instead, Joseph took in my leather pants and bustier—I'd left the blazer draped over the back of my chair. "Nice outfit, Nicole."

"Seriously, that's what you have to say?" I exploded. "How dare you embarrass me like that at a business dinner?"

"Business dinner? Business dinner?" Joseph yelled, louder each time. "If that's a fucking business dinner then *Sugar* is some real bullshit."

Joseph had clearly taken my decision to edit *Sugar* personally, as some sort of rejection. And as we faced each other in the middle of the quiet narrow street, I realized, for the first time, that maybe it was. After Alonzo, my almost universally approved relationship with Joseph had given me concrete evidence that I was finally acting like a real adult. But his rigidity and judgment were beginning to make me feel stifled instead of protected, timid instead of mature. Lately, he had felt like one of the soul-sucking yet positive reinforcement–generating things that Teresa and I had talked about.

Watching his expression change from angry to apprehensive, I realized that I'd stayed with Joseph for so long because he had been my security blanket—and I was afraid how leaving him would impact others' opinions of me. My mother would take our breakup as a sign of residual irresponsibility; I would be disappointing Marie yet again, since she'd always joked about Joseph and me naming our first child after her; and most of my friends would think I had lost my ever-loving mind to let that high-quality man go. But, for once, I had the clarity and confidence to make the hardest choice.

I took his hand and said gently, "Joe, this just isn't working out anymore. I love you, but I need to see what life is like without you right now. I'm so sorry."

Joseph stared at me, his understanding of what I'd said sobering him up. "Nicole, is this really what you want?" he asked slowly. "Do you really want to choose *Sugar* over me?"

I kissed his cheek, surer than ever about my decision. "That's the problem. I shouldn't have to choose."

Joseph backed away, shaking his head. "Don't regret this and come crawling back. This is it, you know."

"I know," I said, trying to ignore the tightness growing in my stomach, the prospect of being alone becoming more frightening as it became more real. I turned and walked into the restaurant, forcing myself not to look back.

I'd half expected JJ to be out of there, but he was waiting patiently at the table. When I sat back down and tried to explain, he waved my apology away.

"Don't worry about it, ma," he told me. "He's your man, so he has a right to be a little protective."

"I guess," I muttered, not yet ready to contradict him about my having a man. "Thanks for being nice about it."

"You sure you're all right?" JJ asked gently. "Want to call it a night?"

I shook my head. Allowing a tight smile, I said, "No, I'm fine. It was a misunderstanding."

"Well, your boy seemed real heated for a misunderstanding. But if you're good, we'll keep it moving."

Relieved, I smiled for real at JJ. It was obvious I was not "good," but I liked him for not dwelling on my embarrassment. "So, where were you before we were interrupted?" I prompted.

"Marketing campaigns," JJ said, handing me a new glass of champagne.

Two hours later, JJ put me in a chauffeur-driven Escalade to take me back to Brooklyn. There was no discussion about whether I needed a car; it simply showed up. He didn't try to kiss me or follow me into the car. He just put his information into my new Motorola two-way pager and disappeared into his own chauffeured car. The only time JJ touched me all evening was when he lightly rested his hand on my lower back while I waited for the Escalade driver to open my door. It was only there for a few seconds, but I still felt the residual sensation as we crossed the Brooklyn Bridge and rolled down Flatbush toward my apartment.

Later that night, I robotically took off and folded my clothes, removed my makeup, washed my face, dotted on eye cream, and applied hand moisturizer until I had no more tasks left to distract me from my emotions.

My pillowcase was still damp when I woke up the next morning.

EIGHTEEN

Joseph wanted me to remove everything from his apartment that weekend. Even though I wasn't ready, I moved through his space, throwing my clothes, toiletries, and books into unglamorous plastic garbage bags. I ran my hands across the cool marble counters in the kitchen, the pebbled leather of the B&B Italia sofa, the cashmere throw at the base of the Armani linen–covered bed. For the hundredth time since that fateful Chakra dinner, I wondered if I was crazy. Nothing like leaving one of the most coveted jobs in publishing and dumping one of the most coveted men in New York City in quick succession to make you question your sanity.

My resolve started to crumble; I thought about staying until Joseph got home, greeting him at the door naked, and earning his forgiveness the old-fashioned way. Then I saw a note attached to the mirror in the master bathroom: *"Nicole, I was pretty upset at Chakra, and I had one awful sleepless night. Then I thought about your total disregard for my opinions and disrespect of our relationship. And I realized that we would have been a miserable married couple. So, thanks for helping me dodge a bullet. Good luck with whatever it is you're doing with your life."*

With that, Joseph delivered the coup de grâce to our relationship. I took one more look around the apartment that had been my second home for the past year, placed my set of keys on Joseph's coffee table, and left, closing the door firmly on all the self-doubt and indecisiveness of my twenties. Still, the pitiful walk down the hall toward the elevator, lugging four heavy bags, reminded me of my equally miserable expulsion from Park Ave Pub.

"You did this," I told myself while I struggled to the corner to hail a cab. As I unloaded the contents of the bags into my little studio apartment, each jacket, dress, and book felt like a rebuke.

I'd been so busy at work that I'd forgotten that my lease was up in a couple months. Usually around this time of the year, I'd be in my landlord's office, begging him not to raise the rent. But now I didn't want to stay in my studio one day longer than I had to. There were too many memories gathered in the corners of that place. I planned to call a real estate agent first thing Monday morning. But as the tsunami of tasks and problems (handled at most other magazines by a staff three times the size of *Sugar*'s) crashed over my office, I couldn't focus on anything but the professional triage that had come to characterize the start of my weeks.

Plus, I needed to clear my plate because Kiara was bringing a new PR client—a young R&B artist—by the office to give an acoustic concert for NuVoices staffers at lunchtime. Kiara sounded excited about working with this singer, so we rolled out the red carpet. We hired a local caterer to deliver food and ordered flowers, a tablecloth, candles, and colorful paper plates to warm up the black leather and steel conference room.

At 12:30, Kiara swept into the NuVoices office looking so red carpet–ready (minus the makeup that she never wore and didn't need) that she almost eclipsed her client. Her hair was plaited in two thick braids so long they brushed her ass, lovingly encased in a white miniskirt. There were only a few inches of skin between her mini and a pair of white suede thigh-high boots. A demure black turtleneck and a white shearling coat made her outfit somewhat appropriate for a midday business appointment.

In contrast, her client had more of an all-American vibe. Even her name—Betty Brown—evoked backyard barbecues, college football rivalries, and a pouf of pink cotton candy at an amusement park. Betty's burnished butterscotch skin, copper-colored eyes, golden corkscrew hair, and Jessica Rabbit body were causing some neck-snapping. But with her baggy cargos, cropped hoodie, and Jordan high-tops and a speaking voice so soft she had to introduce herself twice, Betty initially gave off shy tomboy.

The staff of NuVoices was packed tightly in the conference room, taking every available seat and lining up along the walls. Betty tuned her guitar and warmed her vocal cords. I soon found out that what I'd mistaken for shyness was preperformance "energy-gathering," as she later explained. After a plaintive version of Prince's "Adore," Betty had our full attention when she launched into her own repertoire: a sweet, lilting song about first love, a gritty song about a bad breakup, a melancholy song about fitting in as a biracial girl.

The culturally attuned crew at NuVoices, notorious for making snap decisions about whether something was hot or not, didn't move for the full half hour that Betty sang. When she was done, the thunderous clapping only stopped after Betty put her guitar down, pressed her hands together in front of her, and bowed a few times. As she got ready to be interviewed by *Decode*, *Bella*, and *Sugar* staffers, I pulled Kiara into a corner to talk.

"Girl, she is *it*!" I exclaimed, grabbing her by the shoulders.

"Isn't she?" Kiara grinned back at me. "Eternal Records is throwing everything at her—it's going to be a huge marketing push."

According to JJ's tutelage, this meant the label was trying to make her into a star. I had an inexplicable tingling, a warm excitement, a gut feeling that they would succeed. "Kiara, I want *Sugar* to be the first magazine to give her a cover," I said in a rush. "I want to give her a style makeover that will make the fashion world pay attention. And if we can time it so the issue comes out right when the CD hits stores, I guarantee this will be huge—for both of us."

As I said this, I prayed Barbara wouldn't be too furious. Betty was a complete unknown, so we had no idea how she would sell on a cover, which was a huge chance to take on the issue that would come out halfway into my six-month trial. But if I was right and *Sugar* was the first magazine to crown the next R&B phenom, it would make our reputation. Plus, the issue could piggyback off the label's marketing efforts to drive sales.

She paused, so I wrapped an arm around her waist and entreated, "Come on, girl. You know Betty's not going to get another cover until she proves herself. The other magazines that might eventually put her on their covers are too big to take a chance like that. *Sugar* can."

Kiara nodded but lowered her voice and whispered, "Listen, she played at *Groove*'s office last Friday. They said they needed the weekend to think before they could decide what kind of coverage to offer her." Kiara and I both looked back at Betty, who was handling all the attention like a pro already. "The single is going out to radio in July and the label is pushing for an early August release of her full album," Kiara continued. "It's short notice, so I'm looking for something big."

"Great!" I exclaimed. I was already mentally picturing Betty's makeover for our cover. "I haven't booked my August cover yet. I need to put that issue to bed soon so we'd have to shoot her and do the interview next week. But I know we can make this happen. You know there's no way *Groove* can offer you a cover that fast, so give me the exclusive."

"Exclusive?" Kiara's head tilted to the side. She loved me, but this was her job and she needed to figure out what was best for her client.

"If I give Betty a cover, I don't want her to do any interviews with *Sugar*'s competitors until after my issue is off sale." Every monthly magazine hit the newsstands on a different date, usually at least two weeks before the issue's official month. If another magazine's September issue had an early on-sale date, it might overlap with *Sugar*'s August issue and cannibalize our newsstand sales. "*Groove* or someone else can do an October cover. And the offer is only good until tomorrow morning because I have to nail down a cover ASAP," I replied. I loved Kiara, but this was my job too, and I had to figure out what was best for my magazine.

Kiara and I grinned at each other. "I'm liking EIC Nikki," she said. "Done! I just have to clear it with the label, but since this is our only firm offer, I can't imagine they'd object."

"Great! I can't wait to tell Barbara. She'll be excited," I replied, mentally crossing my fingers that this risk would be worth it. Barbara had bobbed her head appreciatively during the performance but disappeared into her office right after. Regardless, I knew she'd hear about the August cover before the day was over, and all I could do was hope that she'd be able to see my vision and not fire me on the spot for ignoring her cover directive. Also, Alonzo would be furious if he had intended on offering Betty a cover. *Groove*'s next several cover subjects had likely been booked but he'd be enraged that someone else got the scoop on a major new artist—more so if it was me. So, I'd be making the target on my back even bigger.

"Perfect," Kiara said decisively, shaking my hand. Lowering her voice again, she said, "On to more important things: How was dinner with Jerome?"

I shook my head and widened my eyes. "Girl, it was totally fine until Joseph showed up, drunk as hell and wanting to fight."

"Tell me they did not throw down in the middle of Chakra." Kiara gasped, eyes wide too.

"Damn near. Joseph knocked over my drink and was making a scene. I had to drag him out before he got his ass beat since half of urban music was there that night."

"Good job, love. A scene in Chakra would have been hid-e-ous. Although two attractive men duking it out for you in public is not the worst look. Page Six would have eaten it up."

"Always the PR maven," I exclaimed, swatting Kiara's arm. "So, we ended up fighting outside and I broke up with him." I spoke as nonchalantly as I could, trying to hide the slight quiver in my lips.

Kiara's smile faded. "Oh no. I'm so sorry. Here I am, making light of the whole thing. You all right, love?" she asked, reaching out to hug me.

"It wasn't pretty, but this has been coming for a while," I said, hugging her back. "I really needed to make some life changes. My lease is up soon and I was thinking of moving back into Manhattan."

"Really?" she asked. "You know... Ricky just finished a luxury rental property in Tribeca. It's not fully occupied yet so you could still get in."

"You think?" I asked excitedly, then sighed when I remembered who I was talking to. "Girl, what am I saying? I probably can't afford to rent a parking space."

Kiara winked. "Friends and family discount, love." She named a rental price that was only a few hundred dollars more than what I was currently paying.

"You serious?" I asked, grabbing her hand.

"Yep. And they're ready, so you could move in whenever."

"Kiara, you have a knack for bailing me out," I told her, sincerely grateful for this beautiful, generous powerhouse.

"And I am lucky to have such an excellent new friend," she replied, squeezing my hand. Then she went over to Betty to tell her she got her first cover offer. Betty's yelp was loud enough to turn every head in the office in her direction. She turned toward all the curious faces, pumped her fist in the air, and yelled, "I'm gonna be on the cover of *Sugar*!"

"My goodness, this is certainly very, very *posh*," Teresa kept saying in a thick British accent. I'd asked her to come with me to check out Matsumoro Tribeca and was now almost regretting it. She hadn't stopped commenting about how *luxurious* the building was since we'd walked into the expansive lobby. Between the twenty-five-foot-high ceilings, indoor Japanese garden, sauna and Jacuzzi in the building's gym, and the rooftop deck with water views, it was impressive. But Teresa's reaction was not what I'd expected: Instead of being excited, she was unmoved, even disdainful of the building and its amenity overkill. And she kept using the word *posh*. Definitely not a Teresa word.

"Tee, what is your problem?" I whispered as the building manager led us through a small lounge and down a wide carpeted hall toward the one-bedroom apartment we were here to see. With the break Kiara gave me on the price, I could finally upgrade from a studio, and I was dying to see how it would feel to not sleep in my living room.

"Nothing," Teresa whispered back as the manager pointed out the zebrawood accents, the Noguchi light fixtures, and the tropical floral arrangements on a hall table that were, apparently, changed every week. "This is simply to die for, *dahling*."

The manager paused in front of the apartment door, taking extra long for dramatic effect. When he swung it open, I understood why. We were on the penthouse level and the first thing we saw as we entered the living room was a wall of floor-to-ceiling windows through which there was an unobstructed view of downtown Manhattan. Even Teresa couldn't pretend to be blasé about the view.

"Okay, wow," she said incredulously.

"Wow is right," the manager chimed in. "And wait until you see this." He walked us to the bedroom, where he motioned toward French doors that led to a small deck. I'd never even dreamed that I could have outdoor space in Manhattan, and I was already imagining drinking a glass of wine overlooking the twinkling cityscape. Meanwhile Teresa was in the next room, freaking out over the stainless-steel Viking and Bosch appliances.

"I know the kitchen's just gonna be home for your vast collection of cereal boxes," Teresa said, coming to check out the deck. "But if you suck up to me enough and let me sun on your deck, I'll come over and make arroz con pollo."

"Deal," I said, running my hand over the sleek glass railing.

After we left, Teresa and I stopped at Rosa Mexicano. I had to put down my margarita mid-sip when Teresa offered to help me pack. "So, you've finally seen the light?"

Teresa shrugged and bit into a chip. "Girl, the apartment is gorgeous. It really is..." She trailed off and took a sip of her drink.

"But," I prompted her, realizing my reaction was premature.

"But I just don't want you to get caught up in all of this," she said, waving her hand in the vague direction of my new life.

"All of what?"

"This," she said, gesturing more emphatically this time. "The parties and the people and the weird paper lamps."

"They're Noguchi, and hella expensive."

"So? They're made of fucking paper," Teresa retorted. "Look, the apartment is obviously fabulous, courtesy of your *fabulous* new buddy, Kiara," she added with a touch of bitterness. "But you're making a lot of changes in your life all at once. All I'm saying is to be careful not to let your head get turned around."

I was getting annoyed, in part because I knew Teresa resented Kiara for facilitating my entry into a world she didn't trust, and in part because she had a point. "Thanks for the heads-up," I finally said, taking a big gulp of my margarita. "I'll try not to transform from a Denise into a Whitley."

"I'm not saying don't enjoy it. I just don't want you to go from a cage right on into some kind of gilded aviary." I was distracted by the high-pitched giggles coming from a pink-sashed bridal party that had entered the room, so Teresa had to grab my hand to pull my attention back. "Listen, you let go of the anvil around your neck, so it must feel like you're free to fly as high as you want. But this shiny new lifestyle is going to trap you like a chicken in a fancy coop if you let the stupid shit become too important."

I couldn't help but chuckle. "Did I hear you call Joseph an anvil?"

Two things I knew for sure about Teresa: I could never get anything past her, and, no matter what, she always had my back. She'd been the only person who hadn't questioned my breakup with Joseph.

"You already know that man really wanted you to be a fancy fashion editor at a fancy magazine that would impress his fancy friends. He liked to listen to hip hop but he didn't want you to bring the culture into his immaculate home. The *Sugar* thing was never going to work for him."

"But damn, an anvil?" I tried to keep it light though her expression was serious. "Okay, I hear you. I won't let my head get turned around by the industry bullshit, no matter how many bouncers at exclusive clubs wave me past the velvet rope or how many chauffeur-driven Escalades I ride in or how many penthouse apartments I live in . . ."

"Girl, shut up!" Teresa finally laughed. "You had better be listening. But I'm not gonna deny that this is all mad sexy." She ordered us two more margaritas. "My treat," she said when I protested. "It's not every day that my girl finally gets a piece of the pie." Then she started humming the theme song to "*The Jeffersons*." We cracked up and any leftover tension between us disappeared.

Teresa loaded a terrifyingly large dollop of the spiciest salsa on a nacho chip. My eyes watered just thinking of how much that would burn my tongue. "Hey, did Derek ever reach out to you?" she asked, not flinching at all as she chewed.

"Derek who?" I returned nonchalantly, although I knew Teresa was referring to the public defender she'd introduced me to at the Vietnamese restaurant.

Teresa waggled her finger. "You can't fool me, chica. You know exactly who I'm talking about. Derek just started a gang assault trial. Some prosecutor is trying to use hip hop lyrics to pin a crime on a kid, and I mentioned that you may be able to give him some info because of your new gig."

"Okay, I'll look out for his call," I said, loading a nacho with the same lava-hot salsa Teresa had casually popped in her mouth. My lips were on fire before I could swallow.

"I bet you will!" Teresa hooted. She gave me a knowing look, then winked as she heaped more of the salsa-from-hell onto her plate.

As I got ready for bed, Teresa's words rang in my mind. How *was* I going to stay grounded? I didn't want to wake up one day and see a "party hag" like Serena or Luna cackling back at me in the mirror. Von had started to bring me enough invitations to music release parties, club openings, private tastings at expensive restaurants, fashion shows, and celebrities' birthdays to keep me out on the town almost every night. And now that I'd be living in one of the most stylish buildings in New York, I'd surely meet swanky neighbors in the sleek marble elevators who would lure me to even more exclusive events. I hadn't even been at *Sugar* three months, and it was already hard to imagine returning to my former life.

After a few sleepless hours, I grabbed a pen and the notebook on my bedside table. Since my college days, I'd kept a journal by my bed to jot down ideas I didn't want to forget or thoughts about my life. The pages were a mix of fleeting inspirations, half-formed plans, and the kind of raw honesty I couldn't share with anyone else. Writing had always been a way for me to untangle the knots in my head, each word loosening the tension until even my most fraught emotions could find release.

Eventually, my pen started to move, almost on its own, and my writing ended up taking the form of a message to my *Sugar* readers. So I decided to turn it into my August editor's letter.

> *Hey, girlfriend. I hope you like this issue! It's only my third as editor-in-chief and I'm still working out the kinks. Sugar is a work in progress—and, as I've recently realized, so am I. Confession: I'm very new to this game and I'm so not perfect. I'm really trying*

to make the right decisions for myself and for this magazine that I've come to love like a sister. But sometimes it's hard to get clear on what's right, what's real, and what are my own insecurities whispering that I shouldn't even bother trying.

Here are some of the major decisions I've personally made within the past few months: I quit a huge job right after I got a big promotion; I broke up with my serious boyfriend; I'm moving out of the Brooklyn apartment I've lived in for the past four years and into a new borough; and I started this glorious new gig as the editor-in-chief of Sugar. *My head is spinning, and I've been second-guessing myself. One thing I do know for certain is that I need* Sugar—*and a fresh start.*

That's why I'm particularly excited to feature Betty Brown, a brand-new R&B artist, on our August cover. Betty's fresh sound and Bed-Stuy-meets-apple-pie look are like nothing I've ever seen before. Some people thought it was risky to put an untested artist on the cover. But I think it is the most Sugar *thing ever to be the first to get behind a dope artist who we believe people across the country will love.*

It is a little scary to push through all this personal and professional change at once. Yet I'm more aware than ever that the only way to grow as a person is to challenge yourself—and to feel a little afraid. Adventure, fulfillment, and success lie outside your comfort zone. If you let fear of the unknown limit you, you can't possibly become the greatest person you could be or *live the best life you could have.*

Still, knowing that and acting on it are vastly different things. And, like I said, I stay second-guessing myself…

I'll make a deal with you: I promise you transparency if you promise me not to listen to that pesky voice telling you what you can't do. I'll give you the real deal about what's happening in my life on this page every single month. And you go out there and do some stuff that scares you. Please send me a letter or an email letting me know what cool new adventures you're having and what you're learning in the process. In the meantime, stay strong and be true to your true self always.

Love, Nikki

I had no idea how long it took me to write the letter because it flowed out of me. When I was done, I felt much calmer and clearer, like I'd just had a good long talk with Teresa. Sitting on my tiny sofa in my dark studio, lit only by my bedside lamp, I decided that instead of writing a boring editor's letter about why you should turn to page 126 or 73 or 29 for whatever was in the magazine, like I had in my first two issues, I would share my real stories and let our readers see me as a real human being—flaws, insecurities, and all. I decided to call it "Nikki's Notes."

NINETEEN

Between organizing Betty Brown's August cover shoot, getting the September issue assigned, and packing up my apartment, it was a *Wizard of Oz* tornado of a week with powerful swirls of activity touching down across my life. I felt like Dorothy desperately holding on to a spinning house hundreds of feet in the air while unpacked boxes and unedited magazine features swirled around me.

JJ had developed a habit of sending me two-way messages multiple times every day to check in. I'd let him extract a commitment to hang out again sometime, but I made no promises about when that would be, telling him that since I'd just broken up with my boyfriend, I wouldn't be ready to date for a while. I'd even told JJ about my upcoming move to explain why I'd be even more busy than usual. So, his daily outreach was sweet, but a little pushy. This was clearly a man used to getting what he wanted when he wanted it.

Occasionally, JJ would call, so I wasn't surprised when Von told me there was a guy for me on the external line. Expecting his gravelly Brooklyn-tinged accent, I stifled a flicker of exasperation. I'd warned JJ this day would be hectic. "Hi there. This is Nikki," I purred, my tone overly sweet to compensate for my irritation.

"Well, hello there. This is Derek."

My involuntarily giggle was mortifying. Although Teresa had given me a heads-up that he'd be calling, I was flummoxed by Derek's presence on the other end of the line. "Oh, hey. Sorry about that. I was expecting someone else."

"Lucky guy." I could hear the amusement in his voice. My cheeks reddened, but before I could decide how to respond, Derek got down to business. "Listen, I know you're at work, so I won't take up too much of your time. Not sure how much Teresa told you, but I've got a new client, a teenage hip hop artist, who a prosecutor claims is gang-affiliated. Even though the kid swears he made everything up, the prosecutor is using lyrics from his latest single as proof that he assaulted a rival gang member. I'm inclined to believe my client, but I need to get some proof."

"Well, that sounds crazy," I exclaimed. "How can they use someone's art as evidence, anyway?"

"Happens all the time. Well, it happens to *us*," Derek corrected himself.

I let out a mirthless chuckle. "I guess you don't have prosecutors quoting honky-tonk songs about gun racks to prosecute any white kids from the sticks. Nobody came after John Lennon for 'Happiness Is a Warm Gun.'"

"What do *you* know about country or rock music?" he snorted. "I thought I was calling an OG hip hop head."

I hesitated. He was right that I loved hip hop to my core. But growing up on a mix of my mom's Isley Brothers, Smokey Robinson, and Stevie Wonder records along with my dad's Thelonious Monk, Rolling Stones, and Janis Joplin records had given me an appreciation for all music. More than one person at Howard had mocked the second cassette case I hid under my bed that was filled with everything *but* hip hop and R&B. So I had learned to keep the full diversity of my musical taste quiet lest my Black card be revoked. But I figured that I had nothing to lose with Derek, a virtual stranger I'd likely never see again. "You got it right about hip hop. That's my heart," I began cautiously. "Country's not my jam, but I am into a lot of different types of music, definitely including rock."

"A'ight, prove it! What was the last non–hip hop album you listened to?" he asked with no small amount of skepticism.

"I have the Smashing Pumpkins' *Siamese Dream* in my Discman right now," I replied, fully expecting him not to know what the hell I was talking about.

"Wait, *you* like the Smashing Pumpkins?"

"*You* know who the Smashing Pumpkins are?"

Both of us uttered a drawn-out "interesting" at the same time, then burst out laughing.

I didn't know a single other Black person who was into that band and was now genuinely curious about this man. "Okay, Derek, I know what my excuse is, but how is it that you come by your alt-rock knowledge?"

"Whew, complicated story," he stalled. "Well, I got into a little trouble coming up, so my folks sent me to a super strict Catholic school in a 'good' neighborhood. Of course, it was full of pissed-off rich troublemakers who cut classes to smoke weed and steal shit from the bodega. I was buddies with kids who expanded my musical repertoire."

"So, you're into the Smashing Pumpkins because of some wealthy pothead shoplifting high schoolers?"

"Add Led Zep, Sinéad O'Connor, and Soundgarden to that list. But yeah, it was a *whole* new world for me."

I loved all the artists he listed, but the emphasis he'd placed on the word *whole* had piqued my curiosity. "Sounds like it. What other repertoires did they expand, or dare I ask?"

"I'm going to save those stories for another day so they don't color your entire impression of me," Derek demurred. "Let's just say that I became a lawyer to right a few wrongs."

"Come on. You can't leave me hanging like that. Are we talking a little petty theft, or did you get in a fight with one of the Catholic schoolboys?" When silence greeted my laughter, I quickly cleared my throat. "Hey, um, I have a knack for sticking my foot in my mouth. And I know I'm prying."

"Nah, it's cool. I don't really mind telling you," he replied slowly. "I got talked into buying weed in Washington Square Park with some guys from school. Right when we were buying, the narcotics squad ran up on us. Everyone took off and this one fat cop fell and busted his face. Because I was the only Black kid there, he said that I hit him. Then one of the other kids flipped on me to get out of trouble." Derek inhaled deeply before continuing. "My folks spent too much money on a shitty lawyer who talked me into a shitty plea. It took a good public defender years to overturn it on appeal. By the time I finally got into college, most of my friends were graduating."

"I can only imagine how frustrating that was," I said, trying to envision how it must have felt to get so derailed while the real culprits were living their lives. "And here I thought it was the end of the world when I got detention for passing notes in class."

"Detention is the most trouble you've ever been in?"

"I've just never been caught," I said with strident bravado, overcompensating for the fact that Dr. Ann Rose would have never let me out of her sight long enough to get into any real trouble. "I mean, my mom kept me on a tight leash."

It was Derek's turn to chuckle. "You didn't strike me as a hardened criminal, so I'm not surprised."

"Uh, you either! I bet you're listening to something like *Fumbling Towards Ecstasy* right now!" I guessed.

"Hey, don't be disrespecting Sarah McLachlan!" The album reference had been a low-key test that I couldn't believe he'd passed. Then again, any Black man who admitted to liking Sinéad O'Connor had an undeniable penchant for folksy singer-songwriters—along with some serious confidence *and* cojones. "Am I going to regret telling you all of this?" His voice was playful, but I sensed he wanted a real reply.

"How could I possibly judge you?" I replied. "Especially if it all went into you becoming a lawyer."

Derek drew a long breath. "My moms didn't have the money to

grease the appeals process and I had to support myself while I waited. I was barely making it, and I watched a lot of guys from my neighborhood get sucked into the system. And I can't say that there weren't times when I was tempted myself to go for the easy money. There but for the grace of God," he admitted. "It definitely inspired me."

"To advocate for the underdog," I added.

"And to defend the underrepresented, absolutely," he responded firmly. "Which brings us back to my gang assault case with the hip hop lyrics."

"Okay, I'm down to fight the good fight too. How can I help?"

"That's nice of you, Nikki." I could hear Derek's smile. "I need to prove that this kid isn't a hardened gangbanger whose lyrics are a diary of his violent crimes." There was an almost imperceptible pause before he continued. "I'm seeing someone who works in the music industry, but she's never heard of this artist. Teresa thought you might have more info since you have better hip hop connects."

I don't know why I was surprised. Of course he had a girlfriend. "Okay, email me your client's name and I'll ask around without letting anyone know what it's about." My voice sounded faintly glum, so I added more energy. "I'll get back to you ASAP!"

It only took a couple calls to figure out that the baby-faced rapper Derek was representing was known in the community for being a poser. He'd hid his White Plains private school background from everyone—including Derek—out of fear of being exposed as a fraud; he might have even *wanted* to go to jail for the street cred.

When I called Derek the next day to let him know, he yelped, "I knew it! You are a lifesaver."

"Really happy to hear that," I responded sincerely.

"You may have kept an innocent kid out of jail." Derek sounded so relieved. "I appreciate you, Nikki! How can I repay you? Lunch or dinner on me?"

As tantalizing as that was, I was being pulled in way too many directions to break bread with my girl's coworker. "Don't worry about it. I'm glad I could help. And I see why you and Teresa are so cool. It all makes sense now."

"And I see why you and Teresa have been best friends for so long. You have a good heart, rock star." His voice was like a classic guitar riff, raw and mellow. "There will be a meal on me at some point, though. You're not getting away that easy."

Even with everything going down, I was determined not to miss my move-in date at Matsumoro Tribeca. Every day I'd grind for twelve hours in the office, then go home and pack for another hour or so. Within ten days, I'd hired a man with a van and was ready to go. That Saturday, Teresa, Sofie, and Denyse came to Brooklyn to help me move.

"Girl, this is how you know we love your ass," Teresa said, leaning against the wall of my Brooklyn apartment building and brushing crumbs off her hands. We'd just taken my television down to the van and were splitting a huge peanut butter cookie as our reward. I was fast discovering that on moving day, all your belongings mysteriously multiply like hamsters or gray hairs—and one man with a van was not nearly enough. If my girls had not come to my rescue, I never could have finished.

"I know it," I said gratefully as Sofie and Denyse emerged from the doorway, carrying my coffee table between them.

"I know you lazy bitches aren't taking a break," Denyse called out as she and Sofie struggled to the curb.

Teresa rolled her eyes while I laughed. "I was bribing our girl with a cookie so she wouldn't bug out," I yelled back.

Denyse walked over, wiping her moist forehead. "I am sweating out my perm for you, heffa," she wheezed, joining Teresa against the wall.

"I know, I know." I passed her a chocolate-chip cookie. "You love me, but I had better name my firstborn after you."

"Shoot, forget the name. I'll take some cash." Denyse laughed and passed half her cookie to Sofie, who was now leaning next to her.

"She doesn't have enough money to pay me for this," Sofie said, shaking the dust out of her hair. "You seriously couldn't throw out your manga collection that I just hauled down to the van in the world's heaviest box?"

"But I've had some of those books since I was in junior high," I said as all three of them groaned.

"Um, so?" Teresa said through a mouthful of cookie. "You're only going to throw them into your big-ass walk-in closet and forget they exist."

"Oh, leave her alone," Denyse said, laughing. "It's not her fault she's got weird taste."

"Wait a minute now, Marcus Garvey. I've never complained about your five-hour lectures on financial literacy and keeping wealth in the Black community."

"Nikki's got a point there." Teresa suppressed a laugh.

"I still don't understand why we aren't moving you into Joseph's apartment," Sofie said as she tightened her ponytail holder.

"Girl, what are you talking about? He was such a tool!" Teresa exclaimed, then clapped a hand over her mouth.

"And I still can't believe Teresa held her tongue all those years," Denyse said with a side-eye.

"You think all good guys are tools, Teresa." Sofie wasn't ready to let it go.

"I do not!" Teresa protested. "I just get bored easily."

"You have the sexual attention span of a toddler," Denyse chimed in.

"Weird analogy, Dee." I crinkled my nose. "I think she's more like one of those insects that eats their mate."

Sofie tapped her forehead, searching for the word in English. "What's it called? Oh yeah, a praying mantis!"

"Now I've gone from bored to straight cannibalistic!" Teresa protested.

We ignored her, giggling, and pried ourselves off the wall to go back upstairs just as the man with the van appeared in the doorway, rivulets of sweat running down his face and pooling in the hollow of his throat before slipping lower. It was a sweltering day and he'd been hauling boxes and furniture out of my studio all morning. At some point, he'd stripped off his shirt and was now wearing nothing above his belt but a silver Coptic cross, his thick locs swinging at his waist while he lugged two chairs to the curb. We all nudged one another, scoping out his glistening chest and bulging biceps. "I know you want some of that hot chocolate," I whispered to Teresa.

"Yeah, mon," she whispered back, twisting a curl next to her ear and jutting out a hip.

The man grinned at all of us. "We're almost done. How about you ladies take a rest and meet me outside the apartment building in Manhattan in an hour?"

"If you insist," I said gratefully.

"You're sure you don't need any help getting there?" Teresa purred.

"Nah, I'm straight, but if you want to keep me company..." He looked her up and down appreciatively.

Teresa turned to us and winked. "I'm going to head into the city with, uh..."

"Dexter," he supplied helpfully.

"Yeah, Dexter," she said to us, practically licking her lips. "So, I'll see you there. Save me a sandwich."

"How's about I save you some Ho Hos," Denyse said, elbowing me.

"I think she'd rather have a Ding Dong." Sofie snickered.

"Come on, let's grab my luggage and lock up before you bitches throw an entire Hostess factory at her." I saluted Teresa before turning toward the front door. "Don't do anything I wouldn't do, Tee."

"Don't hate, congratulate," Teresa called back, blowing us a kiss and climbing into the passenger seat of the van.

Sofie, Denyse, and I waved at her as we headed back inside to have a picnic on the floor of my empty apartment. But when we pulled up to Matsumoro Tribeca in Denyse's car a couple hours later, Teresa was standing on the sidewalk.

"What's up, Tee?" I asked as I climbed out of the car. "Where's Dexter?"

"Girl, he's gone. And your stuff is unloaded already." She looked very confused.

"Wait, how? He couldn't have gotten all that done so quickly. He didn't even have a key."

"You tell me," Teresa replied, putting both hands on her hips. "When we got here, there were three burly guys waiting for us who said they'd been hired to move you in. They'd even convinced the building manager to give them a key."

"Shit, were they thieves?" I asked nervously, envisioning all my stuff selling on a street corner in the Bronx for thirty-two dollars.

"Hell no, I'm not that stupid. I watched them put everything away in your apartment and I got the key they had," Teresa said indignantly, handing it over to me.

"That's weird," Denyse said as she and Sofie walked over. "Did you hire extra people, Nikki?"

"No, I didn't," I told her, now totally baffled. "Did they say who hired them?"

Teresa shook her head. "No, but you have an enormous bouquet of flowers sitting on your kitchen counter."

Denyse and Sofie oohed and aahed as we walked through the plush lobby to the elevators, but I barely noticed because I was wondering who my fairy godmother (or -father) was. They would have to have known when I was moving and where I was moving to. How many people had that information? Had Barbara or Kiara hooked me up with some moving-day love? Maybe my parents wanted to surprise me? But I didn't think so when I saw the flowers in the apartment: four dozen perfect red roses.

"Whoa, these are amazing." Denyse sighed when she saw the bouquet. "Someone's got a crush on you."

"I hope they're not from Joseph," I said, opening the card. I hadn't heard from him since I'd removed my things from his apartment.

"Well? Who's your secret admirer?" Sofie asked impatiently as I read the card.

There's a bottle of champagne in your fridge. I'd like to open it with you later to celebrate your move but understand if you're still not ready. Yours when you want me,

JJ

P.S. You know Biggie is my man, but tonight would be all about Tupac...

"Um, it's from this producer I had dinner with. The guy from that night at Chakra," I said, blushing deeply. I opened the refrigerator. Sure enough, a bottle of Cristal was chilling inside. When I turned around, my girls were clustered together, reading the card.

"Hey!" I exclaimed.

"Don't even start," Teresa said, waving away my protest. "You know we needed to check it out for ourselves. So, JJ is the guy you were out with the night you broke up with Joseph, right?"

"Yeah, that's him," I said, snatching the note from Teresa and plopping down on the sofa to reread it.

"The champagne is for real?" she asked.

I motioned with my chin toward the kitchen. "In the fridge."

"Impressive," she reluctantly acknowledged. "You going to call him?"

"Might," I admitted. "You know, sometime."

Teresa grinned at me. "Okay, Nikki. Give these guys a tour of your place so we can get out of here."

"What are you talking about? I thought you were going to stick around for a while," I said as Denyse and Sofie took their cue from Teresa.

"We'll come back over the weekend to help you unpack some more, although those guys made serious progress," Sofie said, glancing around the mostly box-free apartment.

"They even made your bed. So tonight, maybe you should relax on your own," Denyse said, winking at me.

The three of them glanced at one another, smiling while I pretended not to see. After a few more weak protestations, I gave up trying to get them to stay. I showed Denyse and Sofie the apartment and the rest of the building, and they were gone within the hour. As she left, Teresa whispered in my ear, "Have some fun, Nik. This is not the night to be concerned about rumors or reputation. Just do whatever the hell you want, for once."

When I was alone, I surveyed the scene before me. The movers JJ hired had unpacked the biggest boxes and put away the most obvious items. But clearly their mandate had been to get in and out as quickly as possible. I walked around, putting away the odd sweater and fork and towel taking in my new space. The bouquet was so big that the smell of roses chased me from room to room.

Peeling off my grungy T-shirt and jeans, I ran a hot bath with some lavender oil. My hair was filthy, so I washed it, letting the curls spring back in, then scrubbed my skin with a loofah I'd stashed in my bathroom box. I put on some low-slung lounge pants, a silky tank top, and perfume, then found myself sitting at a kitchen chair with JJ's card on the table in front of me. Yeah, the movers and flowers and champagne were a little presumptuous, but he'd gone way out of his way for me. So what if he'd done it when he was aware I was at my most vulnerable? I still liked that he'd taken charge. I picked up my phone and dialed his number.

JJ arrived with takeout from Nobu. To his credit, he only spared a quick glance at my braless breasts before popping the bottle of Cristal and heaping a plate with rock shrimp tempura, yellowtail sashimi, and miso cod. After we ate, he whipped out some jojoba massage oil and dug into my back muscles that ached from packing and lifting and cleaning. By the time he was putting on his jacket to leave, I was the one looking forward to a goodnight kiss. I kept thinking JJ would make a move, but when he was almost at the door and I realized that he really was about to go, I touched his sleeve and shook my head. That was all he needed.

JJ pressed me against the front door he was about to open and grabbed a handful of my hair, tilting my head back and kissing the base of my neck as I melted into his hard body. He brushed the top of my nipples until they poked through my thin top, then slid a hand under the waistband of my pants to feel a slippery welcome. His fingers rubbed back and forth until the wetness soaked through my thong and I could barely stand. Then he flipped me around so my ass was firmly nestled against his groin, bent my head forward, and gently nibbled the back of my neck. Even with both palms against the door for balance, I was dizzy as I begged for more, gasping as I felt his hard dick slide inside me. My hands balled into fists as he thrust into me. It crossed my mind that my introduction to my neighbors might be pounding on the inside of my door mixed with our guttural moans. But that thought quickly left my mind as one deep thrust made me explode into a million pieces.

JJ pulled his pants back on while I sank into a nearby chair, breathing heavily. Before he left he inclined his head toward my burning pussy, looked deep into my eyes, and said, "That's mine now, Nikki." Then he kissed my forehead and walked down the hallway toward the elevator without looking back.

TWENTY

"Your flowers, madam," Von said with a flourish as he deposited the orchid plant on my desk next to a fat bouquet of purple hydrangeas. To make room, I had to move another extravagant arrangement of tropical flowers outside to Von's desk. Given that I was getting deliveries every third day from Jerome Jermaine and my office was starting to resemble a botanical garden, it was becoming more and more difficult to pretend nothing was going on.

I learned the cardinal rule of dating within the circle that he (and now I) inhabited from Kiara, my urban entertainment Yoda: Do not tell anyone who you're sleeping with because public relationships are a very bad idea. Not that JJ and I were in a relationship, of course; we'd only been seeing each other for a few weeks. But our chemistry had only gotten more intense since the evening I moved into Matsumoro Tribeca. My fragrant office and buzzing pager telegraphed accelerating romantic interest, as did JJ's insistence that he had the right of first refusal for all my weekend evening plans.

So I was a little insulted when one night JJ casually mentioned that he thought it best if we keep our "thing" (as he put it) to ourselves for the time being. The next morning, I called Kiara, who'd echoed his perspective.

"Don't give the haters any more ammunition, love. Serena and those bitches would be too happy to use the information to their advantage," Kiara said, a hard tone creeping into her usual honeyed voice. "Like it or not, you're the hot new thing on the scene, and every baller worth their salt will want to see if he can get some bragging rights. It's an incestuous little world, and their bragging rights would deal a deathblow to your professional reputation."

I knew what she was alluding to. Since the music industry's calloused thumb smudged the line between professional and personal for anyone in or near its vortex, Alonzo's fabrications about me must have been truly outrageous. So often when I met someone, I swear I'd catch a flicker of recognition in a raised eyebrow, a cocked head, the hint of a smirk, the slow repetition of my name in the form of a question. I'd become skilled at concealing my embarrassment behind an unperturbed smile and a crisp follow-up about something related to *Sugar*. A comment about how I hoped to feature them or their famous artists in the magazine usually worked like a charm to turn dismissive bemusement into receptive curiosity.

Although Kiara had insisted that circumspection about dating partners was a good overall rule, I knew that I was working against my reputation. Clearly, giving Serena and Luna, and therefore Alonzo, ammo as they plotted my downfall would not be the best idea. So, JJ and I spent a lot of time hanging out in our respective apartments; when we did go out, we made sure to arrive and leave separately. And I didn't tell anyone other than my best friends. I didn't even tell Von, who kept bringing in my flowers and not-so-subtly waiting for some explanation. But that day, along with the orchid plant, Von had something else tucked under his arm. With an even greater flourish, he whipped out *Sugar*'s August issue, with Betty Brown on the cover.

"The first box of these just came in, hot off the press," he squealed while I grabbed it and hugged it to my chest. "The team jumped me the minute the box hit my desk. I barely got one for you."

DJ Cassius and Latika's pregnancy reveal had driven the June issue's newsstand sales past all prior NuVoices' records. Sinclaire's July issue was about to hit stores, and it had promising advance buzz. The July cover shoot had taken place in a sunny West Side studio overlooking the Hudson. Gaultier pulled through with some colorful summery dresses, and we photographed Sinclaire against equally bright backdrops with a fan that whipped her tawny-brown weave around her face as she laughed for the camera with the practiced ease of a multihyphenate star who knows her angles. I added cover lines about summer fun, and the result was a vibrant cover guaranteed to make the July issue stand out.

But Betty's August issue took *Sugar*'s cover game to a whole new level. I'd called Tyger, a young photographer who'd recently shot a cool sneaker feature for *Vogue Brasil* with Foxy Brown. Freddy and I pitched him the idea of shooting Betty in high-end designer gear mixed with urban streetwear. Tyger loved the concept and suggested doing it on location in Brooklyn. Freddy styled Betty in door-knocker bamboo earrings with a tweed Chanel suit, hooked an Alexander McQueen bag on her shoulder over a Karl Kani jacket, popped a furry Kangol bucket hat on her head to accessorize a silky Versace dress, and even laced up some Timberland boots to go with La Perla lingerie and a Burberry raincoat. Tyger had her pose in the lush wilds of Prospect Park and against the backdrop of gritty Flatbush Avenue. It was a gorgeous study of contrasts that positioned *Sugar* on the cutting edge of fashion and culture.

I kept the cover design mostly monochromatic, adding cover lines in silver and white so only the neon-pink *Sugar* logo popped. The magazine looked chic and current, and, with the marketing buzz that would surround Betty's impending music video and album release, I knew it would make her a style muse. I flipped to my editor's letter and read the heartfelt message, hoping it wasn't a mistake to open myself up so much. "Maybe I should have written a regular letter," I murmured.

"Are you serious?" Von practically yelled in return. "Sure, the cover is dope, but everyone was talking about your letter when I grabbed your flowers."

Imani knocked on the door, talking loud before I could fully wave her in. "Nikki, this issue is fire! I knew it when we sent it to the printer, but people are going crazy out there." She stopped to catch her breath, then high-fived me. "And all the women in the office are talking about Nikki's Notes. Everyone identifies with at least one part of what you wrote."

"For real? I was getting nervous that I'd gone too far." I figured that I may as well be open with Von and Imani.

"For real," Imani said with Von *uh-huh*ing in the background. "I don't know of any EIC who has ever done anything like that. You're breaking ground and our readers will love it."

"And they're going to love you, boo!" Von exclaimed.

Sondra burst through the door without knocking. "We are *so* in business! If Tika's reveal and Sinclaire's fabulosity didn't make the industry sit up and take notice, this sick Betty cover sure will." She was pacing my office excitedly. "And your letter . . . it's like you were in my head. I mean, I'm dealing with a breakup and a new job too."

Sondra sat down on my sofa next to Imani, who put an arm around her shoulders, pointed to herself with her free hand, and said, "New job too, obviously. And I moved to NYC a year ago with my son, as a single mom. I'm having serious trouble opening my heart again." Imani looked up at me. "Your editor's letter gave me courage, Nikki. Not because you said that you have all the answers, but because you admitted that you don't."

I sat next to them for a group hug. With my arms around Sondra and Imani, I grasped for the first time the sisterhood that *Sugar* could truly become. Our shared optimism felt as deep and fragile as our trust in the future.

Von had enough and draped himself across all our laps to break up the suddenly subdued mood. "Um, can we get back to celebrating this ri*donk*ulous issue and our *fah*bulous new EIC!"

He pulled me outside to the floor, where I was swallowed in a sea of hugs and high fives.

That night, JJ took me out to celebrate. I'd wanted to go home and change first, but he insisted on picking me up right after work, baggy denim, cropped T-shirt, high-tops, ponytail, and all.

"You look so cute," he exclaimed as I climbed into his Porsche 911. He rarely drove himself around the city, so this was the first time I'd seen his cobalt-blue sports car. I was unsure what to do with the large rectangular box I'd had to move aside to sink into the buttery tan leather when JJ said, "That's for you, gorgeous."

Ripping it open, I discovered a Louis Vuitton crossbody bag. "No way, it's perfect! I love it!" I wrapped my arms around JJ and wove my fingers through the curls at the back of his neck. He smelled woodsy and sweet, like s'mores melting over a campfire in the forest. I noticed he was wearing jeans and sneakers too. "Where we going, Daddy?" I asked, knowing that was his favorite nickname—even though I had to suppress memories of Alonzo every time I used it.

"MC RedHot just opened a sports bar, and he's having a small opening party tonight." Passersby turned to stare as JJ gunned the engine and swung the Porsche into traffic. "I thought we'd roll through there and then decide what's next for the evening."

"A whole MC RedHot party? Um, I don't know about all that, JJ. Fab new bag notwithstanding, I'm dressed like I'm going to a picnic in Central Park."

"That's the vibe, gorgeous," JJ assured me.

"Wait, are we going there together?"

"There may be drama at the door. RedHot's events always get stupid and you're not on the list, so I should walk you in." As he sped around a corner on two wheels, I started to understand why he had a driver.

"Whatever you say, Mario." I was trying to be chill, but I had a white-knuckle grip on the door handle.

"Mario?" His expression was quizzical.

"Mario Andretti!"

JJ's face clouded for a minute, and I worried that he might misinterpret my reference to the famous Italian Formula One driver as an insult. Then recognition crept across his face. "A'ight, boo. Imma show you what racing looks like." He chuckled as he whipped past cars on Seventh Avenue like they were parked. I'd never been so grateful to see a valet stand in my life.

The sports bar's name, Red, was illuminated in red neon lights across the side of a building that was surrounded by a throng of photographers swarming a red carpet.

"Shit, JJ, it's a total scene," I said, taking in the flashing bulbs and commotion. We had climbed out of the car and were waiting for the valet ticket.

"Yeah, I didn't think it would be all this." JJ shrugged. "He said it would be chill."

"Jerome Jermaine, it's MC RedHot. Even I know that the man does not know what chill looks like," I yelled over the din as I dug in my bag for a lipstick.

"You used my government name, so I know you're annoyed." JJ surveyed the thick line of people waiting to walk the carpet. While most of the men were dressed like they were at a Knicks game, predictably, the women looked like they going to an upscale club. My face must have appeared panicky because he put a finger under my chin and tilted my face upward. "Nicole Rose, you look better than all these women combined," he whispered, then he bent down to press his lips against mine.

For a minute, I closed my eyes and let my lips relax into his, feeling his tongue lightly exploring my mouth. Then I remembered where we were. My eyes snapped open just in time to catch Luna over JJ's shoulder, watching us with an expression so venomous I could practically see the green heat glimmering in her eyes. I pushed JJ away, but it was too late.

"JJ, let's just go," I told him, motioning with my chin toward Luna. He'd obviously forgotten himself as well since he'd already informed me that he didn't want to go public as a couple.

"Oh snap," he said, turning me around so neither of us was facing the curious crowd. It didn't matter how chaste we appeared as the valet searched for our car keys because the damage was done. The rumor mill had started, and Luna would make sure that everyone would be talking about my "thing" with JJ in the least flattering terms.

We ended up having dinner at a discreet restaurant in Tribeca, trying to enjoy the quiet before the storm. My two-way was blowing up before we got to dessert. The only message I opened was from Kiara. It read: *I'm trying to do damage control, love, but Luna is running around this RedHot party telling everyone that she saw Jerome Jermaine with his tongue down your throat and his hand on your ass. She and the other party hags have folks taking bets on whether you slept with him to get one of his artists on your next cover or for clout. Remember that this too shall pass.*

I came in the next morning to find Barbara waiting for me in my office. Her red leather pantsuit told me she meant business.

"Hey, Barbara, I thought you were in Chicago for some sales meetings," I said, trying for a casual tone.

"I was, but since I'm hearing tales about my new editor that I simply do not want to believe, I flew back at the crack of dawn this morning." I chewed my nails as I waited for her next words. "So, I'm hearing that you're sleeping with Jerome Jermaine."

Barbara searched my face. It was her turn to wait while I struggled to find an appropriate answer.

"Well, yes, JJ and I are seeing each other," I replied. "We were trying to keep it a secret, but Luna caught us sharing a moment outside MC RedHot's sports bar opening." Barbara did not move, continuing to regard me with an eerie calm. I hazarded a defiant comment. "I'm not sure why it's such a big deal, though. Neither of us is married, so who cares if we're dating?"

At that, Barbara's expression finally shifted into disbelief. "Are you serious right now? I know I call you newbie a lot, but I did expect you to have more common sense than this. I thought you would have learned your lesson after whatever went down with Alonzo." She closed her eyes and inhaled slowly. "You are aware that being EIC of *Sugar* has you on full display, and you already know that half of the urban world thinks you're one step up from a video ho. So, you thought that openly dating JJ, who is one of the most promiscuous music executives in the business, was a good idea? What do you think that says about you?"

I was too busy turning over the words *most promiscuous music executives in the business* and *one step up from a video ho* to immediately process what she was saying about my reputation.

Not getting the reaction she was looking for, Barbara went on. "Nikki, I took a chance on you. You already know that we can't afford any mistakes, and we only have a short time to prove that this company is viable. So, the first thing you do is fuck the person I introduced you to in order to help you better understand the urban music business?"

"That's not fair, Barbara."

"Um, so what, Miss *StyleList*? I never promised you fair. What I did tell you is that I see everything that happens in my office." She pointed her index finger at me. "You promised me that you understood how important this job is. *Sugar* is a million times better than before you got here, but we are very, very far from being out of the woods." I started to reply, but Barbara interrupted. "I do not want to hear it. Get back to work, keep your head down, do what you're supposed to do."

With that, she stomped out of my office. I could see people on the floor, so proud of me and of *Sugar* just yesterday, looking skeptical once again as they watched Barbara slam the office door of their new EIC, no doubt knowing exactly why.

TWENTY-ONE

The energy at NuVoices' blowout to celebrate *Sugar*'s successful July issue reached a crescendo long before Sinclaire's trademark whistle note rang out over the rapt audience. The next day, Page Six would describe the party as the "event of the season." The hyperbolic headline wasn't too far from the truth—which was a miracle, given how slow the evening began.

Urban parties were nerve-rackingly unpredictable. That crowd was notorious for not RSVPing and waiting to see who was going before deciding to pull up with their friends. If there was no buzz, you could have an empty room with trays of congealing appetizers. If folks started to hear that it was a hot party, rappers and actors and models would show up with huge crews, the line to get in would extend up the street, and the fire marshals would eventually be called.

Barbara pulled out all the stops for Sinclaire's cover party, even engaging Kiara's PR and event firm (at my behest) to handle the affair. On the night of the event, we had everything in place: a buzzy DJ, a sexy stage design for Sinclaire's performance, a step and repeat banner with *Sugar*'s logo and sponsor names, press lined up to interview famous attendees, huge bougainvillea arrangements that added bursts of purple and pink to the Caribbean-themed décor, signature rum cocktails, and Kiara ready to guard the door with a long list of invited names attached to a clipboard. The problem was that the list held almost no confirmed RSVPs, so we had no idea if the party would hit the in-crowd's two-way pagers or if Sinclaire would be singing to an echoey room of NuVoices employees and caterers.

Because she was on the cover, Sinclaire caused a commotion when she hit the red carpet, the flashbulbs going off as she'd entered the cavernous Lower East Side venue and settled into the prime banquette next to the DJ stand. Since no one else arrived with her, for a while we thought her performance might be the only highlight of the evening.

"I don't know, love," Kiara had said after she and I did a quick walk-through of the near-empty high-ceilinged former bank that was now one of the most sought-after event locations in the city. I'd given Sinclaire an optimistic thumbs-up as we moved through the space, regretting that I'd asked her to arrive so early; then Kiara and I trotted to a back room to put the last touches on our outfits—hers a floral-print Roberto Cavalli jumpsuit and mine a silky yellow dress with a plunging neckline so low she'd had to beg me to wear it. Kiara's trademark bare face was gorgeous, so she was keeping me company while I touched up my makeup. "I haven't heard much about the party on the grapevine."

"Tonight cannot be a flop, Ki," I moaned.

I hadn't told Kiara about NuVoices' precarious status, but my panicky tone must have conveyed a profound level of concern because Kiara nodded and pulled out her two-way. "Okay, I've got you," she said. "Let me call in some favors."

Just then, we heard a racket on the street. We rushed out to see multiple chauffeur-driven SUVs pulling up. Apparently, Freddy had spent the day styling a music video that Tyger directed for MC RedHot. The shoot wrapped early, and she'd convinced RedHot, Tyger, and all the dancers that it would be fun to hit the *Sugar* party for some cocktails. Kiara and I stared at each other as the rapper's next music video spilled out of three Escalades.

That's how the "event of the season" got started, and soon, the line of town cars, SUVs, and limos snaked up Houston Street.

Kiara pulled me onto the red carpet and called out, "Nikki Rose, editor-in-chief of *Sugar*, is on the carpet. This is her party!"

The photographers flashed away at me while I attempted to wrangle my limbs into a suitable pose. Kiara had convinced me to wear my hair curly, which I hadn't done in months. It fanned out over the sunny silk covering my shoulders. I'd forgotten how good it felt to look in a mirror and see my natural hair texture, to feel it shrink as it dried and frizz in the humidity, to have stray curls escape a hair tie. But as I pried ringlets off my lip gloss, I realized my inner bookworm would always feel a little awkward in front of the camera.

Of course, JJ would be the first person I ran into as I finally made it to the end of the red carpet. I was grateful to see him climbing out of a chauffeured Escalade instead of the driver's side of his 911. After my conversation with Barbara, I'd tried to distance myself from him, but JJ continued to show up at my door almost nightly. He'd charmed (likely bribed) the Matsumoro Tribeca doorman into letting him upstairs unannounced, so I would have no warning other than a soft knock at my door. The sight of JJ leaning against my doorjamb with a sheepish smile dispelled my annoyance every time.

We'd decided against hanging out in public, so this would be the first night we were at the same event since that fateful valet stand kiss. But when I saw JJ's sleek white suit and cornrows, I almost lost my resolve. Fortunately, I noticed how the crowd between us was looking from him to me to see how we'd react. Running up to him would have added an exclamation point behind the question mark to my name. Instead, I let myself get pulled inside the venue.

I grabbed my first rum punch of the evening from a passing waiter's tray as I searched the crowd for a friendly face. Von appeared at my left shoulder with a beautiful but sour-faced woman whom he introduced as "Paula the dancer." Paula rolled her eyes and skulked off.

"Oh my god, Von. What happened this time?" I asked, hooking

my arm through his as we made our way toward my reserved banquette.

"Same old, same old. I drove us to the party in her new white Benz and sideswiped a red Jeep on the way. Now her car looks like it's bleeding." He shrugged. "I did try to tell her I've only driven, like, three times since college. I'm a New Yorker!" His second shrug told me that after tonight, Paula the dancer would join the unfortunate ranks of Von's exes.

The swell of arriving guests, who had no doubt heard that MC RedHot was in the house, made it impossible to move five feet without someone coming up to me for an air-kiss or an introduction. But the whispers behind my back made it clear that too many people knew about my "thing" with JJ. I grabbed another rum punch from a passing tray, and then another.

Von was the perfect handler, giving me intel on everyone while shielding me from the worst gossipers and steering me toward friendlies. Between avoiding rumormongers and JJ, who seemed to pop up around every corner, we were walking an endless Fibonacci sequence of a path. By the time we finally spiraled to my banquette, I had finished my third drink, my hair had expanded into a cumulus cloud, and I really wanted a break from standing in my new stilettos. No such luck. I'd arranged for premium bottle service so I could entertain in my own space, and I limped up to find none other than Luna and Serena enjoying my Belvedere. How they'd slipped in past Kiara was beyond me, but there they were, in matching skintight minidresses, making cocktails with my mixers. I was too buzzed and annoyed to edit myself.

"What the fuck!" I exclaimed loud enough for several people to turn my way. "You two can feel free to leave."

"Oooh, you all right, boo?" Serena purred, leisurely sipping her drink and twirling her long straight hair. "Did your finger get stuck in an electric socket?"

Luna's glittering eyes never left my face as she and Serena cackled together. "Waiting on someone?" she asked, then lightly slapped her forehead. "What am I thinking? You stay waiting on someone to save you."

"Captain Save-a-Ho!" Serena chimed in. More cackling.

I hadn't seen Von quietly gesturing to the security guards, so I was startled at suddenly being flanked by two mountainous men ready to rumble. At the sight of security, Luna and Serena stood up, clearly not wanting a scene. Serena flounced out first, smirking and still holding her drink. Luna followed close behind but paused to utter in my ear, "Have you heard the good news about Betty Brown? Her album will make such a great Christmas gift."

Her smug look told me something was up, but I had no time to ask what she was talking about because right as Luna melted into the crowd, Barbara appeared with a lanky chocolate-skinned man sporting a long black ponytail. "Nikki, this is Serge. He's the genius behind the fabulous women's line Reine." Barbara and I had just had a meeting about our biggest fashion advertisers, and Reine was at the top of the list. Serge preened, smoothing his white shirt, unbuttoned to the waist, and flipping his ponytail over his shoulder.

"It's a pleasure to meet you, Serge. Reine is one of my absolute favorite brands!" The DJ had put on "Ms. Fat Booty," and the whole party was rapping along with Mos Def. Serge put a bejeweled hand to his ear to indicate that he couldn't hear me. I tried again but he shook his head. I vaguely remembered that he was from the Côte d'Ivoire, so I dusted off my college French. "C'est tellement bruyant ici! J'adore vos créations, Serge. Merci d'être venu à la fête," I yelled over the music, hoping my accent would hold up at top volume.

Serge put a hand to his chest in shock. "Je suis impressionné, Mademoiselle Nikki. And I do like where you are going with *Sugar*."

My relief briefly made me forget that my feet were on fire. Barbara was beaming at me for once, so I tried my luck again. "I would love to work with you on an exclusive style feature."

"Absolument!" Serge snapped his fingers, beckoning his petite greyhound of an assistant, who sped over. She and Von worked out the details of a lunch in our office, then Barbara led him away to meet DJ Cassius and Latika, who'd just walked in.

Within thirty seconds of Serge's ponytail disappearing from view, I was sitting down with my heels off, holding a fresh drink. Sinclaire's incredible five-octave range and prepared set of Billboard #1 hits gave me a few moments to gather myself. I was so grateful for the break that I was initially annoyed at the feel of warm arms hugging me from behind. Then I looked down and saw Teresa's signature white nail polish. I yelped and turned to kiss her cheek, pulling her, along with Sofie and Denyse, who were standing behind her, into a group hug. Sofie had brought her man, MC WhiteHot, so I fist-bumped him as well.

"Chica, this party is fire!" Teresa hollered, but I was looking past her to one more person I hadn't greeted in their group: Derek. While his party gear—black leather pants, a fitted black polo, square-toed boots, silver jewelry—was less lawyer and more music artist, Derek had grown a neatly trimmed beard, which took his look in a more serious, grown-ass man direction. Slipping on my shoes, I stood up and, without thinking, reached out my hand, which he kissed as if I were royalty.

"So, you are the queen of this little shindig," Derek said, looking around, impressed.

"My team might say that I'm more of a despot," I yelled back. My inner bookworm high-fived my use of that word, but the supposed queen of the shindig cringed at my geekiness.

Derek just laughed. "After all the help you gave me with that gang assault case, I know you're not really cruel. Maybe we can split the difference at czarina."

I could feel my girls' eyes boring holes into my skull as they watched the exchange. At that moment, I realized that Derek was still holding my fingers. I yanked my hand back and stuck it in my pocket, gesturing with my other hand toward the banquette. "Make yourselves some drinks and hang."

Von emerged from the dance floor and was motioning for me to follow him. "Barbara," he mouthed, pointing across the room. There would be no rest.

"I have to spend some time schmoozing with my boss," I told my crew. "This whole area is mine, so you guys are good here. I'll be back."

I downed my drink and started to walk toward Von, stumbling after two steps. WhiteHot caught me and winked. I winked back gratefully, squared my shoulders, and took a deep breath to get myself together. I needed water and some time off my feet; instead, Von and I threaded through the crowded dance floor, air-kissing the friendlies and dodging the assholes. Then I felt a hand firmly grab my ass. I whipped around and came face-to-face with JJ, grinning wickedly. I couldn't afford to react, so I pressed my lips together and shook my head, gently pushing him away, even though I was tired of avoiding him.

"My friends are in my banquette," I told him quickly. "Go say hi and I'll be over in a sec." I took a sharp breath at the mental picture of JJ in his fresh whites chewing the fat with Derek in his all-black outfit. That was a lot of masculine energy in one place, but it was too late to pull back the invitation.

He put a finger under my chin, his signature move, but pulled it away before I could swat it away. "Okay, babe. Don't keep me waiting," he replied.

Von led me through the crush to Barbara and the power brokers she wanted me to meet. I must have looked a little worse for wear because he slipped me a bottle of water instead of another drink. I swayed again, grabbing Von's arm for support, hoping no one noticed. But Barbara's keen eye caught the whole thing.

"We good, newbie?" She leaned forward so her forehead was nearly touching mine and spoke low in my ear. I could smell the whiskey on Barbara's breath, but she seemed totally sober and steady. "I'm about to introduce you to my connect at Warner Music, so I need you to be on your A game."

"I got it, Barbara. Don't worry about me," I told her, trying to enunciate so she wouldn't process how buzzed I suddenly felt.

After shakily glad-handing several potential advertisers, I heard a disturbance near the DJ booth. Even over the dancehall mix the DJ was playing, I could make out angry shouting and wildly waving red-clad arms. Von and I looked at each other; it was MC RedHot. He was known for provoking many a party brawl.

"You get security and I'll go see what's up," I told Von and took off toward the fracas. The raised voices led me to my own banquette, where I saw RedHot standing over WhiteHot and my girls.

"I repeat, what is this muthafuckin' poser doing here?" RedHot was yelling at my friends, who were frozen in place, unsure how to handle the unreasonable fury of an entitled rapper. His ire was directed at WhiteHot. RedHot was a much bigger star, but WhiteHot was recognized as a better lyricist—plus he'd come up with his rap name first. Years ago, a music critic called out RedHot in *Vibe* magazine for biting WhiteHot's name, launching a bitter feud.

"Yo man, it's all good. Let's just chill." WhiteHot was trying to take the high road.

"Bitch, who are you telling to chill?" RedHot was apoplectic. "What I want you to do is take your ashy self and your washed-out woman out of this party."

That's when I knew everything was going left because WhiteHot did not like Sofie's name in anyone's mouth. All of a sudden, Barbara appeared at my side. "What the hell is MC WhiteHot doing here?" she fumed.

"I invited him along with his girlfriend—she owns a music industry hangout," I replied, understanding that I'd somehow screwed up and not wanting to confess that Sofie was my girl.

"What were you thinking, Nikki? Those two in the same room are a disaster waiting to happen."

"In my defense, I had no idea MC RedHot would show up." My slurred words undermined the already unconvincing message.

"So... you didn't think the party would be good? Because RedHot shows up at any decent event in the city. Never mind now. Just get WhiteHot out of here."

"But RedHot is the one who started acting crazy!"

"So? We need RedHot's cred more," Barbara insisted. "I want WhiteHot out."

At that moment, RedHot swung on WhiteHot but missed. Before he could swing again, Derek jumped between them. "Guys, it doesn't have to go down like this. We can all still enjoy the night."

Barbara dug a sharp elbow into my side, so I reluctantly said, "Actually, I'd like for you to leave, WhiteHot. I'm so sorry, it's just too much drama."

Derek frowned in confusion, while my friends stared at me, stunned. "Are you for real?" Sofie asked me incredulously.

Teresa chimed in, "Yeah, that's pretty uncool, Nik."

Only WhiteHot, recognizing that there was no win, gathered his white leather jacket to leave. We'd known each other through Sofie for years and I considered him a friend—which was likely why he was leaving calmly, and why it was especially hard to watch him do so.

"I'm out too," Sofie stood and grabbed her purse.

"Me too," Teresa said as Denyse nodded vigorously. "How are we supposed to stay and party after you freakin' kicked out our friends for doing nothing?" She caught sight of Kiara surveying the scene from a safe distance and rolled her eyes. "Have fun with your new crew."

Under Barbara's watchful gaze, there was no point in trying to explain. Teresa's ideas of right and wrong were unyieldingly black and white. There would be no easy convincing her in that moment that my boss had given me no choice, that I was still getting my bearings in a world that had already been biased against me, and that I couldn't afford to have both Barbara and MC RedHot mad at me. So I had to watch my crew file out angrily. Only Derek stopped on his way to the door to give me a quick hug. "That seemed complicated," he whispered. "Hope you're okay."

Seeing the crisis defused, the DJ put on a West Coast mix and the crowd rapped along with Ice Cube: "Today, I didn't even have to use my AK. I gotta say it was a good day!"

As I sat down in my now-empty banquette, the dense room tilted and spun; I could feel the humid air vibrating along with the pounding bass line. I tried to get my bearings and process what had just happened, but my internal compass was as impaired as my balance.

I wasn't alone for long as MC RedHot and his crew swarmed the space. They waved Sinclaire and her friends over. Von came back, then JJ showed up as well. Since I couldn't leave my own party, I gave in to the raucous energy. Rounds of shots were passed around until I no longer cared that everyone I actually loved had left. I no longer cared that RedHot was gloating. I no longer cared that the whole venue could see JJ's hands around my waist. The last thing I remember clearly was climbing on top of the table to gyrate in front of JJ and MC RedHot as the DJ played Missy Elliott's "Hot Boyz."

In that moment, the thrill of dancing on top of the table at a cover party for my magazine, in front of the biggest rapper in the world and the most powerful producer in the game, engulfed any other emotion. I let myself feel like the queen of all I surveyed, never once considering that maybe the right word was *despot* after all.

TWENTY-TWO

I expected to find the *Sugar* team in good spirits the next morning after the triumphant cover release party. Instead, our side of the Nu-Voices floor was strangely quiet, and no one would look at me as I wobbled down the hallway, late and nursing a pounding headache. I'd dunked my head under a frigid shower and mainlined two cups of coffee, but it had still taken all my strength to pull on a Juicy Couture tracksuit, gather my hair into a bun, and schlep to the subway. That rapturous Page Six write-up had declared that it had been the "event of the season." But the fact that I had woken up on top of my bed, dizzy and dehydrated, still in my yellow dress and fake eyelashes—and the total silence from Teresa and my other girls—told a different story.

Von's head was in his hands when I shuffled over to his desk to ask what was going on. He pointed to Sondra, who was lurking by my office door. Her hard-driving energy and staccato delivery would be taxing for my barely functional brain, but clearly something was up.

"That was quite an event, Nik. I can honestly name more celebs who were there than who weren't, so *Sugar* will for sure be the topic of conversation today. And you too, girl. None of us knew that you were going to end up being the life of the party!"

"Yeah, well, neither did I," I groaned as I sank into my sofa cushions, not yet able to face my desk. "Von, would you please, please get me some coffee," I called out, rousing him from his stupor. Normally, I would have gotten it myself, but the room suddenly listed to the side like a sailboat in a swell, so I figured I'd better not move.

"I am so not surprised that you need coffee. You were dancing your ass off when I left." Sondra plopped down next to me, then ruefully added, "I wished so hard that I'd stayed until the end when I read in Page Six that Jennifer Lopez showed up."

"Well, right now I'm wishing that I'd walked out with you," I replied, rubbing my temples.

"Well, you may need to add some hair of the dog to that cup when I tell you what's going on." Sondra turned to face me, her expression shifting from amused to serious. "It's about Betty Brown." I'd forgotten Luna's ominous statement about Betty at the party, but it came flooding back now. She continued, "I got a call from her label, and they're pushing her album release from August to December. They're even pulling her first single back so it won't have any airplay until November."

That would explain the six two-way messages I'd received from Kiara that morning that I hadn't read because I was too busy forcing myself to get ready to work. "But why would they do that?" I wailed. "The market in December will be full of major artists' releases that will totally swallow up her little album. And her single was supposed to go to radio tomorrow."

"I know, it was crazy to me too." Sondra shook her head. "I mean, all of her promotion is on deck, including our August issue."

Shit, *Sugar*'s August issue with Betty's cover was supposed to hit stores the week before her album was released. I was banking on her single being in heavy radio rotation along with the music video and all the accompanying marketing to drive our newsstand sales. Without it, our relatively unknown magazine with a totally unknown cover subject would be competing on newsstands with other established magazines and their very famous cover subjects. *Groove*'s August issue with Destiny's Child was starting to appear on newsstands in anticipation of their lead single from the *Charlie's Angels* soundtrack, "Independent Women"; it would eclipse *Sugar*'s sales even more than usual.

"Wait, what reason did the label give?" I asked.

"Apparently, the CEO of the label is cool with Alonzo Griffin." Sondra looked out toward the floor, her chest visibly rising as she took a deep breath. "I'm not supposed to know this, but it was Alonzo who convinced his buddy to push Betty's release. He wanted to time it with the holiday cover they're giving Betty and promised all kinds of special promotional stuff to seal the deal."

So, Luna *had* been gloating last night. I rolled my shoulders back and forth as I tried to think of a solve for the unmitigated disaster that *Sugar*'s August 2000 issue was about to become. It was made worse by the fact that Barbara had warned me about this exact thing. What Barbara said to me after she'd heard about Betty covering the August issue now rang in my ears: "Okay, newbie, you can't say that you don't know how cover sales work, so whatever happens as a result of this decision is on you." And it had turned out that putting a new artist on the cover had been a gamble that would now tank a critical issue.

I asked Sondra to leave so I could think. Fingers trembling, I called Kiara. She picked up after one ring. "Girl," she uttered.

"Girl," I moaned, our Black girl shorthand conveying heavy emotion.

"Did you see my messages? I've been trying to get you all morning." Kiara sighed. "I got called into Eternal Records first thing. Everyone's scrambling over here. Betty's crying. It's a mess."

"Trust me, it's about to be a bigger mess here," I whispered, figuring there was likely a small crowd outside my office door. "I guess I know what happened . . . but what happened?"

Kiara hesitated. "What I heard was that ya boy Alonzo told Eternal's CEO that he'd put Betty on *Groove*'s winter double issue with a sponsored release party, holiday merch, and everything. He even said he'd see if his boy who runs the Recording Academy would make an exception on the eligibility window and consider Betty for Best New Artist Grammy next year so she wouldn't have to wait until 2002."

"There's nothing you can do?" I cried. I knew the answer, but the magnitude of the situation was starting to sink in.

"You don't think I tried?" she exclaimed. "I pled our case all the way up to the CEO. Thought I might have a chance because Ricky's helped him out with venues for last-minute events." Kiara paused again and drew in a loud breath. "The real story is that Alonzo also threatened to withhold coverage of Eternal artists. The CEO probably shared that little tidbit with me so Ricky wouldn't be too pissed."

"That's the Alonzo playbook, all right. He always told me that it was easier to shake down your friends than your enemies," I uttered weakly.

"I'm so sorry, girl. I really wish there was more I could do," Kiara murmured. "I can only imagine the chaos this will cause on your end."

She had no idea. "Yeah, let me go face that music before it gets any worse."

The fact that I was freshly showered didn't make the trek to Barbara's office feel any less like a walk of shame. While I could see folks digging elbows into each other's sides as I passed, no one would look directly at me. I couldn't tell whether they felt sorry for me because the news had spread about Betty's album release or if they were all embarrassed for me after my tabletop shenanigans. Either way, it was a reminder of how mercurial urban publishing was, and that the vibe could switch from triumphant to tragic in a flash.

Barbara's back was to me as I approached, so I could only see the expanse of her wide shoulders, the coral leather of her sleeveless sheath dress, and the coiled cord to her desk phone stretched taut with the receiver missing, so I knew she was on a call. Hearing my soft knock on her door, Barbara spun around, said five words into the phone, "Here she is right now," and slammed the receiver back onto the base. "So, newbie, you had quite a night and now you're having an equally eventful morning, I hear," she said in a flat tone, her face unreadable.

In gearing myself up to tell Barbara about Betty Brown's release date, I had almost forgotten that she might have a lot to say about watching her new editor-in-chief body roll on a table in front of the man she'd cautioned me to avoid. And it seemed that she'd already heard about Betty. The pounding in my head got louder as I wished I'd had the presence of mind to come up with an opening gambit during my trek across the NuVoices floor.

"Barbara, I couldn't have known that Betty's single and album would get pushed." I quickly realized that my defensive tone was a mistake.

She blinked several times before responding. "That's how you're going to play this, Nikki? A'ight, let's go." She stood up, her high heels adding four inches, so she towered over me in my sneakers. "You're saying that you didn't think that booking Betty for a cover right after she visited *Groove*'s offices would make Alonzo retaliate?"

The glint in her eye told me that her question was rhetorical. "I guess I didn't know Alonzo could do this," I replied weakly.

"So, you didn't possess the good sense that God gave you to know that Alonzo has powerful relationships after two decades in the business, and that he wasn't about to let himself get scooped by a woman he still blames for getting him kicked out of the ivory tower?"

Another rhetorical question, but this time I stayed silent...because she was right. I was arrogant and presumptuous and naïve—a bad combination in a cutthroat world whose rules I was only now learning.

"I suppose this is my fault too. I'm the one who should have known better, but I let it slide because I was excited about Betty." Barbara heaved a sigh and shook her head. "And I liked your instinct to try to get her a cover first. Under normal circumstances, it was an aggressive risk that might have paid off big."

"Right? Betty could have put us on the map," I started, but Barbara held up her hand.

"But these are not normal circumstances, Nikki. I hired you despite your damaged reputation and fractured relationships. And now I have to deal with an August issue that is DOA on the newsstand, plus the fact that the industry is abuzz with not only our Betty cover humiliation but also my new EIC who thought it was a good idea to do a striptease at a cover party."

"It wasn't exactly a striptease..." I trailed off as Barbara's eyes widened.

"You are so consumed with fairness, newbie. When are you going to realize how weak that makes you sound? Everything you do will be judged behind the filter of your past transgressions. It is what it is."

All the fight in my body was replaced by fatigue. "What do I do, Barbara?"

"This August issue is going to cancel out the strides you were making. So, you fucking focus on doing your fucking job in the time that you have left, Miss *StyleList*," she replied slowly, carefully enunciating every word. Then she walked back around her desk and sat down. Without looking up, she told me, "You can go. In fact, go home. You look like hell."

I crept out of the office, into a cab, into my apartment, and under my covers. Another day that should have been victorious had turned to shit. I tried to call Teresa, Denyse, and Sofie to vent, but none of them picked up.

I got week-two sales figures for the August issue on the day that Serge visited the office to discuss a September fashion issue collab between Reine and *Sugar*. The numbers were predictably dreadful. It didn't matter how cool the design looked; most people won't buy a magazine if they don't recognize either the brand or the cover subject. *Sugar* was new and Betty Brown didn't even have a single out yet. At least the June and July issues had sold more than anyone thought, so we had a little wiggle room for August. But it was still a blow to my team's mojo; they'd been the darlings of the office for a couple months but were now walking around with hangdog looks as *Bella* and *Decode*'s August sales surpassed ours by a huge margin.

The one bright spot was the bales of mail addressed to me that had been delivered every day for a week. Those who had bought the August issue loved it, and many of them were writing in because of my editor's letter. I got mail about my readers' breakups, their scary new beginnings, the adventures they were having, and how much my message inspired them. The reaction was beyond anything I'd expected—which helped bolster my confidence at a moment when I needed it most. And that made what I wrote in Nikki's Notes even more true; I needed *Sugar* as much if not more than my readers did.

I tried to channel that energy as Serge breezed into our reception area like the embodiment of a sunny summer afternoon. His sky-blue linen shirt was unbuttoned to the waist to expose layers of gold and diamond chains; his white linen pants were oddly crisp, like he hadn't sat down all day; his long, straight hair was loose and flowing as if a fan were trained on him at all times; and the scent of bergamot and sage trailed him as he and his assistant walked down the hall.

"Salut, Serge. Welcome to our office." I double-kissed his cheeks in the French style. As he cast a critical eye across our floor, I was grateful that I'd strategically placed several oversized arrangements of pink and white peonies to break up the man cave décor, and that I'd had a caterer prepare a pretty lunch in the conference room.

"Merci, Nicole." Serge batted his eyes at me. He was wearing more mascara than I was. "I've been looking forward to our meeting, especially after I saw your August issue. I love how you styled that random girl. It was quite interesting. And Tyger is a fabulous photographer."

Von had asked Imani, Freddy, and Sondra to join us in the conference room for lunch to chat about the collab. We winced in unison at Serge's characterization of Betty as "that random girl."

"Betty Brown is going to be a huge star when her album comes out," Sondra started, but I put a hand on her arm. Serge clearly didn't care, and I could see that his attention was already wandering toward his assistant, who was piling blackened salmon and grilled vegetables on his plate. To get Serge's attention back, I motioned for Von to pour him some of the crisp Sancerre I'd put on ice.

"Très jolie." Serge sighed as the glass was placed in front of him. "How did you know that I simply cannot eat fish without white wine?"

"A lucky guess," I said, hoping the wine would relax him. "We'd love to show you our idea for a September issue spread for Reine's fall line."

Freddy pulled out a mood board that we'd worked on until the wee hours the night before. Serge's fashion line, Reine, featured edgy silhouettes in classic, quality fabrics. Each piece had a distinctive crown logo embroidered somewhere visible yet inconspicuous. Our idea was to do a shoot where we used models of all sizes to showcase how Reine would make every woman look like a queen. We would build sets with elaborate floral backdrops, and we'd have a few diamond crowns and tiaras on hand to mix in with the accessories. The detailed mood board reflected the lush regal vibe we envisioned for the shoot.

Freddy explained the concept, then proudly placed the mood board on the table in front of Serge. As a size-fourteen fashion stylist, this concept was especially close to her heart.

Serge's face contorted, then he squinted and tapped on an image of one of the plus-sized models. "What is that?"

Freddy thought he was indicating the flowers. "That's a representation of one of the oversized floral backdrops we would create."

"No, this woman." Serge tapped the board a little harder. "What is that?"

Imani sat up and frowned, clearly displeased at his use of the word *that* to describe the model. "That's a beautiful Black woman, Serge, who would look gorgeous in your designs," she explained patiently.

He rolled his eyes at her and took an audible gulp of his wine. "Yes, I can see it's a woman, but why on earth do you think that she"—more loud tapping—"would look good in my clothes?"

Freddy's face crumpled. "These are your customers," she said through slightly trembling lips. "They, I, love Reine, and we thought that all women would like to see themselves represented as the queens that they are."

"So, you really are proposing that you put my clothing on this... this fatty?" Serge looked incredulous, then waggled his index finger. "Absolument pas! Absolutely not!"

As he calmly picked up a fork and speared a piece of salmon, the rest of us froze, only our eyes darting toward one another's, making contact then skating away before we could convey more than collective disbelief.

I was seething but thinking of the advertising dollars Reine had already contributed to *Sugar*'s coffers. "Your clothing is sized up to sixteen. Don't you want all of Reine's potential consumers to see themselves in your clothing?" I asked carefully, keeping my expression neutral.

"T'es fou? Why would I want that? And who even wants to see that?" Serge downed his wine and motioned to Von to pour him some more. "No, I am selling them fantasy, not reflecting the sad reality of their undisciplined lives."

I could see the tears forming in Freddy's eyes and Imani's fists balling up. Sondra hadn't said much until that moment, when she muttered, "The nerve of this mofo," under her breath. It came out much louder than she must have intended because Serge swung toward her and slowly asked, "Excusez moi?"

I shook my head at Sondra before she could reply. Von was about to pour more wine into Serge's glass, but I motioned for him to stop and stood up. "Serge, we are done here. I'd be happy to make you a to-go plate, but I'm not going to sit here and let you insult my team or my readers," I said, much more decisively than I felt.

"Suit yourself." Serge gathered his things and stomped out of the conference room without a backward glance.

I expected him to walk toward the reception desk. Instead, Serge marched across the NuVoices floor and right into Barbara's office. None of us spoke as we watched him through her glass wall, clearly relaying his umbrage-filled version of what had just happened via cartoonishly animated gestures. I sat heavily back into my chair, contemplating the gravity of what I'd done.

Suddenly, I heard snapping behind me, then light clapping, then thunderous applause. I turned to see Von, Imani, Freddy, and Sondra giving me a standing ovation. Even though I hadn't considered this when I was kicking our biggest fashion advertiser out of the conference room, I hoped the pendulum of office opinion about me might briefly swing in a positive direction again.

I tried to hold on to that optimism when Barbara beckoned me into her office. She pointed to her sofa, so I sat down and watched her pace back and forth, her long legs covering the length of the room in a few steps. Finally, in a low, even voice that I now understood indicated the depths of her fury, she said, "Please consider yourself to be officially on thin ice, Nikki. Serge pulled his ads from both *Sugar* and *Bella*. So, you just cost us hundreds of thousands of dollars, at a time when the company cannot afford to lose a single penny. And your August issue is circling the drain."

Barbara stopped in front of the sofa, but instead of looking down at me, she closed her eyes and rubbed her forehead with the palm of her hand. "The only thing saving you is how much your June and July issues exceeded our sales projections."

I started to say something, but Barbara shook her head. Her last words to me that day were: "Thin ice, Nicole Rose. Very thin fucking ice."

I trotted to the ladies' room as fast as I could without attracting attention. My tears flowed the minute I locked myself in a bathroom stall, the sting of Barbara's words as sharp and unexpected as stepping on a piece of sea glass on a New York City sidewalk. My responsibility was to defend and represent my audience, or so I thought. I hadn't known that, as the EIC of *Sugar*, I'd still be getting caught between my values and my job.

I stayed in the stall for a long time, at a loss about what to do. What finally got me out of the bathroom was remembering the promise I'd made to my readers in my last editor's letter. Wasn't this a moment to be transparent? I decided to rewrite the September Nikki's Notes while the emotions were fresh, so my eyes were still red and puffy as I sat at my desk, scribbling my internal monologue into a notebook.

Hey, girlfriend. I used to be a senior editor at a mainstream fashion magazine that almost never featured women who look like us on its pages. Most of the models were white, six feet tall, and not over size two. My editor-in-chief wouldn't even consider putting Tyisha on the cover—which is partially why I'm extra honored to have the host of America's Next Cover Girl *be on the cover of Sugar's first September fashion issue! Sure, I occasionally succeeded in getting stories about Black women into the mainstream mag. But more often, I'd pitch ideas that would be shot down. When that happened, I'd protest, then give up.*

When I became the EIC of Sugar, *I decided that, no matter what, I would create a magazine that represented us—and that I would defend this audience of dope, fun, goal-oriented women of color without compromise.*

Well, today I was asked to compromise that vision by none other than the designer of a popular women's fashion brand. I was told that beautiful Black women with real curves aren't good enough to be photographed in their clothes. I'm so freakin' tired of people imposing beauty standards on women of color that don't jibe with how we feel about ourselves. So, girlfriend, this time I risked it all to protest—even though I knew the designer was a major advertiser, which meant our business could lose a lot of money.

Although it was scary to anger the bean counters at my company, it felt amazing to finally stand strong for what I believe in— and to defend the right of every woman to see herself looking like a queen. I hope you feel the love that I and the entire Sugar *team put into this September issue. And I hope you keep your integrity intact and walk your talk this month. I've got your back if you've got mine.*

Love, Nikki

Although writing the letter had calmed my nerves, I knew I was done for the day. As if he had read my mind, I heard a light tapping at my door, then Von peeked into my office.

"Ready to get the fuck out of here, boss?" he asked softly. "Your team wants to buy you a drink."

Anything in which friendly faces and tequila were involved sounded good to me. I grabbed my bag.

TWENTY-THREE

Golden light the same color as the champagne that JJ and I had been drinking the night before blazed through my bedroom window, waking me. The sun had just started rising as I'd fallen asleep, but that hadn't kept me up like the intense beams now roasting my closed eyelids. I was so tired, it felt like I'd slept only as long as it took for me to roll from one side of my bed to the other. But my clock told me that six hours had passed, and that I was running late to meet my friends for brunch.

Only the thought of the maple-glazed bacon and crispy skillet potatoes at Sofie's Café gave me the motivation to haul myself out of bed. There would be no shower because I couldn't be late for the first time I was seeing my girls since *Sugar*'s July cover party a month and a half ago. I threw on timeworn jeans with faded thighs, a crumpled vintage Metallica T-shirt, and flip-flops; then I grabbed my new Louis Vuitton crossbody and shambled to the elevator. I was already in a taxi before I realized that I'd forgotten to brush my teeth or comb my hair.

Sofie hadn't taken any of my calls, so I was surprised when I got the message that she and the girls wanted to meet at her café for brunch. Though I'd managed to get Teresa and Denyse on the phone since the party, they'd made excuses to end the conversation after a few minutes. My friends had never been this mad at me before, but my schedule of twelve-hour workdays followed by near-nightly dinners and parties made it easier to ignore.

Von was still bringing me invitations to sexy events every day; if I wasn't invited to something, JJ was, so there was nowhere that we couldn't or didn't go. Since the rumors that JJ and I were seeing each other had already been confirmed at the *Sugar* party, we no longer made it a point to arrive and leave separately. And I stopped caring what people thought—even though I knew that hanging out with JJ put me in the same category as an uncomfortable number of music video dancers and other random hangers-on. We never talked about the status of our "thing," and the nights started to blur together in a haze of dance floors, drunken sex, and way too little sleep.

I was getting sucked into a fever dream that was unlike anything I'd ever experienced, while my former life seemed less and less familiar. I leaned my head against the worn leather seat and closed my eyes as TLC's "Unpretty" came on the radio, the lyrics hitting home in a new way. When the taxi turned down Grand Street and pulled up in front of Sofie's Café, I realized how long it had been since I'd been here. I stopped before opening the café door, listening to the DJ mix '80s disco hits and willing my body to relax before I faced the music inside.

Sofie had cleared the entire back half of her café for us, no small feat at peak brunch time on a weekend. Teresa met me near the door and enveloped me in a silent hug, then led me to a circular table, where Denyse was already sitting. The table and surrounding area had been cordoned off from the rest of the café by a dense line of chairs. Denyse remained seated as I approached, her eyes widening at my bedraggled appearance.

"What in the actual hell?" she exclaimed, ignoring Teresa's not-so-subtle headshake. "What? She looks awful." Denyse turned back to me, unabashedly looking me up and down. "When is the last time you slept? And why does your hair look like there might be some twigs lodged in there somewhere?"

Denyse reflexively smoothed her own neat bob. Among my girls, she'd been the one with the most appreciation for my straightened hair. My wearing it curly again seemed to add to her impression that urban music and publishing was one big den of iniquity. In fairness, my coif was looking extra chaotic this morning.

"Let her be, Denyse," Teresa chimed in, always ready to defend my hair at its most unruly. But then she leaned in to sniff my shoulder and her nose wrinkled. "But why do you smell like a nightclub bathroom? You're giving off booze, smoke, and despair."

I was desperate for a cup of coffee so I could be fully awake for the drubbing I was apparently going to receive. "Well, hello to you too," I croaked, looking around and catching the eye of my favorite waiter. After I pantomimed pouring a cup of coffee followed by prayer hands, he gave me a thumbs-up and went off to get me my usual double-shot latte. "I was out super late last night or, rather, this morning," I admitted. "So yeah, I rolled out of bed and came directly here."

"Um, no shit," Denyse deadpanned.

"Oh, leave her ass alone," I heard from behind me, and turned to see Sofie gracefully winding her way around the line of forbidding chairs. As we all took in her satin baby-blue Enyce tracksuit, pink high-tops, and blond cornrows, Sofie laughed. "I'm going to be an extra in WhiteHot's music video shoot later," she told us, although her outfit wasn't that different from her normal look.

Until that moment, I hadn't realized how much I'd missed her. My emotions bubbled up as a loud exclamation: "Sof!" I ran over and wrapped her in a strong hug that must have smelled unpleasant. "I'm so sorry, Sofie," I whispered, holding her tight.

"All right, all right," Sofie said as she pried my arms from around her waist. "Let's go sit and talk it out."

The waiter had placed my coffee at the seat next to Denyse, but Sofie moved it to the other side of the table. She and Teresa clustered near Denyse, leaving my seat with a suspicious amount of space around it.

"Is this an intervention or what?" I asked, my voice rising. The last thing I wanted was a pile on from my closest friends after the tough workweek I'd just survived.

The three of them glanced at one another sheepishly. Then Teresa piped up. "Not an intervention, Nik. But we need to know what is going on with you."

Seeing that this would be a two-latte brunch, I downed my coffee and pointed to my cup so the waiter would bring me some more. I drank my second while we ordered our food, waiting until our menus had been cleared to launch into a caffeine-fueled declamation.

"Okay, I know that party was an awful situation, but I seriously didn't know what to do. My boss was in my ear about how much we needed RedHot at the party, and she literally ordered me to ask WhiteHot to leave. You guys know I would have never done that otherwise, but I was up against a wall. That event had to be a success, or it might have been my job." I said all of that with one breath, then braced for their reaction. When none of them said anything, I added, "I really am sorry."

"What are you sorry for, Nikki?" Sofie finally asked, disapproval chasing any warmth or mercy from her tone. "For kicking my man out of your party because he's apparently not famous enough for you and *Sugar*? For not saying anything when your boss dissed him? Or for being part of a culture that only respects knuckleheads and not real artists?"

Sofie's words were a knife in my side. "I mean, I'm still trying to understand this whole world, Sof. I would never diss your man."

"But you did," Teresa chimed in. "And it was so unlike you that now we're all concerned."

"Yeah, you know we love you, but you haven't exactly been sitting at home sad for the past few weeks." Denyse's judgmental tone was really starting to get on my nerves.

My annoyance must have been visible on my face because Teresa quickly added, "Don't be upset, Nikki... but you did stay at that party all night, right? And you've called us maybe once or twice since, on your way to another party or in between meetings. I mean, these are not the actions of someone who is particularly contrite." Teresa's comments stung more than Sofie's angry questions and Denyse's cool observations.

"You guys didn't want to talk to me," I exclaimed. "So I gave up and focused on dealing with the stress of my new job and my crazy boss at my failing company that I have a little over three months left to save."

"You've also been preoccupied with your fancy apartment and your shiesty new friend, Kiara, your shiesty new man, JJ, and your... standing in this shiesty new world," Teresa flung back.

Thinking about how different her attitude had been toward JJ the night of my move and feeling defensive of Kiara, I snapped, "Are you serious right now? Why does everyone and everything in my 'new world' have to be shiesty?" I looked directly into Teresa's eyes. "And you of all people know that Alonzo has been talking shit about me for years, and he made sure my reputation was a mess before I'd even moved into my new office."

"And you decided to handle it by partying until dawn with sketchy dudes and ignoring your real friends?" Denyse interrupted.

"Again, you guys haven't wanted to talk to me, remember? Every time I tried, you would all make excuses to sign off. Except you, Sofie, since you wouldn't even pick up when I called." I pressed my lips together so they wouldn't quiver. "I really feel like you guys aren't even trying to hear me right now."

I'd lost my appetite, so when our food arrived, I could only watch my friends tuck into their eggs and French toast while I nibbled on a piece of bacon. Mimosas arrived for all of us, but my stomach flipped over at the thought of drinking any more champagne.

"Wait, what do you mean by 'I have three months to save *Sugar*'?" Sofie asked.

I had hoped to never let them know that NuVoices was a ticking time bomb, but I'd let it slip. "When Barbara hired me, she told me that the company was in trouble and that I would have about six months to significantly increase *Sugar*'s revenue or NuVoices would go under."

Denyse did a double take. "And you still took the job? What were you thinking?"

"I was thinking that I would finally get to realize my fucking dream, Dee," I hurled back, tears of frustration gathering in my eyes. "Do you have any idea how brutal this has been? And I can't even talk to my team about what's going on. They think I'm responsible for the success of *Sugar*, but they have no idea the goddamned future of the company is at stake."

"Nik, I'm sorry about that. I know what it's like to run a business in tough times. I get that you've been stressed," Sofie acknowledged. "But it doesn't just excuse everything."

"Listen, bonita," Teresa said in a softer tone, "none of us have ever seen you like this, and we are legitimately worried about you."

"I know Jerome Jermaine's reputation from being around rappers," Sofie added. "I also know how easy it can be to get caught up in the industry and all the stupid shit that goes on."

"Everyone thinks JJ is such a bad guy, but he's been cool with me." It was easier to defend him than myself.

"You really think he's only 'cool' with you?" Sofie used air quotes around the word *cool*.

"Also, what does that even mean?" Teresa asked me. She put down her fork and crossed her arms. "You're right—of all people, I know how awful Alonzo was, and is. So why are you going down that path again with JJ? I'll admit that he came on real strong at first, but he showed his ass real quick. Do you seriously not see the similarities?"

Her words shifted everything around me out of focus. Denyse was talking, the busboy was refilling water glasses, Sofie was motioning for more mimosas; but I was suddenly unable to concentrate. The only thing that cut through the haze was "Upside Down," the song the DJ had just put on. My thoughts about JJ and Alonzo mixed with Diana Ross singing "... boy, you turn me inside out, and round and round..."

Maybe their respective fondness for being called *Daddy* should have clued me in, but I hadn't seen all the parallels between JJ and Alonzo until that moment. They were both "ballers" with enough clout that most people in urban music and publishing knew their names. And they were both known for being ruthless and charismatic and successful, the kind of men who got everything they wanted. That's why Alonzo couldn't deal with me leaving and why he wouldn't let go of his false impression that I'd betrayed him. JJ had spent more time taking actual care of me, but he'd been no less clear that even though our "thing" wasn't exclusive, my body was his.

I felt Teresa's hand on my shoulder, shaking me back to the present. I hadn't noticed her get up and walk around to my side of the table, so it was a small surprise to look up and see her anxious face so close to mine as she asked, "You okay, chica?"

"No, I'm really not okay, Tee," I replied. I had wanted to see my girls and pad my stomach with some greasy carbs, and now I was sitting there, questioning all my life choices.

"Look, Alonzo was an intense, yearlong emotional roller coaster for you. Even though you and I both know that shit was crazy, I was there for all the highs and lows. And I'm still here while you deal with the consequences of pissing off that woman-hating narcissist," Teresa said, her hand still resting on my shoulder. "I love you, but I do *not* want to do it again, especially when we can all see it coming a mile away."

I shook Teresa's hand off and muttered, "I didn't come here to be attacked." Then I stood up, scraping my chair against the tile floor, threw some cash on the table, and hung the crossbody over my shoulder. "You guys have no idea how completely absurd it is to be me right now. If I'm too aggressive, I'm an asshole. If I'm too submissive, I'm a doormat. If I'm at the office too much, I'm a workaholic. If I'm at the club, I'm a party girl. If I grow the business, I'm a sellout. If I protect my readers and ignore the business, *Sugar* might go away." I put on my sunglasses to hide my damp eyes. "Am I a slut or a boss or a bookworm or somebody's bitch? Honestly, I have no fucking idea. And I don't know what you all want from me." My voice got more and more strident as I realized how much I wanted to get away from this bootleg intervention. "And, for the record, Kiara was the first person to warn me about JJ. So maybe *she's* not the problem here."

Without giving my girls a chance to reply, I spun on my heels and was outside in seconds. The midday sun bore down on my shoulders, but getting into a hot subway or smelly taxi was too oppressive to face. So, I walked through SoHo to Broadway, turned south, and didn't break stride until I got to Tribeca. There was a street festival clogging my neighborhood with rows of food vendors and a DJ scratching his way through an unexpectedly cool mix of Biggie and Busta. Normally, I would have bought a falafel from one of the vendors and hung out for a while. Instead, I threaded my way through the head-bopping crowd, stopped at a bodega to get Tylenol and Gatorade, then traipsed the remaining two blocks home. I immediately climbed back into bed and pulled the covers over my head, feeling much worse than before.

TWENTY-FOUR

Kiara woke me up from my nap by calling four times in a row. I finally picked up to a loud, "Oh, thank God!"

Then she let me know that Ricky had to travel last minute so wouldn't be able to take her to MC RedHot's fashion show that night for the launch of his new sneaker line. Kiara had clients who'd be there so she needed to show her face, and she didn't want to go solo—which I understood because his events were always unruly. It was much easier for women to roll in pairs. I didn't want to leave my apartment, but since Kiara was calling in a favor, I agreed to meet her at the after party.

Kiara told me that the invite requested that everyone wear sneakers, which I interpreted to mean a sporty outfit. My denim shorts, red tank top, and Air Jordans were a sharp contrast to the women in sequined minidresses paired with bedazzled running shoes and men in ice cream–colored suits with white sneakers ringing the Harlem venue's velvet rope. I found Kiara at the bar, wearing a red satin jumpsuit with gold leather high-tops. Her hair was pulled tightly into a bun, showcasing her enormous diamond studs; the only ring she wore was a three-finger gold ring that spelled out her husband's name: RICKY.

"Oh, love, I guess I should've said something." Kiara grinned as she took in my outfit. "Nothing RedHot ever does is casual. Everything he touches is blinged out. When in doubt, think sequins."

"Yep, knew that and inconveniently forgot it tonight. At least I didn't bring a backpack." I wouldn't have had the energy for much more glam anyway, but Kiara didn't need to know that I really wanted to be in my pajamas, eating takeout and popping a rented movie into my DVD player.

"No matter what you have on, you always look great," Kiara told me. Her gaze darted across the room. "I see one of Ricky's clients over there. Let me go say a quick hi. Be back in a sec."

Having hung out with her at many of these events, I knew that could mean five or forty-five minutes. Feeling little desire to circulate, I settled onto a barstool to people-watch and listen to the DJ mixing Goodie Mob, Silkk the Shocker, and OutKast. I hadn't been there long enough to know if Southern hip hop was part of his set or the musical theme of the night, but I was into it.

It seemed as if every major urban entertainment heavy-hitter was milling around in the velvet-walled speakeasy. I didn't think I would ever get used to being around so many arbiters of culture in one place—or to being one of them myself. The hierarchy in the room was as defined as the Hindu caste system, with the most powerful ballers emitting a centrifugal force that pulled pleasure-seekers to their respective VIP sections. They each hung with a crew of formidable guys who were rewarded for their hype-man loyalty with riches and access.

Then there were the lowliest guys in the food chain, with their pants belted mid-thigh to expose Calvin Klein underwear, the only designer item they could afford. These were the worker bees in the industry, hoping to one day catch a break and become a rich hype man or even a baller. They buzzed from banquette to banquette, looking for someone willing to let them stay and enjoy a little nectar in the form of Cristal or cocaine. Because a baller's objective was to pack his area with hot women, it was with a great degree of salty reluctance that any one of them would relinquish a space that a video vixen could be occupying for a worker B-boy on the come up.

As I watched the sagging-pants dudes hovering around the VIP, I realized how rarely I saw couples at any of these events. Save for a very few female music, style, or media executives, these parties were largely populated by naïve women not more than a decade out of puberty, whose goal was to get as close as they could to the primary baller in the most sought-after banquette. They'd arrive in bright, giggling cliques, like a chatter of parakeets, hanging together until the more attractive and opportunistic among them splintered off into smaller groups that reflected their higher pecking order. It was easier for two or three of the prettiest girls to get into a VIP section than a mixed group of six or seven.

Even if one of these pretty girls managed to be on a baller's arm as he walked out, they would never be seen together at the next party. Occasionally, one of the executives (like me) and one of the ballers (like JJ) would be observed together at more than three events and, therefore, deemed a "thing." But these "things" rarely lasted beyond the change of a season, according to Kiara, who was, ironically, in one of the few high-profile marriages in our circle.

My intention had been to order club soda, but the scene was too demoralizing to face without proper social lubrication. I'd guzzled half a too-tart whiskey sour when I glimpsed a familiar muscly bicep and set of fresh cornrows. Hopping off the barstool, I stood on my tiptoes and looked over the expanse of red to see JJ holding court in a banquette. I hadn't told him that I would be at this party, nor had he mentioned that he was going. I was reminded that the status of our relationship was "thing"—and of the uncomfortable comparisons to Alonzo that I'd been pushing to the back of my mind since the morning.

I'd never anonymously watched JJ in a social setting and was impressed anew by the confident way he managed the acolytes clustered around him. He'd laid claim to the VIP section adjacent to RedHot, and their combined energy created the nexus of the party's activity. It was all bobbing heads and hands in the air in their corner, with only the best-looking girls and most determined B-boys getting within twenty yards of either JJ or RedHot. I was debating whether to make my way over there when I saw JJ lean down and whisper into the ear of a woman I couldn't see enough of to recognize. I caught periodic flashes of her profile before it would disappear but couldn't make out who the black hair, glossy red lips, and pointed talon nails belonged to—until she climbed up to stand on the back of the banquette, and I saw that it was Luna.

"They had a 'thing' back in the day." I wasn't sure when Kiara had reappeared next to me, but she'd caught me staring at JJ as he casually draped an arm around Luna while she shook her hips in time to 112's "Anywhere."

"For real?" I swiveled my head to now stare at Kiara, who was nodding at me with an I-told-you-so look. Fatigue and annoyance added some acidity to my tone. I thought about Teresa's comments at brunch that morning. "Is there anything else I should know?"

Kiara cocked her head. "Nikki, I *told* you that JJ has a rep. He used to be one of the biggest modelizers in the city."

I drew in a long breath, feeling contrite; she *had* warned me. As I exhaled, I fully processed the level of Luna's wrath after she saw JJ kissing me. I had now taken two things that she considered to be hers.

I might have stayed put for a while to spy on my lover and my archenemy, but I caught a glimpse of salt-and-pepper locs coming through the door: Alonzo. He always seemed to pick me out in a crowd, so I hopped off my perch and turned toward the bar. As I pressed two fingers against my mouth, Teresa's words skittered across my mind: *I know how awful Alonzo was, and is. So why are you going down that path again with JJ? Do you seriously not see the similarities?*

I turned my head very slightly to view the masses around JJ's banquette part like the Red Sea to let Alonzo through. I watched him clink glasses with JJ and kiss Luna on the cheek, then quickly turned back around before he spotted me. Any certainty that my friends didn't understand what I was up against faded as I wondered why I was attracted to yet another emotionally unavailable, entitled baller. I'd spent years trying to be invisible to Alonzo in the cloistered world of high-end fashion where I'd felt like an interloper. And now I had thrown myself into the center of Alonzo's sphere of influence—where I somehow felt as if I belonged. Why were danger and indifference more compelling to me than stability and prestige?

As more people thronged the area around me, trying to get a bartender's attention, everyone near the bar had to jostle for space. To my left, Kiara was obliviously chatting with an A&R executive who claimed to have discovered Betty Brown. I was still lost in thought, but a few determined shoves on my right side brought me out of my reverie.

"My bad, ma." A man in a red satin button-down and white fedora held up both hands. "I come in peace, pretty lady. Just trying to get a Henny since my assistant forgot to add it to my bottle service." He jabbed a thumb in the air toward a remote corner of the speakeasy where I gathered he had a reserved banquette. "I got a whole table of top-shelf vodka and some fruity-ass mixes that I don't even like."

"All good." I smiled weakly, hoping he'd take the hint and move on.

No such luck. White fedora dude had looked me up and down and leaned in so close, the brim of his hat brushed my forehead, and I could see dark ovals of sweat turning the armpits of his shirt a deep maroon. "Man, I got a roster of dimes over there, but none of them are as cute as you in your little Daisy Dukes. You here with someone?"

I inclined my head toward Kiara, but White Fedora chuckled. "Nah, I mean, are there any men here that I gotta worry about?"

I glanced over at JJ, who was deep in conversation with Alonzo as Luna poured herself another drink. "I guess not," I said reluctantly.

"All right, so I got you for the rest of the night." White Fedora inched closer, which I didn't think was possible. "Let me buy you a cocktail. You don't never need to pull out your wallet around me."

"I think I'm straight," I insisted, but he was already shaking his head.

"Nah, I bet you need something. Let me at least introduce you to my artist," he told me proudly as the enormous hunks of diamond in his ears caught the light. "I bet he'll want to put you in his next video when he sees you."

"I'm not a dancer! I'm the editor-in-chief of *Sugar* magazine," I blurted with an indignant snort.

"Oh, okay, Miss EIC. My bad again. You was just looking so fine." A couple droplets of White Fedora's spittle landed on my cheek. But I was caught in a crush of partiers with no easy escape. "I see a drink isn't gonna impress you. So how about a trip on my PJ to Miami?"

I was trying to figure out a graceful exit when I felt the horde around us being pulled apart and shoved aside. Before I could respond, JJ pushed the last few feet toward us, then clapped a heavy hand on White Fedora's shoulder. "Eddie, my man. When are you going to send me that track?" he boomed. Then JJ wrapped me in an embrace and kissed me. "I see you've met my girl, Nikki," he spoke in White Fedora's general direction while keeping his eyes trained on me.

"Your girl?" White Fedora seemed shook, which told me that JJ was much higher on the food chain. "I didn't know that."

"Neither did I," I told him. I poked Kiara in the back and said low in her ear, "I'm going to the ladies' room. This situation is no bueno."

Kiara spun around and came face-to-face with a flustered White Fedora, a flinty JJ, and me, likely looking as irritated as I felt. She smoothly turned to JJ and said, "Well, hello, stranger. I haven't seen you all night. Ricky told me to tell you wassup."

While she distracted JJ and White Fedora, I slipped away to a nearby bathroom to splash cold water on my face. I stopped to stare at the snowy, owlish combination of my pale puffy cheeks and angry, yellow-tinged eyes in the mirror. I had to get out of there, but JJ was waiting for me.

"'Neither did I.' Really?" he fumed. "What was that about, Nikki?"

Biting back a caustic comment, I tried for frosty ignorance instead. "What do you mean, JJ? You've never called me your girl before. How would I know?"

"You would know because I fucking said it," he riposted. "And even if you were somehow unclear, you decide to play me in front of that joker?"

"Play you? Uh, I think you're the one playing me," I said as calmly as I could, digging my nails into my palms so I wouldn't yell at him in the middle of the party. "I walked in, not expecting to find you here, only to see you hugged up on Luna. I know we're not exclusive, but I don't particularly appreciate an entire MC RedHot party watching you cozy up to someone who publicly hates me."

JJ's mocking laugh made me even more mad. "First of all, you didn't say anything about coming to this party, so I'm the one who wasn't expecting to see you here," he replied, rolling his eyes. "Second, I'm not fucking Luna. She's just been around forever, so I know her."

"In the biblical sense, right?" I interrupted.

"A while back, but yes," he admitted. "Third, I already told you that"—he gestured toward my shorts—"is mine. So, I sure don't want to see you out here letting greasy Eddie push up on you."

JJ wasn't wrong about White Fedora; he was pretty greasy. But I didn't want to give him the satisfaction. "Eddie seemed nice enough to me. I wasn't going to come but Kiara asked me to be her plus-one at the last minute. And I'm glad I did because now I know what's up."

"I keep trying to tell you that nothing is up," JJ started, but I held up my hand to stop him.

"It's cool, JJ. I'm going to leave so you can have fun in peace."

I started to walk away but JJ grabbed me, hard enough that I knew there would be faint markings on my arm the next day. His sweet tone belied his steel grip. "I don't want you to leave like this. Why don't you come and have a drink? Maybe you and Luna can make up."

I looked toward JJ's banquette to see Alonzo watching us intently. With a smug grin, he gave me an exaggerated salute. Instead of turning on my heel and rushing out like I instinctively wanted to do, I brought my hand to the back of JJ's neck and pulled him close for a long kiss. Behind JJ's head, I slowly raised a middle finger in Alonzo's direction.

TWENTY-FIVE

It took me 180 seconds too long to understand everything that our October cover subject's manager was telling me. After I heard him say, "Roxy has decided that she doesn't want to be on your cover," a wave of white noise crested in my brain and washed away all other sound for a few minutes. I knew that I couldn't pull another stunt like I had with Sinclaire and the July cover because Roxy, a number-one Billboard rapper who had also launched a successful beauty empire, was too established to risk burning a bridge with. The fact that we had landed a music artist of Roxy's caliber at all was a miracle, but Sondra and I had pitched the October power theme and promised a concept shoot on the level of Betty Brown's. (Betty's August cover hadn't sold well, but the entertainment and style industries thought it was dope enough to now take my phone calls.)

    I thought I had a killer one-two punch with Tyisha, whom we'd photographed exclusively in Black designers for the September fashion issue cover, followed by Roxy covering October. Now, it was falling apart—again.

    I had both palms over my closed eyes, not processing any words other than "... doesn't want to be on your cover," when I heard the manager say something about *Groove*, the name a faint echo as if he'd yelled it from the other side of a large field. "Wait, what did you say about *Groove*?" I lifted my head.

There was a long impatient sigh, then Roxy's manager slowly repeated, "I said that I'm telling you as a courtesy that Roxy will be on *Groove*'s October icons cover instead. They're letting her guest edit the whole issue, plus they gave her the second cover ad placement for her new skin-care launch for free."

So, Alonzo had pulled out stops to steal this cover from me, even giving up the enormous revenue that the back cover advertising placement normally generates. *Groove* could afford to do that, while *Sugar* could not. Alonzo had been seething after I flipped him off at MC RedHot's party. I'd watched Alonzo's expression change from disbelief to comprehension to pure rage. When I broke free from that spontaneous kiss, I knew three things: I would never be able to fully trust JJ again; Alonzo was not done seeking vengeance; and neither man would let me go easily.

My own anger had already replaced any last vestiges of fear. Imagining Alonzo crowing with Luna over besting me yet again, the competitive spirit I'd honed on my high school track team returned: I would not let him win without a fight. I calmly ended the conversation with Roxy's manager, then called an emergency team meeting.

There was a conspicuously long silence when I explained that Roxy was a no-go for our October cover. The team had likely surmised that *Groove* stealing the cover was driven by Alonzo's hatred for me as much as it was by his desire to dominate the urban publishing world. Even though they had no idea that there were only a couple issues left on *Sugar*'s countdown clock, everyone in that conference room was clearly disappointed.

"I've already pulled all the looks," Freddy finally wailed. "I got so many designers who had never given me the time of day to release their best samples because it was for Roxy."

Von patted her shoulder, even though he seemed more upset than anyone. He'd already confessed to me that Roxy was his latest girlfriend's favorite rapper of all time and that he'd promised her an autographed CD. I wondered if this would be the end of yet another one of Von's thirty-day relationships.

"Look, Alonzo Griffin is obviously gunning for me. And I'm fucking sick of it!" I registered the disbelief in the room as they heard me curse. But that f-bomb involuntarily roared out of me like a heat-seeking missile targeting an infrared Alonzo.

"I know that's right!" Sondra bellowed. As the entertainment director, it had taken a lot of work on her part to get Roxy's team to agree to the deal and iron out all the details of the cover shoot. "I'm not trying to let *Groove* keep pilfering our hits."

"Agreed," Imani added. She felt an affinity with Roxy as a creative businesswoman and had been excited to write the cover story. I knew she was upset.

"So, are we going to lie down and take it, or are we going to fucking fight?" I let another f-bomb fly, sensing that my team needed my passion more than my professionalism. "I say we fight!" The conference erupted into cheers.

"What's the plan, Captainess?" Imani asked.

"We're going to print in two weeks, and we don't have time to get another prestigious artist for the cover." I considered our realistic options. "So, it has to either be a big reveal like Latika's pregnancy, or we find someone provocative. And we need low-hanging fruit because we already paid to book a studio for the cover shoot in five days."

There was more silence, then Sondra slowly said, "You're probably not going to like this, but... Sliq Bishopp was just accused of date rape by a groupie he hung out with after one of his concerts. Bishopp's people called me this morning to see if I wanted to hear his side of the story." Sondra's pursed lips implied her skepticism.

Sliq Bishopp was a notorious rapper whose three albums chock-full of violent and raunchy lyrics had all gone gold. He'd recently released a club banger that was getting major radio airplay and was on every DJ's rotation. The last thing I wanted was to give this asshole a platform, but women in the urban music scene almost never came forward to claim rape, so it would be incendiary when the news broke.

"Ugh, you're right, Sondra. I do kind of hate it." I looked upward, searching for a solve to the ick factor, because I had to admit that a controversial Sliq Bishopp cover might even outsell a Roxy cover. And we desperately needed a bestseller.

"What if we also interview the accuser?" Imani offered. "That way we can present a balanced perspective."

"Now that's a great idea!" I slapped the table. "We can illuminate all sides of the issue."

"If we keep the same photographer and shoot date, I think I can pull together a quick concept cover with loads of statement pieces from Jacob the Jeweler," Freddy added. Bishopp was known for his Mr. T–like excesses of necklaces and his diamond-encrusted mouth grill. I gave Freddy a thumbs-up.

"Okay, let's get on this." I stood up to pace the room. "Von, would you please track down the accuser? Imani and Sondra, do either of you want to interview Bishopp?"

"Um, one more thing," Sondra interjected, avoiding my eyes, so I knew her next statement would be a doozy. "Nikki, apparently Bishopp saw you at some recent MC RedHot party and only wants you to do the interview. That's his condition for an exclusive."

I paused but, seeing no alternative, closed my eyes and let my head fall back. "All righty then, I guess I'm writing the cover story this month. Imani, you're on the accuser's story. Let's go, team!"

Sondra hung around after everyone else had left the conference room. "Look, I didn't want to say anything in the meeting, but you should know that Jerome Jermaine produced most of Bishopp's last album, including his current single. He's not going to like any story about his artist that isn't irrefutably positive."

"How can we be irrefutably positive about an artist who's been accused of rape?" I said. "But okay, good to know... So, we need to keep the fact that we're also interviewing the accuser under strict wraps."

"Aye-aye, Captainess!" Sondra raised her eyebrows but saluted me.

I recalled Alonzo's similar gesture at RedHot's party and thought, *Game on.*

The hotel lobby had been a compromise. Sliq Bishopp had wanted me to interview him in his suite, but I'd declined. He refused to come to the office, so Von had the idea to meet him at the lobby bar, promising that he'd come with me but stay at a discreet distance so Bishopp wouldn't see him. The uniformed doorman who opened the opulent gold doors for us noticeably refused to make eye contact. Since Bishopp was staying there, I imagined all kinds of ratchet activity popped off at every hour of the day and night. The doorman may have assumed we were part of the merry band of troublemakers—or he was a run-of-the-mill racist.

I'd puzzled over what to wear, not wanting to be too sexy but knowing that I should probably not wear a muumuu to get the best story out of Bishopp. So, I settled on body-hugging black jeans, a black tank top, a lightweight cropped leather jacket, and silver pumps. I hoped this would be an inconspicuous outfit, but I stood out in the sea of Muffy clones in their matching floral dresses prancing through the high-ceilinged, ornate lobby.

It was a mystery to me why Bishopp chose such an old-school Midtown hotel until he emerged from the elevator, flanked by six men. Equal parts handsome and menacing, they were dressed in matching white linen suits paired with a rainbow of pastel shirts. The violent and misogynistic thread that ran through Sliq Bishopp's lyrics was echoed in his infamous music videos in which he and his crew, wearing long white tanks, bandannas, and loose denim with Glocks tucked in the waistbands, would plunder neighborhoods then throw their cash spoils at women's bare and bouncing asses. But now, they strutted through the lobby like a genteel hip hop Rat

Pack on their way to a lawn party in the Hamptons. They fit right in to the gold-dipped lobby, with its marble floors, crystal chandelier, and birds of paradise–printed wallpaper.

Beaming like a benevolent king, Bishopp palmed hundred-dollar bills to the elevator operator, the bellman, the front desk attendant, and a few other uniformed hotel employees who hastily emerged from the shadows. Everyone was deferential, addressing him as Mr. Bishopp and basically kowtowing as he passed. Bishopp's comfort and familiarity made it clear that this was not his first time staying there.

"Isn't it a trip how white folks will lose their shit over a C-note? They damn near forget to be racist," Bishopp whispered conspiratorially as he sank into the soft couch next to me. He gave me a small smile showing teeth that were devoid of his omnipresent grill, not seeming to notice that I was still struck dumb at his entrance. He gestured to the bartender, then took my hand, and said, "So, Nikki Rose, editor-in-chief of *Sugar* magazine, you are even prettier than I remember." He reached up to twirl one of my curls around his finger. "And you are here to figure out how anyone could possibly think that Sliq Bishopp, a leader of the hip hop community, would need to rape anyone."

I had been gazing at the flawless tawny brown of Bishopp's cleanshaven pate; I'd never noticed how attractive he was underneath the gangbanger gear, and I had the absurd urge to lick his shiny head to see if it tasted like the chocolate truffle it resembled. But his comment brought me back to reality. Withdrawing my fingers and removing my hair from his grip, I pulled out my recorder and said, "Nice to meet you, Bishopp. Do you mind if I tape our conversation?"

"Right down to business, huh?" Bishopp downed the entire flute of champagne the bartender had placed in front of him. "I thought we could get to know each other a little before we get to the interview."

"Getting to know you is part of the interview." I smiled at him in what I hoped was a charming way, but Bishopp just blinked at me as he drank half of a second flute that had appeared. I guessed his gesture to the bartender meant some version of "keep 'em coming."

"Nah, Nikki Rose." Pointing at my untouched champagne, he said, "I need you to have at least one drink with me before I spill my guts."

This wasn't the first time I'd been offered a drink during an interview. Normally, I turned them down, but Bishopp was looking at me like a drug dealer who needed me to sample the wares to prove I wasn't a cop. So I took a small sip and immediately furrowed my brow. "Why does the champagne taste like that?"

Bishopp laughed at my grimace. "There's a big shot of vodka in the Cristal. That will get you right."

"Whew, glad I asked." I tried to smile back but wondered whether this was Bishopp's go-to drink when he was trying to disarm a woman. I'd been drinking so much champagne lately that I quickly tasted something else in that flute. Someone else may have thought it was just a brand they didn't recognize. "Think I'm going to stick to Perrier."

"Man, why you acting like a prude?" Bishopp looked annoyed but signaled to the bartender again. "The way people talk about you in these streets, I figured you'd be up for more than a fancy club soda."

I didn't know if he was referring to Alonzo's character assassination or my now-public "thing" with JJ, his producer. Either way, Bishopp was clearly comfortable aggressively hitting on me. I felt like a pawn in a game I barely understood.

"People talk about you in these streets too. I think that's why we're here," I replied sharply, although I was less annoyed at Bishopp than at myself for being distracted by his dimples and deep green eyes.

"Oh, okay, I see you, Miss EIC. I guess you did not come to play." Bishopp downed the rest of his second champagne-and-vodka mix and motioned for a third. "That's too bad, though. We could have had some fun, you and I."

Something in his tone made that comment feel like a threat. Then Bishopp winked over my shoulder at his white-suited crew, who had clustered near the bar, throwing back tequila shots. It seemed as if they'd been waiting for some kind of cue from Bishopp because his boys, swollen with prison-yard muscles and implicit power, guffawed and nodded knowingly toward me. I subtly turned my head in the other direction to make sure that Von was still there, wanting to cry with relief when I saw him sitting in a corner looking back and forth from me to the book he'd brought to pass the time. Without Von, I would have been truly uneasy, likely how Bishopp's accuser had felt as she was sucked into a situation she couldn't control.

"You do know that I'm here to write a cover profile on you for a national magazine? You sure this is how you want to start?" I asked him, turning my tape recorder on. "We are now on the record."

Bishopp stared at me over the top of his glass, his expression darkening. I'd never seen a man in a white linen suit and Gucci slides look so dangerous. "You're nothing like I'd thought you'd be. But I guess I should have known when you wanted to meet in the lobby that you'd be taking this way too seriously."

Listening to Bishopp go on and on about how disappointed he was that I was so straitlaced and how he'd been ready to show me a good time brought to mind my first experience with Alonzo, five years ago at a Midtown hotel not that far from where Bishopp and I were now. I remembered thinking that I'd arrived early, but Alonzo was already ensconced in a quiet area of the hotel's sleek Italian eatery, nursing a tumbler of bourbon and yelling at someone on his cell phone. I'd seen him at a couple family functions but had lumped him together with my mother's old friends so never paid him much attention. But since he had the potential to get me a job in publishing, Alonzo Griffin had become much more compelling on that winter afternoon.

I hadn't wanted to interrupt, so I'd loitered near the door, spying on Alonzo as he'd punctuated his loudest points with indignant hand gestures. His ponytailed locs and silvery Italian suit were already distinctive, but the unabashed brutality and volume with which he dispatched the unlucky soul on the other end of his call set him far apart from everyone else in the conservative room. There had been a fearlessness in Alonzo's carriage that exuded authority.

I remembered being startled by how potent his energy had felt when his eyes met mine across the room. By the time Alonzo had waved me over, I was already a little intoxicated by him. Which made it that much easier to give in to everything that came next: his hand brushing my hair off my shoulder, his knee touching mine under the table, his fingers absently rubbing my arm as we talked about how he could help me achieve my professional dreams, the invitation to the room, my shirt over my head, Alonzo thrusting into me from behind as both of my palms were pressed against the floor-to-ceiling window, not caring if any tourists below could see us.

I was doing the same thing with Bishopp, getting lost in his brutal good looks. My attraction to dominance tinged with ruthlessness was spinning me in concentric circles that got smaller as I neared a perilous center. If I didn't break out of this pattern, I would implode.

With greater resolve, I pulled Bishopp back to our conversation by asking with faux innocence, "So, if I'd agreed to do the interview in your suite, would you have assumed that I was down to have some 'fun'?"

"Well, yeah, Nikki," Bishopp growled. "If a female accepts an invite to the crib, she knows what's up."

"What if I hadn't understood what you meant by the invitation to your room?" I was getting somewhere, but he didn't know it.

"Why else would a bitch think I want her up in the suite? I'm not a dental assistant. I'm a fucking rapper."

"What do you mean by that? Why does it matter that you're a rapper?"

Bishopp sighed deeply and drained his third flute. The more alcohol he drank, the more he sounded like his song lyrics—and the less attractive he became. I tried not to dwell on the thought that he was likely packing. "Look, if a bitch wanna mess with the music industry, a bitch had better learn how we get down. We get money and 'we don't love them hoes,'" he emphasized, quoting Snoop Dogg.

"You think that music is different than other industries?" I kept probing, hoping he was too buzzed to recognize that I was leading him in a specific direction.

"Most of these nine-to-five niggas is soft." Bishopp's speech was starting to slur. "I don't know any real G's who would invite a female to their crib for a fucking tickle party."

"But what if I was up in your suite tonight and I really thought I was only there to do an interview, so I told you no?" I pushed a little more. "Also, I think you mean 'woman,' not 'female,' right?"

Bishopp smirked at me, then loudly sucked his teeth. Ignoring my last comment, he continued, "What's a *no* to a G? If you're in my house, you're mine."

I glanced down to make sure my tape recorder was still running. "Is that what happened with your accuser? She didn't know the deal, so she said no and you weren't trying to hear it?"

"Seriously, what did she think I wanted when I pulled her out the crowd at my concert and invited her to my place? Like, what did she think was going to happen? Why was she dancing in the front row in some booty shorts and a bra if she didn't want my attention?" Bishopp tapped his forehead to indicate his accuser's obvious naïveté. "And now she wants to cry rape because she's mad I don't want to be her boyfriend or something? Man, fuck that. She knew what was up."

"So why do you think she's saying that you raped her? That's a serious accusation for someone to make from some hurt feelings."

He leaned forward and whispered, "I know you're smarter than this, Miss EIC. It's a shakedown. She's using the court system to launch an expensive civil suit. This bitch is after my money."

"But Bishopp, did she say no?" I held my breath.

He gazed at me for a few seconds, sizing me up. Then he rolled his eyes. "Come on, Nikki. I don't know what the hell she said. We was partying and a lot of stuff was said. But, like I told you, what's a *no* to a G? If I want to hit, I'm going to hit. And if a *female*"—he emphasized the word—"goes up to my suite, she can't act confused about what that means and then cry rape." Bishopp shrugged, unaware that he'd just incriminated himself *and* indicted the entire music industry.

His answer was like a gut punch. Memories of having reluctant sex with Alonzo in his Range Rover outside the Krispy Kreme streaked across my mind like a runaway firecracker. Bishopp's accuser's *no* was nothing to him; and my *no* had been nothing to Alonzo. Until that moment, I had chalked the incident up to just another time when Alonzo expected me to get off on his sexual dominance. But after I left Bishopp frustrated in the lobby and made it home that night, I stared at my shadowy bedroom ceiling, unable to sleep as I kept turning over in my mind whether I had also been raped.

It was risky calling my girls in the wee hours of the morning, especially when they were still upset with me, but this couldn't wait. I tried both Denyse and Teresa and left a version of the same message when I got their answering machine: "*I know you love me, and I also know that you're worried about me. I'm so sorry for taking you for granted, for being stubborn when you were just trying to help, and for not prioritizing our sisterhood. Thank you for being my support system through all the mistakes I've made, and I ask that you please don't lose patience because I'll definitely be making more. I hope you can give me a little grace this time because I really have been under some crushing pressure. I promise to make it up to you. I love you.*"

Only Sofie, who was probably just getting in from closing her café, picked up. Understandably, her first words were, "Why are you calling me at this hour, Nikki? You *are* buggin' out!"

"Sof, I know you love me and that you were worried—" I only got a few words into my prepared spiel before Sofie groaned loud enough to shut me up.

"You have got to be kidding me." She let loose. "Are you seriously calling me at three AM to peacock back our last conversation?"

"I think you mean 'parrot,'" I interjected.

Normally, Sofie appreciated when we corrected her rare language slip-ups, but at this moment, she couldn't have cared less. I could practically hear her death stare through the phone. "Whatever, Nikki. This is hella weird and I don't think I want to have this conversation now."

"Please, Sofie, I'm feeling pretty bad right now. Can I just talk to you for a minute?" I took her silence as reluctant consent. "I know I fucked up. You and WhiteHot have every right to be mad at me. I've never felt less like I know what I'm doing in my life. You guys bore the brunt of my bad judgment, and I regret it."

I hoped she didn't hear my voice tremble, but Sofie's normal kindheartedness crept into her tone. "What *is* going on?" she asked gently. "All of this is so unlike you."

"I told you about the six-month steeplechase I'm running at *Sugar*. That's been weighing on me." I paused. Sofie and I had the least one-on-on time of all my closest friends, but I was grateful that she was the one who had picked up the phone because I thought she might understand. "And everything that went down with Alonzo back in the day is coming up now, almost worse than before."

"That makes sense, Nik. You're in his domain now. And hip hop culture can be merciless. It's one thing to be a consumer and something else entirely to fully exist in it, when it's your livelihood and your social circle," Sofie replied. "Part of the reason I opened my café was because I felt like I was losing myself in WhiteHot's world. I needed something that I could control, that was only mine."

"I'm scared I'm losing myself too." I took a long drink of water to buy myself time before I spoke again. "Actually, I'm scared I lost myself a while ago and am only now realizing it."

"Why would you say that?"

"I'm just seeing everything with new eyes," I choked out. "I know I was abused, and I think I may have been raped."

Sofie drew in a quick breath. "Oh my god, when? Was it Alonzo?"

"Yes, the last time we had sex, I... didn't want to." Tears were now streaming down my face, but my voice was oddly steady. "But we'd done it so many times where he was ordering me around and telling me that I was his 'good bitch' that I chalked it up to a rough session."

"All this time, I can't believe I didn't know you were hurting like that. Did you tell anyone?" Sofie asked gently.

"I didn't tell anyone because I didn't know either. At least not for sure, not to the point where I was ready to admit it to myself... For some reason, it feels clearer now, maybe because I *am* in his domain, and I can see the monster that he is. I can also see that he's not the only one. And people seem okay with these guys. Or at least they find excuses for them, like blaming the culture." Although my words were now coming out in a shaky stream of consciousness, I couldn't stop talking. "But looking back, I remember saying 'no.' I know I said 'no'..."

Sofie must have heard my voice finally break because she said simply, "I'm on my way over, schatje."

Although she showed up at my door with ice cream and wine, the only thing I really wanted was her hug. After we spent some time chitchatting about everything other than why my face was puffy and my eyes were red, Sofie draped an arm over my shoulder. "Look, I know how hard it is to feel comfortable in a totally new scene. Modeling took me around Europe, but it didn't prepare me for the culture shock of New York City and the music industry."

I regarded her with new respect as I processed how successful a shape-shifter Sofie was. She had acclimated to multiple countries' cultures, then somehow managed to become a fixture in urban entertainment and downtown nightlife, all by her early thirties. I felt a little lame for feeling like a fish out of water in a culture that I'd grown up with in the city where I was born and raised.

"But you never ever have to accept men treating you like shit. And there is no 'cultural' justification for rape." Sofie spun me around so that I faced her. "And even though you did let me down, I forgive you, and I will always be here for you."

I nodded, not trusting myself to speak. Her compassion allowed me to see that I'd never forgiven myself for everything that had happened with Alonzo—and that I'd been blaming myself for the last time he took me in his Range Rover. *No more*, I resolved. That shit was over.

TWENTY-SIX

Imani and Von were waiting in my office when I arrived. Approaching the shut door, I saw the two of them through the glass, seated on the sofa, heads close together. They were so deep in conversation that they didn't hear the door hinge creak. I had to say "Morning, guys," so they'd look up.

"Nikki, thank god you're here," Imani said. "Close the door."

"Jeez, who died?" I threw my bag on the desk and dragged a chair in front of the sofa.

"I found Sliq Bishopp's accuser," Imani replied simply.

"So fast? You are a magician!" I extended my fist to give her a pound, then took in Imani's and Von's grave expressions. "Okay, what's going on? Was it worse than we thought?"

"Much," Von groaned, eyes downcast, his pale cheeks making the freckles seem more prominent.

"Nikki, she's a child," Imani said softly.

"What do you mean? She's naïve?"

Imani shook her head slowly. "No, she's a literal child. I found her at an after-school job at Burger King. She told me she was seventeen, which is the age of consent in New York. But I looked up her records and, Nik, she just turned seventeen last week."

"So, she was sixteen when..." I sat silently for a minute, remembering how much Bishopp's crew had intimidated me. I couldn't even imagine trying to navigate that by myself as a child. "Did she tell you what happened?"

"Yeah, as she cried into her strawberry shake." Imani inhaled deeply. "Apparently, she snuck out of her house to go to the concert with some of her friends. She's a cute, curvy girl, and when she caught Bishopp's eye, he sent one of his crew to bring her backstage. They wouldn't let her bring her friends, so she was by herself when Bishopp's boys offered her booze and passed her a joint. She says she was so wasted that she barely noticed where they were taking her, and she ended up in Bishopp's hotel suite. The next thing she knew, she was no longer a virgin."

My vision blurred with unexpected tears. I'd lost my own virginity in a college dorm room with a lumbering fellow freshman who'd talked a good game about his manhood and prowess but had clearly never had sex. It was clumsy and frenetic, and I'd been dismayed by almost every aspect of the inelegant affair. But I wasn't scared or shell-shocked or regretful the way this girl likely was.

I pressed a finger to the corner of my eye. "How on earth did she get out of there?"

"Her story is that Bishopp got pissed when she started to cry so he kicked her out. She literally took the subway home. When she tried to sneak in, her older sister caught her and told her mom, who, correctly, freaked out."

"That poor kid." The details kept painting a worse picture. "Were there any witnesses or anyone who can corroborate her story?"

"I ran her pic over to the hotel where he's staying now," Von interjected. "I figured his simple ass was a regular, and sure 'nuff one of the lobby attendants recognized her. But I didn't say anything about Bishopp, so I hope dude's memory doesn't get fuzzy if he knows those hundos might stop flowing."

"Nice work, Von!" I hesitated because I hated to ask the next question. "Either way, this is statutory rape, but did she definitively say no to him?"

"That's what she told me," Imani replied. "And I believe her. I mean, I can totally see it. She had a round baby face, but her uniform was a size too small, and she had on a bunch of makeup. Not saying any of this is her fault, of course. But I bet she felt grown, like she could handle whatever. And then that precocious kid found herself in a situation that no one could have handled." Imani paused, then closed her eyes. "I can still see how hard she was weeping. It was awful."

"This whole thing is awful," I agreed. "Has she pressed charges?"

"She said that her mom went to the police, so I assume so." I nodded, then rested my chin in my palm, staring upward and thinking about what to do. I didn't move for several long minutes until Imani finally asked, "Do you want to pull the story?"

This cover story had morphed into an atomic bomb, and I closed my eyes to picture the impact it would have when it hit newsstands, the devastation to Sliq Bishopp's career and his label. I thought of the advertising dollars from Bishopp's record label that NuVoices would lose. I imagined JJ's furious face when he realized that I'd torpedoed his prize artist.

But I recalled the glint in Bishopp's eye as he unflinchingly told me, "What's a *no* to a G?" I remembered Alonzo taking me in his truck even after I tearily told him, "No, I don't think I want to right now." And I thought about having to prove to an entire industry that I was a serious editor because I'd been labeled a ho while the men I'd been with were considered charming Lotharios.

"No, no, I don't," I said firmly. "We're not going to name the girl in the article, but we are going forward with the cover. And we're going to blow it up so everyone knows where *Sugar* stands. Somebody has to have her back."

I reached out to each of them and the three of us sat there for a few minutes, holding hands in silence.

I was dialing Teresa's number before I put my bag down. I'd stayed late to do some edits on the cover story, eating a vending machine dinner of potato chips and a Snickers bar, and dragged my spent body home at 11:00 PM. It was late but I missed my best friend so much my chest hurt. I knew my apology voicemail had softened her, but it hadn't been enough. Although she and I had mostly fallen back into our old rhythm of talking several times a week, tension now marbled our conversations. But that night, I needed my girl. Teresa picked up after one ring.

"Teresa, thank god," I blurted before she could say hello. "It's been a helluva couple days."

"Hi, Teresa. How was your day? Did you keep any innocent people from going to jail?" she deadpanned.

"That's any given Tuesday for you! But are you good?"

"Yeah, chica. It's same old same old over here." I could hear water running in the background and assumed she was getting ready for bed.

"Shit, I'm sorry, it is super late. But do you have a sec for me to tell you what's up with this rapper Sliq Bishopp?"

"Sure, it's cool. You can keep me company while I do my skin care routine. You know a bitch got serums." I was relieved to hear Teresa's smile through the phone. "Sliq Bishopp... Doesn't he have a fresh rape charge?"

I paused with a forkful of cold leftover Chinese food halfway to my mouth. "Wait, how did you know that? My entertainment editor just brought it up a few days ago and said it was still on the low."

"I got a buddy in the DA's office who was gossiping at the dirty water dog guy outside the courthouse yesterday. He did say it hadn't gone public yet."

"Um, you didn't want to call your journalist best friend with that scoop?"

"That would have been un-eth-i-cal," Teresa said, enunciating each syllable. "Besides, it's not like you'd cover that asshole in *Sugar* anyway."

My heart sank. "Actually, he's our October cover."

"Are you fucking serious right now?" I could hear Teresa's smile disappear.

"Tee, Alonzo stole another cover from me, which is catastrophic since I'm two-thirds of the way through my six-month trial. I needed a big seller, and I knew the rape accusation would be buzzworthy when it comes out," I started. "Look, I know it sounds awful, but we found the accuser and I'm going to publish an interview with her as well. It turns out she was only sixteen when it happened."

There was a heavy silence. "Let me get this straight. You're giving Sliq Bishopp a national platform to defend himself after he raped a child?"

"No, I mean, I guess so." It sounded vastly different when she said it. "But I'm writing the story myself, so it's not going to be some glowing profile, Tee. I'm really going there."

"So, you're also giving this bastard the respect of having the editor-in-chief of the damn magazine write his profile?" Teresa managed to convey her dismay through the drone of her electric toothbrush.

"I'm making sure the story is done right," I protested. "Actually, could I walk you through some of the legal stuff? I'm not sure I know how to talk about date rape versus statutory rape."

"Uh, no! First of all, I'm totally against this Sliq Bishopp guy getting a *Sugar* cover. I don't care how you tell his story," Teresa exclaimed. "But I also have a morning hearing, so I've got to crash."

"Please don't leave me in the lurch, Tee," I begged. "NuVoice's legal department will do a review but it's up to me to get the profile right. I'm walking a really fine line here."

Teresa spat out her toothpaste before replying firmly, "Then you should kill it."

I sighed. It wasn't as if I wasn't fighting my own misgivings. "I know you hate this, but I think you also know that I can't kill it now. I don't have anyone else for this cover and, even if I did, I wouldn't be able to get the money back for the studio and photographer already booked for tomorrow's shoot. What I can do is use every tool I have as a journalist to take him to task for his actions. And I can bring more awareness to the issue of rape culture. But if I get any of the legal facts wrong or accidentally defame him, then it will all be for nothing. Not to mention, my reputation will be screwed."

For a minute, I only heard rustling sounds as I assumed Teresa was changing into the flannel pj's she liked to wear. I knew better than to push her while she was weighing a decision, so I waited for her to speak. When the rustling stopped, I imagined her climbing into bed and staring at her bedroom ceiling, thinking. I risked a few sniffling noises until she finally said, "Okay, okay, jeez. I obviously don't want you to get yourself into trouble. I have an idea: I'm going to give you Derek's number. He's tried lots of rape cases and he'd be a great resource."

I hadn't seen Derek since the MC RedHot party, and this was a less-than-ideal way to reconnect. "You think he'll want to talk to me?"

"Puleeze, Nikki. Did you really not see the way he was eyeballing you at that party? Trust me, he'll talk to you."

I swallowed my surprise. I'd been distracted by the situation with MC RedHot—and Derek had told me that he had a girlfriend. "Okay, I appreciate it. Thanks, girl," I replied.

"Nah, don't thank me," Teresa objected. "I'm just hoping he talks you out of this."

TWENTY-SEVEN

The next morning, I woke before my alarm went off, buzzing with nervous energy. Sliq Bishopp's cover shoot was that day, and I was going to stop by the studio. I'd asked Freddy to sneak in some solemn shots with subdued dark suits with the imbecilic shots of Bishopp in full gangsta gear, and to double his normal thick stack of jewelry. I didn't yet know how I wanted Bishopp to look on the cover: like he was going to his own funeral or like a preposterous clown. Either way, this cover story was about to be the topic of conversation around the industry. It would be explosive and divisive and important—and I only had three more days to finish it.

Wanting to catch Derek before he got into his workday, I walked to the office instead of taking the subway so I could call him. I swung northeast toward NoHo and my favorite coffee shop, where I bought a cappuccino and a chocolate croissant. Then, juggling the cup, my stuffed tote bag, and my phone, I dialed Derek's number.

"This is Derek Mills."

I hadn't expected him to answer in such a professional tone; when I heard his deep voice utter those crisp words, the phone call suddenly felt intimate. I froze halfway across Lafayette Street, my prepared opening gambit leaving my brain.

"This is Derek. Who is this, please?" he tried again.

"Derek, hey. It's Nikki, Teresa's friend." The blaring car horns jolted me back to reality and I hustled over the crosswalk.

There was a moment of silence so fraught with energy it was almost audible. In a much warmer, slightly surprised voice, Derek said, "I know who you are, rock star. This is a very pleasant surprise." He paused, waiting for a reply that didn't come fast enough. "Did I lose you? You still there?"

"Hi, yes, no—I'm here," I stammered. "I'm calling because I could use your help. I'm writing a tough piece and I need to get the legal points right." Without adding any detail about my experience interviewing Bishopp, I told Derek about the cover profile, the rape accusation, and the underage accuser.

When I finished explaining the context, Derek responded with a bitter laugh. "Well, Sliq Bishopp seems like an upstanding citizen. And you are putting him on your cover because . . . why?"

I bristled at his implicit judgment. "As you can imagine, Bishopp wasn't my first choice. But my profile of him will be more of a takedown, and we're including the interview with his accuser. That's why I'm calling you, to make sure I'm getting any legal stuff right, but if you don't want to help, I understand."

"No, no, I didn't mean that. My bad." Derek sighed. "I recently came off a rape case and I guess I'm still mad."

"Teresa told me. You won, right?"

"Actually, I lost. But let's just say that it was the right outcome." There was pain in Derek's voice. "Rape 1 is a class B felony and dude had no priors, so the asshole judge who hates me gave him the minimum of five to spite me. He'll likely be on parole after four years and then he'll have to register as a sex offender."

"Doesn't seem like much time," I said. "Maybe that's why Bishopp was so cavalier about the case. Isn't it super hard to get a rape conviction in the first place?"

"No, Bishopp is probably looking at doing real time if he's convicted. I'm betting he has a prior violent felony conviction or two, so he could get up to twenty-five years. Then there's statutory rape; even though it's a lower-level felony, it still carries mandatory prison time. So even if he beats the top charge, as long as they can prove they had sex and that he's older than twenty-one and she's under seventeen, he'll get a statutory charge." I heard something muffled in his background. "It's not like the seventies, when rape charges couldn't be brought at all unless the complainant could prove they resisted." He trailed off and I heard more muted noises.

"You good over there?" I asked.

"Yeah, hang on," Derek replied. Over the now more distinct background clatter, I heard him say, "Chocolate frosted doughnut and a hazelnut latte with three sugars."

"For real? A chocolate frosted doughnut *and* three sugars in your hazelnut coffee?"

"What? I've got a sweet tooth," he exclaimed. "Listen, I love what I do for a living, but being a public defender is not for the faint of heart. These can be some very long, very tough days. My coping mechanism is to start my mornings with a little treat."

I had detoured to a park bench in Union Square to continue the conversation. I was making my way through my coffee and chocolate croissant, feeling too silly to tell Derek that I was eating almost the same breakfast. "Well, you obviously stay in the gym because I don't see those doughnuts anywhere."

I clapped my hand over my mouth, but Derek quickly replied, "I'm glad you noticed." I couldn't come up with a reply, so I was grateful when Derek continued, "So, what are you listening to on your walk?"

"How did you know I'm walking?"

"My brilliant power of deduction and low-key psychic abilities." He laughed. "It's New York and the streets are cacophonous."

Just hearing the word *cacophonous* used in an actual sentence made my geeky heart swell. I hadn't yet slipped my headphones over my ears, but Derek had guessed correctly that I had some music cued up. "I've got some *Black on Both Sides* in the Discman. You?"

"Mos Def. Nice," Derek acknowledged. "I was going to play some Massive Attack before *someone* called me."

"I just bought *Mezzanine* the other day."

"And I was about to play *Protection*," Derek replied.

"No way," I blurted. "That album is definitely on my desert island top ten."

"Your what?"

"The ten albums you would choose to have if you were stuck on a desert island. Duh!"

"Okay, so, what else would be on your personal *TRL*? Now I have to know."

"MTV does songs, not albums," I stalled.

"Out with it!"

"You have me on the spot here, but... for sure *The Miseducation of Lauryn Hill*; *Nevermind* because Nirvana; Tupac's *Greatest Hits*, if that's not cheating; and *Ready to Die* because I stay lying when I say I love Pac more than Biggie." I chewed my croissant contemplatively. "Can I choose the *Waiting to Exhale* soundtrack? I mean, it has TLC, Whitney, Aretha, Mary J...." I trailed off.

"I'll let these greatest hits and soundtracks go, but you already know you're cheating!" Derek replied through his own mouthful of doughnut. "Keep going, because this is fascinating."

I couldn't read his tone and hoped he wasn't ragging on my picks. "Um, four more, right? Let me see... Well, I'd need some Jimi Hendrix with me and I'm thinking *Band of Gypsys* over *Electric Ladyland*, but that's a tough choice. I'd want Stevie too and would probably go for *Hotter Than July* over *Songs in the Key of Life*, which is another impossible choice. Whew, just two more? Definitely Led Zep; I guess I'll say *IV* so I don't catch heat for another greatest hits album; um, Sade's *Love Deluxe*, and I'll stand by my Massive Attack choice."

"You weren't lying! You do have some diverse musical taste," he acknowledged. "But where's Bob Marley or Miles Davis? And no Arrested Development or De La Soul? How about Fiona or Sinéad? No house music or anything international..."

"Okay, okay," I groaned. "I only had ten choices and they were off the top of my head!"

"This was your game, so no excuses!" Derek retorted warmly. "All bullshit aside, your list is dope. You're still 'rock star' to me."

Chatting with someone who didn't ridicule music that wasn't on Hot 97 or WBLS was rare. And hearing Derek talk about how he loved being a public defender was irrationally magnetic. It reminded me that I had originally wanted to become a journalist to tell positive, impactful stories. Teresa and I basically grew up together, so I took our shared values for granted. With Derek, the parallel between our professions and passions felt fresh.

As I balanced the rest of the pastry on my knee and sipped my cappuccino, I felt jealous of the passersby in their commuter sneakers and casual Friday slacks, blithely strolling to their places of work. They were probably not contemplating the nuances of rape charges or the stress of dealing with our flawed justice system. They could probably flirt with a cute boy in peace.

Derek broke into my thoughts. "Hey, off the subject of music: I forgot to ask you whether the Bishopp assault happened recently."

"Under a year ago."

"Okay, good. Because the statute of limitations for rape is five years."

Five years. How long ago had Alonzo cornered me in his Range Rover? Had it been four years or were we coming up on five? I found myself doing the mental math. My silent calculations must have gone on longer than I realized because the next thing I heard was Derek asking me "Hey, Nikki, now I need to know if you're good over there."

I was grateful he couldn't see me. "Yep, all good. I'm...um...It's just that this story is important to me" was all I trusted myself to say.

I could hear Derek calmly munching his doughnut, waiting for me to continue. "There are all these rules and relationships and politics in this new world that I'm barely managing. And everything is more complicated as a woman. That RedHot party disaster was a small taste."

"Well, that small taste was hard to watch. It seemed like a no-win situation for you."

"That's exactly it! It was no-win. But I chose the path of least resistance, so that's on me," I murmured, flushing as it dawned on me how little responsibility I'd taken for the RedHot party when I was at Sofie's Café.

"So now you want to resist?"

"Now I want to resist. I am resisting."

"Okay, I feel that." I could hear Derek nodding. His voice made me want to keep talking.

"I'm just . . . sick of being a pawn. Honestly, I'm sick of how damn near every woman is a pawn in this world. We get judged and cornered and casually discussed." My voice caught, so I took a big gulp of my coffee.

"And now you want to use your platform to make sure that Bishopp doesn't get away with rape or that his accuser isn't maligned," Derek offered. "Look, if no one else says it, I'm impressed. Way to take back the power, Nikki."

That night, I watched everyone else leave the office while I worked on Bishopp's profile. It had been enraging to see him mugging for the camera at the photo shoot, oblivious to having laid waste to a child's innocence and thinking that after propositioning and threatening me, he was still getting a glowing cover story. I was rage-typing long after the last person vacated the NuVoices floor, so focused that I jumped when the lobby attendant called to tell me I had a pizza downstairs.

"I didn't order anything," I told him, although I hadn't eaten and was starving.

"You tell that to the delivery guy, miss. He's on his way up."

The medium pie was delivered with a CD and a note that read:

Figured you'd be working late tonight. Speaking truth to power isn't a 9-to-5 job under normal circumstances, and I know you're on a deadline. Plus, I still owe you a meal. Sending good energy and pepperoni. You got this! (The CD is pretty far afield from the Smashing Pumpkins, but I think you'll be into it, rock star.)

Warmly, Derek

Walking down the dark and deserted halls to my office with the lukewarm pizza in hand, I couldn't make up my mind whether to feel empowered or sorry for myself. Derek was right: There was no way to get around the discomfort of resistance. Normally, a cover subject is the most celebrated person in a magazine, which is what everyone—Barbara, JJ, the industry—expected me to do with Sliq Bishopp. But I was going renegade. The more I typed, the more it felt like one of the most meaningful and powerful things I had ever done as a journalist. On the flip side, both NuVoices and my career were on the bubble. And, more importantly, my best friend was questioning my judgment.

I needed a distraction, so I put on the CD Derek had sent along with the pizza: *Hôtel Costes, Vol. 1*. The eclectic mix of lounge-y electro house music curated by a French DJ named Stéphane Pompougnac paired throbbing beats with a chill vibe. Perfect writing music. Derek's kind gesture made me regret even more everything I'd done to cause a rift with my best friends.

I had an inspiration for my October editor's letter and grabbed a notebook and pen to scribble with one hand while I ate my pizza with the other.

Hey, girlfriend. I'm writing this letter late at night, from my deserted office, feeling more alone than I have in a long time. I don't feel this way because I'm by myself working late; I feel alone because I made some bad decisions that have messed up some of the relationships I care most about.

Lately, I've been doing a lot of talk about resistance: how important it is to resist a culture that disregards women, how important it is to resist anyone who disrespects the Sugar *audience, how important it is to resist giving in to the people with power and money who always seem to get their way. And I really am trying to walk that talk. That's why I wrote to you last month about sacrificing the advertising dollars my company would have made by collaborating with a bullying fashion designer. That's why I'm in the office at 11 pm right now, crafting a story on a powerful rapper who is accused of a heinous crime. It's also why we have included an interview with this rapper's accuser to make sure that she's allowed to tell her truth as well.*

But resistance is hard. It's messy and exhausting and risky—and often comes with very little support. I'm trying to have the courage to stay the course, to protect myself and you, my Sugar *girls, at all times. But I recently behaved exactly opposite of everything I'm talking about.*

At the last Sugar *party, I asked a brilliant music artist and friend who is dating one of my closest girls to leave because his presence was unreasonably upsetting another rapper at the event. I didn't feel secure enough in my new job, in my music industry status, or in myself to do what I knew was the right thing, so I took the path of least resistance, and I disrespected people I love. To make matters worse, when my friends called me to task and told me they were worried about me, I was defensive and selfish.*

I'm in the office at 11 by myself writing a potentially incendiary cover story. But the real reason I'm feeling very alone right now is because I did not have the courage to defend my friends when it counted. This is a mea culpa to everyone as well as a public apology to my friends, who always had my back, even when I didn't have theirs.

Your convictions mean nothing if you can't maintain them in all areas of your life. And I will try to do better.

Love, Nikki

With that off my chest, I restarted the *Hôtel Costes* CD, letting the chill music chase the stress from my mind so I could refocus on Bishopp's profile. The piece was difficult to write, the photos would be difficult to edit, and the cover lines would have to be very carefully crafted. But nothing would stop my arrow from finding its target.

TWENTY-EIGHT

I almost turned away when the waiter approached me at the entrance with a tray of brimming champagne flutes. Since I had developed a habit of disappointing everyone, including myself, when I partied too hard, I'd cut my carousing way back. But even with Von at my side, I needed some liquid courage to walk into that room. Ricky Matsumoro's annual after party for the MTV Video Music Awards was renowned for being a VIP-only affair. He always held it at his newest hotel, and this year the winners posed with their Moonman trophies on a red carpet that stretched in front of the just-opened Matsumoro SoHo building. Waiting handlers swept awardees to an expansive penthouse that opened onto a rooftop deck surrounding a black-bottomed pool, covered for the evening with frosted acrylic to create an exterior dance floor. Of course, Kiara oversaw her husband's guest list, and she made sure that the Moonman winners were surrounded by only A-list fellow artists, music label executives, actors, fashion designers, editors, models, and other notable culture creators.

This was my first time attending the VMAs and, therefore, my first time at the Matsumoro after party. (At *StyleList*, I wasn't even close to being senior enough for an invite.) And it would be my first event since the October issue with Sliq Bishopp hit newsstands a few days ago. When Barbara saw the shadowy pic that

I'd chosen for the cover of a scowling Bishopp picking his diamond grill with a knife and realized how far I'd gone in the profile, she'd shrieked loud enough for all activity to stop on the NuVoices floor. The only thing that had calmed her down was the news that stores were already selling out of their October copies. Even in her fury, Barbara knew that the incendiary story would put *Sugar* on the map.

Since Sliq Bishopp had been nominated for a VMA, he and his boys would be at the party—as would JJ and the rest of his label. The thought of facing Bishopp, JJ (whose calls I'd been avoiding for weeks), and the whole industry at the same damn time made my stomach hurt. But Barbara had informed me in no uncertain terms that I'd already jeopardized too many ad dollars to miss any opportunity to glad-hand potential new advertisers and other important people with marketing budgets.

I also wanted to support Kiara and her publicity firm's signature event. So, after I got my makeup done and combed my hair into a tight bun, I put on the one-shouldered leopard-print Norma Kamali dress that Freddy had pulled for me, clasped a gold snake cuff to my upper arm, and made myself walk out the door.

Now that I was about to literally face the music, I decided to accept that glass of champagne.

Von grabbed my elbow. "Let's go for a grand entrance, shall we?" he said. But he faltered after just a few steps inside. "Am I tripping, or is literally everyone gawking over here?"

He wasn't wrong. The sudden attention felt like a riptide pulling us to the center of the party. Men were studying us as we passed, their faces largely unreadable, while women were whispering to each other.

Squaring my shoulders, I tugged the back of Von's shiny purple-and-black jacquard jacket so he'd focus on me. "They're looking at us because we did something that no one else in the industry dared to do."

As we debated whether to hit the bar before we did a loop around the party, someone touched my waist. With her smooth walnut skin, the petite woman who'd materialized at my side appeared dipped in chocolate. Her voice was low and conspiratorial, so I had to lean down to hear her say, "Excuse me, you are Nikki Rose, right? Editor-in-chief of *Sugar*?" When I nodded, a smile broke across her face and her tone turned shy. "Oh, wow, okay. I'm so excited to meet you. I swear Nikki's Notes is talking directly to me. You're so real and inspiring. It's the first page me and my girls read every month!"

She must have been surprised by the force of my hug. I gripped my poor unsuspecting fan for several long beats until she tactfully wriggled her shoulders to indicate that she'd appreciate a lungful of air. I released her with a warm chuckle. Some understanding had passed between us because she looked into my eyes and said, "You know you're a role model, right? Especially after that Sliq Bishopp story. That took guts. You got a lot of people in your corner, sis."

"Thanks so much, sis." I didn't want to freak her out with another bear hug, so I briefly clasped her hand. "You have no idea how much I appreciate you, especially tonight."

She took in the number of people still observing us. "You got this, Nikki," she told me with a firm squeeze to my sweaty hand. She walked away a couple feet, but doubled back. "Hey, I forgot to tell you, I'm in the publicity department at Eternal Records. Betty Brown's label. That cover was the shit! I know it was early, but you're gonna look like a genius when her album drops." She winked and took off.

I relaxed for the first time that night. I'd been so caught up in the Sliq Bishopp drama that I'd forgotten everything else I'd done with *Sugar*. I beamed at Von and was about to suggest we hit the dance floor when I saw JJ rushing through the crowd toward us.

"Nikki, why the hell are you here?" JJ grabbed my arm, his eyes darting around the room as if looking for a place to hide or a fast escape. "This isn't safe."

I took a page from Teresa's book and said evenly, "Hi, Nikki. You look fabulous. How've you been since I last talked to you nearly a month ago?"

JJ stopped glancing around to regard me intently. "Okay, Nikki, you wanna play this game? Yeah, you look good—except maybe your hair."

I took the bait. "What's wrong with my hair?"

"I'm not feeling the ballet-dancer bun thing." JJ shrugged, his face expressionless. "But can we stop talking about stupid shit? You know I'm here with Bishopp's crew, right?"

I nodded, too hurt to immediately process his warning.

"Okay, well, I've been trying to talk that nigga off a cliff all night. I don't know if he's angrier at you for playing him with that profile that made him sound like the East Harlem Rapist—or at me since he's convinced that I knew about the story in advance. Of course, I didn't know anything about the story in advance, now, did I?"

I looked down at my hands, studying the red nail polish. JJ had a right to be indignant; if I'd trusted him, I would have given him a heads-up. But even though I'd put him in a bad position, it still felt as if he held the power in this conversation. "I'm not sure what to say," I finally sputtered. "I just didn't want you to try to talk me out of doing what I had to do."

"Yeah, well, now Bishopp thinks that *he* has to do something. And I don't like you being in the same venue with him and his stupid boys when he's this fucking angry."

JJ spun me around like he was going to frog-march me to the door, but a loud commotion to our right stopped him. As Bishopp stormed over, flanked by his crew, JJ let go of me, took three steps to the side, and faded into the crowd. By the time I realized he was gone, the total solar eclipse of Bishopp and his posse in their color-coordinated suits and durags blocked out the rest of the party. Next came Bishopp's voice booming over Madonna's "Ray of Light," so loud I almost thought the DJ had mixed in a rap song.

"I'll be goddamned, Nikki Rose. You're the last fucking person I thought I'd see tonight. I have to admit that I'm low-key impressed by your cojones."

I was in full tonic immobility, unable to budge my limbs or form words. Barbara's claim that she'd stared down multiple strapped gangstas over the years popped into my mind as I tried to figure out what to do. No wonder she'd become unflappable. In the same way I'd often speculated why Barbara had asked me to meet with JJ, since she clearly knew that he was a rake, I now had to question why Barbara would send me into this den of lions, knowing full well that Bishopp would be here. Yet here I was, at the most exclusive VMAs after party, getting screamed at by a highly combustible rapper she must have known would confront me. It felt as if Barbara were teaching me to swim by throwing me into big-wave surf.

"What, you don't have anything to say to me now?" Bishopp was just winding up. "For such a pretty girl, you have a fat fucking mouth, don't you? And I guess I found that out the hard way."

Von stood gamely next to me during Bishopp's verbal onslaught. He took a big gulp of air and squeaked, "Hey yo, don't talk to her like that."

Bishopp glanced at Von like he was a misbehaving puppy, then rhetorically asked the growing crowd of spectators, "I'm sorry, who is *this* fool?"

That restored my voice. "Bishopp, would you please relax. I'd be happy to discuss this—"

"Bitch, did you just tell me to fucking relax?" Bishopp interrupted, his voice rising again. "You fucking come for my reputation in your little article where you repeat every fucking word of our conversation out-of-fucking context. And you interviewed that gold-digging liar." I tried to take a step back but was blocked by one of Bishopp's boys.

"I taped our interview, and I told you that it was on the record," I insisted, although I was quaking with fear.

"I don't give a fuck about your tape. You seem real confused by the fact that this ain't a game. I'm about to sue the shit out of you."

Kiara elbowed her way over to stand next to me. She put up a warning finger and said, "Bishopp, this is not cool. You need to back off now."

"Bitch, you better get your finger outta my face. I don't give a fuck who your husband is," Bishopp bellowed, making Kiara rear back. As she regained her balance, only a slight twitch in her right eyebrow betrayed any nerves. She calmly turned and flicked her chin once toward a corner of the room. In eight seconds, what looked like the entire Giants' defensive line dressed in black suits appeared, ringing Kiara.

"Well, somebody cares," Kiara spoke carefully, not taking her eyes from Bishopp's face.

"Yeah, all right, ma. No need to trip." Bishopp smoothly switched his tone. Then he looked back at me. "But this bitch..."

Out of nowhere, a man appeared and stepped between me and Bishopp. I was so shocked to see him that it took me a second to process who it was standing in front of me with balled-up hands and a livid expression. But when he spoke, I immediately recognized Derek's voice—and registered the absolute absurdity that our last conversation had been about the very person he seemed about to confront.

"Yo, if you call one more woman a bitch," Derek said with more bass in his voice than I'd heard before. "I think you heard the ladies. You need to back up and chill out."

Bishopp sized him up. Derek stood a full four inches taller and was filling out his royal-blue suit and crisp white shirt. His beard made him seem older than Bishopp, but his clenched fists implied youthful reckless energy. Bishopp hesitated but quickly remembered that half the party was watching their exchange. He jabbed a finger in Derek's chest. "I don't know who the fuck you are, but you probably don't want any part of this."

"I'm sure you're right," Derek told him, batting away his finger. "But you probably don't want to try me."

"Man, fuck this shit," Bishopp yelled. "Square up, nigga." He swung on Derek, who blocked his fist with a quick move that left Bishopp on the floor.

I could feel a surge from Bishopp's crew as they pushed forward to defend their boy, but the defensive line around Kiara intervened too quickly for any more fists to be thrown. One of them grabbed Bishopp's lapel and lifted him off the floor like a rag doll. The rest muscled Bishopp's crew toward the door. When they were gone and the spectators dispersed, Von, Kiara, Derek, and I stood there for a minute, staring at each other in disbelief. My hands were shaking, and I was surprised by the sudden wetness on my cheeks. Von was the first to speak. "I'm getting us some tequila shots."

"Thank you," I mouthed as I struggled to regain my composure. I let Kiara wrap me in a hug.

"That was legit crazy," Kiara whispered. "But you're good now."

"Shit, I think you handled that, Nikki!" Derek held his hand up for a high five. "Way to not back down."

I gave Derek a weak smile and touched my moist palm to his. "I don't think I handled that at all. But you sure did. I appreciate you jumping in with the karate moves."

Kiara raised her eyebrows and looked thoughtfully from me to Derek and back. "Actually, that looked like aikido," she said. "Ricky's been studying it for years."

Derek nodded, clearly impressed. "Good eye. I'm a black belt. Comes in handy when people get out of hand in court," he quipped.

I'd forgotten they'd never met. "Ki, Derek works with my girl Teresa at the New York County Defender Services. Derek, this is Kiara Matsumoro. She runs a PR firm—and this is her husband's party."

They shook hands, then Kiara gave me one more quick squeeze. "All right, folks, crisis averted." She pointed to her headset as someone was evidently talking to her. "I'm off to deal with more drama."

When she left, Derek led me to a chair. "Hey, what are you doing at this party?" I asked him. "Doesn't seem like your scene."

Derek paused. "Remember I told you that I'm dating someone who works in music? She's a producer at MTV. In fact, I should probably go find her. I was just going to make a cocktail run and now I've been gone for twenty minutes."

I blinked at him a few times before realizing I needed to say something. "Oh, cool. Well, I mean, don't leave her waiting," I said, instead of what I really wanted to ask: *Who is she? What exactly does she produce at MTV? What does she look like? How long have you been together? What's her astrological sign?*

Von had returned with four tequila shots, so I grabbed two and handed them to Derek. "Here, Kiara's gone, so bring these to your girl." My tone was a little too clipped, so I softened it. "You can say you wanted to get the party going before you guys start cocktailing."

Derek stood there, holding both shots, exploring my face. The longer he stood there, the less I wanted him to walk away. I downed the tequila shot Von brought me and moved to give Derek a hug goodbye. But suddenly, a frantic energy rippled through the room, and a weird number of rings and beeps quickly grew into a reverberating roar. My two-way went off right as Von's started to buzz.

"What the hell," I said, flipping open the pager. There was an all-caps message from Sondra: *JUST HEARD FROM A LABEL SOURCE THAT BOBBIE WASHINGTON DIED IN A CAR CRASH. I'M CONFIRMING WITH HER MANAGER BUT THIS IS REAL.*

I looked at Von on his phone and asked, "Bobbie?" He nodded, eyes wide. My heart broke.

The news of Bobbie's death was a conflagration that engulfed the party. It was mayhem. People were rushing around, gripping each other, and weeping. She wasn't only my favorite singer; Bobbie Washington was one of the most beloved neo soul artists charting on Billboard. Bobbie had not only recorded multiple critically acclaimed albums and several major hits; she'd written "Independent Heart," an anthemic song that got every woman to the dance floor whenever a DJ played it. Denyse liked to request "Independent Heart" anytime we'd all meet up at Sofie's, and my girls and I had danced to it more times than I could remember. This loss was a jagged tear in both the fabric of the culture and in my emotional universe.

I saw Kiara near the DJ booth, then the music went silent. Without thinking, I walked over and asked if I could have the mic for a minute. She wordlessly handed it over, too upset to ask what I was about to do. I surprised myself by tapping the mic and saying clearly, "Everyone, may I ask you to be still for a minute so we can honor Bobbie Washington? Let's take a moment of silence for this inspiring artist who empowered so many women to stay strong and follow their dreams."

I handed the mic back to the DJ, grabbed Kiara's hand, and walked to the dance floor where a cross section of women at the event—platinum artists to label execs to video vixens to bartenders—were spontaneously gathering. Instead of the usual skeptical speculation, I saw respect and appreciation in their collective gaze. The woman from the Eternal Records publicity department sidled up to me and looped her arm through mine. Another woman I didn't recognize linked arms with me on my other side. It continued until we all locked arms in a large circle that felt like a group hug.

After a few minutes, I reluctantly broke free, shook off my heartache, and got to work. I found Sondra, asked Von to call the team to have everyone meet us at the office. We were a week away from putting the November issue to bed, and we would now have to pull the entire issue apart to crash a tribute special for Bobbie. It was about to be all hands on deck for the next seven days.

With the whole party now spilling onto the street below, I knew we wouldn't be able to get a taxi. JJ hadn't reappeared since Bishopp accosted me, but I didn't have time to dwell on why he'd abandoned me. I needed a ride. Sondra, Von, and I were casting about for a solution when my eyes met Derek's across the room. I didn't have to wave him over; he leaned down to say something to a beautiful but scowling woman with red box braids, then hurried my way.

"What do you need?" Derek asked as he approached.

"A ride to our office," I told him. "I'm meeting my team there tonight to figure out what we're doing for Bobbie."

"My Jeep is parked a few blocks away. I'll meet you downstairs in ten."

As we made our way outside Matsumoro SoHo and up the street so Derek could pull his Jeep over more easily, I saw JJ hanging out of his parked Porsche, waving his hands to get my attention. I told Von and Sondra I'd be right back.

"For real, JJ? I am *not* in the mood," I told him, leaning into the passenger window so only he could hear me. "You fucking left me there, knowing full well that Bishopp was on the attack. And now you show up after Bobbie Washington dies? I don't have time for this right now."

"You know, Nikki, despite how you've been treating me lately, I'm here to do you a favor." JJ's expression was annoyed instead of contrite, which made me even more mad.

"How I've been treating *you*? I know you're mad that I didn't give you a heads-up about the Bishopp story. But what did you expect? I didn't want to hear anything about 'innocent until proven guilty' or how important Bishopp is to the label."

JJ snorted derisively. "Oh, word? You didn't want to hear the truth? Gotcha."

"Jerome Jermaine, that was statutory rape at the minimum. And you know it."

"I don't know shit," JJ insisted, his eyes hard. "Do you not even think there's a possibility that chick is just waiting to file a civil suit that will set her kids' kids up for life? I been around these hos and I know how they think."

"'These hos'? That was a sixteen-year-old high school junior in her big sister's clothes." I hit his car window for emphasis. Sondra and Von were trying not to stare so I breathed deep to calm down. "And the way Bishopp was rolling up on me at the hotel, I can see exactly how the whole thing went down."

"Wait, why were you at his hotel? Now I gotta worry about you too?"

My mouth fell open. "Worry about me? Or worry about me getting with your boy? I mean, so you know, he did make his best effort, JJ. But I was there for work."

"That hasn't always stopped you in the past."

And there it was: the Alonzo reference I'd been waiting for this whole time. "You know what, JJ? You definitely do not have to worry about me anymore."

"What are you saying? You don't want to hang out?" He was incredulous.

"I don't trust you, JJ."

JJ nodded slowly, his outrage only evident in the stiff set of his jaw. "You don't trust me? After I showed you the ropes? Man, I really was trying to give you a leg up. I even showed you off. You think I normally do that shit?"

I didn't feel like asking why I should be honored that he wasn't ashamed to be seen with me. I was about to turn and leave when he said, "A'ight, Nikki. But let me give you a heads-up about Bishopp. That muthafucka was serious when he said he was going to sue you. I tried to reason with him, but he wasn't trying to hear it. That boring-looking suit going all Bruce Lee on him did not help."

The fine hairs on my neck bristled. "That boring-looking suit might be the only reason that Bishopp didn't haul off and hit me."

"You're being dramatic, Nik. He wasn't gonna hit you in the middle of an event." JJ rolled his eyes at me. "Don't get me wrong, Bishopp was mad as a mofo. But I doubt he would have actually hit you."

"You 'doubt'? Because you seemed pretty shook at the idea of a confrontation," I retorted. "And you think I'm being dramatic about what happened? I guess that explains why you haven't apologized for doing nothing while Bishopp jumped down my throat."

JJ and I glared at each other, breathing heavy. "Are you going to get in this fucking car or what?" he snarled.

The last time I saw the inside of Alonzo's Range Rover flashed through my mind. "Why are you so pressed? You were the one who wanted this to be an undefined 'thing.'"

JJ briefly closed his eyes. Then he pressed his lips together and exhaled before saying, "I did, and now I don't. As much as I wish it were different, you stay on my mind."

The weird thing was that even though I believed what he was saying, it made me trust him even less. JJ had grown up in the industry and it was clear that the baller had been baked into him. His moral compass was too skewed to even process what loyalty looked like. Then again, I'd still betrayed our friendship by not giving him some advance warning of my takedown of Bishopp.

"We're not... good together, JJ." I shook my head and sighed. "I mean, we are, but this isn't going to end better down the road, so we might as well call it quits now."

After a long silence, JJ shrugged and put his hand on the gearshift. I could feel the car coming to life. "You know who needs to apologize?" JJ pulled his seat belt over his shoulder. "You do, to Bishopp." I must have looked taken aback because he nodded exaggeratedly. "Yes, Nikki, you. You should try to say you're sorry before this blows up even bigger."

"You know I won't do that."

"Your choice, then. I guess I won't worry about you." The passenger window rose in my face. The last thing I saw before he peeled away was my uneasy reflection in the glass.

TWENTY-NINE

Imani beat me to the office. I walked in to find her pacing in front of the Wall. We were going into week four of production on the November issue, so it was nearly full.

"Okay, I have a plan," she said without turning around. "If we kill the vegetarian Thanksgiving thing and push the holiday girls' trips feature, the accessories story, and obviously the cover to December, we free up twenty pages in the well. You think that's enough for Bobbie's tribute?" Her voice broke on the word *tribute*.

"I know," I said simply. "I hate this so much. I hate everything about it."

"I profiled Bobbie once for *Essence*. She spoke in the most enlightened perfect sentences. All I had to do was transcribe them. And she went out of her way to be kind to me." Imani turned her head, and I could see the smear of runny eye makeup bruising her cheek. "I don't know, it changed me or something. I started my locs after I met her."

"Bobbie had that impact on folks." Sondra was now standing on Imani's other side. "And she was the nicest. I remember one year I was a baby entertainment reporter covering the red carpet for the Grammys. Bobbie walked past all the mainstream outlets until she got to me. Then she gave me the best interview. I had all the dopest clips of her, and that was the year she won best new artist. She got me a promotion."

"I styled the music video for the lead single of her second album," Freddy said in a hushed tone next to me. "First of all, her body was bananas. She looked sick in, like, every single thing. And she was super sweet, posed for pics with the whole glam squad, and even hired me once on the side to style her for the BET Awards."

The rest of the team was starting to file in, a sad parade of people whom Bobbie had touched, directly or indirectly, in some way. I looked around the shattered and sniffling group assembled in the conference room and wished I could reminisce with them. But we had work to do. All the relevant magazines would be in a race for the biggest writers, so I'd spent the car ride to the office calling entertainment journalists I'd worked with at *StyleList*. I'd managed to lock down Joan Morgan, Nelson George, Lola Ogunnaike, Scott Poulson-Bryant, and Touré to write about different aspects of Bobbie's life and impact. But we still had to map out the rest of the issue.

"Okay, team, you already know how much work this is going to be. We have seven days to produce a tribute worthy of Bobbie Washington. And I have a crazy idea," I said, looking from face to face. I needed them to get inspired so they could channel their sadness into doing their best work—for Bobbie. "I want to redo the whole issue from Bobbie's perspective. Let's salvage what we can because there are some completed pieces that might still work. We'll have to push or kill the rest."

"So almost as if Bobbie were the guest editor," Sondra said, nodding.

"Exactly, you totally got it!" I exclaimed. "Bobbie was the original *Sugar* girl. So, let's remake this issue from her point of view. But we're also doing a proper tribute. I want to call the famous folks she's worked with to get their favorite experience with her. Sondra, you're running point on that. Freddy, I'd like to do a style spread with all her best looks. Imani, I'd like you to write the main cover story. You can talk about your experience profiling her years ago." I thought for a minute. "We also need a visual timeline of Bobbie's life events to run along the bottom of the stories in her tribute. And we need some space in the book for you guys to share your Bobbie memories. If we keep them to a few sentences, they can be a design element along the timeline or they could be on a running sidebar throughout the issue."

"That's fucking genius!" Von cried out, hitting his hand on the table. When some people turned to stare at him, he said, "What? You know it is."

I smiled at him gratefully. "We're going to meet tomorrow at noon for everyone to present any additional ideas you have for the issue."

"What are we going to use for the cover image?" Freddy interjected. "Bobbie only had a couple of photographers she liked to work with, and *Groove* has most of the rights to those images."

I sighed and looked toward the ceiling.

"I don't know the whole story," Freddy continued, "but when Barbara ran *Groove*, she bought a few photographers' catalogs, and I know the best Bobbie images were in those archives."

"Damn it. But okay, let me try to think of something."

I was surprised that Luna and I were in near-matching outfits when we met the next morning: tracksuits, white high-tops, ponytails, and hoop earrings. My tracksuit was powder blue and Luna's was flamingo pink; her nails were so long and bright, they looked like crab legs, while I had bitten mine to the quick overnight. Otherwise, we were twinning. We started when we saw each other, an involuntary smile flashing across both of our faces before we remembered that we had beef.

I'd emailed Luna with the subject line *For Bobbie* asking to meet up, figuring that she probably had a Bobbie story too, so maybe she'd humor my request. Luna had agreed to meet at a diner on the same block as the *Groove* headquarters at 10 AM; I'd arrived at 9:30 to get good and caffeinated before dealing with Lunatic.

Reaching out to her had been my very last option. We'd mocked up covers with different red carpet images from Getty that made the magazine look cheap. We'd reached out to secondary photographers who'd shot Bobbie for her music label and found nothing but overused publicity pictures and unflattering outtakes. We'd even tried still shots from her music videos. None of it did Bobbie justice. We needed those images that *Groove* owned. Luna was my Hail Mary.

"Well, that's not the ugliest outfit I've seen you wear." Luna's backhanded compliment reminded me of Lucinda and Barbara. "Please explain what is so goddamned important that you dragged me to this dive in the middle of crunch time—for both of us," she said.

There was no need to remind her that this "dive" was her choice. "Thanks for meeting me on such short notice. It's definitely a tough week," I started. Luna's tense jaw and furrowed brow told me I'd better get to the point. "Obviously, we're both working on tributes to Bobbie."

"Obviously, Nikki. I fucking slept in these clothes." She squinted at me, creasing the day-old concealer I now spied circling her eyes. "Seriously, what is it that you want? You're wasting time I don't have."

I'd only thought about Luna on a runway or out on the town; I'd never considered how much time she must spend in her office. She'd stopped modeling a decade ago to transition into writing for *Hot Hair*; then she'd worked her way up to eventually become the editor-in-chief. Even though *Hot Hair* wasn't the most highbrow title, that ascent must have still taken hard work, focus, and talent. And now Luna was the deputy editor of what was still the biggest urban entertainment magazine. Just because we didn't have the same taste didn't make her lazy or even bad at her job. So, yeah, Luna Baxter would be working her ass off right now too, same as me.

"My bad, Luna," I said, and meant it. "I know you're busy. Bobbie's death plus putting together the tribute is wearing on me. We were in the last week of production on November, and now we're pulling the whole issue apart. There's no time to even think about missing Bobbie." My breath came out more ragged than I thought, and I quickly glanced at Luna to see if she'd noticed, but she was intently examining her nails. I would have normally thought she was ignoring me, but I could see how tightly Luna was clasping her hand.

"At least you have a week. I got into it with Alonzo because we'd already shipped November, so we had to pay a stupid amount of money to pull it off the presses. But our cover was Sliq Bishopp. You know, telling the 'real story.'" She looked up and made air quotes, then continued. "I was, like, no fucking way everyone else has Bobbie Washington tributes on the stands and we're out with an accused rapist."

Luna and I shared a brief, knowing look. "Yeah, Bobbie would absolutely not have liked that," I said.

"At all," Luna replied. "You knew her?"

"Nah, not really. But she came to Howard when I was there, and it was hugely inspirational. Hard to explain, but I felt different after she left."

Luna closed her eyes for a beat too long. "Bobbie was my first-ever interview," she murmured. "We grew up in the same neighborhood and started doing what we do at the same time. Bobbie always had something very different about her. So when she was a local artist playing dive bars and I was modeling while trying to get people to pay me for my words, I interviewed her on spec. It took me weeks to get, like, fifty bucks for the piece."

I didn't want to give her the satisfaction, but I was legit impressed. "So you have some real perspective on Bobbie's life."

"Yes, I have real perspective," she intoned in a Steve Urkel voice. "Nikki, I just told you that Bobbie was my homegirl." Luna rolled sad eyes.

I could see I'd made another mistake, and I was about to lose

Luna. "You did. You're right. I'm thinking about Bobbie's impact, but you literally grew up with her. That's a different kind of hurt."

She grunted at me, her eyes still hooded. "Can you tell me already why the hell I am here? We only have twenty-four hours to make any changes to the November issue before we gotta get it back to the printer. I am not missing my on-sale date humoring the great Nicole Rose."

"Listen, I wanted to talk to you because *Sugar* doesn't have access to good images of Bobbie for our cover."

"Uh, why would I want to help you, Nikki?" Luna blinked at me.

"First of all, it's more for Bobbie, so we can all do her justice," I replied. Luna's eyebrows softened, but her lips remained pressed into a tight line. "But you also just told me that you only have a day. What if I could get you a fifteen-hundred-word feature on Bobbie from Nelson George? Could we trade for a cover image? I'll pay for both," I said, thinking on my feet and fervently hoping Barbara wouldn't throw me through a wall for making such an expensive deal. But without a great picture on the cover, I knew *Sugar* wouldn't be able to compete on newsstands.

"You already assigned the story to Nelson? I guess that's why he screened my calls," Luna acknowledged begrudgingly. "I'm actually not mad at this idea. I gotta run it by Alonzo, and we would get to choose the *Groove* cover image first."

"Of course, you choose *Groove*'s cover first. But is there any way we can do an under-the-table deal where you tell Alonzo that you were able to get through to Nelson? We'll blame Barbara for getting the picture directly from the photographer or something." This was a huge risk, because I was giving trigger-happy Luna a lot of ammunition. "Look, it's for Bobbie. Plus, you'll look like a hero for securing a Nelson George story in less than two days."

She drummed her fingers a few times on the highboy table, crab-leg nails clacking loudly. "You know what? Yeah, let's do it. Alonzo Griffin can go fuck himself."

I couldn't hide my shock. Luna noticed and tried to rephrase what she'd said, but I waved her cleanup efforts away. "Uh, you know, of all people, I don't care what you say about him," I told her. "I'm sure you've heard how Alonzo talks about me."

"Yeah, I have, a lot. And I believed him for a long time," Luna replied slowly.

"Believed?" I asked. "Until?"

"Until one night in his Range Rover."

There was no need to ask the obvious, so I waited to see if she'd elaborate.

"It was what it was. We'd been flirting a little, but I didn't want it to get too messy in the office. Alonzo didn't agree and cornered me in his truck after our October issue cover party for Roxy." That story was too familiar; I knew she saw the same ache, shame, and, yes, defiance on my face that I saw on hers. "You might know what I'm talking about."

"It's like I was there," I replied calmly, though the twinge in my chest was preventing me from taking a full breath. "But it sounds like you did a better job than me of separating business from pleasure."

"You were young." She shrugged. "When Alonzo told me that shit happened five years ago, I started to understand how hard he was tripping. I mean, I was wildin' all through my twenties. But it wasn't until that night in the Range Rover that I put it all together." Luna hesitated. "That muthafucka even said some stupid shit like: 'I keep having to train bitches not to turn Daddy down,' which said everything I needed to know about how long Alonzo's been running game on women."

"Not a lesson I would have wished on anyone."

"Not even me?" she asked with a mirthless smile.

"Not even you," I told her. Luna flinched as I placed my hand on hers, withdrawing her fingers like she'd touched fire. It was a premature gesture and, clearly, neither of us was ready for a kumbaya moment. I grabbed my coffee and switched the topic. "So, you're going to push your Sliq Bishopp cover to December?"

Luna held up her palms. "Guess so."

"That timing's not going to work as well for the rape case," I said, giving her a sideways look.

"True," she replied, with another oh-well lift of her hands. Clearly, Luna was not into Bishopp's story. "I do hate that we'll have to push the Betty Brown cover to January. I mean, we worked so hard to get that cover." This time she gave me a sideways look.

"You could always kill it," I tried. "Best-case scenario is that Bishopp is a bad dude. Worst case, he's a rapist. I think we both know it's the latter."

Luna pursed her lips. "You didn't seem to be worried about that when you put him on the cover."

"And I may have made a mistake," I admitted. "But my profile story all but accused him *and* we talked to the girl he raped. You said he gets to tell the 'real story'"—I made air quotes—"for *Groove*'s cover."

"Yeah, well, obviously not ideal. But Alonzo and JJ made some kind of informal agreement at RedHot's sneaker launch where JJ will feed *Groove* exclusives in exchange for conveniently positive coverage."

"So, JJ gave you that Sliq Bishopp cover?"

"Who else?" Luna looked bemused. "We crashed it after your October issue came out. I guess Bishopp went rogue to get your cover, then he was up JJ's ass about the, um, result. JJ paged me and Alonzo to call in the first favor."

So that's why JJ had been so quiet: He'd struck a deal with Alonzo that could ultimately hurt *Sugar*'s access; and he and Luna were in cahoots on a Bishopp cover for *Groove* that might immediately discredit *Sugar*'s authority.

The revelation must have been all over my face because Luna rolled her eyes and leaned forward. "Look, I heard the conversation, and if it makes you feel any better, Alonzo strong-armed JJ. He promised him positive coverage but he also threatened no coverage at all if JJ didn't agree."

When I glanced up, Luna's eyes locked on to mine. Though she didn't seem insincere, there was a trace of exasperation, as if my naïveté was testing her patience. What she didn't realize, though, was how intimately I understood Alonzo's extortion tactics. I was still seething. "Yeah, well, JJ still didn't bother to tell me," I shot back, my voice laced with anger.

Luna stabbed my arm with one of her talons. "You gotta remember, it's not personal. It's always business with those ballers."

"I guess you would know better than me."

"For real, Nikki? That's how you want to play it?" Luna's eyebrows shot up to her hairline, and I realized I was about to screw up our fragile peace.

"I just meant that we both know I'm pretty green in this world," I replied quickly, realizing there was no need to shoot the messenger.

"Well, that's true," Luna said in a more relaxed tone. "Let me give you a little advice. Don't get too caught up, and never forget that, even if you don't see it at first, there's always some kind of transaction and a big trade-off when you're fucking with a baller."

"Thought you and JJ weren't fucking." I was instantly embarrassed by the tinge of jealousy in my voice.

Luna only snorted. "Don't trip. I aged out of JJ's bed a decade ago. But not before that muthafucka gave me traction alopecia from all the glue-in weaves he paid for."

"Wait, are you serious?" I asked. "Why was he paying for you to get a weave?"

"Because he liked that I was a model but didn't like my natural hair," she said, glancing with no small amount of bitterness at my thick curls. I hadn't processed that her pony was a weave, but now I saw the mesh part.

"That's so—" I began, unsure how to finish my sentence.

"—fucking crazy?" Luna interrupted. "Yeah, it is. I'm madder at myself than anyone, though. I knew better modeling all those years and then working at *Hot Hair*. These fucking weaves snatched all my edges, so I literally have to wear a weave now." She abruptly stood up to go. "Consider yourself warned."

"No need. That ship has sailed."

A thoughtful look passed between us as we both realized that we were the ones now in cahoots. Before she walked out, we agreed to talk in a couple hours to work out the details. Luna nodded stiffly at me, then pasted a smile on her face and hit the street. I ordered my third coffee to go so I could call Nelson George as I walked south to the NuVoices office.

Before we put *Sugar*'s Bobbie Washington tribute to bed, I sat in my darkened office, staring at every letter and punctuation mark. There could be no mistakes when I sent it to the printer, so I scrutinized every detail—from the cover with the bartered beauty shot of Bobbie in glamorous makeup, her blond locs twisted into an elaborate updo, to the BOB where we'd added pages of staff reminiscences. Even Barbara said the issue was beautiful.

I'd dug up the picture of me with Bobbie on the Howard campus that I'd had on my bulletin board at *StyleList* to use on my editor's letter page, but I had yet to write the text. When I finished poring over the rest of the pages, I uncapped a pen and let the words flow.

Hey, girlfriend. This has been the hardest issue to put together of any magazine I've ever worked on. Bobbie Washington was an insightful, generous, stunning unicorn of a woman who impacted so many people—myself included. It's because Bobbie inspired me at a young age to be myself and to follow my passions that I'm writing this letter to you, my Sugar *girls. My kick-ass team and I pulled out all the stops to make sure we honored Bobbie's life and her death, and I'm so grateful to everyone who contributed to this beautiful, painful issue.*

In addition to the tribute to Bobbie's life and impact, we produced the rest of the issue in a way that we felt would reflect her values and perspective, as if she were Sugar's *guest editor. The team and I made sure that all the other stories venerated and empowered the independence and potential of women of color everywhere.*

I want to walk my talk in my own career and life. And so, I've decided that it's time to shed some light on misogyny in the corporate world, starting with an editorial series on sexual harassment and assault in the music industry. Not only have I seen how women—from video dancers to female executives—are treated poorly, I've personally experienced sexual harassment and, yes, sexual assault. This will come as news to many people because I've been afraid for a long time to talk about it. But early in my professional life, I was pressured into having sex with a powerful man who had the ability to influence my career. I acknowledge that I made a mistake by getting involved with this person in the first place. But I now realize that our ongoing interaction, and one incident in particular, went far beyond a youthful transgression and into dangerous territory.

I thought I'd learned my lesson, but recently I found myself seduced by money and power and access again. I know, girlfriend, I should be able to date a powerful man without being afraid that I'm going to be put in a position where my no *won't mean anything. I know…*

I'm telling you this because I'm hoping that if I share my story, others will too. Then we can work together to make a difference for all women. Bobbie was a moral center for so many of us. Now that she's gone, I want to try to embody her values and figure out how Sugar *can impact your life as much as Bobbie impacted mine. It's time for something new—for me, for* Sugar, *and for all of us.*

If you want, please send me your own stories. I promise to read every one. Stay strong, sisters. Be brave. We're in this together.

Love, Nikki

I capped the pen and finally, finally allowed myself to cry—for the death of my idol, for the culture, and for my lost innocence.

THIRTY

After watching household-name celebrities snort lines of coke off video vixens' asses in the VIP area at various MC RedHot parties, I thought I was unshockable. But getting Lucinda's card was even more astounding than seeing the star of last summer's box office blockbuster lift his white powder–covered face from a dancer's nether regions and yodel over Big Pun's "I'm Not a Player." I ripped open the black envelope to find a brief note in barely legible cursive. I could hear Lucinda's voice as I read:

Dear Nicole,

I feel compelled to reach out after perusing your Bobbie Washington tribute. You certainly learned a lot under my tutelage. If you had adequate resources, your November issue would have been an even better homage to an artist that you obviously held in high regard. Just this year, Bobbie refused to shoot an inside feature for StyleList *because we didn't have a Black editor to work on her story. It was a questionable career move for her (much like your decision to leave Park Ave Pub), but she displayed considerable integrity.*

   I also read your editor's letter with some interest, as I believe I know to whom you were referring... It was courageous to write about a situation that so many women have faced. You always did have more nerve than you gave yourself credit for.

I've been asked to put forth suggestions for new ASME members, and I've sent them your name. I'm sure the organization will reach out shortly. I hope that you appreciate this opportunity and will not squander it as you have others. Marie says hello.

Fare thee well,

Lucinda

When I got to the end, I exhaled the breath I'd been holding and placed the card face down on my desk. Lucinda's name was a verb, and as I sat there, feeling anxious, insulted, and honored at the same time, I realized that I'd been Lucinda-ed. Still, there could be no question that the woman was a goddamned industry legend. And she'd given the American Society of Magazine Editors, the most prestigious organization in our industry, my name? I was floored. You had to be at the top of the masthead at a "respected" publication to even be considered for ASME membership.

That it had even reached Lucinda's marble desk was a testament to the amount of attention the November issue had generated. The October issue with Sliq Bishopp's provocative cover had sold well, but the November tribute to Bobbie was gone from newsstands within days.

People in the industry suddenly reached out with what I now understood were the *real* invitations. I had assumed you could spot the power brokers by who occupied a VIP banquette at a party. But then I started hearing about the *other* gatherings—the intimate dinner cooked by a celebrity chef at a platinum artist's Alpine, New Jersey, mansion; the leadership retreat for the fifty most powerful women in music and media; the private jet a label CEO was chartering to fly three hundred of his closest industry friends to Jamaica for his birthday. That's when I realized: The party scene was only the surface layer.

There were levels to this kind of cultural power: At the outermost layer, you might hear about an MC RedHot party. A step deeper, you might actually get an invitation. Securing a VIP banquette at that party meant you had some influence. But true power existed much further in, in the spaces you wouldn't even know existed unless you were part of them—where invitations weren't about being seen but about being counted among the real players. Getting a seat on that jet to Jamaica wasn't just another level; it was five layers deeper into a world where real decisions, alliances, and deals were made.

As much as the industry was taking notice, so was *Sugar*'s audience. I'd been recognized a few times by excited fans of the magazine in the corner bodega and in the drugstore (where I'd been on an inglorious errand to buy tampons and Tums). When I went to a music festival in Marcus Garvey Park, so many people came up to me, I almost felt like one of the performers. DMX was the headliner and Ruff Ryders Entertainment had given me access to the VIP tent along with four extra tickets, so I invited Teresa, Denyse, Sofie, and Kiara. While my besties had acknowledged that they may have rushed to judgment, they still needed to get to know her. When Kiara showed up with a couple fat joints, I knew we were about to bond for real.

Sofie and Teresa lit up right away while Denyse took some convincing. By the time DMX hit "Ruff Ryder's Anthem," we were all toasted and singing "Stop, drop, shut 'em down, open up shop. Oh, no, that's how Ruff Ryders roll" at the top of our lungs.

When the song ended, Denyse poked me and murmured, "Nik, I think people are staring at you."

I'd just laughed. "It's the weed, girl. You're not used to being high and you're paranoid!"

But I glanced around to see a few women looking my way. I'd been questioning how strong that joint was when a woman who looked young enough to still be in college padded up to me. "Hey, Nikki. Sorry to bug you," she said, so low I had to put my ear next to her lips to hear her. I must have frowned as I strained to hear her because her volume increased as she blurted, "Your Bobbie Washington issue was da bomb!"

Before I could properly thank her, another young woman hesitantly approached. "Excuse me, Ms. Rose," she mumbled. "Just wanted to say that I have every one of your editor's letters."

My friends had watched bemusedly as more women wandered over to me while I struggled to sober up enough to respond. This was different from the industry crowd at Ricky Matsumoro's VMAs after party; these were my readers, my *Sugar* girls.

The mail that referenced Nikki's Notes had also increased every month, and with the tribute issue, my editor's letter generated almost as many letters as the articles on Bobbie. I'd ignited a firestorm as people debated which industry was worse for women and who the powerful man I'd referenced was. Women wrote to me from every state in the country with their own tales of being hit on, overlooked, objectified, assaulted, afraid, and pissed off.

As we were flooded with letters and emails, I questioned my promise to read every one of them. At least much of the December issue had been pushed from November, so it would be less work to produce. But I still found myself in the office late every night, going through story after story that many of the women said they'd never shared with anyone before.

One of those nights, I decided to take a break from sifting through the tens of letters we'd received just that day to check my insistently buzzing two-way pager. It was an ominous message from Barbara: *I'd like to see you first thing in the morning. Please be in my office at 10 am.*

The next day, Tisha was blasting a local hip hop station in the Nu-Voices reception area like she did every morning. As I crept by her desk, hoping I'd beat Barbara to the office, I heard a familiar voice. It was Betty Brown's first single, its catchy, driving beat instantly distinctive whenever it came on the radio—which felt like every thirty minutes. Eternal Records' marketing machine had finally kicked in, and Betty's song had been rapidly climbing the charts, like I thought it would.

Tisha was bopping her head and warbling along, snapping her fingers to the syncopated rhythm. "Hey, Nik, have you heard the second single yet?" she called out when she saw me. "They played it a few minutes ago. I guess it's Betty day!"

I gave her a thin smile. I was reserving energy for my conversation with Barbara. It felt as if I were running a gauntlet as I walked the NuVoices floor to my office: Congratulations on the prescience of *Sugar*'s August cover were coming from every side, but the words were like blows, highlighting my success identifying a rising star but also my failure to translate it into newsstand sales. The August issue had been like an indie movie at an artsy film festival, a critically acclaimed tour de force with precious little actual audience.

I dropped onto the sofa in my office with a yawn, resisting the urge to close my eyes. Sleep had eluded me as I played out all the possible scenarios of the 10 AM meeting while staring up at the dark ceiling. Barbara hadn't commented on any of my Nikki's Notes but had been openly begrudging my presence ever since I'd obliquely called her a "bean counter" in my September letter; she'd loudly exhale every time she had to address me in the office but still crowed about how well *Sugar* was doing during every call with NuVoices' board.

Von stuck his head in my door, but I dismissed him with a small head shake. I'd emailed him to cancel my morning appointments sans mentioning that Barbara had summoned me. My mind was racing enough without having to manage the whirling dervish Von would have become had he known about my meeting with our CEO. When the clock ticked to 9:59, I dusted off the white pantsuit I'd broken out for the occasion (though I now had the sleeves rolled up and was wearing it with orange dunks and a Knicks tank top) and trudged toward Barbara's closed door.

I heard Barbara's muffled voice, talking low into the phone as I knocked. I made out the barely audible words "She's here, be ready" before opening the door.

I flung my low braid over my shoulder and tried a bright smile and brighter tone. "Morning, Barbara. Have you heard Betty's new single? It's all over the radio and the whole office is buzzing about it."

Barbara looked at me quizzically as she straightened the front of her black leather tee. The thought that this woman was single-handedly contributing to climate change with her leather obsession distracted me for a second, until she said, "You seem to be feeling pretty successful today, Nikki." I couldn't tell if it was a question or a statement.

"I didn't mean...I wouldn't say all that," I responded, immediately wishing that I hadn't started off so cheerily.

"Tell me, why do you think your first six months at NuVoices have been successful?" This was a question, and Barbara waited expectantly for an answer.

"Um, well, *Sugar* looks much better overall. We've increased our style coverage, improved the journalism, added new writers..." I petered out because I could see the plumes of resentment spreading underneath Barbara's innocent expression.

"Don't stop," she said in a syrupy tone. "You're on a roll."

"Barbara, I..."

"No, no." She wagged a finger. "I really do want to hear this. Go on."

My incisor nipped my lower lip as I worked out what to say next. "Okay, um... *Sugar* broke the story on DJ Cassius and Latika's pregnancy in the June issue; we saved the Sinclaire profile in July; we gave Tyisha her first-ever cover in September; and our November Bobbie Washington tribute is selling out everywhere." I left off Betty's August issue and our bestselling October issue with Sliq Bishopp on the cover.

Barbara stared at the wall behind my head, not saying anything. Since I was already tickling my tonsils with my toes, I was afraid to break the uncomfortably long silence. Finally, she slid her eyes in my direction and motioned for me to sit in the chair in front of her desk. "I'd like to offer you an alternative perspective, newbie."

Barbara swiveled in her chair to grab a stack of *Sugar* issues from the shelf next to her desk. She spread my first six issues on the desk in chronological order. "Producing some nice-looking magazines with 'more style coverage' and 'better journalism' is not success to me. Have you not noticed that I'm a Black woman in a man's world trying to grow a tough business? This shit is not easy." She picked up the August issue and shook it at me. "I don't care about Betty's single climbing the charts. What did that do for us? Your dicey past with Alonzo fucked this issue." Barbara tossed the magazine toward the desk where it skittered off onto the floor. "You know what success is to me? It's my bottom line, pure and simple."

"*Sugar*'s newsstand sales are up so much," I interrupted, but she wagged her finger again, this time to shut me up.

"The increase in newsstand sales was offset by the ad dollars you cost us when we lost Reine after you decided to go all hip hop feminist on Serge." Barbara snorted begrudgingly like she did every time she was forced to address me. "I still let you do basically what you wanted because newsstand sales and subscriptions are getting better. But now I have to deal with Sliq Bishopp suing us?"

My heart sank. "Oh, wow. I guess I was hoping he'd change his mind."

"Nikki, you knew about this?" She crossed her arms. "You could have given me a heads-up before Bishopp's lawyer called yesterday."

"I guess I thought it would go away—which was stupid," I admitted. "But the legal department vetted my profile and the interview with Bishopp's accuser before we went to print. They said it was only nominally risky."

"Only nominally..." Barbara covered her eyes with both hands. "Legal really should have flagged it so I could sign off. I knew I'd hear from his people once the issue came out. But getting sued is on another level." Barbara rose to pace the room, her black leather-clad legs squeaking with every stride. She stopped in front of her bookcase and ran a finger along her collection of Walter Mosley's novels. "I'm sure you can imagine that hiring you gave me some pause. Yes, Alonzo is a pimp, but he said a *lot* about you, Miss Nicole Rose." I did not mistake Barbara's low-pitched tone for kindness. She picked up a copy of *Devil in a Blue Dress* and flipped through it as she continued talking. "Obviously, I decided that you were worth the risk. But I didn't just give you a six-month probation because the company was in trouble; I also wanted to have enough time to see how you'd handle major temptation and tough decisions." Barbara put the book back and sat on the edge of her desk in front of me. "If you think I've been testing you . . . it's because I've been fucking testing you. And you've failed every single test."

Barbara was too close for me to dab my eyes, so I had to let them well up. "I've been working so hard," I whined stupidly.

"Oh my god, pull it together. So have we all. But you're too caught up in your own little world to see it." Barbara's gaze was steely, so I suppressed a sniffle. "And let's not forget that your very first questionable decision was letting JJ run game on you." Barbara's voice had been rising and she paused to inhale deeply through her nose. When she continued, her voice was low and even again. "I cut you some slack when your past with Alonzo cost us covers, when you ignored my advice and tanked our August issue, when you told Serge to kick rocks, and when you went behind my back to get that picture of Bobbie." She was counting off my offenses on her fingers. Then she dramatically hit her forehead. "And let's not forget when you wrote about me in your editor's letter and made me out to be a money-grubbing asshole."

"I'm really sorry, Barbara." I had no choice but to wipe the tears crisscrossing my cheeks.

She returned to her chair and pushed a box of tissues across the desk. "But I have to admit that your little Nikki's Notes is gaining some kind of cult following. Which is why I hope you'll do the right thing so you can still be successful here."

"What do you want me to do?"

"Apologize!" Barbara exploded. "Print a retraction of the Sliq Bishopp profile. Say you got some facts and quotes wrong."

I pressed a tissue into the inner corners of my eyes. "Please don't make me do that. Bishopp is rotten to the core. And it would be terrible for *Sugar* anyway. If we don't stand up for our readers, what's the point?"

Barbara shook her head. "Nikki, you're at the end of your six-month probation. You want to stay? You want to win? This is how."

I weighed it. I wish I hadn't, but I sat there and thought about whether there was a way I could craft an apology to Bishopp that wouldn't feel like selling my soul—or selling out my readers. "I just... can't do that," I finally croaked.

"And I can't let you take the company down." Barbara sighed. "You probably cost us half a million dollars of advertising from Serge. If Bishopp sues, it could be millions more."

My hackles rose. "Take the company down? I put *Sugar* on the map. Everyone in the industry is talking about the November issue. Random women are coming up to me in stores to thank me for my editor's letters."

"And you have now confirmed that this is the perfect time for us to have this conversation, because it's obvious that you have the misguided impression that *you* are *Sugar*." Barbara gave me a calculating look. "Frankly, if you're not here, I can pin both the Serge and Bishopp situations on you, and I can try to recoup the relationships and the money. I'm afraid that this is your last day at NuVoices."

"Wait, you're seriously firing me—"

"—in the middle of your November tribute issue victory lap," she interrupted. "Yes, I am. I don't want to do this, but you can't keep going rogue because you think you know better than everyone else. And if I can get the Reine ad dollars back and avoid Bishopp's lawsuit, the improved newsstand sales over the last few months will buy me enough time to find a new EIC." Barbara picked up her phone and said simply, "It's time."

Our regular security guard came in, mouthing an apology to me behind Barbara's head. He escorted me to my office, where, like my undignified departure from *StyleList*, I had exactly ten minutes to pack everything up. Von looked like he was going to cry as he flew around my office, throwing my books, magazines, and knickknacks into the bags and boxes he sourced from bewildered onlookers. I sat, stunned, on the sofa, looking around the room from the yellow bookcase I'd found at Ikea, to the matching sunny rug, to the wall I'd repainted and covered with framed pictures of my favorite female heroes. I'd stuck to my guns with Barbara and refused to compromise my integrity, but I still felt as if I'd managed to let that entire wall down. And now I would have to leave this place that felt like my home.

THIRTY-ONE

Failure was a distorting mirror through which everything looked uglier: the industry, the ballers, Barbara, NuVoices, and me. Definitely me. People who loved me kept repeating how strong I was to not let myself be bullied into betraying my values and my sisters. But when I examined the warped fun-house reflection of my six months stewarding *Sugar*, I looked drawn, defeated, and foolish. The more time that passed since I was fired, the less powerful I felt.

Getting escorted out of the office wasn't the hard part. It was embarrassing, to be sure. But I'd kept my head held high and walked out like Angela Bassett in *Waiting to Exhale*. I'd nodded goodbye to my team as I rode the wave of my convictions out the door and into a taxi, where everything sank in. The cab driver had Bob Marley on blast, which normally would have cheered me up. But during that fifteen-minute ride, I played out scenarios where I'd never get another job in publishing, I wouldn't be able to afford my rent, my credit card debt would pile up even higher...

The hard part wasn't telling my closest friends or my parents. Even though they had some ambivalence about both NuVoices and the industry as a whole, they supported my decision not to apologize to Bishopp. Their certainty that I'd done the right thing should have made it easier to deal with calls from acquaintances and colleagues who might not understand my sudden departure from what outwardly seemed like a victorious run at *Sugar*.

But that wasn't an issue, because they didn't call. And that was the hardest part: the isolation.

The scores of people I'd met as editor-in-chief of the buzziest new magazine in the urban world had only known me at a career peak—with the power to grant favors in the form of coverage and access. Now there were no more favors to be had, only speculation about why I'd been dethroned. I thought my two-way and email and voicemail would be blowing up with folks wanting to know the real deal. But it was the exact opposite. Now that I was a nobody again, I had instantly become uninteresting to anyone who didn't genuinely love me—or hate me.

So, I found out, the painful way, that failure was also a filter, permitting authentic emotion to pass through while retaining the solid particles of transactional bullshit.

One of the few messages I got was from Marie, who reached out with an email that was meant to be sympathetic, though I could hear *I told you so* in her tone. Still, I was grateful for any shreds of caring—which was why I made the mistake of picking up a call from an unknown number.

I was lying on my sofa with a throw over my head to block the mid-afternoon light and a plate with a half-eaten PB and J resting on my stomach. The call had been the only sound in my apartment all day, so I answered on the first ring. Hearing Alonzo's smoky voice jolted me straight up, knocking the sandwich to the floor.

"Well, babygirl, I guess you really thought you could play with the big dogs," he said gleefully. A retort didn't form fast enough in my mind, so Alonzo just chuckled. "But I saw you trying hard. You really put your shoulder to the wheel for your November issue. Although, it probably wasn't *too* hard to get Luna to give up that Bobbie pic you used on the cover. She's such a dizzy bitch."

"That wasn't me..." Though tremulous, I found my voice. I was about to toe the party line that Luna and I had agreed upon, but Alonzo cut me off.

"Don't bother telling me that Barbara miraculously made a deal with the photographer on the side. You and I both know that's ridiculous, and I don't want to get mad all over again." I could picture Alonzo's pinky pressed against his mouth, his tell when he couldn't decide between amusement and fury. "It was kind of adorable to see you two chickenheads striking up a little frenemy deal. That is, until I read your editor's letter where you stopped just short of calling me a fucking rapist."

"I know it was almost five years ago, but you know exactly what I was talking about."

The phone line crackled with furious energy, the same intensity that used to infuse our illicit hotel room sex. But now we were panting from anger instead of lust.

"You know what I know? That it's teases like you who are dangerous, Nikki. That's why it was so important to me—well, to me and JJ—that Bishopp get to tell his real story in *Groove*," Alonzo growled. "But that's not why I'm calling."

Morbid curiosity prevented me from hanging up. "That's pretty gross, even for you, Alonzo."

"You and Luna and the rest of you bitches who think you can just throw it in a real man's face and then walk away *are* teases, Nicole. But as much as I'm enjoying doing a jig on your professional grave, I'm actually calling to see if you have any dirt you want to share on Barbara."

"Why would I have dirt on Barbara?"

"Jesus, Nikki. Either you are stupidly loyal or just stupid. But that's cool. I guess I'll have to enjoy watching NuVoices and Barbara implode from afar."

"Wait, what are you talking about? Barbara told me NuVoices was going to be all right."

Alonzo snickered. "Man, you are still Annie's naïve little minx, aren't you? Have a good afternoon, babygirl. Maybe you should think about showering and getting your shit together." He hung up, leaving me to wonder how he knew soap hadn't touched my body in days.

It was my love for Teresa that finally got me under a shower and out of my apartment. Her thirty-first birthday was coming up in a month, and Derek had reached out to see if I wanted to help him plan a party for her. I agreed to meet him in person before I processed that I'd have to wash my hair and figure out something cute to wear for the first time since I'd been escorted out of the NuVoices offices two weeks prior. We'd exchanged a few emails, but the last time I actually saw Derek was when he dropped me at the office after the Matsumoro VMAs after party. The contrast between the leopard-print number I had on that fateful night and the yogurt-crusted sweatpants that had become my uniform would have been a little too much.

We were meeting at Party City to pick up some supplies, so I surveyed my neglected closet for a big-box-retailer-chic outfit. Since the weather had gone from chilly to wintry while I'd been holed up in my apartment licking my wounds, I threw on a black turtleneck, charcoal jeans, and a black Canada Goose coat. I shook off the thought of Denyse, whose wardrobe had remained consistently conservative since freshman year, telling me I looked goth whenever I wore all black.

When I rounded the corner of the decór aisle, Derek gave my ensemble a quick once-over and lifted an eyebrow. "You in mourning?"

"Nah, I'm just a native New Yorker," I said stiffly, not sure if he was making fun of me.

"Touché," he replied with a warm smile that defused my defensiveness. "Well, me too. Born in the North Bronx and raised in Co-op City. You're from Harlem, right?" I must have looked startled because he said sheepishly, "Teresa mentioned that we're both uptown kids."

"Yeah, I guess so," I murmured, wondering what else Teresa had told him. Still unused to interacting with anyone other than whoever answered the phone at my favorite Chinese restaurant, I didn't have my social sea legs. I tugged down the brim of the baseball hat I'd put on to avoid brushing my still-wet hair and fingered some paper dice in the casino theme section.

"You read my mind," Derek continued kindly. "I was thinking a Vegas party could be cool. We could get some playing cards, scatter around fake gold coins..."

"Are you looking for an excuse to get some strippers?" I ventured a small smile in his direction. In his blue sweatpants and blue hoodie under a brown leather puffer jacket, Derek looked as handsome dressed casually as he did in a suit.

"Not sure that Teresa and I have the same taste in strippers, but I'm not going to object."

"Well, you already know that Tee would not enjoy participating in the sexual objectification and commodification of women." I lifted both hands up in a mock oh-well gesture.

"Male strippers it is," Derek exclaimed, pumping the air with his fist.

This time, I laughed. "Nah, that's not my speed. Too corny."

After a pause, Derek asked a little too casually, "So what is your speed, Nikki? Jerome Jermaine?"

His back was to me as he carefully put heart and spade wall garlands into a basket, so I couldn't read his facial expression. He'd never asked me about JJ or anyone else I might have been dating. I wondered again how much Teresa had shared.

"Not anymore—especially now that I'm not at *Sugar* or really in that world at all." I tried to match the studied casualness in Derek's tone, but I knew he could hear my voice catch when I said *Sugar*.

"I'm sorry, I didn't mean to be nosy. I haven't even asked how you're doing." Derek looked back at me, remorse knitting his brows together.

"I'm...not that good, I guess. This is the first time where I really don't know what to do with myself," I told him, surprised by my honesty. I pivoted so that I was facing stacks of plastic poker chips and dollar sign–imprinted paper plates that I started to pile into my own basket. "It's weird. It's only been a couple weeks, but *Sugar* and even JJ seem so distant. Like the whole thing was a surreal dream."

It was true: Kiara and Von were reaching out as much as Teresa and the girls. But the less I heard from everyone else at *Sugar* and the fewer invitations to industry parties I received, the more my memories of being a sought-after urban wunderkind blurred.

Derek scratched his beard. "For what it's worth, Bishopp deserves everything that's coming to him and I'm glad you didn't fold."

So, Teresa had been talking to him about me. "I know I did the right thing, but what good did it really do? Did I really serve the *Sugar* reader by giving up the platform?"

"Why not create a new platform?" Derek had filled a basket with enough playing card–themed decorations to re-create a small casino on the Vegas Strip and was now gazing at me thoughtfully.

"I wouldn't even know where to begin to launch a new magazine." My own basket was now brimming with paper plates, cups, napkins, and a gold table cover. I pointed to the balloon display, and we walked over to preorder a few dozen.

"I don't believe that, Nikki," Derek countered as he waved away my offer to chip in for the balloons. "But I didn't mean a whole magazine. What about a blog? There's this platform called Open Diary where you can publish writing that readers can comment on. Or you could start your own website."

I stopped in the middle of the aisle on the way to the checkout area. "My own blog." I said the words slowly, testing how they felt in my mouth. "I do miss writing. And I could focus on issues that affect women of color."

"See? And you can build an audience of true fans, and even sell ads."

I felt a prickle of excitement for the first time in weeks. Bouncing on my toes, I considered the possibilities. "I could even call it Nikki's Notes, like my editor's letter."

"Now you're on to something!" Derek's smile was inspiring.

"This is kind of a dope idea. I could do social commentary but also write articles on style. No fashion shoots, of course, but think pieces about the meaning of beauty for Black women, the politics of our hair." I wryly lifted my damp ponytail and let it drop back to my shoulder.

"That's a good one," he exclaimed. "You could interview women with both long and short styles—and someone like Joan Morgan to get different perspectives." I gazed at Derek's enthusiastic face as another idea started to form. But he continued before I had a chance to say anything. "Listen, I'm here if you want to talk through all of this, and I can do a legal review on your thornier topics, like we did with the Bishopp profile."

Although my breath quickened as he amiably placed both hands on my shoulders, I stiffened and pulled away, not yet prepared for any man to touch me, even as a friend. Plus, as far as I knew, Derek had a girlfriend—although I could still see his date's angry face as he left the Matsumoro party with me. I had no appetite to untangle a bunch of relational knots in yet another complicated romantic situation. Either way, Derek had come to my rescue too many times now. It was time for me to prove that I could rescue—and trust—myself.

Derek had jammed a hand back in the pocket of his jacket and picked up his basket with the other. As we walked together toward the cash registers at the front of the store, I peeked at him from the corner of my eye. His jaw was set but I could see a muscle twitching above his eyebrow.

"That would be amazing, Derek," I said, hoping I hadn't upset him. "Let me work on this idea a little bit, and I'll let you know."

He stopped in his tracks and looked into my eyes. "Like I said, I'm here for whatever you need. Although maybe the idea was enough for a rock star like you."

I followed him to the checkout, standing up a little straighter. I would write a proposal for Nikki's Notes with the same detail that had been in the one I'd put together for *Sugar*—but this time, it would only be for me.

THIRTY-TWO

Summer 2001, Six Months Later

"Can you believe she broke up with me because of that? I mean, I can't be the only guy who has regifted a present." Von dropped his freckled forehead onto the table.

"But Von, you regifted the present *she* got *you* for your birthday back to her!" I couldn't stop laughing as I pictured the poor girl opening the same lava lamp she'd given Von one month prior. "Did you even change the wrapping paper?"

Von moaned without lifting his head while Imani rolled her eyes. He'd begun the story of his latest relationship disaster right after we ordered, and our waiter was now clearing our entrees. As per usual, Von spared no detail, and this was likely not the first or even second time Imani had heard the story. The three of us were having lunch at a tiny West African restaurant equidistant from my apartment and the NuVoices office. I'd been in the middle of editing my latest blog post, but they'd insisted on getting together right away. Von had me cracking up since we sat down in the booth, and I was starting to wonder what the big emergency was.

"Von, you are totally burying the lede. This is not why we wanted to have lunch with Nikki today." Imani's singsongy tone promised juicy news.

"Ugh, I know. I just miss our Nikki so much." Von lifted his head and briefly draped an arm around my shoulder. "But we do have some shit to talk about."

Imani pursed her lips and bobbed her head while Von rubbed his palms together.

"Will one of you please tell me what's going on?" I looked from Imani to Von and back. "Hellooo?"

"Girl..." Von and Imani spoke at the same time. I crossed my arms.

"Okay, I'll go." Imani dragged her chair closer and lowered her voice. "NuVoices is totally out of money. If we don't find another major investor, the company may even have to file for bankruptcy."

"What? I'm super confused. I thought NuVoices got back all the advertising dollars they lost last year. And, obviously, Bishopp never moved forward with the lawsuit."

"Yeah, Barbara pulled the Reine campaign back in, and you know why Bishopp didn't sue the company." Imani sighed as we both recalled the apology to Bishopp she'd been forced to run as *Sugar*'s interim EIC. Imani had reached out before the issue had gone to print to explain that her son had just been diagnosed with type 1 diabetes and that, as a single mom, she couldn't afford to lose her job and medical insurance. I'd understood, but that didn't ease the sting of seeing the retraction in the December issue, the same month that Bishopp appeared in *Groove* with his "real story."

The only positive was that my frustration accelerated my desire to get my blog up and running. I launched Nikki's Notes that same month with the think piece on misogyny and sexual harassment in the music industry that I'd wanted to run in *Sugar*. I wrote it myself, after cajoling Sondra to help me find female music executives, models, dancers, stylists, and even singers to share their stories on the record; and Derek had come through as promised to add an insightful legal perspective. The ripple effect after I posted the article put my fledgling blog on the map. CNN even interviewed me to talk about how women in entertainment are treated—which led to television appearances whenever I published notable blog pieces. My audience was growing, and I was even starting to get some advertising dollars.

Imani covered my hand with hers. "Our *Sugar* girls didn't like that retraction at all. We got tons of angry letters and subscription cancellations. Getting the ad dollars back didn't matter because we lost so many readers."

"Now *you're* burying the lede, Imani," Von broke in. He'd been drumming his fingers on the table and had obviously had enough. "The real reason that NuVoices might go bankrupt is the woman Barbara was sleeping with embezzled money from the company!"

I almost fell off my chair. "Are you serious? I don't even understand."

"Girl, it's a crazy story," Imani cut in. "Barbara was hooking up with some wannabe who ran an 'image development agency' that was code for a few raggedy hairstylists and makeup artists. Long story short, Barbara hired her lover to work on shoots across all the NuVoices magazines, and this chick submitted fake invoices along with the real ones. We think she had an accomplice in accounting because no way would that much money go unnoticed for so long."

"I know Barbara wasn't in on it. She's way too ferocious about that company. But how could she not see what was going on?"

"Pussy blindness," Von replied with a knowing smirk as Imani elbowed him. He gave her a sidelong glance. "Well, you know it's true!" Von faced me again. "Of course, the board is blaming Barbara, so..."

"...so they're forcing her out of her own company," I finished, as I saw how the whole thing must have played out.

"Apparently, she decided that she's over publishing and wants to go into television." Imani sipped her chai latte. "Last I heard, Barbara launched Porter Productions and is developing a reality TV show that pits men against women on a remote island or something."

"Shit, I might actually watch that." I laughed. "And how did you two figure all this out?"

"I know where all the bodies are buried at NuVoices," Von whispered. "Remember, I was Barbara's assistant before she moved me to *Sugar*. So, the board involved me when they figured out that the books didn't balance. I'm not supposed to tell anyone, but no way was I not gonna tell you and Imani."

"I am stunned," I said, pressing a hand to my chest.

"I was too when I first heard. But it explains so many things," Imani said. "There was always a fire drill over NuVoices' finances, even when we came in under our production budget. Our newsstand numbers were way over projection, and we had incremental ad dollars that replaced Reine, at least at *Sugar*. But I counted *Bella* and *Decode*'s ad pages and they were holding their own too."

"You counted their ad pages?" I interrupted, impressed.

"I sure did." Imani gave a half shrug as both Von and I gaped at her. "As far as I could tell, we were exceeding the goals that the board and the investors set, so I could never figure out why we were always in so much financial trouble."

"Tell her the rest," Von urged Imani.

She drew in a long breath and sat back in her chair. There was a long pause, as evidently neither wanted to share the rest of the information.

"Guys?" I spoke into the tense silence.

Imani's shoulders sagged. "Alonzo Griffin wants to buy NuVoices. He gave a presentation to the board and the investors about the potential economies of scale of producing *Groove* along with NuVoices' titles."

"He's already submitted a bid and I overheard the head of the board say that they're seriously considering it," Von added. "And now we're freaking out that we'll all lose our jobs."

"Von! That's no longer Nikki's problem."

Von threw his hands in the air. "Yeah, okay. But we all know that if Alonzo buys NuVoices, he's going to fire anyone he thinks was in Nikki's camp first."

My heart was beating so hard in my throat that I thought it must surely be visible. I rubbed my hands on my thighs, then inspected my fingernails. Anything to avoid looking up. As hard as I'd tried, I'd never stopped thinking about it as my magazine, and the *Sugar* readers as my community. I had been getting at least ten emails a week asking why my name was no longer on the masthead, and I always wrote the same thing back: *"Even though you don't see my name, I am forever a* Sugar *girl in spirit."*

Plus, Von was 100 percent correct: As the new owner of NuVoices, Alonzo would get rid of anyone he thought was still loyal to me right away. And when he gutted the *Sugar* team, my former assistant and my former number two would be first on the chopping block. I don't know how much time passed as I reluctantly contemplated what Alonzo might do with the *Sugar* brand and my former team, both of which I still loved.

Then an idea started to form in my mind. "Von, do you have the contact number for the head of the NuVoices' board?"

"I sure do."

"Okay, give me a sec. I have a crazy idea." I walked outside to get some fresh air and privacy. As I paced the sidewalk in front of the restaurant, I made a call. "Hey, Kiara. Remember when Ricky was telling us over dinner last month that he wanted to diversify his business? I may have a time-sensitive opportunity for him. Can I come by tonight?"

Barely one month later, Ricky Matsumoro had a majority stake in NuVoices. I'd pulled every bit of data on NuVoices I could and then begged Imani to come with me to the Matsumoros' house to help explain the strength of the current business. After I talked about the important niches that *Decode* and *Bella* occupied and the fast-growing strength of the *Sugar* brand, Ricky saw the acquisition as the perfect extension of his VMAs after party—and a chance for Kiara to flex her PR and marketing muscles. He'd reached out to

NuVoices' board the next day to put his name in the hat, reviewed the P&L and financial projections, and outbid Alonzo and Groove Media by almost half a million dollars within a week. Ricky's legal team negotiated the terms at top speed, and three weeks later, the documents were finalized.

Then Ricky went for a hat trick that even I hadn't anticipated: He bought Groove Media as well. Before she'd left, Barbara had sold her stake in Groove to an investor who apparently had no desire to be part of a company that would now have to compete with the growing Matsumoro empire. Ricky was going to consolidate the two publishing companies into one media conglomerate with the intention of expanding his after party into an event franchise and launching a music festival to complement the magazine brands.

Because the negotiation between Ricky, the investment bank, and Groove Media had been so contentious, Ricky's first act after acquiring the company was to fire its combative president, Alonzo Griffin. Unlike his exit from Park Ave Pub, this time I fervently wished it were my doing. But it wasn't. I actually had no idea Alonzo was out until I received a gleeful message from Luna, who told me that he'd screamed and cursed as he was escorted out of the Groove Media building.

Although I knew he was now wandering these unemployed streets, I was taken aback to see a dejected Alonzo waiting for me outside Sofie's Café on Sunday. His clothes were wrinkled, his locs looked dusty, and the bags under his eyes told me he hadn't slept well in days. It was the first time that Alonzo seemed old to me.

My apprehension must have been visible because he shook his head. "Relax, babygirl. This time, I know you didn't get me fired. You probably cost me the NuVoices deal, but you didn't make Ricky let me go. That was all my doing."

I backed away from him and looked around me. "How did you know where I was?"

"JJ told me that this is where you have brunch with your girls on the weekends."

I wondered how long Alonzo had been lingering outside the restaurant. "Okay, well, what do you want?"

He twisted the wedding ring on his finger. "Look, I know you're tight with the Matsumoros. Can you talk to Ricky about reinstating me to run all the magazines? I should be president of NuVoices."

I swayed on my feet, the shock making me feel unsteady. "You can't possibly be serious."

"Yes, I am fucking serious." Alonzo drew closer, then stopped short. "He obviously listens to you. And you owe me."

My anger mixed with pity as I watched Alonzo pluck imaginary lint from the sleeve of his sweater. Having now been fired twice in a row under dubious circumstances, he would have a difficult time getting another job in publishing. His desperation should have made me exultant. Alonzo Griffin, the person who'd turned me out and then tormented me for years, had hit rock bottom. Instead, I felt an unexpected sadness for my mom's oldest friend. Alonzo was a monster who'd assaulted several women I knew, and he deserved everything that was now coming to him. But my mom had told me too many stories about the virulent racism and bullying they'd survived growing up, and I'd spent too many nights in this man's arms to rejoice at his downfall. Alonzo was the worst thing that had ever happened to me, but I had no idea who I would be if I hadn't had to evolve and toughen up to deal with him. And I really liked myself now.

"Yeah, I do owe you... because now I know better," I finally told him. "You're on your own, Alonzo."

"'You little ingrate,'" he said, seething. "You do realize that I put you on."

"And then you tried to take me out, multiple times."

Alonzo had expected me to cave. I could see it all over his face.

"You know what? I've been on my own, babygirl. So that's cool, I'll figure it out."

"I bet you will," I shot back. "But you'll probably have to ask one of your boys for help. I would try JJ first."

Alonzo flinched. "Aren't you the quick learner," he said coldly.

It wasn't a question, but I answered anyway. "No, I'm a slow learner. Because it took me too long to really understand that you're the problem, Alonzo. You tried to convince everyone, and maybe yourself, that it was me. But it's always been you. And now, I am not going to be your solution."

With that, I strode down the street, leaving him behind.

Ricky mentioned that he wanted to bring in an executive with fresh eyes to help him restructure NuVoices and integrate Groove Media, and I immediately thought of Marie. I didn't believe that she'd be able to extricate herself from Lucinda's powerful grasp, but Ricky convinced her to take the chief operating officer role at NuVoices.

"I didn't know how much more I could do at Park Ave Pub, and I've been trying to figure out my next move for a while," she said excitedly when she called to share the news. "I killed myself over all those years to push through diversity hires. And I just got them to bring in a Black EIC, their first ever, for *TravelList*, which was huge. But since then, Park Ave Pub has been acting like they're maxed out on people of color. I was exhausted."

"When Ricky said he needed someone to rethink NuVoices' org and culture, you were the first person I thought of. But I honestly never thought he'd get you," I told her truthfully. "How did Lucinda react?"

Marie snorted. "You already know that Lucinda lost her mind when I told her. I kept trying to remind her that I don't even work for her directly, but she thinks she runs all of Park Ave Pub. Poor Mary-Kate must still be cleaning up the drink and broken glass."

I laughed. "I think Mary-Kate has Stockholm syndrome or something. How's *StyleList* doing now? Lucinda was so stressed about the decreasing audience, but she's still there, so..."

"Well, that was a big part of why Lucinda was so upset when you left. You were supposed to be her magical negro. In my effort to get you promoted, I may have encouraged that," Marie admitted. "I found her a Latina editor who helped her make inroads into that market. It probably saved her job."

"Nice! But you're wrong, Marie. *You* were always her magical negro. No wonder she didn't want you to go."

I heard Marie's sharp intake of breath. "Oh my god, I never thought of it that way. Which makes the NuVoices opportunity even more perfect!" Marie's voice was warm and sincere. "I really appreciate the connect, Nikki. Thank you."

"Don't thank me yet. NuVoices is a shit show and I can only imagine how crazy it is at Groove Media. And you're supposed to bring them together. That's a hell of a job."

"Oh, I know." Marie chortled. "I'm sure I'll be missing Park Ave Pub's marble lobby within weeks. But I'm psyched for the challenge." She paused for effect. "And since we seem to be trading professional favors, I have one for you: I'd like to offer you your job back. Ricky wants you to return to *Sugar*, and I couldn't agree more."

I had a feeling Marie would try to get me back, but I wasn't yet prepared to have that conversation. "I... I have to think about it."

"What? Nikki, come on. I hated to admit it while I was still mad at you, but you were crushing it as *Sugar*'s EIC. We'd get to work together again. And it could be a fresh start for both of us."

"But that's just it, Marie. I've already made a fresh start." I spoke haltingly, shifting the phone from one hand to the other. "Look, it was hard as hell to pick myself up after everything that went down at NuVoices. But I did it. I built a blog from the ground up that lots of people actually read. And now, I don't want to go backward."

Marie was silent for a minute. "Okay, I get it. What if I talk to Ricky about acquiring your blog, and adding staff to help you keep it going along with *Sugar*?"

The idea of finally being able to pay off the last of my credit card debt was tempting. And I had to admit that I missed being in the inner circle of music and publishing power. But I was not excited about going back into baller culture with all its sexist bullshit. Plus, I liked being my own boss. "I also don't know that I want to give up the ownership of this thing that I built by myself."

Marie thought some more. "What if Ricky gave you an equity stake in NuVoices? That way you'd have a piece of your blog and *Sugar* and all the other titles. Now that would be a real fresh start."

I couldn't deny how much I missed *Sugar*. In the mere half a year I'd worked there, it had gone from being a job to being a mission. It would definitely be easier to continue that mission with a larger platform—and to change the industry from the inside. That wasn't going backward, especially if I owned a piece of NuVoices.

But I wasn't the only one who deserved a fresh start. I thought for a minute, then said, "What if Ricky gave all NuVoices employees some equity? So that everyone has a stake in the company's success?"

"That's brilliant!" Marie exclaimed. "Let's get on a call with Ricky tomorrow to talk it through. How does it feel to actually live your dream, Nikki?"

I'd been walking back and forth in my living room, and I stopped to appreciate the view of the Manhattan skyline. The midafternoon winter sun cast a crisp, pale light over the city, giving the normally chaotic streets below a pristine and hopeful glow. I looked north toward my childhood home in Harlem and then south toward my last apartment in Brooklyn. "I'm not gonna lie, it feels pretty good," I replied slowly. But I knew that I wasn't quite ready. To truly move forward, I would have to do something different; I would have to *be* different. "There's one more thing I need to take care of before I go back to NuVoices."

THIRTY-THREE

"Girl, you know you crazy," CeCe exclaimed, putting one hand on her hip and looking around the hair salon as if she couldn't believe this was happening.

"I'm not crazy, Ce. I'm a woman on a mission!"

"A mission to do what? Give me a heart attack?" Whenever a Black woman cuts off her hair, it's a major event and CeCe was swiveling her head from left to right as if she were searching for the camera that must be documenting this insanity.

"I thought you'd be excited to do something different." I suppressed a nervous laugh. "You're the one always telling me to switch it up."

CeCe gave me an incredulous look, then pointed a long purple fingernail in my direction. "I meant get some layers or highlights, not chop it all off. Most of these heffas in here would give a limb or at least a digit for all this hair."

I'd walked into her salon that day with a stack of pictures of Halle Berry and Toni Braxton that CeCe barely glanced at before walking away while emphatically shaking her head no. But when she realized that my mind was made up, she'd gotten an excited look on her face. I figured she was telling me I was crazy just to cover her ass—like a doctor qualifying a risky surgery to avoid a malpractice suit.

"They can have it, Ce," I said, shrugging as if I didn't care that she was about to cut off thirty years of hot oil treatments, careful trims, leave-in conditioners, and silk pillowcases.

CeCe gathered my hair into a low ponytail. "This is it," she exclaimed. "No going back." When I nodded, she said, "Okay, here we go!" and cut it off right at the rubber band.

I was grateful that CeCe's first cut had been so decisive because, truth be told, I *was* freaking out. I thought about the entire month my mother had grounded me during my freshman year of high school, after I'd cut ragged bangs with kitchen shears in an act of teen defiance. "You're going to be happy for this hair one day," Mom would say as she braided my hair at night, silencing any protests I made at her rough treatment of my tangles. "Appreciate what you have and don't go chopping it off on a whim."

But this wasn't a whim. It was a mission—to have my exterior match what I now felt like on the inside. I was no longer interested in scraping back my curls to be invisible or getting a blowout to be catcalled by random men. I'd stopped wearing my hair down anyway; the weight had been bothering me for months. My first day back at NuVoices was that Monday, and I didn't want my fresh start to feel weighed down.

After CeCe finished cutting and shaping and gelling and spraying, she spun me around to look in her mirror. I caught my breath. My eyes looked huge, my mouth full, my neck long. I reached up to feel the soft wisps of hair in the back, then I touched the bangs that swept over one eye, the delicate layers around my ears. I felt as if I were looking at my true self for the first time. A stylish woman as opposed to a pretty girl. I eyed my outfit—white turtleneck, jeans, tan boots—and thought about how a plunging neckline would look with my hair, how I could now carry off heavy chandelier earrings and wrap cool scarves around my neck.

Everyone was staring at me. All motion had ceased as the women who'd seen CeCe do my hair the same way for years waited for my reaction.

"It's fabulous, Ce. I can't believe how different I look. I love it, I really love it," I said, turning my head to examine my new pixie cut from every angle. As I jumped up and hugged her, an upbeat single from Betty Brown's album suddenly blared from the radio. The ladies in the salon perked up when it came on, singing along, seat dancing, and head bobbing. Ce had copies of *Sugar* all over the salon, and when one of her clients spied the August issue with Betty on the cover, she squealed, "Oh shit, this is the girl singing right now! Don't think I saw this before."

"This cover is fire!" The woman's friend lifted the hood dryer to get a closer look. She held out her hand to get the magazine, but her girl wasn't giving it up.

CeCe noticed and passed her a second copy of the August issue from a low coffee table near her station. "You know that's the editor-in-chief right here," she told her, tilting her head in my direction.

I was about to say *former editor-in chief* when the sensation of being *Sugar*'s EIC again overwhelmed me, both electrifying and familiar. I just smiled and introduced myself to the woman under the dryer. Monday couldn't come fast enough.

That evening, Derek came by to review my latest blog post. I had written a piece on a series of troubling sexual harassment claims at a major music label, and I needed to be sure I wasn't publishing anything inadvertently defamatory. Over the past six months, Derek had been my partner in crime on Nikki's Notes. He knew I couldn't afford to take any legal risks, so he had insisted on reading every one of my posts. Sometimes I'd email him the text, but we met in person more frequently. In the beginning, we'd go to coffee shops, but after a while, it became easier for him to stop by my apartment after work, since it was so close to the courthouse.

Though Derek never mentioned it, I think he was worried about my money situation without my EIC salary. He'd always show up with dinner from a local restaurant. We had a ritual where I'd open my front door with a cocktail for him, while he passed me the bag with our food. I hadn't yet told Derek that I was going back to *Sugar*, so that night, I made a festive mix of prosecco and St-Germain. After a moment of hesitation, I put on the *Hôtel Costes* CD he'd sent me, feeling a bit self-conscious as the sensual music filled my apartment. When I opened the door, flute in hand, Derek didn't move to take it; he was riveted to the spot, staring at me, open-mouthed.

"Ya like?" I asked timidly. I wouldn't see my girls and my parents until that Sunday, when we'd made plans to meet for brunch and celebrate my return to NuVoices. So Derek was the first to see my makeover. Although I'd already gotten plenty of reactions from the streets. Like some Samson story remix, I'd felt more powerful walking home from the salon with my pixie cut than with long hair. Given how much unwanted attention I used to get whenever I got a silk press, I'd half expected to be totally ignored. But my confidence had been like catnip to passersby. I'd gotten more looks than ever, but a different kind. The catcalls were less "Give me a smile, baby" and more "You go, girl!" It seemed as if the people nodding appreciatively in my direction were seeing me and not only my hair—maybe because I felt more like myself than ever.

"I . . . It's . . . It's just . . . I mean, you look amazing," Derek stuttered, and I felt my face flush. I'd never seen him lose his cool.

"Phew! Now that I have your stamp of approval, I can rest easy," I joked, hoping he hadn't noticed my bright red cheeks.

"Well, then you can rest easy because this look suits you beautifully." Derek found his composure and handed me the pizza box while he took a sip from the flute I'd given him. "Oh wow, and this is delicious. If I'd known it was a special night, I would have brought something more interesting than a pepperoni pie."

"No, that's perfect, and I'm starving," I told him as we walked toward the kitchen. "Come on, let's eat first. I have news."

"There's more happening than your fire-ass haircut?"

"Just a little bit." I perched on a kitchen counter stool, grabbed a slice, and told him about my conversation with Marie, and that Ricky had agreed to my terms to return to NuVoices.

"Are you sure you're not a lawyer?" Derek asked, grinning, after I finished. "You've somehow managed to negotiate the literal best of all worlds."

"To be honest, I was hesitant at first. The blog is doing so well."

"Uh, yeah—and now it's about to blow up with all the extra resources. You're on your way to full-on media moguldom."

It was the second time Derek had pointed out a possibility I hadn't fully grasped myself. Turning away to hide the warmth rising in my cheeks, I busied myself pouring us more prosecco and St-Germain. "I'll admit, I was starting to feel burnt out trying to scale the blog on my own," I said. "But what if people think it's weak to go back to NuVoices?"

"First of all, fuck anyone who isn't supportive," Derek replied, his voice sharp. "Second, how is this not a power move? You're returning to *Sugar* after building a fast-growing blog and, oh yeah, as part owner. Shit, Nikki, give yourself some credit." He chuckled, but the serious look in his eyes didn't waver. Rising from the stool where he'd been sitting, Derek placed a hand on my shoulder. "Plus, your *Sugar* girls need you," he added, his tone now quiet and sincere.

"You think so?" I whispered, enjoying the warm pressure of his hand.

"Yes, they need you." Derek replied softly, then put his other hand on my right shoulder. Like tendrils of light in a plasma globe, the energy between us danced from his fingertips through my body. "Nikki, I can't take it anymore. I need you too." He leaned in to place his mouth on mine.

I hadn't been kissed in more than six months, and my body responded like I'd gotten a taste of water after hiking through the Sahara. I reached a hand to the back of Derek's neck and pulled him closer, pressing my lips against his, my back arching to meet his touch. One of his hands made its way to the back of my head, and I lost myself in the sensation of his fingers playing with my short hair. I made myself pull away for a second to look at him. "Wait, are you still seeing that woman who works at MTV?"

"That was over the night of the party." Derek kissed his way across my cheek to nibble at my ear. "I haven't dated anyone seriously in a very long time."

"Why is that?" I moaned as his hand crept lower to the waistband of my jeans.

"Because you're all I think about," Derek murmured into my neck. I didn't say it back. I didn't need to. Instead, I pulled my turtleneck over my head.

Derek took his time, driving me wild with his barely there caresses across my stomach, the light trail of his fingers down my inner thigh, the soft flick of his tongue on my hard nipples. He gently peeled off my jeans, then kissed and licked his way down to my soaking thong. By the time he nudged it aside, my hips were grinding the air, desperate for more. But Derek would not be rushed. He lay his tongue in the center of the wetness and didn't move until I begged.

Then slowly, so slowly, he moved his tongue—enough to send spasms of pleasure through my body but not enough to make me come. He placed the tip of his index finger inside me, and I could feel my muscles grasping at it, trying to pull it farther inside me. Every time the muscles clenched around his finger, he'd insert it a tiny bit more and faintly increase the pressure of his tongue until he turned me into a feral animal. The feeling built from somewhere low and deep, and when Derek finally let me climax, the release was higher and more ferocious than anything I'd ever experienced.

When he replaced his finger with his penis, I moaned so loud I thought the neighbors might call the police. The next orgasm was another slow ascent. He brought me to the brink several times before neither of us could take it anymore and we exploded together, losing control in the frenzied press of our bodies.

After we dozed off, then made unhurried love again, we rested on my bed, our chests rising and falling in unison as we caught our breath. I lay awake, long after Derek kissed me on my forehead and gave in to sleep, thinking about how sensual the experience had been. Later on, I would look back and wonder if this was the moment when I finally let myself fall in love with him.

"Nicole Rose, oh my goodness, what have you done?" my mother wailed as she and my father approached our table in the back of Sofie's Café, their outmoded and messy professor gear standing out among the chic brunch crowd.

I'd texted my girls Saturday night about my new do and asked them to meet me before my folks were supposed to arrive so they could check it out. Since they'd been dropping hopeful hints for months about me giving Derek a chance, I also wanted to share the news—although I'd already squealed the story to Teresa when I called her the next day after Derek left my apartment. I'd invited Kiara to join our normal brunch crew that Sunday, so by the time my parents arrived, she, Teresa, Sofie, and Denyse had already processed my new look and my love life.

When I'd first walked into the café, they'd shrieked so loud, half the restaurant turned around. Sofie waved her Baby Phat–clad arm at her customers so they'd relax and turn back, but by then my girls had encircled me and the volume had risen to howler-monkey levels. Between my new look, my new man, and my new ownership status at NuVoices, the reactions from our table were thunderous for at least thirty minutes. I'd shushed them as soon as I saw my parents amble through the café door.

"Hey, Mom. What do you think?" I asked unnecessarily as her horror was all over her face. My dad, who had a dismissive attitude about hair length, looked unconcerned. But he had a firm grip on my mother's elbow, possibly to restrain her from rushing toward me.

"You look like a teenage boy!" Mom lamented as she inspected my hair from different angles.

"Okay, well, nice to see you too," I muttered.

"Come on now, Dr. Rose. I think Nikki's hair looks awesome!" Teresa exclaimed. She'd known my mother since she was in high school, and they'd developed a warm relationship over the years. Every now and then, Teresa could make Mom understand something more easily than I could. But not today.

After more squawking about how I'd regret cutting my hair off, Mom finally asked, "Can you please tell me why you would do this to yourself?"

"I just didn't want to go back to being the EIC of *Sugar* like nothing's changed. I can't be the same and expect everything to be different, right?" I blew out my cheeks. "Well, now, folks at NuVoices and in the industry are going to know that they're dealing with a new Nikki."

"I'm here for that, love," Kiara piped up, but fell silent when my mother whirled around and stared daggers at her.

Denyse had always been my mother's favorite, so she jumped in to help me. "Now Miss Ann," she started, the only person in my friend group Mom would allow to use her first name. "You know I always preferred your baby with a blowout. But I've been doing this corporate thing long enough to know that she's right. Nikki can't walk back into NuVoices the same person because they won't respect her. She has to show them that she's different and that she means business—which this new look signals. It's very confident."

I smiled gratefully at Denyse while my mom considered what she'd said. "Well, that is true. It is a confident look," she acknowledged.

"And Nikki needs to walk in like the badass boss and company co-owner she is," Kiara declared, snapping her fingers loudly in the air.

"Which is what we're here to celebrate, right? Our brilliant Nikki, who is returning to her rightful place as editor-in-chief of *the* magazine for urban women," Teresa said as she walked over and hugged me from behind. "I'm so happy for you, bonita. Wepa!"

"Right on time, Tee! I've got champagne coming now," Sofie said, motioning to a waiter who hurried over with a couple ice buckets holding chilled bottles of Veuve Clicquot.

When we all had flutes in hand, my dad said that he'd like to propose a toast. He raised his glass. "To my favorite daughter, Nicole, who I've always been proud of, even when I didn't understand what the heck she was doing." He laughed knowingly, then took my hand in his. "Your mom and I have watched you learn and mature, and you've displayed such tenacity and work ethic. We both respect who you've become," he said as I fought the tears welling in my eyes. "Congratulations on this next journey, sweet pea. You've got a lot of folks rooting for you!"

As everyone clinked glasses, platters of French toast, bacon, and frittatas, along with a spinach quiche and a bowl of freshly cut fruit were placed on the table. We were about to dig in when I heard the first chords of "Independent Heart" by none other than Bobbie Washington. I jumped up, grabbed Teresa and Kiara, and headed to the open area in front of the DJ booth. Sofie and Denyse were close behind us. As we started to dance, I looked back at my mother still seated, bopping her head to the beat. As unalike as we were, there was no one I admired more than this beautiful, intelligent, determined woman. I doubled back, grabbed her hand, and dragged her to the dance floor. She swayed shyly, her loafers shuffling in a self-conscious two-step. But then Mom seemed to be transported by the driving beat and Bobbie's empowering lyrics. She started to spin and snap her fingers with me and the girls. And when the chorus came, the five most important women in my life and I held hands and sang it together:

"I won't back down, won't be confined,
My time has come, gonna redefine,

*This independent heart, glowing free and bright,
Breaking through the dark, lighting up the night."*

As the song was ending, I saw Derek standing to the side of the room, watching us. Instead of following Mom and the girls back to the table, I walked over to him, feeling the energy between us spark as I approached.

"Hi," he mouthed with a half smile.

"Hi," I mouthed back, not yet trusting myself to say more.

I snuck a quick look toward the back of the restaurant to see my friends casting sidelong glances our way as they whispered among themselves while my parents watched us curiously. Teresa winked at me, then turned and motioned with her head toward the ladies' room. My girls got up to go, giving me a moment of privacy with my parents.

I took a deep breath and slipped my hand into Derek's, realizing that this was the first time we'd touched in public. We wound our way through Sofie's Café, the newness of it all making us awkward at first, then our hands tightened together, and our grins widened until we were both beaming. As we got close to our table, I spoke: "Mom, Dad, there's someone I'd like you to meet..."

EPILOGUE

Since I hadn't stepped foot in the NuVoices offices for almost eight months, I'd expected an aloof welcome on Monday. Instead, I was treated like the returning prodigal daughter. I didn't know Marie had made it known to the entire floor that it was my idea for the company to offer all employees equity, so the standing ovation took me off guard—as did the loud reaction to my transformation. The same crew that had skeptically watched me thread my way through the cubicles in a stiff white pantsuit on my first day now exclaimed over my hair and clapped me on the back as they checked out my Moncler puffer, oversized Enyce sweater, camo jeans, and Jimmy Choo boots. I'd finished the look with large gold bamboo earrings that read NIKKI in the center, a nod to the signature jewelry of the platinum-selling female rapper I'd already tapped for *Sugar*'s next cover.

Greeting my NuVoices colleagues and hugging my *Sugar* team, I felt back in the flow before I even made it to my office. But I was also struck by how true the adage was: The more things change, the more they stay the same. The absence of Barbara's mercurial energy was evident in everything from the soft R&B that was now playing in the reception area instead of blaring gangsta rap to the lemongrass wall diffusers masking the vague smell of weed that used to permeate the floor. Yet the overall mood was as boisterous as ever. Neither the new Matsumoro ownership nor Marie's additional infrastructure could prevent soccer balls from being kicked around, fashion editors from dragging rolling racks at top speed down the halls, or clusters of writers from gathering at each other's desks, joking and playing music.

My own office had been preserved like a museum, with every decorative throw pillow still in place. As much as I'd still loved the makeshift furnishings I'd cobbled together to erase Luna's presence, I decided that I wanted to redecorate. My space deserved a fresh start too. I spent the morning with Von, getting settled in and deciding what color to paint the walls next. Then I took my team to lunch to celebrate our new beginning and to strategize how we were going to crush our goals for the rest of the year. They needed to know that I was not playing.

At the end of the day, I let everyone leave the office without me so I could sit with my thoughts. I was supposed to meet Derek for a celebratory dinner, but I was exhausted. I'd forgotten the stamina it took to be an editor-in-chief, to be conspicuously in charge, to be always "on." All I wanted to do was kick back with him at home, and I knew he wouldn't care because that was our happy place anyway.

I was about to pack up my stuff when I suddenly had a brainstorm for my first editor's letter as the returning EIC of *Sugar*. I picked up the Montblanc pen that Ricky Matsumoro had given me as a welcome-back gift and let my thoughts flow onto the page:

The French fashion designer Coco Chanel once said: "A woman who cuts her hair is about to change her life." Well, girlfriend, she was right...

ACKNOWLEDGEMENTS

I began writing this book many years ago on the deck of a beautiful apartment in New York City. Kara Bajuk, to whom this book is dedicated, spent many days on that deck with me, working on her own projects and keeping me company. She has read and edited every word of every draft, contributing insightful suggestions and giving me much-needed sisterhood over our forty-plus-year friendship. Gratitude does not begin to express how I feel.

It was my wonderful partner, Richard Brooks, who read and loved this book, then encouraged me to finish it after the partially written draft had been sitting in a proverbial drawer for over a decade. His support, love, confidence, and creative genius were critical to my deciding to bring a story to fruition that had stayed in my mind for so many years. None of this would have happened without you, my love.

Nicole Jefferson Asher, your insightful, whip-smart, and unequivocal notes were invaluable as I worked to make the plot compelling and bring my characters alive. You are a gifted storyteller, a generous editor, and a terrific friend. I'm excited to see what our creative partnership will yield. Let's do this!

My extraordinary agents, Sarah Passick and Mia Vitale at Park, Fine & Brower Literary Management, saw the potential in my unfinished manuscript, gave astute editorial direction, and guided me across the finish line with patience, wit, optimism, and strategy. You manifested my wildest dreams with me and made them, and every aspect of this novel, a reality. I am also indebted to everyone at PFB, and specifically those who work on international rights: Abby Koons, Kat Toolan, Angela Lee, Ben Kaslow-Zieve, and Melissa Rodman. First the UK and then the world! I am eternally thankful and beyond relieved to have this exceptional and supportive team.

My brilliant editor Caroline Bleeke is the smart, intuitive, thoughtful partner of my dreams. Caroline, you believed in this book but, more importantly, you believed in me. You made my novel more propulsive and incisive, and you handled difficult material with sensitivity and care. I am honored and thankful to be on this journey with you. I'm also grateful to the rest of the tireless team at Flatiron Books: Megan Lynch, Mary Retta, Elisa Rivlin, Esther de Araujo, Andrea Morales, Laywan Kwan, Alexus Blanding, Leah Carlson-Stanisic, Emily Walters, Carla Benton, Eva Diaz, and Maris Tasaka.

Many more thanks to my lovely editor Clare Hey at Simon & Schuster UK and the rest of the team across the pond, including Ella Lewis and Rowan Lawton at the Soho Agency. Because of you, I can say that I'm an international novelist.

As I wrote this novel, I saw every scene play out in my mind: the visual details, the sounds, the subtle shifts in lighting. I've always envisioned it on-screen, and I'm thrilled to be working toward that goal with film/television industry legend Howie Sanders at Anonymous Content, along with the indefatigable Ali Lefkowitz at Kaplan Perrone. From our very first meeting, I felt that you truly saw me and understood my promise as a multimedia creator. We are about to make some magic together!

I am enormously indebted to Krishan Trotman, without whom I may not have connected with my literary agents. Your generosity and cheerleading were the wind beneath my wings as I gathered the confidence to complete my book. I sincerely hope that you and I get to work together in the future.

I'm also thankful to my friend and Delta Sigma Theta soror Mara Brock Akil, for giving me the gift of inspiration, time, and a breathtakingly radiant space in which to crack open a manuscript I hadn't read in years and begin the editing process. My time as an artist-in-residence at the Writer's Colony, Mara's brainchild and just one of her many contributions to our cultural community, allowed me to rediscover my creative voice. I appreciate the entire gifted and kind team at the Writer's Colony: Natalie Guerrero, Jazmin Johnson, Brooklynn Fields, and Ayana Anene.

This novel is the fulfillment of my first true dream. After post-college experiments in the finance and fashion industries, I succumbed to the pull of my true passion: writing. I decided that I wanted to go to grad school so I could write the great American novel. But first, I took a yearlong detour to the literary stronghold of Ireland to study fiction at University College Dublin. The portfolio of writing I put together there helped me gain admission to Columbia University's MFA program in creative writing. I am forever grateful to the teachers and fellow students at Columbia, UCD, and every writing workshop I've ever taken who helped me hone my craft and inspired me to push harder.

I won a literary fiction prize from the Hurston/Wright Foundation for a short story I wrote while working on my MFA. The accomplished novelist and founder of Hurston/Wright, Marita Golden, may not know how much that changed my life. Monique Greenwood, then editor-in-chief of Essence magazine, presented the award to me; we stayed in touch, and she eventually offered me a senior role at *Essence*. That was the foundation for a two-decade career in media—including three of my own stints as an editor-in-chief. The first, at *Honey* magazine, inspired the fictional *Sugar* and a few of the events in this novel. I'm grateful to you, Monique, and to so many people in media who supported my career in ways big and small. This partial list includes former colleagues and current friends: Byron Allen, Doreen Arriaga, Todd Brown, Zena Burns, Angela Burt-Murray, Maureen Carter, Keith Clinkscales, Johnny Cooper, Darhil Crooks, Arem Duplessis, Terry Glover, Lynette Galloway, Jennifer

Hunt, Eliot Kaplan, Marie Johnson, Debra Langford, Jeanine Liburd, Nina Malkin, Kierna Mayo, Claire McIntosh, Scott Mills, Denene Milner, Isolde Motley, Susan Morey, Cori Murray, Connie Orlando, Kim Paige, Richard Parsons, Anne Sempowski Ward, Susan Taylor, Elaine Welteroth, Tia Williams, Cortney Wills, and Wendy Wilson.

From New York to Chicago to Los Angeles to Paris, thank you to my family—chosen and otherwise—who've cheered me on as I change my career and my life: James Andrews, Jennifer Baltimore, Steve Barnett, Emily Barnett, Maurice Bernstein, Maitrayee Bhattacharyya, Gina Barge, Traci Blackwell, Raquel Brooks, Roxanne Brooks, Rhonda Brown, Donna Byrd, Philip Cope, Dominique Cristall, Lisa Gelobter, Isla Garraway, Tamara Gregory, Robinne Lee, Manuel Macarrulla, Sheila Marmon, Amber Mike, Mitzi Miller, Marissa Nance, Sango Ndedi Ndolo, Dion Peronneau, Jodie Patterson, Jessica Sbarsky, Christy Tanner, Latham Thomas, Geneva Thomas, Dawanna Williams, and my Montclizzie crew. I miss my groundbreaking rock star mommy Dr. Marguerite Ross Barnett every single day.

Max Brown, being your mom is the joy of my life. You have made me a better person and therefore a better writer. I'm so fortunate to not only love you but truly like you—and I'm hopeful that one day you'll be the music supervisor for a screen adaptation of one of my books! In the meantime, everything I do, I do for you.

ABOUT THE AUTHOR

Amy DuBois Barnett is an award-winning media executive and author who earned national acclaim as editor-in-chief of *Honey, Ebony* and *Teen People* – where she made history as the first Black woman to helm a major mainstream US magazine – and as deputy editor-in-chief of *Harper's Bazaar*. She has held senior leadership roles at Paramount, Hearst, Disney, Time Inc. and several independently owned media brands. Barnett has a BA from Brown University and an MFA in creative writing from Columbia University. She resides in Los Angeles. *If I Ruled the World* is her debut novel.

NEWS & EVENTS | BOOKS | FEATURES | COMPETITIONS

Follow us online to be the first to hear from your favourite authors

booksandthecity.co.uk @TeamBATC

Join our mailing list for the latest news, events and exclusive competitions

Sign up at
booksandthecity.co.uk